In times of danger, survival isn't easy. It takes intelligence, strategy—and a certain ruthlessness on the part of leaders who know that public safety depends on public strength.

Every society will have its wars. Thus every society must have its army—or be prepared to surrender to one.

CREATED BY J.E. POURNELLE

MEN OF

WAR

A TOM DOHERTY ASSOCIATES BOOK
NEW YORK

Research for the essay "The Technological War," as well as for other non-fiction portions of this book, was supported in part by grants from the L-5 Society and the Vaughn Foundation.
Responsibility for opinions expressed in these works rests solely with the authors.

MEN OF WAR

A Tor Book
Published by Tom Doherty Associates, Inc.
49 West 24th Street
New York, N.Y. 10010

Cover art by Alan Gutierrez

ISBN: 0-812-50902-1   Can. ISBN: 0-812-50903-X

First edition: January 1984

Printed in the United States of America

0 9 8 7 6 5 4 3

For Jenny, my favorite captain.

CONTENTS

PREFACE
To Provide For The Common Defense
Jerry Pournelle

"WE THE PEOPLE of the United States, in order to form a more perfect Union, establish justice, insure domestic tranquility, provide for the common defense, promote the general welfare and secure the blessings of liberty to ourselves and our posterity, do ordain and establish this Constitution for the United States of America."

In the hot summer of 1787 a remarkably talented group of men met in Philadelphia to institutionalize the first—and in some ways the last—real revolution in history. The Framers set out their goals in the Preamble. Now that we're approaching the 200th anniversary of the Convention of 1787, it's appropriate to see how well they accomplished what they set out to do.

The first goal, a more perfect Union, seems secured, although it took the bloodiest war in our history to prove it. Not long ago, few would have doubted their success with the others. Now things don't seem quite so certain.

It would be interesting to look at what we've done to justice, domestic tranquility, general welfare, and the blessings of liberty. Liberty, in particular, was a primary goal of the Framers. However—important as the other goals may be, if we cannot provide for the common defense, we will not survive to celebrate the 200th anniversary of the Philadelphia Constitution.

When I was young, defense was not a real problem. There was no realistic possibility of invasion, from this

11

continent or any other. Indeed, we could have survived quite comfortably without any overseas contacts at all. As a maritime nation we had some interest in "freedom of the seas", but those interests could be protected by naval forces. There was no need for a large peacetime army.

In those days it was easy to provide for the common defense, and Congress was able to do so. There were plenty of debates on whether it was done well. There were more debates and much acrimony when we adopted peacetime conscription prior to World War II. Whatever we did, though, could only affect the security of others. The United States was never at hazard, nor was world survival at risk.

We all know things have changed. Now not only the blessings of liberty, but our posterity themselves, are threatened.

Simply put: forget how well or how badly the Congress is doing with justice, and welfare, and liberty. Can it provide for the common defense?

Most of the evidence says no.

In the early 1960's, the Ballistic Systems Division of the US Air Force Systems Command began Project 75. This study pulled together into one document everything known and predictable about ballistic missile technology: structures, guidance, accuracy, warheads, yields, basing, security, command and control, and communications.

Project 75 examined every then-forseeable question of strategic deterrence. It looked at basing options. It examined multiple-warhead technology and multiple independently targetable re-entry vehicles (MIRVs). It looked into hypothetical circumstances: given that the Soviets have such-and-such capability, what does this do to our force requirements, and what must we do *now* to meet various threats in the future.

Project 75 was highly classified, because it dealt with the real and projected capabilities of the US, and contained the best estimates we had of what the Soviets could do. In 1968, the Air Force funded an unclassified study on "Stability and Strategic Doctrine"; this study took general capabilities, such as accuracy and weapon yield, and examined their effect on deterrence and world stability.

As it happens, I was editor of the Project 75 final report, and principal investigator of the stability study. In a later part of this book, we'll look at Project 75's conclusions.

During the 60's and early 70's there was furious debate on what we ought to do about nuclear war. Now, in 1983, the Congress of the United States is finally thinking about the problem. They're awfully late; very nearly too late. What could have been a series of orderly steps taken over a period of years must now be done as crash programs at outrageous costs—that is, if we do anything at all. It hasn't been proven that the Congress will make *any* decision.

Some aspects of the strategic problem are highly technical; but the principles, and most of the facts, are comprehensible to any interested citizen of average intelligence. The information needed for intelligent debate about nuclear war will be given in this book.

True: nothing is certain in war. The first lesson they teach at West Point is that "No battle plan ever survives contact with the enemy." Von Clausewitz put it even more succinctly: "In war, everything is very simple, but the simplest things are very difficult."

What is certain is that Soviet capabilities are growing, while ours stand still. We don't have a lot of time before the Marshal of the Soviet Union can predict, with some confidence, precisely what will happen if the war starts. This doesn't mean that the war will start the instant they believe they can win it; of course not. But until they have confident predictions of what will happen, the Politburo has no decisions to make; once predictions are possible, they do.

That doesn't sound like a comfortable world to me; but then it didn't sound comfortable back in 1964 when we tried to look into the future.

For fifteen years Congress has ignored the problem. Now, at long last and in some haste, they seem almost ready to take up their Constitutional task.

The question remains: is this a proper way to provide

for the common defense? Or is it time the citizens of this
Republic become directly involved? Who *is* responsible
for our defense?

I hope you'll enjoy the stories in this book. I also hope
you'll learn from the non-fiction. Clemenceau said, "War
is far too important to be left to the generals." He was
right. It is also far too important to be left to politicians.

EDITOR'S INTRODUCTION TO:

THE WEAPON
by
Fredric Brown

The late Fredric Brown was an important writer of short fiction. He was best known as a mystery writer. Sometimes classified as an "absurdist" writer, Brown's best known novel is *Martians Go Home!*, in which the men from Mars really do turn out to be little green men.

This story raises questions that it cannot answer. How do you put the djinni back in the bottle? And what happens if you cannot . . .

THE WEAPON
by
Fredric Brown

The room was quiet in the dimness of early evening. Dr. James Graham, key scientist of a very important project, sat in his favorite chair, thinking. It was so still that he could hear the turning of pages in the next room as his son leafed through a picture book.

Often Graham did his best work, his most creative thinking, under these circumstances, sitting alone in an unlighted room in his own apartment after the day's regular work. But tonight his mind would not work constructively. Mostly he thought about his mentally arrested son—his only son—in the next room. The thoughts were loving thoughts, not the bitter anguish he had felt years ago when he had first learned of the boy's condition. The boy was happy; wasn't that the main thing? And to how many men is given a child who will always be a child, who will not grow up to leave him? Certainly that was rationalization, but what is wrong with rationalization when— The doorbell rang.

Graham rose and turned on lights in the almost-dark room before he went through the hallway to the door. He was not annoyed; tonight, at this moment, almost any interruption to his thoughts was welcome.

He opened the door. A stranger stood there; he said, "Dr. Graham? My name is Niemand; I'd like to talk to you. May I come in a moment?"

Graham looked at him. He was a small man, nondescript, obviously harmless—possibly a reporter or an insurance agent.

But it didn't matter what he was. Graham found himself saying, "Of course. Come in, Mr. Niemand." A few minutes of conversation, he justified himself by thinking, might divert his thoughts and clear his mind.

"Sit down," he said, in the living room. "Care for a drink?"

Niemand said, "No, thank you." He sat in the chair; Graham sat on the sofa.

The small man interlocked his fingers; he leaned forward. He said, "Dr. Graham, you are the man whose scientific work is more likely than that of any other man to end the human race's chance for survival."

A crackpot, Graham thought. Too late now he realized that he should have asked the man's business before admitting him. It would be an embarrassing interview; he disliked being rude, yet only rudeness was effective.

"Dr. Graham, the weapon on which you are working—"

The visitor stopped and turned his head as the door that led to a bedroom opened and a boy of fifteen came in. The boy didn't notice Niemand; he ran to Graham.

"Daddy, will you read to me now?" The boy of fifteen laughed the sweet laughter of a child of four.

Graham put an arm around the boy. He looked at his visitor, wondering whether he had known about the boy. From the lack of surprise on Niemand's face, Graham felt sure he had known.

"Harry"—Graham's voice was warm with affection—"Daddy's busy. Just for a little while. Go back to your room; I'll come and read to you soon."

" 'Chicken Little?' You'll read me 'Chicken Little'?"

"If you wish. Now run along. Wait. Harry. This is Mr. Niemand."

The boy smiled bashfully at the visitor. Niemand said, "Hi, Harry," and smiled back at him, holding out his hand. Graham, watching, was sure now that Niemand had known; the smile and the gesture were for the boy's mental age, not his physical one.

The boy took Niemand's hand. For a moment it seemed that he was going to climb into Niemand's lap, and Graham pulled him back gently. He said, "Go to your room now, Harry."

The boy skipped back into his bedroom, not closing the door.

Niemand's eyes met Graham's and he said, "I like

him," with obvious sincerity. He added, "I hope that what you're going to read to him will always be true."

Graham didn't understand. Niemand said, " 'Chicken Little,' I mean. It's a fine story—but may 'Chicken Little' always be wrong about the sky falling down."

Graham suddenly had liked Niemand when Niemand had shown a liking for the boy. Now he remembered that he must close the interview quickly. He rose, in dismissal. He said, "I fear you're wasting your time and mine, Mr. Niemand. I know all the arguments, everything you can say I've heard a thousand times. Possibly there is truth in what you believe, but it does not concern me. I'm a scientist, and only a scientist. Yes, it is public knowledge that I am working on a weapon, a rather ultimate one. But, for me personally, that is only a by-product of the fact that I am advancing science. I have thought it through, and I have found that that is my only concern."

"But, Dr. Graham, is humanity *ready* for an ultimate weapon?"

Graham frowned. "I have told you my point of view, Mr. Niemand."

Niemand rose slowly from the chair. He said, "Very well, if you do not choose to discuss it, I'll say no more." He passed a hand across his forehead. "I'll leave, Dr. Graham. I wonder, though . . . may I change my mind about the drink you offered me?"

Graham's irritation faded. He said, "Certainly. Will whisky and water do?"

"Admirably."

Graham excused himself and went into the kitchen. He got the decanter of whisky, another of water, ice cubes, glasses.

When he returned to the living room, Niemand was just leaving the boy's bedroom. He heard Niemand's "Good night, Harry," and Harry's happy " 'Night, Mr. Niemand."

Graham made drinks. A little later, Niemand declined a second one and started to leave.

Niemand said, "I took the liberty of bringing a·small gift to your son, doctor. I gave it to him while you were getting the drinks for us. I hope you'll forgive me."

"Of course. Thank you. Good night."

Graham closed the door; he walked through the living room into Harry's room. He said, "All right, Harry. Now I'll read to—"

There was sudden sweat on his forehead, but he forced his face and his voice to be calm as he stepped to the side of the bed. "May I see that, Harry?" When he had it safely, his hands shook as he examined it.

He thought, *Only a madman would give a loaded revolver to an idiot.*

EDITOR'S INTRODUCTION TO:

TIME LAG
by
Poul Anderson

We are told that interstellar conquest can never happen, because it cannot be profitable. This seems a bootless objection. Even Soviet economists recognize that Western Europe is more valuable to the Soviet Empire as a free trading partner than as a subject state; does this mean that Europe is safe?

The impulse to power is a stronger motivation than simple greed or gain. Why else would those who have more than they can ever spend risk all to gain more?

In a recent interview Poul Anderson said, "No human institutions have yet developed that didn't contain the seeds of their own destruction, and I doubt any ever will. Of course, here in America in the last hundred years we've been witnessing that sort of thing happening. It's still grinding on, but it probably hasn't far to go now.

"I should add, too, that I don't want to preach a sermon to anyone. I'm just a storyteller."

TIME LAG
by
Poul Anderson

522 Anno Coloniae Conditae:

Elva was on her way back, within sight of home, when the raid came.

For nineteen thirty-hour days, riding in high forests where sunlight slanted through leaves, across ridges where herbal and the first red lampflowers rippled under springtime winds, sleeping by night beneath the sky or in the hut of some woodsdweller—once, even, in a nest of Alfavala, where the wild little folk twittered in the dark and their eyes glowed at her—she had been gone. Her original departure was reluctant. Her husband of two years, her child of one, the lake and fields and chimney smoke at dusk which were now hers also, these were still too marvelous to leave.

But the Freeholder of Tervola had duties as well as rights. Once each season, he or his representative must ride circuit. Up into the mountains, through woods and deep dales, across the Lakeland as far as The Troll and then following the Swiftsmoke River south again, ran the route which Karlavi's fathers had traveled for nearly two centuries. Whether on hailu-back in spring and summer, through the scarlet and gold of fall, or by motorsled when snow had covered all trails, the Freeholder went out into his lands. Isolated farm clans, forest rangers on patrol duty, hunters and trappers and timber cruisers, brought their disputes to him as magistrate, their troubles to him as leader. Even the flitting Alfavala had learned to wait by the paths, the sick and injured trusting he could heal them, those with more

21

complex problems struggling to put them into human words.

This year, however, Karlavi and his bailiffs were much preoccupied with a new dam across the Oulu. The old one had broken last spring, after a winter of unusually heavy snowfall, and 5000 hectares of bottom land were drowned. The engineers at Yuvaskula, the only city on Vaynamo, had developed a new construction process well adapted to such situations. Karlavi wanted to use this.

"But blast it all," he said, "I'll need every skilled man I have, including myself. The job has got to be finished before the ground dries, so the ferroplast can bond with the soil. And you know what the labor shortage is like around here."

"Who will ride circuit, then?" asked Elva.

"That's what I don't know." Karlavi ran a hand through his straight brown hair. He was a typical Vaynamoan, tall, light-complexioned, with high cheek-bones and oblique blue eyes. He wore the working clothes usual to the Tervola district, leather breeches ending in mukluks, a mackinaw in the tartan of his family. There was nothing romantic about his appearance. Nonetheless, Elva's heart turned over when he looked at her. Even after two years.

He got out his pipe and tamped it with nervous motions. "Somebody must," he said. "Somebody with enough technical education to use a medikit and discuss people's difficulties intelligently. And with authority. We're more tradition-minded hereabouts than they are at Ruuyalka, dear. Our people wouldn't accept the judgment of just anyone. How could a servant or tenant dare settle an argument between two pioneers? It must be me, or a bailiff, or—" His voice trailed off.

Elva caught the implication. "No!" she exclaimed. "I can't! I mean . . . that is—"

"You're my wife," said Karlavi slowly. "That alone gives you the right, by well-established custom. Especially since you're the daughter of the Magnate of Ruuyalka. Almost equivalent to me in prestige, even if you do come from the other end of the continent." There they were fishers and marine farmers rather than woodsfolk. His grin flashed. "I doubt if you've yet learned what awful snobs the free yeomen of Tervola are!"

"But Hauki, I can't leave him."

"Hauki will be spoiled rotten in your absence, by an adoring nanny and a villageful of ten wives. Otherwise he'll do fine." Karlavi dismissed the thought of their son with a wry gesture. "I'm the one who'll get lonesome. Abominably so."

"Oh, darling," said Elva, utterly melted.

A few days later she rode forth.

And it had been an experience to remember. The easy, rocking motion of the six-legged hailu, the mindless leisure of kilometer after kilometer—where, however, the body, skin and muscle and blood and all ancient instinct, gained an aliveness such as she had never before felt; the silence of mountains with sunlit ice on their shoulders, then birdsong in the woods and a river brawling; the rough warm hospitality when she stayed overnight with some pioneer, the eldritch welcome at the Alfa nest—she was now glad she had encountered those things, and she hoped to know them again, often.

There had been no danger. The last violence between humans on Vaynamo (apart from occasional fist fights, caused mostly by sheer exuberance and rarely doing any harm) lay a hundred years in the past. As for storms, landslides, floods, wild animals, she had the unobtrusive attendance of Huiva and a dozen other "tame" Alfavala. Even these, the intellectual pick of their species, who had chosen to serve man in a doglike fashion rather than keep to the forests, could speak only a few words and handle only the simplest tools. But their long ears, flat nostrils, feathery antennae, every fine green hair on every small body, were always aquiver. This was their planet, they had evolved here, and they were more animal than rational beings. Their senses and reflexes kept her safer than an armored aircraft might.

All the same, the absence of Karlavi and Hauki grew sharper each day. When finally she came to the edge of cleared land, high on the slopes of Hornback Fell, and saw Tervola below, a momentary blindness stung her eyes.

Huiva guided his hailu alongside hers. He pointed

down the mountain with his tail. "Home," he chattered. "Food tonight. Snug bed."

"Yes." Elva blinked hard. *What sort of crybaby am I, anyhow?* she asked herself, half in anger. *I'm the Magnate's daughter and the Freeholder's wife, I have a University degree and a pistol-shooting medal, as a girl I sailed through hurricanes and skindove into grottos where fanfish laired, as a woman I brought a son into the world . . . I will not bawl!*

"Yes," she said. "Let's hurry."

She thumped heels on the hailu's ribs and started downhill at a gallop. Her long yellow hair was braided, but a lock of it broke loose, fluttering behind her. Hoofs rang on stone. Ahead stretched grainfields and pastures, still wet from winter but their shy green deepening toward summer hues, on down to the great metallic sheet of Lake Rovaniemi and then across the valley to the opposite horizon, where the High Mikkela reared into a sky as tall and blue as itself. Down by the lake clustered the village, the dear red tile of roofs, the whale shape of a processing plant, a road lined with trees leading to the Freeholder's mansion. Old handhewn timbers glowed with sun; the many windows flung the light dazzlingly back to her.

She was halfway down the slope when Huiva screamed. She had learned to react fast. Thinly scattered across all Vaynamo, men could easily die from the unforeseen. Reining in, Elva snatched loose the gun at her waist. "What is it?"

Huiva cowered on his mount. One hand pointed skyward.

At first Elva could not understand. An aircraft descending above the lake . . . what was so odd about that? How else did Huiva expect the inhabitants of settlements hundreds of kilometers apart to visit each other? —And then she registered the shape. And then, realizing the distance, she knew the size of the thing.

It came down swiftly, quiet in its shimmer of antigrav fields, a cigar shape which gleamed. Elva holstered her pistol again and took forth her binoculars. Now she could see how the sleekness was interrupted with turrets and boat housings, cargo locks, viewports. An emblem was set into the armored prow, a gauntleted hand grasping a planetary orb. Nothing she had ever heard of. But—

Her heart thumped, so loudly that she could almost not hear the Alfavala's squeals of terror. "A spaceship," she breathed. "A spaceship, do you know that word? Like the ships my ancestors came here in, long ago. . . . Oh, bother! A big aircraft, Huiva. Come on!"

She whipped her hailu back into gallop. The first spaceship to arrive at Vaynamo in, in, how long? More than a hundred years. And it was landing here! At her own Tervola!

The vessel grounded just beyond the village. Its enormous mass settled deeply into the plowland. Housings opened and auxiliary aircraft darted forth, to hover and sweep. They were of a curious design, larger and blunter than the fliers built on Vaynamo. The people, running toward the marvel, surged back as hatches gaped, gangways extruded, armored cars beetled down to the ground.

Elva had not yet reached the village when the strangers opened fire.

There were no hostile ships, not even an orbital fortress. To depart, the seven craft from Chertkoi simply made rendezvous beyond the atmosphere, held a short gleeful conference by radio, and accelerated outward. Captain Bors Golyev, commanding the flotilla, stood on the bridge of the *Askol* and watched the others. The light of the yellow sun was incandescent on their flanks. Beyond lay blackness and the many stars.

His gaze wandered off among constellations which the parallax of fifteen light-years had not much altered. The galaxy was so big, he thought, so unimaginably enormous. . . . Sedes Regis was an L scrawled across heaven. Tradition claimed Old Sol lay in that direction, a thousand parsecs away. But no one on Chertkoi was certain any longer. Golyev shrugged. Who cared?

"Gravitational field suitable for agoric drive, sir," intoned the pilot.

Golyev looked in the sternward screen. The planet called Vaynamo had dwindled, but remained a vivid shield, barred with cloud and blazoned with continents, the overall color a cool blue-green. He thought of ocherous Chertkoi, and the other planets of its system, which were not even habitable. Vaynamo was the most beautiful color he had ever seen. The two moons were also visible, like drops of liquid gold.

Automatically, his astronaut's eye checked the claims of the instruments. Was Vaynamo really far enough away for the ships to go safely into agoric? Not quite, he thought—no, wait, he'd forgotten that the planet had a five percent greater diameter than Chertkoi. "Very good," he said, and gave the necessary orders to his subordinate captains. A deep hum filled air and metal and human bones. There was a momentary sense of falling, as the agoratron went into action. And then the stars began to change color and crawl weirdly across the visual field.

"All's well, sir," said the pilot. The chief engineer confirmed it over the intercom.

"Very good," repeated Golyev. He yawned and stretched elaborately. "I'm tired! That was quite a little fight we had at that last village, and I've gotten no sleep since. I'll be in my cabin. Call me if anything seems amiss."

"Yes, sir." The pilot smothered a knowing leer.

Golyev walked down the corridor, his feet slamming its metal under internal pseudogravity. Once or twice he met a crewman and accepted a salute as casually as it was given. The men of the Interplanetary Corporation didn't need to stand on ceremony. They were tried spacemen and fighters, every one of them. If they chose to wear sloppy uniforms, to lounge about off-duty cracking jokes or cracking a bottle, to treat their officers as friends rather than tyrants—so much the better. This wasn't the nice-nelly Surface Transport Corporation, or the spit-and-polish Chemical Synthesis Trust, but IP, explorer and conqueror. The ship was clean and the guns were ready. What more did you want?

Pravoyats, the captain's batman, stood outside the cabin door. He nursed a scratched cheek and a black eye. One hand rested broodingly on his sidearm. "Trouble?" inquired Golyev.

"Trouble ain't the word, sir."

"You didn't hurt her, did you?" asked Golyev sharply.

"No, sir. I heard your orders all right. Never laid a finger on her in anger. But she sure did on me. Finally I wrassled her down and gave her a whiff of sleepy gas.

She'd'a torn the cabin apart otherwise. She's probably come out of it by now, but I'd rather not go in again to see, captain."

Golyev laughed. He was a big man, looming over Pravoyats, who was no midget. Otherwise he was a normal patron-class Chertkoian, powerfully built, with comparatively short legs and strutting gait, his features dark, snubnosed, bearded, carrying more than his share of old scars. He wore a plain green tunic, pants tucked into soft boots, gun at hip, his only sign of rank a crimson star at his throat. "I'll take care of all that from here on," he said.

"Yes, sir." Despite his wounds, the batman looked a shade envious. "Uh, you want the prod? I tell you, she's a troublemaker."

"No."

"Electric shocks don't leave any scars, captain."

"I know. But on your way, Pravoyats." Golyev opened the door, went through, and closed it behind him again.

The girl had been seated on his bunk. She stood up with a gasp. A looker, for certain. The Vaynamoan women generally seemed handsome; this one was beautiful, tall and slim, delicate face and straight nose lightly dusted with freckles. But her mouth was wide and strong, her skin suntanned, and she wore a coarse, colorful riding habit. Her exoticism was the most exciting thing: yellow hair, slant blue eyes, who'd ever heard of the like?

The tranquilizing after-effects of the gas—or else plain nervous exhaustion—kept her from attacking him. She backed against the wall and shivered. Her misery touched Golyev a little. He'd seen unhappiness elsewhere, on Imfan and Novagal and Chertkoi itself, and hadn't been bothered thereby. People who were too weak to defend themselves must expect to be made booty of. It was different, though, when someone as good-looking as this was so woebegone.

He paused on the opposite side of his desk from her, gave a soft salute, and smiled. "What's your name, my dear?"

She drew a shaken breath. After trying several times, she managed to speak. "I didn't think . . . anyone . . . understood my language."

"A few of us do. The hypnopede, you know." Evi-

dently she did not. He thought a short, dry lecture might
soothe her. "An invention made a few decades ago on
our planet. Suppose another person and I have no language in common. We can be given a drug to accelerate
our nervous systems, and then the machine flashes images on a screen and analyzes the sounds uttered by the
other person. What it hears is transferred to me and
impressed on the speech center of my brain, electronic-
ally. As the vocabulary grows, a computer in the machine figures out the structure of the whole language—
semantics, grammar, and so on—and orders my own
learning accordingly. That way, a few short, daily sessions make me fluent."

She touched her lips with a tongue that seemed equally
parched. "I heard once . . . of some experiments at the
University," she whispered. "They never got far. No
reason for such a machine. Only one language on
Vaynamo."

"And on Chertkoi. But we've already subjugated two
other planets, one of 'em divided into hundreds of language groups. And we expect there'll be others." Golyev
opened a drawer, took out a bottle and two glasses.
"Care for brandy?"

He poured. "I'm Bors Golyev, an astronautical executive of the Interplanetary Corporation, commanding this
scout force," he said. "Who are you?"

She didn't answer. He reached a glass toward her.
"Come, now," he said, "I'm not such a bad fellow. Here,
drink. To our better acquaintance."

With a convulsive movement, she struck the glass
from his hand. It bounced on the floor. "Almighty Creator!
No!" she yelled. "You murdered my husband!"

She stumbled to a chair, fell down in it, rested head in
arms on the desk and began to weep. The spilled brandy
crept across the floor toward her.

Golyev groaned. Why did he always get cases like
this? Glebs Narov, now, had clapped hands on the jolli-
est tawny wench you could imagine, when they conquered Marsya on Imfan: delighted to be liberated from
her own drab culture.

Well, he could kick this female back down among the
other prisoners. But he didn't want to. He seated himself across from her, lit a cigar out of the box on his

desk, and held his own glass to the light. Ruby smol-
dered within.

"I'm sorry," he said. "How was I to know? What's
done is done. There wouldn't have been so many casualties if they'd been sensible and given up. We shot a few
to prove we meant business, but then called on the rest
over a loud-speaker, to yield. They didn't. For that matter,
you were riding a six-legged animal out of the fields, I'm
told. You came busting right *into* the fight. Why didn't
you ride the other way and hide out till we left?"

"My husband was there," she said after a silence.
When she raised her face, he saw it gone cold and stiff.
"And our child."

"Oh? Uh, maybe we picked up the kid, at least. If
you'd like to go see—"

"No," she said, toneless and yet somehow with a dim
returning pride. "I got Hauki away. I rode straight to
the mansion and got him. Then one of your fire-guns hit
the roof and the house began to burn. I told Huiva to
take the baby—never mind where. I said I'd follow if I
could. But Karlavi was out there, fighting. I went back
to the barricade. He had been killed just a few seconds
before. His face was all bloody. Then your cars broke
through the barricade and someone caught me. But you
don't have Hauki. Or Karlavi!"

As if drained by the effort of speech, she slumped and
stared into a corner, empty-eyed.

"Well," said Golyev, not quiet comfortably, "your people had been warned." She didn't seem to hear him.
"You never got the message? But it was telecast over
your whole planet. After our first non-secret landing.
That was several days ago. Where were you? Out in the
woods?—Yes, we scouted telescopically, and made clan-
destine landings, and caught a few citizens to interrogate.
But when we understood the situation, more or less, we
landed openly in, uh, your city. Yuvaskula, is that the
name? We seized it without too much damage, captured
some officials of the planetary government, claïmed the
planet for IP and called on all citizens to cooperate. But
they wouldn't! Why, one ambush alone cost us fifty
good men. What could we do? We had to teach a lesson.
We announced we'd punish a few random villages. That's
more humane than bombarding from space with cobalt

missiles. Isn't it? But I suppose your people didn't really believe us, the way they came swarming when we landed. Trying to parley with us first, and then trying to resist us with hunting rifles? What would you expect to happen?"

His voice seemed to fall into an echoless well.

He loosened his collar, which felt a trifle tight, took a deep drag on his cigar and refilled his glass. "Of course, I don't expect you to see our side of it at once," he said reasonably. "You've been jogging along, isolated, for centuries, haven't you? Hardly a spaceship has touched at your planet since it was first colonized. You have none of your own, except a couple of interplanetary boats which scarcely ever get used. That's what your President told me, and I believe him. Why should you go outsystem? You have everything you can use, right on your own world. The nearest sun to yours with an oxygen atmosphere planet is three parsecs off. Even with a very high-powered agoration, you'd need ten years to get there, another decade to get back. A whole generation! Sure, the time-contraction effect would keep you young—ship's time for the voyage would only be a few weeks, or less—but all your friends would be middle-aged when you come home. Believe me, it's lonely being a spaceman."

He drank. A pleasant burning went down his throat. "No wonder man spread so slowly into space, and each colony is so isolated," he said. "Chertkoi is a mere name in your archives. And yet it's only fifteen light-years from Vaynamo. You can see our sun on any clear night. A reddish one. You call it Gamma Navarchi. Fifteen little light-years, and yet there's been no contact between our two planets for four centuries or more!

"So why now? Well, that's a long story. Let's just say Chertkoi isn't as friendly a world as Vaynamo. You'll see that for yourself. We, our ancestors, we came up the hard way, we had to struggle for everything. And now there are four billion of us! That was the census figure when I left. It'll probably be five billion when I get home. We have to have more resources. Our economy is grinding to a halt. And we can't afford economic dislocation. Not on as thin a margin as Chertkoi allows us. First we went back to the other planets of our system and worked them as much as practicable. Then we started re-exploring the nearer stars. So far we've found two useful planets. Yours is the third. You know what your population is? Ten million, your President claimed. Ten million people for a whole world of forests, plains, hills, oceans ... why, your least continent has more natural resources than all Chertkoi. And you've stabilized at that population. You don't want more people!"

Golyev struck the desk with a thump. "If you think ten million stagnant agriculturists have a right to monopolize all that room and wealth, when four billion Chertkoians live on the verge of starvation," he said indignantly, "you can think again."

She stirred. Not looking at him, her tone small and very distant, she said, "It's our planet, to do with as we please. If you want to breed like maggots, you must take the consequences."

Anger flushed the last sympathy from Golyev. He ground out his cigar in the ashwell and tossed off his brandy. "Never mind moralizing," he said. "I'm no martyr. I became a spaceman because it's fun!"

He got up and walked around the desk to her.

*   *   *

538 A.C.C.:

When she couldn't stand the apartment any more, Elva went out on the balcony and looked across Dirzh until that view became unendurable in its turn.

From this height, the city had a certain grandeur. On every side it stretched horizonward, immense gray blocks among which rose an occasional spire shining with steel and glass. Eastward at the very edge of vision it ended before some mine pits, whose scaffolding and chimneys did not entirely cage off a glimpse of primordial painted desert. Between the buildings went a network of elevated trafficways, some carrying robofreight, others pullulating with gray-clad clients on foot. Overhead, against a purple-black sky and the planet's single huge moon, nearly full tonight, flitted the firefly aircars of executives, engineers, military techs, and others in the patron class. A few stars were visible, but the fever-flash of neon drowned most of them. Even by full red-tinged daylight, Elva could never see all the way downward. A fog of dust, smoke, fumes and vapors, hid the bottom of the artificial mountains. She could only imagine the underground, caves and tunnels where workers of the lowest category were bred to spend their lives tending machines, and where a criminal class slunk about in armed packs.

It was rarely warm on Chertkoi, summer or winter. As the night wind gusted, Elva drew more tightly around her a mantle of genuine fur from Novagal. Bors wasn't stingy about clothes or jewels. But then, he liked to take her out in public places, where she could be admired and he envied. For the first few months she had refused to leave the apartment. He hadn't made an issue of it, only waited. In the end she gave in. Nowadays she looked forward eagerly to such times; they took her away from these walls. But of late there had been no celebrations. Bors was working too hard.

The moon Drogoi climbed higher, reddened by the hidden sun and the lower atmosphere of the city. At the zenith it would be pale copper. Once Elva had fancied the markings on it formed a death's head. They didn't really; that had just been her horror of everything Chertkoian. But she had never shaken off the impression.

She hunted among the constellations, knowing that if she found Vaynamo's sun it would hurt, but unable to stop. The air was too thick tonight, though, with an odor of acid and rotten eggs. She remembered riding out along Lake Rovaniemi, soon after her marriage. Karlavi was along: no one else, for you didn't need a bodyguard on Vaynamo. The two moons climbed fast. Their light made a trembling double bridge on the water. Trees rustled, the air smelled green, something sang with a liquid plangency, far off among moon-dappled shadows.

"But that's beautiful!" she had whispered. "Yonder songbird. We haven't anything like it in Ruuyalka."

Karlavi chuckled. "No bird at all. The Alfavala name— well, who can pronounce that? We humans say 'yanno.' A little pseudomammal, a terrible pest. Roots up tubers. For a while we thought we'd have to wipe out the species."

"True. Also, the Alfavala would be hurt. Insofar as they have anything like a religion, the yanno seems to be part of it, locally. Important somehow, to them, at least." Unspoken was the law under which she and he had both been raised: the green dwarfs are barely where

man was, two or three million years ago on Old Earth,
but they were the real natives of Vaynamo, and if we
share their planet, we're bound to respect them and
help them.

Once Elva had tried to explain the idea to Bors Golyev.
He couldn't understand at all. If the abos occupied land
men might use, why not hunt them off it? They'd make
good, crafty game, wouldn't they?

"Can anything be done about the yanno?" she had
asked Karlavi.

"For several generations, we fooled around with electric fences and so on. But just a few years ago, I consulted Paaska Ecological Institute and found they'd
developed a wholly new approach to such problems.
They can now tailor a dominant mutant gene which
produces a strong distaste for Vitamin C. I suppose you
know Vitamin C isn't part of native biochemistry, but
occurs only in plants of Terrestrial origin. We released
the mutants to breed, and every season there are fewer
yanno that'll touch our crops. In another five years there'll
be too few to matter."

"And they'll still sing for us." She edged her hailu
closer to his. Their knees touched. He leaned over and
kissed her.

Elva shivered. *I'd better go in*, she thought.

The light switched on automatically as she re-entered
the living room. At least artificial illumination on
Chertkoi was like home. Dwelling under different suns
had not yet changed human eyes. Though in other
respects, man's colonies had drifted far apart indeed. . . .
The apartment had three cramped rooms, which was
considered luxurious. When five billion people, more
every day, grubbed their living from a planet as bleak as
this, even the wealthy must do without things that were
the natural right of the poorest Vaynamoan. Spaciousness,
trees, grass beneath bare feet, your own house and an
open sky. Of course, Chertkoi had very sophisticated
amusements to offer in exchange, everything from multi-
sensory films to live combats.

Belgoya pattered in from her offside cubicle. Elva
wondered if the maidservant ever slept. "Does the mistress wish anything, please?"

"No." Elva sat down. She ought to be used to the

gravity by now, she thought. How long had she been here? A year, more or less. She hadn't kept track of time, especially when they used an unfamiliar calendar. Denser than Vaynamo, Chertkoi exerted a ten percent greater surface pull; but that wasn't enough to matter, when you were in good physical condition. Yet she was always tired.

"No, I don't want anything." She leaned back on the couch and rubbed her eyes. The haze outside had made them sting.

"A cup of stim, perhaps, if the mistress please?" The girl bowed some more, absurdly doll-like in her uniform.

"No!" Elva shouted. "Go away!"

"I beg your pardon. I am a worm. I implore your magnanimity." Terrified, the maid crawled backward out of the room on her belly.

Elva lit a cigaret. She hadn't smoked on Vaynamo, but since coming here she'd taken it up, become a chainsmoker like most Chertkoians who could afford it. You needed something to do with your hands. The servility of clients toward patrons no longer shocked her, but rather made her think of them as faintly slimy. To be sure, one could see the reasons. Belgoya, for instance, could be fired any time and sent back to street level. Down there were a million eager applicants for her position. Elva forgot her and reached after the teleshow dials. There must be something on, something loud and full of action, something to watch, something to do with her evening.

The door opened. Elva turned about, tense with expectation. So Bors was home. And alone. If he'd brought a friend along, she would have had to go into the sleeping cubicle and merely listen. Upperclass Chertkoians didn't like women intruding on their conversation. But Bors alone meant she would have someone to talk to.

He came in, his tread showing he was also tired. He skimmed his hat into a corner and dropped his cloak on the floor. Belgoya crept forth to pick them up. As he sat down, she was present with a drink and a cigar.

Elva waited. She knew his moods. When the blunt, bearded face had lost some of its hardness, she donned a smile and stretched herself along the couch, leaning on one elbow. "You've been working yourself to death," she scolded.

He sighed. "Yeh. But the end's in view. Another week, and all the obscenity paperwork will be cleared up."

"You hope. One of your bureaucrats will probably invent nineteen more forms to fill out in quadruplicate."

"Probably."

"We never had that trouble at home. The planetary government was only a coordinating body with strictly limited powers. Why won't you people even consider establishing something similar?"

"You know the reasons. Five billion of them. You've got room to be an individual on Vaynamo." Golyev finished his drink and held the glass out for a refill. "By all chaos! I'm tempted to desert when we get there."

Elva lifted her brows. "That's a thought," she purred.

"Oh, you know it's impossible," he said, returning to his usual humorlessness. "Quite apart from the fact I'd be one enemy alien on an entire planet—"

"Not necessarily."

"—All right, even if I got naturalized (and who wants to become a clodhopper?) I'd have only thirty years till the Third Expedition came. I don't want to be a client in my old age. Or worse, see my children made clients."

Elva lit a second cigaret from the stub of the first. She drew in the smoke hard enough to hollow her cheeks.

But it's all right to be launching the Second Expedition and make clients of others, she thought. *The First, that captured me and a thousand more (What's become of them? How many are dead, how many found useless and sent lobotomized to the mines, how many are still being pumped dry of information?) . . . that was a mere scouting trip. The Second will have fifty warships, and try to force surrender. At the very least, it will flatten all possible defenses, destroy all imaginable war potential, bring back a whole herd of slaves. And then the Third, a thousand ships or more, will bring the final conquests, the garrisons, the overseers and entrepreneurs and colonists. But that won't be for forty-five Vaynamo years or better from tonight. A man on Vaynamo . . . Hauki . . . a man who survives the coming of the Second Expedition will have thirty-odd years left in which to be free. But will he dare have children?*

"I'll settle down there after the Third Expedition, I

think," Golyev admitted. "From what I saw of the planet last time, I believe I'd like it. And the opportunities are unlimited. A whole world waiting to be properly developed!"

"I could show you a great many chances you'd other-wise overlook," insinuated Elva.

Golyev shifted position. "Let's not go into that again," he said. "You know I can't take you along."

"You're the fleet commander, aren't you?"

"Yes, I will be, but curse it, can't you understand? The IP is not like any other corporation. We use men who think and act on their own, not planet-hugging morons like what's-her-name—" He jerked a thumb at Belgoya, who lowered her eyes meekly and continued mixing him a third drink. "Men of patron status, young-er sons of executives and engineers. The officers can't have special privileges. It'd ruin morale."

Elva fluttered her lashes. "Not that much. Really."

"My oldest boy's promised to take care of you. He's not such a bad fellow as you seem to think. You only have to go along with his whims. I'll see you again, in thirty years."

"When I'm gray and wrinkled. Why not kick me out in the streets and be done?"

"You know why!" he said ferociously. "You're the first woman I could ever talk to. No, I'm not bored with you! But—"

"If you really cared for me—"

"What kind of idiot do you take me for? I know you're planning to sneak away to your own people, once we've landed."

Elva tossed her head, haughtily. "Well! If you believe that of me, there's nothing more to say."

"Aw, now, sweetling, don't take that attitude." He reached out a hand to lay on her arm. She withdrew to the far end of the couch. He looked baffled.

"Another thing," he argued. "If you care about your planet at all, as I suppose you do, even if you've now seen what a bunch of petrified mudsuckers they are . . . remember, what we'll have to do there won't be pretty."

"First you call me a traitor," she flared, "and now you say I'm gutless!"

"Hey, wait a minute—"

"Go on, beat me. I can't stop you. You're brave enough for that."

"I never—"

In the end, he yielded.

*   *   *

553 A.C.C.:

The missile which landed on Yuvaskula had a ten-kilometer radius of total destruction. Thus most of the city went up in one radioactive fire-gout. In a way, the thought of men and women and little children with pet kittens, incinerated, made a trifle less pain in Elva than knowing the Old Town was gone: the cabin raised by the first men to land on Vaynamo, the ancient church of St. Yarvi with its stained glass windows and gilded bell-tower, the Museum of Art where she went as a girl on entranced visits, the University where she studied and where she met Karlavi—*I'm a true daughter of Vaynamo,* she thought with remorse. *Whatever is traditional, full of memories, whatever has been looked at and been done by all the generations before me, I hold dear. The Chertkoians don't care. They haven't any past worth remembering.*

Flames painted the northern sky red, even at this distance, as she walked among the plastishelters of the advanced base. She had flown within a hundred kilometers, using an aircar borrowed from the flagship, then landed to avoid possible missiles and hitched a ride here on a supply truck. The Chertkoian enlisted men aboard had been delighted until she showed them her pass, signed by Commander Golyev himself. Then they became cringingly respectful.

The pass was supposed to let her move freely about only in the rear areas, and she'd had enough trouble wheedling it from Bors. But no one thereafter looked closely at it. She herself was so unused to the concept of war that she didn't stop to wonder at such lax security measures. Had she done so, she would have realized Chertkoi had never developed anything better, never having faced an enemy of comparable strength. Vaynamo certainly wasn't, even though the planet was proving a hard-shelled opponent, with every farmhouse a potential arsenal and every forest road a possible death trap. Guerilla fighters hindered the movements of an invader

with armor, atomic artillery, complete control of air
and space; they could not stop him.

Elva drew her dark mantle more tightly about her
and crouched under a gun emplacement. A sentry went
by, his helmet square against the beloved familiar face
of a moon, his rifle aslant across the stars. She didn't
want needless questioning. For a moment the distant
blaze sprang higher, unrestful ruddy light touched her,
she was afraid she had been observed. But the man
continued his round.

From the air she had seen that the fire was mostly a
burning forest, kindled from Yuvaskula. Those wooden
houses not blown apart by the missile, stood unharmed
in whitest glow. Some process must have been developed at one of the research institutes, for indurating
timber, since she left. . . . How Bors would laugh if she
told him! An industry which turned out a bare minimum of vehicles, farm machinery, tools, chemicals; a
science which developed fireproofing techniques and
traced out ecological chains; a population which deliberately held itself static, so as to preserve its old customs
and laws—presuming to make war on Chertkoi!

Even so, he was too experienced a fighter to dismiss
any foe as weak without careful examination. He had
been excited enough about one thing to mention it to
Elva—a prisoner taken in a skirmish near Yuvaskula,
when he still hoped to capture the city intact: an officer,
who cracked just enough under interrogation to indicate
he knew something important. But Golyev couldn't wait
around for the inquisitors to finish their work. He must
go out the very next day to oversee the battle for Lempo
Machine Tool Works, and Elva knew he wouldn't return
soon. The plant had been constructed underground as
an economy measure, and to preserve the green parkscape
above. Now its concrete warrens proved highly defensible,
and were being bitterly contested. The Chertkoians meant
to seize it, so they could be sure of demolishing everything. They would not leave Vaynamo any nucleus of
industry. After all, the planet would have thirty-odd years
to recover and rearm itself against the Third Expedition.

Left alone by Bors, Elva took an aircar and slipped off
to the advanced base.

She recognized the plastishelter she wanted by its

Intelligence insignia. The guard outside aimed a rifle at
her. "Halt!" His boyish voice cracked over with nervousness. More than one sentry had been found in the morning with his throat cut.

"It's all right," she told him. "I'm to see the prisoner
Ivalo."

"The gooze officer?" He flashed a pencil-thin beam
across her face. "But you're a—uh—"

"A Vaynamoan myself. Of course. There are a few of
us along, you know. Prisoners taken last time, who've
enlisted in your cause as guides and spies. You must
have heard of me. I'm Elva, Commander Golyev's lady."

"Oh. Yes, mistress. Sure I have."

"Here's my pass."

He squinted at it uneasily. "But, uh, may I ask what,
uh, what *you* figure to do? I've got strict orders—"

Elva gave him her most confidential smile. "My own
patron had the idea. The prisoner is withholding valuable information. He has been treated roughly, but
resisted. Now, all at once, we'll take the pressure off. An
attractive woman of his own race. . . ."

"I get it. Maybe he will crack. I dunno, though, mistress.
These slant-eyed towheads are mean animals—begging
your pardon! Go right on in. Holler if he gets rough or,
or anything."

The door was unlocked for her. Elva went on through,
into a hemicylindrical room so low that she must stoop.
A lighting tube switched on, showing a pallet laid across
the floor.

Captain Ivalo was gray at the temples, but still tough
and supple. His face had gone haggard, sunken eyes and
a stubble of beard; his garments were torn and filthy.
When he looked up, coming awake, he was too exhausted
to show much surprise. "What now?" he said in dull
Chertkoian. "What are you going to try next?"

Elva answered in Vaynamoan (Oh, God, it was a year
and a half, her own time, nearly seventeen years cosmic
time, since she had uttered a word to anyone from her
planet!): "Be quiet. I beg you. We mustn't be suspected."

He sat up. "Who are you?" he snapped. His own
Vaynamoan accent was faintly pedantic; he must be a
teacher or scientist in that peacetime life which now
seemed so distant. "A collaborator? I understand there

are some. Every barrel must hold a few rotten apples, I suppose."

She sat down on the floor near him, hugged her knees and stared at the curving wall. "I don't know what to call myself," she said tonelessly. "I'm with them, yes. But they captured me the last time."

He whistled, a soft note. One hand reached out, not altogether steady and stopping short of touching her. "I was young then," he said. "But I remember. Do I know your family?"

"Maybe. I'm Elva, daughter of Byarmo, the Magnate of Ruuyalka. My husband was Karlavi, the Freeholder of Tervola." Suddenly she couldn't stay controlled. She grasped his arm so hard that her nails drew blood. "Do you know what became of my son? His name was Hauki. I got him away, in care of an Alfa servant. Hauki, Karlavi's son, Freeholder of Tervola. Do you know?"

He disengaged himself as gently as possible and shook his head. "I'm sorry. I've heard of both places, but only as names. I'm from the Aakinen Islands myself."

Her head dropped.

"Ivalo is my name," he said clumsily.

"I know."

"What?"

"Listen." She raised her eyes to his. They were quite dry. "I've been told you have important information."

He bridled. "If you think—"

"No. Please listen. Here." She fumbled in a pocket of her gown. At last her fingers closed on the vial. She held it out to him. "An antiseptic. But the label says it's very poisonous if taken internally. I brought it for you."

He stared at her for a long while.

"It's all I can do," she mumbled, looking away again.

He took the bottle and turned it over and over in his hands. The night grew silent around them.

Finally he asked, "Won't you suffer for this?"

"Not too much."

"Wait. . . . If you could get in here, you can surely escape completely. Our troops can't be far off. Or any farmer hereabouts will hide you."

She shook her head. "No. I'll stay with them. Maybe I can help in some other small way. What else has there been to keep me alive, but the hope of— It wouldn't be any better, living here, if we're all conquered. There's to be a final attack, three decades hence. Do you know that?"

"Yes. Our side takes prisoners too, and quizzes them. The first episode puzzled us. Many thought it had only been a raid by—what's the word?—by pirates. But now we know they really do intend to take our planet away."

"You must have developed some good linguists," she said, seeking impersonality. "To be able to talk with your prisoners. Of course, you yourself, after capture, could be educated by the hypnopede."

"The what?"

"The language-teaching machine."

"Oh, yes, the enemy do have them, don't they? But we do too. After the first raid, those who thought there was a danger the aliens might come back set about developing such machines. I knew Chertkoian weeks before my own capture."

"I wish I could help you escape," she said desolately. "But I don't see how. That bottle is all I can do. Isn't it?"

"Yes." He regarded the thing with a fascination.

"My patron . . . Golyev himself—said his men would rip you open to get your knowledge. So I thought—"

"You're very kind." Ivalo grimaced, as if he had tasted something foul. "But your act may turn out pointless. I don't know anything useful. I wasn't even sworn to secrecy about what I do know. Why've I held out, then? Don't ask me. Stubbornness. Anger. Or just hating to admit my people—our people, damn it!—that they could be so weak and foolish."

"What?"

"They could win the war at a stroke," he said. "They won't. They'd rather die, and let their children be enslaved by the Third Expedition."

"What do you *mean?*" She crouched to hands and knees.

He shrugged. "I told you, a number of people on Vaynamo took the previous invasion at its word, that it was the vanguard of a conquering army. There was no official action. How could there be, with a government as feeble as ours? But some of the research biologists—"

"Not a plague!"

"Yes. Mutated from the local paracoryzoid virus. Incu-

bation period, approximately one month, during which
time it's contagious. Vaccination is still effective two
weeks after exposure, so all our population could be
safeguarded. But the Chertkoians would take the disease
back with them. Estimated deaths, ninety percent of the
race."

"But—"

"That's where the government did step in," he said
with bitterness. "The information was suppressed. The
virus cultures were destroyed. The theory was, even to
save ourselves we couldn't do such a thing."

Elva felt the tautness leave her. She sagged. She had
seen small children on Chertkoi too.

"They're right, of course," she said wearily.

"Perhaps. Perhaps. And yet we'll be overrun and
butchered, or reduced to serfdom. Won't we? Our forests will be cut down, our mines gutted, our poor Alfavala
exterminated. . . . To hell with it." Ivalo gazed at the
poison vial. "I don't have any scientific data, I'm not a
virologist. It can't do any military harm to tell the
Chertkoians. But I've seen what they've done to us. I
would give them the sickness."

"I wouldn't." Elva bit her lip.

He regarded her for a long time. "Won't you escape?
Never mind being a planetary heroine. There's nothing
you can do. The invaders will go home when they've
wrecked all our industry. They won't come again for
thirty years. You can be free most of your life."

"You forget," she said, "that if leave with them, and
come back, the time for me will only have been one or
two years." She sighed. "I can't help make ready for the
next battle. I'm just a woman. Untrained. While maybe
. . . oh, if nothing else, there'll be more Vaynamoan prisoners brought to Chertkoi. I have a tiny bit of influence.
Maybe I can help them."

Ivalo considered the poison. "I was about to use this
anyway," he muttered. "I didn't think staying alive was
worth the trouble. But now—if you can— No." He gave
the vial back to her. "I thank you, my lady."

"I have an idea," she said, with a hint of vigor in her
voice. "Go ahead and tell them what you know. Pretend
I talked you into it. Then I might be able to get you
exchanged. It's barely possible."

"Oh, perhaps," he said.

She rose to go. "If you are set free," she stammered, "will you make a visit to Tervola? Will you find Hauki, Karvali's son, and tell him you saw me? If he's alive."

* * *

569 A.C.C.:

Dirzh had changed while the ships were away. The evolution continued after their return. The city grew bigger, smokier, uglier. More people each year dropped from client status, went underground and joined the gangs. Occasionally, these days, the noise and vibration of pitched battles down in the tunnels could be detected up on patron level. The desert could no longer be seen, even from the highest towers, only the abandoned mine and the slag mountains, in process of conversion to tenements. The carcinogenic murkiness crept upward until it could be smelled on the most elite balconies. Teleshows got noisier and nakeder, to compete with live performances, which were now offering more elaborate bloodlettings than old-fashioned combats. The news from space was of a revolt suppressed on Novagal, resulting in such an acute labor shortage that workers were drafted from Imfan and shipped thither.

Only when you looked at the zenith was there no apparent change. The daylit sky was still cold purplish-blue, with an occasional yellow dustcloud. At night there were still the stars, and a skull.

And yet, thought Elva, you wouldn't need a large telescope to see the Third Expedition fleet in orbit—eleven hundred spacecraft, the unarmed ones loaded with troops and equipment, nearly the whole strength of Chertkoi marshalling to conquer Vaynamo. Campaigning across interstellar distances wasn't easy. You couldn't send home for supplies or reinforcements. You broke the enemy or he broke you. Fleet Admiral Bors Golyev did not intend to be broken.

He did not even plan to go home with news of a successful probing operation or a successful raid. The Third Expedition was to be final. And he must allow for the Vaynamoans having had a generation in which to recuperate. He'd smashed their industry, but if they were really determined, they could have rebuilt. No doubt a space fleet of some kind would be waiting to oppose him.

He knew it couldn't be of comparable power. Ten million people, forced to recreate all their mines and furnaces and factories before they could lay the keel of a single boat, had no possibility of matching the concerted efforts of six-and-a-half billion whose world had been continuously industrialized for centuries, and who could draw on the resources of two subject planets. Sheer mathematics ruled it out. But the ten million could accomplish something; and nuclear-fusion missiles were to some degree an equalizer. Therefore Bors Golyev asked for so much strength that the greatest conceivable enemy force would be swamped. And he got it.

Elva leaned on the balcony rail. A chill wind fluttered her gown about her, so that the rainbow hues rippled and ran into each other. She had to admit the fabric was lovely. Bors tried hard to please her. (Though why must he mention the price?) He was so childishly happy himself, at his accomplishments, at his new eminence, at the eight-room apartment which he now rated on the very heights of the Lebadan Tower.

"Not that we'll be here long," he had said, after they first explored its mechanized intricacies. "My son Nivko has done good work in the home office. That's how come I got this command; experience alone wasn't enough. Of course, he'll expect me to help along his sons. . . . But anyhow, the Third Expedition can go even sooner than I'd hoped. Just a few months, and we're on our way!"

"We?" murmured Elva.

"You do want to come?"

"The last voyage, you weren't so eager."

"Uh, yes. I did have a deuce of a time, too, getting you aboard. But this'll be different. I've got so much rank I'm beyond criticism, even beyond jealousy. And second— well, you count too. You're not any picked-up native female. You're Elva! The girl who on her own hook got that fellow Ivalo to confess."

She turned her head slightly, regarding him sideways from droop-lidded blue eyes. Under the ruddy sun, her yellow hair turned to raw gold. "I should think the news would have alarmed them, here on Chertkoi," she said.

"Being told that they nearly brought about their own extinction. I wonder that they dare launch another attack."

Golyev grinned. "You should have heard the ruckus. Some Directors did vote to keep hands off Vaynamo. Others wanted to sterilize the whole planet with cobalt missiles. But I talked 'em around. Once we've beaten the fleet and occupied the planet, its whole population will be hostage for good behavior. We'll make examples of the first few goozes who give us trouble of any sort. Then they'll know we mean what we say when we announce our policy. At the first suspicion of plague among us, we'll lay waste a continent. If the suspicion is confirmed, we'll bombard the whole works. No, there will not be any bug warfare."

"I know. I've heard your line of reasoning before. About five hundred times, in fact."

"Destruction! Am I really that much of a bore?" He came up behind her and laid his hands on her shoulders. "I don't mean to be. Honest. I'm not used to talking to women, that's all."

"And I'm not used to being shut away like a prize goldfish, except when you want to exhibit me," she said sharply.

He kissed her neck. His whiskers tickled. "It'll be different on Vaynamo. When we're settled down. I'll be governor of the planet. The Directorate has as good as promised me. Then I can do as I want. And so can you."

"I doubt that! Why should I believe anything you say? When I told you I'd made Ivalo talk by promising you would exchange him, you wouldn't keep the promise." She tried to wriggle free, but his grip was too strong. She contented herself with going rigid. "Now, when I tell you the prisoners we brought back this time are to be treated like human beings, you whine about your damned Directorate—"

"But the Directorate makes policy!"

"You're the Fleet Admiral, as you never lose a chance to remind me. You can certainly bring pressure to bear. You can insist the Vaynamoans be taken out of those kennels and given honorable detention—"

"Awww, now." His lips nibbled along her cheek. She turned her head away and continued:

"—and you can get what you insist on. They're your own prisoners, aren't they? I've listened enough to you, and your dreary officers when you brought them home. I've read books, hundreds of books. What else is there for me to do, day after day and week after week?"

"But I'm busy! I'd like to take you out, honest, but—"

"So I understand the power structure on Chertkoi just as well as you do, Bors Golyev. If not better. If you don't know how to use your own influence, then slough off some of that conceit, sit down and listen while I tell you how!"

"Well, uh, I never denied, sweetling, you've given me some useful advice from time to time."

"So listen to me! I say all the Vaynamoans you hold are to be given decent quarters, recreation, and respect. What did you capture them for, if not to get some use out of them? And the proper use is not to titillate yourself by kicking them around. A dog would serve that purpose better.

"Furthermore, the fleet has to carry them all back to Vaynamo."

"What? You don't know what you're talking about! The logistics is tough enough without—"

"I do so know what I'm talking about. Which is more than I can say for you. You want guides, intermediaries, puppet leaders, don't you? Not by the score, a few cowards and traitors, as you have hitherto. You need hundreds. Well, there they are, right in your hands."

"And hating my guts," Golyev pointed out.

"Give them reasonable living conditions and they won't. Not quite so much, anyhow. Then bring them back home—a generation after they left, all their friends aged or dead, everything altered once you've conquered the planet. And let me deal with them. You'll get helpers!"

"Uh, well, uh, I'll think about it."

"You'll do something about it!" She eased her body, leaning back against the hard rubbery muscles of his chest. Her face turned upward, with a slow smile. "You're good at doing things, Bors," she said languidly.

"Oh, Elva—"

Later: "You know one thing I want to do? As soon as I'm well established in the governorship? I want to marry you. Properly and openly. Let 'em be shocked. I won't care. I want to be your husband, and the father of your kids, Elva. How's that sound? Mistress Governor General Elva Golyev of Vaynamo Planetary Province. Never thought you'd get that far in life, did you?"

* * *

584 A.C.C.:

As they neared the end of the journey, he sent her to his cabin. An escape suit—an armored cylinder with gravity propulsors, air regenerator, food and water supplies, which she could enter in sixty seconds—occupied most of the room. "Not that I expect any trouble," he said. "But if something should happen . . . I hope you can make it down to the surface." He paused. The officers on the bridge moved quietly about their tasks; the engines droned; the distorted stars of near-light velocity framed his hard brown face. A thin sheen of sweat was on his skin.

"I love you, you know," he finished. Quickly, he turned back to his duties. Elva went below.

Clad in a spaceman's uniform, seated on the bunk, enclosed in toning metal, she felt the inward wrench as the agoration went off and speed was converted back to atomic mass. The cabin's private viewscreen showed stars in their proper constellations again, needle-sharp against blackness. Vaynamo was tiny and blue, still several hundred thousand kilometers remote. Elva ran fingers through her hair. The scalp beneath felt tight, and her lips were dry. A person couldn't help being afraid, she thought. Just a little afraid.

She called up the memory of Karlavi's land, where he had now lain for sixty-two years. Reeds whispered along the shores of Rovaniemi, the wind made a rippling in long herbal, and it was time again for the lampflowers to blow, all down the valley. Dreamlike at the edge of vision, the snowpeaks of the High Mikkela floated in an utter blue.

I'm coming back, Karlavi, she thought.

In her screen, the nearer vessels were glinting toys, plunging through enormous emptiness. The further ones were not visible at this low magnification. Only the senses of radar, gravpulse, and less familiar creations, analyzed by whirling electrons in a computer bank, gave any approach to reality. But she could listen in on the main intercom line to the bridge if she chose, and hear those data spoken. She flipped the switch. Nothing yet, only routine reports. Had the planet's disc grown a trifle?

Have I been wrong all the time? she thought. Her heart stopped for a second.

Then: "Alert! Condition red! Alert! Condition red! Objects detected, approaching nine-thirty o'clock, fifteen degress high. Neutrino emissions indicate nuclear engines."

"Alert! Condition yellow! Quiescent object detected in orbit about target planet, two-thirty o'clock, ten degrees low, circa 75,000 kilometers distant. Extremely massive. Repeat, quiescent. Low level of nuclear activity but at bolometric temperature of ambient space. Possibly an abandoned space fortress, except for being so massive."

"Detected objects identified as spacecraft. Approaching with average radial velocity of 250 KPS. No evident deceleration. Number very large, estimated at five thousand. All units small, about the mass of our scoutboats."

The gabble went on until Golyev's voice cut through: "Attention! Fleet Admiral to bridge of all units. Now hear this." Sardonically: "The opposition is making a good try. Instead of building any real ships—they could have constructed only a few at best—they've turned out thousands of manned warboats. Their plan is obviously to cut through our formation, relying on speed, and release tracking torps in quantity. Stand by to repel. We have enough detectors, anti-missiles, negafields, to overwhelm them in this department too! Once past us, the boats will need hours to decelerate and come back within decent shooting range. By that time we should be in orbit around the planet. Be alert for possible emergencies, of course. But I expect only standard operations to be necessary. Good shooting!"

Elva strained close to her screen. All at once she saw the Vaynamoan fleet, mere sparks, but a horde of them, twinkling among the stars. Closer! Her fingers strained against each other. *They* must *have some plan*, she told herself. *If I'm blown up in five minutes—I was hoping I'd get down to you, Karlavi. But if I don't, goodbye, goodbye.*

The fleets neared each other: on the one side, ponderous dreadnaughts, cruisers, auxiliary warcraft, escorting swarms of transport and engineer ships; on the opposite side, needle-thin boats whose sole armor was velocity. The guns of Chertkoi swung about, hoping for a lucky hit. At such speeds it was improbable. The fleets would interpenetrate and pass in a fractional second. The Vaynamoans could not be blasted until they came to grips near their home world. However, if a nuclear shell should find its mark now—what a blaze in heaven!

The flagship staggered.

"Engine room to bridge! What's happened?"

"Bridge to engine room! Gimme some power there! What in all destruction—?"

"*Sharyats* to *Askol*! *Sharyats* to *Askol*! Am thrown off course! Accelerating! What's going on?"

"Look out!"

"*Fodorev* to *Zuevots*! Look alive, you bloody fool! You'll ram us!"

Cushioned by the internal field, Elva felt only the minutest fraction of that immense velocity change. Even so, a wave of sickness went through her. She clutched at the bunk stanchion. The desk ripped from a loose mooring and crashed into the wall, which buckled. The deck split open underfoot. A roar went through the entire hull, ribs groaned as they bent, plates screamed as they sheared. A girder snapped in twain and spat sharp fragments among a gun turret crew. A section broke apart, air gushed out, a hundred men died before the sealing bulkheads could close.

After a moment, the stabilizing energies regained interior control. The images on Elva's screen steadied. She drew a shaken lungful of air and watched. Out of formation, the *Askol* plunged within a kilometer of her sister ship the *Zuevots*—just when that cyclopean hull smashed into the cruiser *Fodorev*. Fire sheeted as accumulator banks were shorted. The two giants crumpled, glowed white at the point of impact, fused, and spun off in a lunatic waltz. Men and supplies were pinwheeled from the cracks gaping in them. Two gun turrets wrapped their long barrels around each other like intertwining snakes. Then the whole mass struck a third vessel with shattering impact. Steel chunks exploded into space.

Through the noise and the human screaming, Golyev's voice blasted. "Pipe down there! Belay that! By Creation,

I'll shoot the next man who whimpers! The enemy will be here in a minute. All stations, by the numbers, report."

A measure of discipline returned. These were fighting men. Instruments fingered outward, the remaining computers whirred, minds made deductive leaps, gunners returned to their posts. The Vaynamoan fleet passed through, and the universe exploded in brief pyrotechnics. Many a Chertkoian ship died then, its defenses too battered, its defenders too stunned to ward off the tracking torpedoes. But others fought back, saved themselves, and saw their enemies vanish in the distance.

Still they tumbled off course, their engines helpless to free them. Elva heard a physicist's clipped tones give the deduction from his readings. The entire fleet had been caught in a cone of gravitational force emanating from that massive object detected in orbit. Like a maelstrom of astronomical dimensions, it had snatched them from their paths. Those closest and in the most intense field strength—a fourth of the armada—had been wrecked by sheer deceleration. Now the force was drawing them down the vortex of itself.

"But that's impossible!" wailed the *Askol*'s chief engineer. "A gravity attractor beam of that magnitude. . . . Admiral, it can't be done! The power requirements would burn out any generator in a microsecond!"

"It's being done," said Golyev harshly. "Maybe they figured out a new way to feed energy into a space distorter. Now, where are those figures on intensity? And my calculator. . . . Yeh. The whole fleet will soon be in a field so powerful that— Well, we won't let it happen. Stand by to hit that generator with everything we've got."

"But sir . . . we must have—I don't know how many ships—close enough to it now to be within total destruction radius."

"Tough on them. Stand by. Gunnery Control, fire when ready."

And then, whispered, even though that particular line was private and none else in the ship would hear: "Elva! Are you all right down there? Elva!"

Her hands had eased their trembling enough for her to light a cigaret. She didn't speak. Let him worry. It might reduce his efficiency.

Her screen did not happen to face the vortex source, and thus did not show its destruction by the nuclear barrage. Not that that could have been registered. The instant explosion of sun-center ferocity transcended any sense, human or electronic. Down on Vaynamo surface, in broad daylight, they must have turned dazzled eyes from that brilliance. Anyone within a thousand kilometers of those warheads died, no matter how much steel and force field he had interposed. Two score Chertkoian ships were suddenly manned by corpses. Those further in were fused to lumps. Still further in, they ceased to exist, save as gas at millions of degrees temperature. The vessels already crashed on the giant station were turned into unstable isotopes, their very atoms dying.

But the station itself vanished. And Vaynamo had had the capacity to build only one such monster. The Chertkoian ships were free again.

"Admiral to all captains!" cried Golyev's lion voice. "Admiral to all captains. Let the reports wait. Clear the lines. I want every man in the fleet to hear me. Stand by for message.

"Now hear this! This is Supreme Commander Bors Golyev. We just took a rough blow, boys. The enemy had an unsuspected weapon, and cost us a lot of casualties. But we've destroyed the thing. I repeat, we blew it out of the cosmos. And I say, well done! I say also, we still have a hundred times the strength of the enemy, and he's shot his bolt. We're going on in! We're going to—"

"Alert! Condition red! Enemy boats returning. Enemy boats returning. Radial velocity circa 50 KPS, but accleration circa 100 G."

"What?"

Elva herself saw the Vaynamoan shooting stars come back into sight.

Golyev tried hard to shout down the panic of his officers. Would they stop running around like old women? The enemy had developed something else, some method of accelerating at unheard-of rates under gravitational thrust. But not by witchcraft! It could be an internal-stress compensator developed to ultimate efficiency, plus an adaptation of whatever principle was used in the attractor vortex. Or it could be a breakthrough, a totally

new principle, maybe something intermediate between
the agoratron and the ordinary interplanetary drive. . . .
"Never mind what, you morons! They're only flocks of
splinters! Kill them!"

But the armada was roiling about in blind confusion.
The detectors had given mere seconds of warning, which
were lost in understanding that the warning was correct
and in frantically seeking to rally men already shaken.
Then the splinter fleet was in among the Chertkoians.
It braked its furious relative velocity with a near-
instantaneous quickness for which the Chertkoian gunners
and gun computers had never been prepared. However,
the Vaynamoan gunners were ready. And even a boat can
carry torpedoes which will annihilate a battleship.

In a thousand fiery bursts, the armada died.

Not all of it. Unarmed craft were spared, if they would
surrender. Vaynamoan boarding parties freed such of
their countrymen as they found. The *Askol*, under Golyev's
personal command, stood off its attackers and moved
doggedly outward, toward regions where it could use
the agoratron to escape. The captain of a prize re-
vealed that over a hundred Vaynamoans were aboard
the flagship. So the attempt to blow it up was abandoned.
Instead, a large number of boats shot dummy missiles,
which kept the defense fully occupied. Meanwhile a companion force lay alongside, cut its way through the armor,
and sent men in.

The Chertkoian crew resisted. But they were grossly
outnumbered and outgunned. Most died, under bullets
and grenades, gas and flamethrowers. Certain holdouts,
who fortified a compartment, were welded in from the
outside and left to starve or capitulate, whichever they
chose. Even so, the *Askol* was so big that the boarding
party took several hours to gain full possession.

The door opened. Elva stood up.

At first the half-dozen men who entered seemed foreign.
In a minute—she was too tired and dazed to think
clearly—she understood why. They were all in blue
jackets and trousers, a uniform. She had never before
seen two Vaynamoans dressed exactly alike. *But of course
they would be*, she thought in a vague fashion. *We had to
build a navy, didn't we?*

And they remained her own people. Fair skin, straight hair, high cheekbones, tilted light eyes which gleamed all the brighter through the soot of battle. And, yes, they still walked like Vaynamoans, the swinging freeman's gait and the head held high, such as she had not seen for . . . for how long? So their clothes didn't matter, nor even the guns in their hands.

Slowly, through the ringing in her ears, she realized that the combat noise had stopped.

A young man in the lead took a step in her direction. "My lady—" he began.

"Is that her for certain?" asked someone else, less gently. "Not a collaborator?"

A new man pushed his way through the squad. He was grizzled, pale from lack of sun, wearing a sleazy prisoner's coverall. But a smile touched his lips, and his bow to Elva was deep.

"This is indeed my lady of Tervola," he said. To her: "When these men released me, up in Section Fourteen, I told them we'd probably find you here. I am so glad."

She needed a while to recognize him. "Oh. Yes." Her head felt heavy. It was all she could do to nod. "Captain Ivalo. I hope you're all right."

"I am, thanks to you, my lady. Someday we'll know how many hundreds of us are alive and sane—and here! —because of you."

The squad leader made another step forward, sheathed his machine pistol and lifted both hands toward her. He was a well-knit, good-looking man, blond of hair, a little older than she: in his mid-thirties, perhaps. He tried to speak, but no words came out, and then Ivalo drew him back.

"In a moment," said the ex-captive. "Let's first take care of the unpleasant business."

The leader hesitated, then, with a grimace, agreed. Two men shoved Bors Golyev along. The admiral dripped blood from a dozen wounds and stumbled in his weariness. But when he saw Elva, he seemed to regain himself. "You weren't hurt," he breathed. "I was so afraid . . ."

Ivalo said like steel: "I've explained the facts of this case to the squad officer here, as well as his immediate superior. I'm sure you'll join us in our wish not to be

inhumane, my lady. And yet a criminal trial in the
regular courts would publicize matters best forgotten
and could give this man only a limited punishment. So
we, here and now, under the conditions of war and in
view of your high services—"

The squad officer interrupted. He was white about the
nostrils. "Anything you order, my lady," he said. "You
pass the sentence. We'll execute it at once."

"Elva," whispered Golyev.

She stared at him, remembering fire and enslave-
ments and a certain man dead on a barricade. Everything seemed distant, not quite real.

"There's been too much suffering already," she said.
She pondered a few seconds. "Just take him out and
shoot him."

The officer looked relieved. He led his men forth. Golyev
started to speak, but was hustled away too fast.

Ivalo remained in the cabin. "My lady—" he began,
slow and awkward.

"Yes?" As her weariness overwhelmed her, Elva sat
down again on the bunk. She fumbled for a cigaret.
There was no emotion in her, only a dull wish for sleep.

"I've wondered. . . . Don't answer this if you don't
want to. You've been through so much."

"That's all right," she said mechanically. "The trouble is over now, isn't it? I mean, we mustn't let the past
obsess us."

"Of course. Uh, they tell me Vaynamo hasn't changed
much. The defense effort was bound to affect society
somewhat, but they've tried to minimize that, and
succeeded. Our culture has a built-in stability, you know.

"Not that we mean to sit still. In due course, we'll be
sending expeditions of our own out after those devils.
Liberate their slave worlds and make certain they can't
ever try afresh. But that shouldn't be difficult.

"As for you, I inquired very carefully on your behalf.
Tervola remains in your family. The land and the people
are as you remember."

She closed her eyes, feeling the first thaw within herself.
"Now I can sleep," she told him.

Recalling, she looked up a bit startled. "But you had a
question for me, Ivalo?"

"Yes. All this time, I couldn't help wondering. Why

you stayed with the enemy. You could have escaped. Did you know how great a service you were going to do?"

Her own smile was astonishing to her. "Well, I knew I couldn't be much use on Vaynamo," she said. "Could I? There was a chance I could help on Chertkoi. But I wasn't being brave. The worst had already happened to me. Now I need only wait . . . a matter of months only, my time . . . and everything bad would be over. Whereas—well, if I'd escaped from the Second Expedition, I'd have lived most of my life in the shadow of the Third. Please don't make a fuss about me. I was actually an awful coward."

His jaw dropped. "You mean you knew we'd win? But you couldn't have! Everything pointed the other way!"

The nightmare was fading more rapidly than she had dared hope. She shook her head, still smiling, not triumphant but glad to speak the knowledge which had kept her alive. "You're being unfair to our people. As unfair as the Chertkoians were. They thought that because we preferred social stability and room to breathe, we must be stagnant. They forgot you can have bigger adventures in the spirit, than in all the physical universe. We really did have a very powerful science and technology. It was oriented toward life, toward beautifying and improving instead of exploiting nature. But it wasn't less virile for that. Was it?"

"But we had no industry to speak of. We don't even now."

"I wasn't counting on our factories, I said, but on our science. When you told me about that horrible virus weapon being suppressed, you confirmed my hopes. We aren't saints. Our government wouldn't have been quite so quick to get rid of those plagues—would at least have tried to bluff with them—if something better weren't in prospect. Wouldn't it?

"I couldn't even guess what our scientists might develop, given two generations which the enemy did not have. I did think they would probably have to use physics rather than biology. And why not? You can't have an advanced chemical, medical, genetic, ecological technology without knowing all the physics there is to know. Can you? Quantum theory explains mutations. But it also explains atomic reactions, or whatever they used in those new machines.

"Oh, yes, Ivalo, I felt sure we'd win. All I had to do myself was work to get us prisoners—especially me, to be quite honest—get us all present at the victory."

He looked at her with awe. Somehow that brought back the heaviness in her. *After all*, she thought . . . *sixty-two years. Tervola abides. But who will know me? I am going to be so much alone.*

Boots rang on metal. The young squad leader stepped forward again. "That's that," he said. His bleakness vanished and he edged closer to Evla, softly, almost timidly.

"I trust," said Ivalo with a rich, growing pleasure in his voice, "that my lady will permit me to visit her from time to time."

"I hope you will!" she murmured.

"We temporal castaways are bound to be disoriented for a while," he said. "We must help each other. You, for example, may have some trouble adjusting to the fact that your son Hauki, the Freeholder of Tervola—"

"Hauki!" She sprang to her feet. The cabin blurred around her.

"—is now a vigorous elderly man who looks back on a most successful life," said Ivalo. "Which includes the begetting of Karlavi here." Her grandson's strong hands closed about her own. "Who in turn," finished Ivalo, "is the recent father of a bouncing baby boy named Hauki. And all your people are waiting to welcome you home!"

EDITOR'S INTRODUCTION TO:

THE TECHNOLOGICAL WAR
by
Stefan T. Possony and Jerry E. Pournelle

In 1970, Stefan Possony and I published a book called *The Strategy of Technology*. It was a *success d' estim*, which is to say that it didn't make much money, but it did get good reviews. The book was later adopted as a text in the US Air Force Academy and the Air War College. We can hope it had some influence among up and coming officers.

There is, or was, a Brentano's book store in the basement of the Pentagon; over a thousand copies of *Strategy of Technology* were sold there. Alas, we saw no other evidence of our influence on US military policy.

This chapter, "The Technological War", was in some ways the heart of the book. In this essay we try to analyze the nature of war, the nature of technology, and the nature of strategy. No one could do more than introduce these subjects in a brief essay. We hope we have done that.

Dr. Stefan T. Possony received his Ph.D. in political science from the University of Vienna. Following his graduation he was active in the anti-Nazi movement in Austria, and his name was high on the Gestapo's wanted list. After many adventures he came to the United States, where he worked for some twenty years in the intelligence community.

Dr. Possony is Senior Fellow Emeritus of the Hoover

Institution on War Revolution and Peace, and is author of more than a score of books.

The following chapter from *The Strategy of Technology* needed little revision. I have inserted brief comments where they seemed appropriate.

THE TECHNOLOGICAL WAR
by
Stefan T. Possony and J. E. Pournelle

The United States is at war. Whether we consider this
to be the Protracted Conflict initiated in 1917 by the
Bolsheviks or something new brought about by the march
of technology in this country, the war cannot be escaped.
The field of engagement is not everywhere bloody. Except for financial sacrifices, many citizens of the West
and subjects of Communism may be unaware of the
conflict until the decisive moment, if it ever comes, is
upon them. For all that, the Technological War is most
real, and we must understand its nature, for it is decisive.
Our survival depends on our not losing this battle.

The natures of both technology and the enemy dictate
this state of warfare. The U.S.S.R. is a power-oriented
dictatorship, whose official doctrine is Communism: That
is, a chiliastic movement which seeks to liberate—we
would say enslave—the entire earth. It is not necessary
for all of the individual leaders of the U.S.S.R. to be true
believers in this doctrine. Since the Soviet Union is a
dictatorship, the usual dynamics of dictatorship apply.

One fundamental fact of dictatorship is that losing
factions within its ruling structure forever lose their
positions and power. They may retain their lives, but
they retain little else, and often they do not survive.
Thus, such rulers, whether sincere or cynical, have a
powerful incentive to conform to the official ideology or
line of the top man or group. Moreover, they compete
with each other for power. If a powerful faction counsels
aggressive expansion—whether out of sincere belief in
the ideology, because expansion creates more opportuni-

ties for advancement, or because it expects aggression to prop up a tottering regime—failure is the only way through which its influence will be reduced. Every successful aggressive action increases the influence of those who counsel aggression.

If aggressive moves encounter stern opposition, so that the ruling faction is not only not rewarded for its expansionist policies, but finds its national power decreased, changes in the official policy may take place. Such failures, consequent punishment, and resultant troubles for the dictatorship may serve to place in power a more cautious group dedicated to defense of the empire and the status quo; but it is obvious that this turn to pure imperial defense has not yet happened in the U.S.S.R.

We do not mean that the Kremlin's government will necessarily be aggressive. Other Communist states may play a role. As we write this (1968), there is a growing danger of conflict between the U.S.S.R. and Maoist China. However, expansionism is the normal state of affairs for the Soviet Union.

(We did not predict the events that took place in China following The Great Cultural Revolution. No one else did, either. We do note that tyrannies try to remain independent of each other, and it is unlikely that Communist states can ever have "equal and friendly" relations with each other. JEP 1983)

Moreover, aggressive actions may occur because of internal pressures, especially in a period when faith in Communism as an ideological system is declining, and it is possible, although unlikely, that aggressive initiatives will be taken by non-Communist states. Despite all those complications the U.S.S.R. is the single most important and strongest opponent of the United States. Consequently, American strategists must primarily be concerned with Soviet strategy and the threat posed by the U.S.S.R. (1)

The nature of technology also dictates that there will be conflict. Technology flows on without regard for human intentions, and each technological breakthrough offers the possibility for decisive advantages to the side that first exploits it. Such advantages will be fleeting, for although the weaker side does not have weapons based on the new technology yet, it is certain that it will have them in the near future. In such circumstances, failure to exploit the capability advantage is treason to the Communist cause.

It must be emphasized that to the committed Communist, there are no ideological reasons for not exploiting advantages over the capitalists. The only possible objections are operational. No communist can admit that a capitalist government is legitimate; thus there can be no "mercy" to a vulnerable capitalist regime.

Therefore, capability combines with ideology to produce a powerful effect on intentions, which, be they ever so pure before the advantage was obtained, cannot fail to change with the increasing capabilities: if capabilities grow, intentions become more ambitious.

Thus, it is futile and dangerous to base modern strategy on an analysis of the intentions of the enemy. The modern strategist must be concerned with the present and future capabilities of his opponent, not with hopes and dreams about his goals. The dynamics of dictatorship provide a continuing source of ambitious advisors who will counsel the rulers of the Soviet Union toward aggressive action, and only through continuous engagement in the Technological War can the United States ensure peace and survival.

Because the goals of the United States and the U.S.S.R. are asymmetric, the strategies each employ in the Technological War will be different. The United States is dedicated to a strategy of stability, of being a stabilizing rather than a disturbing power; of preserving the status quo and the balance of power rather than seeking conquest and the final solution to the problems of international conflict through occupation or extermination of all opponents.

The U.S.S.R. is expansionist; aggressive; a disturber power which officially states that the only true peace is that of world Communism. The United States has conceded the initiative in the Protracted Conflict, and is to a great extent bound to a policy of reacting to Communist advances, rather than seeking the intiative in undermining Communist power.

Because we have conceded the initiative in the phase of the Protracted Conflict which deals with control of territory and people, (2) we must not abandon the initiative in the Technological War. We are engaged in war, not a race, although it may appear to be a race to many of us. But it is a race in which we must stay ahead, because if we ever fall behind, the opponent will blow up the bridges before our runners can cross them.

Given the opportunity, the Soviets will deny us access to the tools of the Technological War exactly as they have denied access to their territory, which they call the "peace zone" in distinction to the rest of the world which is the "war zone". If we are to be on the defensive in the Protracted Conflict, survival demands that we retain the initiative and advantage in the Technological War. We know that U.S. supremacy does not bring on global war, let alone a war of conquest; we held an absolute mastery during our nuclear monopoly. We can be certain that the Soviets would not be passive were they to gain supremacy.

The Technological War is the decisive struggle in the Protracted Conflict. Victory in the Technological War gives supremacy in all other phases of the conflict, to be exploited either by thermonuclear annihilation of the opponent, or simply demanding and obtaining his surrender. The Technological War creates the resources to be employed in all other parts of the Protracted Conflict. It governs the range of strategies that can be adapted in actual or hot war. Without the proper and superior technology our strategy of deterrence would be meaningless. Without technological advantages, we could never fight and win a small war thousands of miles from our homeland, or prevent the occupation of Europe and Japan.

Up to the present moment, technological warfare has largely been confined to pre-hot war conflict. It has been a silent and apparently peaceful war, and engagement in the Technological War is generally compatible with the strong desires of most of our people for "peace". The winner of the Technological War can, if he chooses, preserve peace and order, act as a stabilizer of international affairs, and prevent shooting wars. The loser has no choice but to accept the conditions of the victor, or to engage in a shooting war which he has already lost.

Technological War can be carried on simultaneously with any other forms of military conflict, diplomatic maneuvers, peace offensives, trade agreements, detente, and debacle. It is the source of the advanced weapons and equipment for use in all forms of warfare. It renders cold war activities credible and effective. Technological warfare combined with psychosocial operations can lead to a position of strategic dominance.

This new form of warfare has its roots in the past, but it is a product of the current environment. World War II was the last war of industrial power and mobilization, but it was also the first war of applied science. The new war is one of the directed use of science. The manner of its use is shown by the changing nature of warfare. Wars of the past were wars of attrition of the military power which was a shield to the civilian population and the will to resist. The new technology has created weapons to be applied directly and suddenly to the national will.

Definition of Technological Warfare

Technological warfare is the direct and purposeful application of the national technological base (3) and of specific advances generated by the base to attain strategic and tactical objectives. It is employed in concert with other forms of national power. The aims of this kind of warfare, as of all forms of warfare, are to enforce the national will on enemy powers; to cause them to modify their goals, strategies, tactics, and operations; to attain a position of security or dominance which assists or supports other forms of conflict techniques; to promote and capitalize on advances in technology to reach superior military power; to prevent open warfare; and to allow the arts of peace to flourish in order to satisfy the constructive objectives of society.

The emergence of this new form of war is a direct consequence of the dynamic and rapidly advancing character of the technologies of the two superpowers and of certain of the U.S. allies. Its most startling application to date has been the Soviet and American penetration of space and the highly sophisticated articulation of specific technical achievements in other aspects of modern conflict—psychological, political, and military.

Its foremost characteristics are dynamism and flexibility, while surprise is its main strategic utility. The superpowers can expand their technologies and employ them unhindered by actions short of all-out war. The nature of the technological process reinforces the uncertainty of war and of the enemy's course of action. The indicators of success in maintaining a position of dominance are vague and inconclusive because of dynamism, variability, and uncertainty; thus, unless this form of warfare is fully understood, it is possible to lose it while maintaining to the last the illusion of winning.

The importance of this new form of conflict lies in the challenge it poses to the continued national existence of the participants. Just as the Romans deliberately increased their national power by adding seapower to landpower, and just as the major nations of the world increased their power by adding airpower to their surface power, the U.S.S.R. is adding technological power to its existing capabilities.

(The above was written in 1968. It is now possible to see the effects of Soviet adoption of a technological strategy. They have an entire new line of intercontinental missiles with accuracies sufficient to threaten the entire US land-based missile force; and they have gone into space in a big way, so that they have far more experience in manned space operations than we do.

They have also built a full line of naval vessels, including nuclear ballistic missile submarines.

The threat of Soviet technological power is much greater now than when we wrote this book; and our time for meaningful response is much shorter. There is still time, but we have little to waste. JEP 1983)

Technological advances can produce a small number of weapons with a decisive capability, as illustrated by the atomic bomb. Since some technological changes can occur unobtrusively and yet be decisive, the real power situations are never transparent and never fully understood, so that the power of the opponent, as well as one's own power, remains partially unknown.

This unavoidable ignorance is the source of direct challenge to the security and existence of the participants in the Technological War. Technology itself does not automatically confer military advantages. Blind faith in technology alone can lead to disaster. Like all wars, the Technological War requires a deliberate strategy, and it must be conducted by commanders who understand fully the objectives they have been instructed to reach.

The Technological War is not synonymous with technological research. The instruments of technological research and development are required for successful participation in the Technological War, but their existence does not ensure their proper use. Research itself does not create technology but is merely one of technology's major prerequisites; and technology by itself cannot bring victory or guarantee national survival.

Foundations of the Technological War

Fundamentals of Technological Strategy

There are four overall aspects to technological strategy. Enumerating them does not constitute a strategy but merely sets forth certain criteria with which to judge the conduct of the conflict. They are:

- Superior Forces In Being
- Modernization of Weapons
- Modernization of the Technological Base
- Operational Capability to Use New Technology

A power that is determined not to end the Technological War by destroying the enemy must constantly maintain superiority and continuously modernize its forces. At all times, the defending nation in the Protracted Conflict must maintain sufficient forces in being to assure that the enemy does not end the conflict by *coup de main*, an overwhelming surprise blow. These forces must *have* the modern weapons they require, and must know how to use them; must have operational familiarity with them.

The result is a highly dynamic process, requiring careful judgment. We certainly cannot depend on our traditional strategy of mobilization, relying on overseas allies to bear the initial brunt of the war while we convert from a peace to a war economy. We must have a force in being which cannot be destroyed by the enemy, and which can *quickly* move to counter the enemy's aggressive actions.

(A recent example is the Falkland Islands conflict: Britain had sufficient forces in being to reverse the initial advantages held by Argentina. Had Britain scrapped its nuclear submarines and surface ships (as was indeed planned for the following year) then there would have been no possible response to the Argentine occupation of the Falklands; certainly no response short of all-out war and actions against the Argentine homelands. This could have been very dangerous. JEP 1983)

Secondly, the force in being must be a *modern* force. It is unimportant if we surpass the enemy in capability to conduct horse-cavalry conduct, or even guerilla war, if we do not have a force that can fight successfully with modern high-energy weapons. The situation is not symmetrical; if we possess superiority or supremacy, we need not end the conflict by destroying the enemy, and will not do so because of our essentially defensive grand strategy. However, we cannot afford to allow the enemy superiority or supremacy, because he could use it to force so many concessions—particularly from our then-unprotected allies—that the contest would be decided in his favor even if he did not employ his decisive weapons to destroy us.

Finally, we must assure that the technological base from which our force in being are derived is truly modern and creative. We must be certain that we have missed no decisive bets in the Technological War, that we have abandoned no leads which the enemy could exploit for a decisive advantage over us. For every weapons system he has, we must have a counter, either through defending against the weapon or riposte against him if he uses it. More important, we must keep a sufficient technological base to allow us to generate the counter-systems to any new weapons he constructs or may suddenly invent.

Dimensions of the Technological War

The dimensions of the Technological War range farther than any conflict previously known in human history. They include the aerospace, from ground-level to trans-lunar space; the ground and the underground deep within the earth; and the surface of the seas and the underwater world we call inner space. The battlegrounds of the Technological War could include every conceivable area in which military conflict can occur. Yet, this is merely the final aspect of the Technological War. Actual military battle may never take place. The dimensions of the war also include the nonmilitary struggles, psychopolitical warfare, ideological warfare, economics and trade, and the educational process. A college campus with students shrilly screaming obscenities at the police, and a quiet laboratory populated with soft-spoken men armed with chalk and blackboards are equally important battlegrounds.

Technological Warfare in its decisive phase will aim at bypassing the other forms of military conflict and striking directly at the will to resist. Military power may be used, and thermonuclear warfare may be necessary to consolidate the victory, but the true aim of the Technological War is the denial, paralysis, and negation of all forms of hostile military power. Often this may be achieved through psycho-political pressure employing tactics of demonstration, terror, despair, and surprise, conducted in concert perhaps with other forms of warfare. Specifically, genuine Technological War aims at reducing the use of firepower in all forms to a minimum.

An Overview of the Nature of Technology

Before we examine the strategy of Technological War, it is necessary to understand the nature of technology. Contrary to what people have often been encouraged to believe, it is not necessary to be a scientist or technologist to comprehend the general nature of technology, or to employ technology in a strategic contest. Indeed, sometimes specialization on one aspect of technology and strategy prevents understanding of technology in its broader sense.

The following discussion is a nontechnical introduction to the general nature of technology and strategy. Later sections of this book develop each of these themes more fully, but because of the interdependence of strategy and technology in modern warfare, it is not possible to organize this book into discrete sections and chapters.

Modern Technological Warfare is a mixture of strategy and technology, and their interrelationships.

The primary fact about technology in the twentieth century is that it has a momentum of its own. The stream of technology flows on endlessly, and it is impossible to dam it. There remain only three choices. You may swim with the stream, exploiting every aspect of technology to its fullest; you may attempt to crawl out on the bank and watch the rest of the world go past; or you can attempt to swim against the stream and "put the genii back in the bottle"

Since nearly every nation, and certainly both superpowers, swim in more or less the same technological stream, only the first course of action makes sense. To continue the analogy for a moment, there is a fog over the surface of the water, so that you cannot know exactly what and how your opponents in the race are doing. An opponent may tell you he has crawled out on the bank and is enjoying the view, while in fact he is either treading water or racing away from you. If you do not intend to lose, you have little choice but to swim with the current as long and as hard as you can.

The impersonal nature of technology makes meaningless the gunpowder era phrase arms race. It is fashionable at present to speak of the action-reaction arms race, in which each power constructs weapons for fear that the other has done so. According to this theory, (4) the primary reason nations arm themselves is that they react to others. In fact, in the Technological War, opposing powers essentially react to the impersonal stream that carries them along. They really have no choice and never will have so long as the current flows and there is asymmetry of information between them.

The fog of war is made denser by confusion caused partly by deliberate deception and partly by self-deceptions. Only when the Communist states have transformed themselves into open societies and there is a complete exchange of information—that is, when the fog has lifted from the stream of technology—can meaningful efforts to arrange the contest on a more economical and less risky basis be successful. Until that time we must engage in the Technological War. It is fairly obvious that rationalization of the conflict will not come in our lifetimes. We would do well to expect that even if the U.S.S.R. were to change its character, other threats might arise in its stead.

Arms races in the nuclear era differ from those in the gunpowder era in one fundamental way: they are qualitative rather than quantitative. In the gunpowder era, numbers of divisions, tanks, battleships, and aircraft gave rough estimates of the strength of the possessor and his capability to defend himself. It was possible to overcome an enemy by sheer numbers of weapons alone. In the nuclear era, numbers remain important, of course, but the primary strength lies in quality of weapons and their survivability. Nuclear weapons can destroy an enemy's entire military power in one strike if the attacker possess sufficient qualitative superiority. This too is a result of the nature of modern technology.

One of the most easily observed phenomena of technology is that it moves by "S" curves. Take for example speed; for centuries the speed of military operations increased only slightly as each side developed better horses. Then came the internal combustion engine. Speed rose sharply for a while. Eventually, though, it flattened out again, and each increase took longer and longer to achieve.

Note that the top of one S curve may—in fact usually will—be the base of another following it. Although the stream moves on inexorably, it is possible to exploit one or another aspect of technology at will. Which aspect to exploit will depend on several factors, the most important being your goals and your position on the S-curve.

To illustrate the S-curve concept, consider the development of aircraft, and in particular their speed. For many years after the Wright brothers, aircraft speeds crawled slowly forward. In 1940, they were still quite slow. Suddenly, each airplane designed was faster, until the limits of subsonic flight were reached. At that point, we were on a new S-curve. Again, the effort to reach transsonic flight consumed many resources and much time, but then the breakthrough was made. In a short time, aircraft were traveling all multiples of the speed of sound, at speeds nearly two orders of magnitude greater than those achieved shortly before World War II.(5)

Technology is interdependent: advances in one sector of technology soon influence areas which might naively have been believed unrelated. For example, the development of molecular chemistry techniques led to the art of microminiaturization, which allows development of computer technology beyond the expectations of only a few years ago. The revolution in computer sciences has made possible the development of on-board computers for missile guidance, and thus of accuracies not previously predicted. Increased accuracy has made possible the destruction of missile silos with much greater ease and smaller warheads, and has led to the development of Multiple Independently Targetable Re-Entry Vehicles (MIRV), each one of which uses on-board guidance computers. The increased kil capability stimulated research into silo hardening techniques, which led directly to the present hard rock silo designs. And that development also made it possible to conduct certain mining operations that were previously financially infeasible. Examples of interdependence can be given without limit.

Thus, technology influences nearly every aspect of national life. In particular, technology influences strategy, forcing strategic revolutions at frequent intervals. There are those who say that strategy never changes. If they mean literally what they say, they have never appreciated the effects of the airplane and the ICBM, the possibilities for surprise attack created by these radical new weapons delivery systems coupled with thermonuclear explosives, and the effect they have on ground battles. If, however, they mean that the principles of strategy have not changed, they are more nearly correct, as we will discuss below.

The important fact is that technology paces strategy to some extent, and forces the development of new military strategies which take the new technology into account. As we will show, it is dangerous to regard this relationship as one-sided. Technology and strategy are interrelated, and strategy can and should also pace technology.

Despite the critical importance of technology, it re-

mains an impersonal force, largely because we have
never made an effort to understand it. Although America is the leading technological power—perhaps because
we are the leading technological power—we do not really comprehend technology. As a consequence, technology remains largely a matter of individual initiative,
and we have failed to develop a strategy of technology,
let alone a strategy for winning the Technological War.

The Decisive War

The technological contest is a war. It is not a game
against an impersonal force, it is a deadly conflict with
an intelligent and implacable enemy. We do not suppose that a military commander who conducted his
battles as they occurred, understanding neither the terrain nor the enemy and preparing only for the battle
that he had already fought, would be properly performing his task. Yet, too often this is precisely what happens in the Technological War, which may be the most
decisive engagement in the history of mankind. Technology has grown into the driving force, dictating to strategy;
and strategy is conceived of as employment of systems
already created by the technologists; that is, strategy is
confined to operational decisions. This is akin to allowing the recruiting and supply officers to decide the conduct of a traditional land war.

The danger in the Technological War is that it is
closely coupled with the Protracted Conflict, and a decisive lead in the Technological War can be converted
into a decisive advantage in military weapons. Note
that military power and technological power are coupled,
but are not identical; military technology is not in and
of itself a weapon system, but it can be used to create
weapons systems. Thus a commanding lead in the Technological War can be achieved before a corresponding
lead in military technology has been obtained.

As an example, the Soviet Union could, through the
development of nuclear defense technology, obtain a
decisive lead in the Technological War at a time when
the United States still possessed a clear superiority in
deliverable weapons. This technology could then be used
to create defense systems, and if the United States took

no countermeasures during the deployment of those defensive systems, we would find ourselves in an inferior military position.

(What actually happened during the 1970's was that the Soviet Union achieved spectacular gains in achievable accuracies, and also built large new missiles capable of carrying a dozen and more warheads over intercontinental distances. The United States relied on Arms Control negotiations for security; when these failed, we found ourselves facing a "window of vulnerability." This increasing strategic inferiority has not been overcome as of 1983.)

Victory in the Technological War is achieved when a participant has a technological lead so far advanced that his opponent cannot overcome it until after the leader has converted his technology into decisive weapons systems. The loser may know that he has lost, and know it for quite a long time, yet be unable to do anything about it. To continue the above example, if the Soviet Union were able to develop the technology in time to deploy systems of his own before ours could be installed and operational, we would be beaten, even though the U.S.S.R. might spend several years in deployment of his own system. Our only choices would be the development of a penetration system that his defenses could not counter (such as manned bombers of very high capabilities), (6) surrender, or preventive war.

(Many believe that development of space laser battle stations will be a decisive move in the technological war. The laser battle station could, at least in theory, destroy an entire ICBM force in flight, then burn down the enemy's bomber fleet for encore. Such a station once in place would give a decisive lead to its owner.

Space based ICBM defenses have also been proposed, as example by General Daniel O. Graham in his Project High Frontier. If such systems could give us a decisive advantage, they would confer no less on the Soviets if we allow our enemies to develop them without any counter on our part. JEP 1983)

This is the unique feature of the Technological War. Military superiority or even supremacy is not permanent, and never ends the conflict unless it is used. The United States is committed to a grand strategy of defense, and will never employ a decisive advantage to end the conflict by destroying her enemies. Consequently, she must maintain not only military superiority but technological supremacy. The race is an alternative to destructive war, not the cause of military conflict.

Proper conduct of the Technological War requires that strategy drive technology most forcefully; that there be an overall strategy of the Technological War, allocating resources according to well-defined objectives and an operational plan, not merely strategic elements which make operational use of the products of technology. Instead of the supply officer and the munitions designer controlling the conduct of this decisive war, command must be placed in the hands of those who understand the Technological War; and this requires that they first understand the nature of war.

Lest the reader be confused, we do not advocate that the Technological War be given over to the control of the scientists, or that scientists should somehow create a strategy of technological development. We mean that an understanding of the art of war is more important than familiarity with one or another of the specialties of technology. It is a rare scientist who makes a good strategist; and the generals of the Technological War need not be scientists any more than the generals of traditional military conflict need to be good riflemen or railroad engineers.

Like all wars, the Technological War must be conducted by a *commander* who operates with a strategy. It is precisely the lack of such a strategy that has brought the United States to the present low point in prestige and power, with her ships seized across the world, her Strategic Offensive Forces (SOF) threatened by the growing Soviet SOF—and with the United States perplexed by as simple a question as whether to attempt to defend her people from enemy thermonuclear bombs, and unable to win a lesser war in South East Asia.(7) Because we have no generals and no strategy, we must muddle through the most decisive conflict in our national history. We are *not* doing a good job.

There have been a few exceptions to this unsatisfactory record of American performance. General Bernard Schriever created a military organization for strategic analysis which was responsible for our early command-ing lead over the Soviets in ballistic missiles, despite the fact that the U.S. had allowed the U.S.S.R. many years' head start in missile development after World War II.(8) The Air Force's Project Forecast and later Project 75, was an attempt to let strategy react to, then drive, technology; it too was a creation of General Schriever's.

In the navy there have also been notable attempts to allow strategy to influence technology and produce truly modern weapons systems. The long-term results on the careers of the officers involved have been similar to those of the officers identified with General Schriever in the Air Force: failure. Our military organizations have not been geared for commanders who understand the Technological War, even though this is the most deci-sive of all wars we have fought. Yet in the few cases where the proper actions have been taken, the payoff in the Technological War has been very great. Unfortunately, the men who were involved in making these contribu-tions to the nation have suffered for doing so.

The Elements of Strategy

What is Strategy?

Because there seems to be little understanding of strat-egy and its effect on the Technological War, we will briefly review some general principles of strategy and warfare. Our purpose is not to teach the elements of strategy, which would require another book, but rather to make the reader aware of strategy and some of its complexities.

According to the traditional concept of military strat-egy it should mean the art of employing military forces to achieve the ends set by political policy. This defini-tion was formulated by [Sir Basil Henry] Liddell Hart in 1929 and it hardly differs from that of Clausewitz. Raymond Aron in his recent book follows it almost word for word. France's leading strategist of the 60's commented:

"In my view this definition is too restrictive be-cause it deals with military forces only. I would put it as follows: the art of applying force so that it makes the most effective contribution towards achieving the ends set by political policy . . .

"In my view the essence of strategy is the abstract interplay which, to use Foch's phrase, springs from the clash between two opposing wills. It is the art which enables a man, no matter what the techniques employed, to master the problems set by any clash between two opposing wills. [It is the art which enables a man, no matter what the techniques employed, to master the problems set by any clash of wills] and as a result to employ the techniques available with maximum efficiency. It is therefore the art of the dialectic of force, or, more precisely, *the art of the dialectic of two opposing wills using force to resolve their dispute.*(9)

In our judgment it would be hard to better the above definition provided that we understand force to include the broader concept of power and force. Examining the definition shows us several important aspects of the Technological War and its strategy.

First, we see that strategy involves two opposing wills. This in itself sets the Technological War apart from the simple development of technology. The development of technology is a game against nature, which may be uncooperative, but which never deceives or actively conspires to prevent your success. The Technology War is a contest with an intelligent opponent who seeks to divert you from seeing his purpose, and to surprise you with his results.

Secondly, strategy involves the use of power and force. In the Technological War, the more power is extant, the less often force needs to be used in the primary or decisive mode of the conflict. In the place of battles, the Technological War general disposes his own resources so as to maximize the power he holds and at the same time compel the enemy to make maximum dispersal of his. To make the enemy counter each move you make, and dance to your tune, is the aim of a Technological War strategy. In the ideal, if the enemy were required continually to build purely defensive weapons which might protect him from your weapons but could not possibly harm you, you could be said to have won a major engagement in the Technological War. In the contest between wills, seizing and holding the initiative is of importance; as indeed it has been for a long, long time:

> You hear that Phillip is in the Chersonese, and you vote an expedition there; you hear that he is in Thessaly, and you vote one there. You march the length and breadth of Greece at his invitation, and you take your marching orders from him.(10)

But if the power ratio is ambiguous, the decision as to who is the stronger will be made by force, which is the application of power in battle. Other things being equal, battles are won by superior technology. But clearly superior technology prevents battle.

The Principles of War

War is an art; it is not an exact science. Precisely because there is an intelligent opponent, there are real uncertainties about war, not merely statistical uncertainties which may be measurable. Every attempt to reduce war to an exact science has ended in a dismal failure. The advent of the computer and systems analysis, useful as both may be, has not changed this fact, although it has often been forgotten.

Part of the traditional method of learning the art of war is studying the principles of war. These principles are a set of general concepts, like holds in wrestling, and no exact group of principles is universally recognized. Some strategists combine several into one or divide one of those we show into several. The following list will serve well enough for our purpose:

- The Principle of the Objective
- The Principle of the Initiative
- The Principle of Surprise
- The Principle of the Unity of Command
- The Principle of Mass (Concentration of Force)
- The Principle of Economy of Forces
- The Principle of Mobility
- The Principle of Security
- The Principle of Pursuit

It will be noted that some of these principles, if carried to their extremes, would be contradictory. They are intended to serve not as a formula for the planning of a battle, but rather as a set of guides or a checklist which the planner ignores only with peril. They are as applicable to the Technological War as to any other war. At first glance, it might seem that one principle or another might be more directly applicable to the Technological War than the others, but in fact none can be disregarded if success is to be achieved. We will have occasion to refer to them from time to time in the analysis below.

Strategy and Technology

The United States today has no technological strategy. We have, instead, a series of independent and often uncorrelated decisions on specific problems of technology. This is hardly a strategy. A technological strategy would involve the setting of national goals and objectives by political leaders; it would be integrated with other aspects of our national strategy, both military and nonmilitary (Initiative, Objective, and Unity of Command); it would include a broad plan for conducting the Technological War that provided for surprising the enemy, pursuing our advantage (Pursuit), guarding against being surprised (Security), allocating resources effectively (Economy of Forces), setting milestones and building the technological base (Objective), and so forth. Lesser conflicts such as that in Vietnam would be governed by a broad strategic doctrine instead of being considered isolated and treated as crisis.

In our national strategy, far too much attention has been given to current affairs and to specific conflict situations at particular times and places. There has been no serious attempt to integrate the individual decisions, or relate them to a comprehensive grand strategy that is adequate to overcome the challenges. The few attempts we have made to manage technological decisions properly were disastrous; examples are the ludicrous "saving" achieved through the TFX and the equally dismal saving through over-management of the C5A program. We have confused a strategy of technology with centralized interference in the design of production of specific weapons and the imposition of a "standard management plan".

The results are that our performance in Vietnam was quite unsatisfactory, we have failed to exploit our superior technology to grasp a commanding lead in either inner space or outer space, our merchant marine where it exists at all flies the proud flag of Panama or Liberia, and many of our young men fight overseas with weapons that make use of principles discovered by Roger Bacon in the thirteenth century.

(Alas, we see no reason to revise the above after a dozen years. Our failure to understand what the Vietnam War was about cost us all the blood and treasure we had previously invested; the Soviets have surpassed us in manned space exploitation and ICBM deployment; and we were unable to use our technology or military power in the Iranian hostage crisis. JEP 1983)

The reasons for this dismal performance are complex; it is not necessary to understand all of them and it is not germane to blame anyone. Events caught up with us, the stream of technology swept us along, and only recently did we begin to realize the nature of the Technological War. In fact, one reason we have no strategy of technology is that not everyone realizes we are at war; but perhaps the most important reason is the basic failure to understand the nature of technology itself, and particularly the problems of lead time which produce a crisis-oriented design process.

Crises have kept coming endlessly, and we have had to meet them. Decision makers at the national level concentrate on fighting today's fire, partly because they hope that the current trouble will be the last but mostly because of the long lead time involved in technology. A president called upon to spend money in any fiscal year actually is spending money to solve the problems of a resident two terms later. But even if we try to find comfort in expenditures for research and development, we must understand that these are oriented to specific projects and tasks and do not result from technological strategy.

(During the 1970's, the expenditures in research and development were cut back; the result was that high technology exports became less valuable than agriculture in our balance of payments. There has been an erosion of our technological base. Fortunately the Soviets have their problems too, caused by their generally bad management practices; but do note that the Soviet military economy is run on an entirely different basis from their notoriously inefficient civilian economy. JEP 1983)

Our misunderstanding of the Technological War is illustrated by our failure to build an organization for conducting technological warfare. The review of the annual budget and of individual projects in basic research, in applied research, in development, and in procurement is the only process by which our technological development is controlled directly. Other influences such as the statements of requirements and the evaluation of military worth are felt only at the level of individual projects. Overall evaluation of the research and development effort and of its relations to strategy is rudimentary.

An example of how irrelevant factors influence our efforts, and perhaps one of the decisive signs of the times: the January 20, 1969 issue of *Aviation Week and Space Technology*, the most influential journal in the aerospace field, included a report entitled "Viet Lull Advances New Weapons". The article makes clear that the budgetary funding level of many new weapons systems, including research and development, basic technology, and actual system procurement, is largely dependent on the continuation of a "lull" in the Vietnam War. Given a proper strategy for the Technological War and proper command of our efforts, the title should read "Advanced New Weapons End Vietnam War."

1983

The previous decade has seen the development of many "smart" weapons; however, few have actually been put in the hands of operational troops. We still do not have a strategy of technology.

Notes

1. Since we wrote this in 1968–69, the Soviets have invaded Czechoslovakia to consolidate the Empire's power there; invaded Afghanistan; placed tens of divi-

sions on the Chinese border; interfered in the Middle East; used Cuban mercenaries to destabilize a great part of Africa; and induced the Communist regime in Poland to enslave its own working class. Is further evidence of Soviet aggressive tendencies needed?

2. Robert Strausz-Hupe et al, *Protracted Conflict* (New York: Harper 1969); Stefan T. Possony, *A Century of Conflict*, 5th ed. (Chicago: Regnery, 1969).

3. We define as technological base the sum total of resources needed to produce and constantly modernize the tools of war and peace. Those resources include scientists, inventors, engineers, laboratories, laboratory equipment, funds, information flow, incentives, etc., as well as industry and the economy as a whole, which we do not discuss in this book.

4. The theory is essentially that of Lewis Richardson, who made up the elaborate differential equations to try to demonstrate the mathematical relationship between the arms expenditures of nations and international blocs, and found a reasonable fit in the single case of the Pre-World War I Entente and Alliance. No empirical confirmation of the Richardson theory has been found, and the specialized assumptions required to make the World War I history fit the theory leave the entire effort in a questionable state. Richardson's theory is presented in L.F. Richardson, *Arms and Insecurity* (Pittsburgh, Boxwood Press, 1960). His most vigorous contemporary champion is Anatol Rappaport, in *Fights, Games, and Debates* (Ann Arbor: University of Michigan Press, 1960). The results of one unsuccessful attempt to find a modern instance of a Richardson arms race are reported in Pournelle, *Stability and National Security* (U.S. Air Force, 1969). We have found that in the nuclear era, expenditures on weapons simply do not fit the Richardson equations.

5. In common engineering parlance, an increase by an order of magnitude is approximately a tenfold increase. Astronomers, be wary.

6. We would, of course, have not only to invent and develop these bombers but build them in quantity, fly them, train the pilots, etc., and do it all within the time limits of U.S.S.R. deployment.

7. Since this book is intended to be a discussion of principles, not of current specific problems, it may be well in print long after the present war in Vietnam is ended. We venture to predict, however, that for many years after this is written (1970) there will be wars in Asia, including South East Asia and the area formerly known as Indo-China.

8. The authors recall the frustration of Wernher Von Braun and other rocketry experts when the last of the V-2 rockets brought to the United States were used, not for the development of rocket sciences, but as supersonic test beds for aircraft parts to avoid spending the funds required for construction of supersonic wind tunnels. This retarded the development of both missiles and supersonic aircraft, of course.

9. General d'Armee Andre Beaufre, *Introduction to Strategy* (New York: Praeger, 1965), p. 22.

10. Demosthenes, *First Phillipic to the People of Athens*.

EDITOR'S INTRODUCTION TO:

MANUAL OF OPERATIONS
by
Jerry Pournelle

In the bad old days of science fiction, a John W. Campbell editorial was certain to have one result: a dozen writers would turn out stories illustrating the point Mr. Campbell had made. Sometimes these were good stories; sometimes they were bloody awful since they'd been churned out quickly in the hopes of catching John W. Campbell with his checkbook open.

There is a sense in which I wrote this story in response to a Campbell editorial: John once said that our attempts to understand truly advanced alien science were likely to be no more successful than would a medieval monk's attempts to understand television were a TV suddenly to appear in his cloister. That intrigued me enough to want to do a story on the theme.

On the other hand, it took me five years, and the result turned out very different from what I had first conceived.

MANUAL OF OPERATIONS
by
Jerry Pournelle

"Harry Logan, stop messing around with that junk and Get a Job!"

"Yes, dear." It used to be a daily ritual. Now it was three or four times a day. If he'd been musically inclined, Harry could have set it to music: Chorale and concerto for percussion and nagging wife. GET A JOB, BOOM BOOM, YES DEAR, YES DEAR, GET A JOB, BOOM BOOM, YES DEAR, YES DEAR . . .

"I mean it, Harry. I can't pay the grocery bills, there's the doctor, and Shirley's orthodonist, and Penny's is sending our account to a collection agency. You've got to Do Something Before I Go Out of My Mind!"

"Yes dear." He didn't raise his eyes from the microscope ($65.00 surplus from Los Angeles City College, a good buy, I *need* it, Ruth. I can use it to make some money.) After a while he heard her retreating footsteps.

This was a preliminary skirmish. She'd be back with the main force attack later. But for now . . . Outside, the rooster squawked loudly and drove a young opossum away from his harem. The dog barked and ran ashamedly to help the scrappy little cock. The dog got a piece bit out of his ear for reward. Harry gratefully left the microscope with its dirty slide and listened to the sounds of peace.

The letters from his last job enquiries were on his desk, but he'd been afraid to tell Ruth. They all said the same thing. Dear Mr. Logan, we are very pleased that you have considered our company as a possible employer. However, at this time we have no position suitable for a man of your unique talents. Please be assured that we will keep your application on file . . .

Harry knew why they didn't want him. He had no college degrees. In fact, he'd never been inside a college in his life, and there were dozens, hundreds, thousands of new engineering graduates looking for work. What chance did a company-trained engineer have for a professional position? He'd tried starting over, but that was no good either: with three published papers on solid state physics and four patents to his credit he was overqualified to be a technician. No engineer wanted a lab tech who knew more than his boss.

Harry was sure that the constant fights he'd had with company administrators had nothing to do with his rejections. He'd been *right* every time. But somehow, after the companies *learned* that, they still wouldn't hire him . . .

His research wasn't going well. His papers were rejected by reputable journals as too far out and he couldn't write down for the popular science magazines. Nothing was going well, and the cold reality gnawed at his guts. What in hell *am* I going to do? he thought. It was a moment of panic.

The house was paid for (Harry, you should have kept title to that patent, not sold it outright! Harry, you have no business sense at all! But Ruth, I wanted to keep the patent and you said we have to have a house . . .) At least they couldn't take the house. But he couldn't raise chickens out here in Tujunga Wash anymore. The Los Angeles City Department of Health had sent a complaint. His house was miles from any other habitation, but somehow it was inside the city limits . . .

He stood for a moment by the desk, then paced nervously to his work bench. The blasted circuit ought to work, why didn't it? But growing integrated circuitry was a tricky thing and he had only the most primitive equipment to work with. He thought about that. Sometimes, Ruth took off her wedding ring to do the dishes, and he could pawn it for . . .

He didn't finish the thought. There was a knock on the workroom door and Logan looked up in surprise.

"Harry Logan?" the man asked. There was an accent to the voice, probably Canadian. An ordinary man: big framed, going bald, dark hair where he had any. Stocky and tough, but well dressed. "You are Harry Logan, aren't you?"

"Yes," Harry admitted. It was an admission: the last guy who came to see him had been a bill collector and this guy was built like one.

"May I come in?"

"You're already in. I don't think I know you."

"David McClellan. Before we waste each other's time, are you the man who published that far-out thing about the future of solid-state physics in Tele-Tech? Also the article speculating about unknown forces?"

"Yes." The unknown forces article had got him fired from his last job. His descriptions of equipment he used in the research made it plain he was working on that problem despite orders to abandon it. Who'd have thought the Director would read a thing like that? "Yeah, I wrote them."

"Good. I've got a consulting job for you."

"What kind of work?" Harry asked. No good to sound too eager. "I'm a little busy, but—"

"You'll be well paid. Besides, you'll learn something new. I guarantee it." The man was assured, and his confidence was infectious. Logan found himself looking forward to whatever McClellan had in mind. What did 'well paid' mean? Anything was good pay now . . .

McClellan was still talking. "But you don't have a working telephone so I couldn't call for an appointment. Glad to find you in."

"Eh—oh, sure." Damn phone company. He'd always paid his bills eventually . . . "Where is this work?"

"Canada. I want you to come with me right away."

Logan brought up the subject of money. It wasn't any problem. McClellan took a thousand dollars from his wallet and handed it over. It was an expensive wallet, and it looked full.

Ruth exploded as expected. McClellan wouldn't say where they were going. He seemed obsessed with secrecy about the whole project, and Ruth took Harry's inability to be precise for deviousness.

"Off to Canada with some bum you just met! Can't say where! Harry Logan, you're Up To Something! You're going off to drink again, and I won't put up with it,

Harry Logan, now you listen to me, you take one drink and you can't stop, I know all about you, you're not going off to any . . ."

She was speechless for the first time in years as Harry shoved a thousand dollars at her. He was tempted to stuff it into her mouth . . .

"Where in hell are we going?" Harry asked. It seemed a reasonable question. They'd landed in Vancouver, taken a small turbo-prop north to Dawson, and immediately drove away from the airport in a Rover. Now they'd left the highway and started off into rugged hill country. McClellan hadn't said three hundred words since they left Tujunga Wash.

"You'll see soon enough." The country got wilder, pine trees and scrub brush, and they turned off the gravel road onto an unmarked dirt track. Harry had to hold on to keep from being jounced out of his seat. After they were a half mile in, the trail vanished. McClellan swung off into the forest, driving over dried pine needles that blew over their tracks in the stiff breeze.

"Timber country," McClellan said. "Nobody comes here but me. I own it."

They passed weathered No Trespassing signs, forded a small creek, bounced across another rocky flat, and plunged into more thick woods; then they topped a small rise at the edge of a tiny clearing, and there it was.

Logan had a brief impression of a logging camp. Log shack covered with mud. A generator trailer. Camp fire, with a wiry bearded man squatting in front of it. None of these really registered, because the little clearing was dominated by an alien shape.

That was the first thing Harry was sure of. It was wrong. Alien. The color was wrong, the shape was wrong, everything about it. Then he looked for details.

The ship was round, about twenty feet in diameter, and swept up in thickness from infinitesimal at the edges to about seven feet in the center. The cross-section shape was part of the alien impression: it thickened in a series of compound curves not smoothly blended into each other.

It wasn't perfectly round. From above it would have

looked like a distorted circle, but there was no conic section that could describe it. One end was elongated and flattened, with its thin edge stretching out another four or five feet, no thicker than a man's hand at the greatest dimension, undulating in waves of curved sections that made no sense.

The whole ship was a dull metallic grey-green, and it shined, not brightly, and not evenly over its surface; when he tried to look closely Harry saw that it was the light pattern that gave an illusion of motion to the hull sections. The ship didn't change shape, but the glowing areas moved in rippling patterns across the surface.

Harry turned to his companion. The man was watching Logan curiously. "A flying saucer," Harry said. "Yours?"

McClellan laughed. "It is now." He raised his voice to shout. "Al, he thinks we're little green men! He asked if it was mine!"

The bearded man laughed with them as he came to the Rover. "I'm Al Parish, Mister Logan." Parrish held out a lumberjack's hand and crushed Harry's. "Do we look like we could build that thing?"

"No. All right, what's the story."

"Come sit by the fire and have a drink," McClellan answered. "We're going to tell you."

David McClellan owned timber lands. He'd inherited them and was happy to live off the income. He also liked to hike in his woods. "And one day—there it was," he finished.

"But—who brought it here? What about the crew?"

McClellan shrugged. "Nothing. It was like you see it here. And there's no strange bones around, nothing here at all. Maybe the crew got killed by rattlers and dragged off by scavengers. Maybe anything, but they're gone. After I poked around for a week I went and got Al."

"I'm an engineer," Parrish added. "Not much of one, maybe, but the only engineer Dave knew. And this thing is driving me crazy. When I talked to the professors at the university about some of the effects I got they told me I'd been drinking. Nothing like that could ever work. So I remembered the articles you wrote and Dave went to get you."

"Thanks," Logan said. He meant it. "But aren't you going to tell the government?"

"Hell no!" McClellan exploded. "They'd thank us and never let us near it again." He spat into the fire. "I want that ship, Logan. It's mine."

Harry could understand that. He'd had his problems with administrators. He didn't care if the government never found out about it. "You think it uses advanced solid state devices, huh?"

"Has to be something like that," Parrish answered. "I can't even find the power source. It's got one, you see things work, but no power. No wires, nothing, just blocks of glop. Lots of those, but I can't see what they connect to or even how they connect." Al poured an enormous mug of coffee, drank half, and filled it to the top with Christian Brothers brandy. Harry looked at it hungrily, but he knew better. Ruth was right more often than he wanted to admit.

"Near as I can figure," Parrish said, "this thing operates with some force nobody on earth ever heard of. And you wrote about that, and about the future of solid state work—hell, at least you'll admit it's possible for the ship to work!"

"Can I look at it?"

"Yeah." McClellan seemed reluctant. "But be careful. We don't know what does which to what. You might put us out in the orbit of Saturn."

It seemed as strange inside as out. The entrance was two doors four feet high with a two foot space between them, an obvious airlock that a man might just barely have crammed himself into. Both sliding doors were open, and somebody had wedged them into their recesses with pine logs.

"Haven't been able to close this ship up," Parrish explained, "but I didn't want to take any chances. Be hell to be trapped in here."

The inside was one big chamber about the shape of the outside of the ship. Three chairs which would have been perfect for small human children were bolted to the steel-gray deck. The chairs swivelled and were equidistant around a circular console in the center of the ship. The console had a shelf two feet off the floor and a sloping panel inboard of that rose nearly to the top of the cabin. The panel was a jumble of translucent plates, many of them marked with squiggles that might have been Arabic but Logan was sure it wasn't.

"Near as I can figure, the panels above the console are some kind of screens," Parrish told him. "But there ain't nothing behind them, so I don't know. Course, they might be kids' greasepaint boards for all I know."

"Kids?"

"Sure. Whole thing could be a toy. Look at the size. Like a doll house. Admit it isn't likely, but then the ship isn't likely either."

"That's for sure." Harry was just able to stand in the space next to the console. Everywhere else the ceiling was too low and he had to crouch.

Parrish showed him around the ship. Under one chair was a gismo with an air scoop sticking out of a solid box to a tank, and a steady stream of air flowed from the tank.

"What kind of air does it make?" Logan asked.

"About like ours, only feel. Hot, and wet as hell. Little more oxygen too."

"What else works?"

"Funny about that," Parrish said. "Sometimes lights flash. Sometimes we hear noises. Nothing predictable, and no way to control any of it. Look, there's not even controls to work, no knobs or switches. Least, nothing we can recognize as a control," he added thoughtfully. "Maybe it's like somebody in the Middle Ages finding a radio—he'd never know what switches and knobs were."

They went back outside, although Logan wanted to remain in the ship. The others persuaded him; he'd have plenty of time to look at it, and it gave them the creeps in the dark. Before they left Parrish lifted a deck plate. The thin grey metal section came away easily to reveal a mass of brightly colored rectangular shapes varying in size from larger than an attache case to smaller than a matchbox. The blocks fitted together perfectly and couldn't be pulled out, but when Parrish touched one corner with a steel screwdriver they popped out easily. There weren't any connections Harry Logan could see; the blocks were of uniform texture, like hardened epoxy. When replaced they fitted together again like a parquet floor, and couldn't be removed by force.

"See what I mean about advanced solid state?" Mc-

Clellan asked. They sat around the campfire and ate shishkebob while Parrish told what he had tried.

He had used every detection device he could think of with no result whatever. Oscilloscope, voltmeter, electroscope, they all gave the same result. "That ship's electromagnetically dead," Parrish said. "It's all at ground potential. Except for one thing, that flat surface dead aft—well, I think it's aft, but what the hell, there being no windows or anything, how would I know? Anyway, that flat place is a south pole. Damn strong one, I had to use the Rover to pull my magnet off it. But it only attracts north poles, repels south ones, and has no effect on non-magnetized iron. It's directional, and there isn't a north pole on the ship. How's that grab you?"

"A monopole?" Harry asked. "Could it be the drive?"

"Damned if I know. I don't think it's strong enough to lift the ship. For that matter, nothing I think of can lift that ship."

"What do you mean?"

Parrish shrugged and pulled another chunk of steak off the skewer. "It's heavy. Or it's rooted in place, take your choice. Tried jacking it up and broke the Rover's jack. Got a big fifty ton hydraulic job and managed to push the jack down into the ground. That ship doesn't lift. It's enough to drive me crazy."

"Yeah." Logan stared into the campfire.

Parrish took the dirty dishes and put them in a bucket to soak. "Wash up in the morning. Now for something I've been waiting for since we found that thing," he said. He went to the Rover and got out a case of brandy. "Didn't have but a couple of bottles to last me and had to stay sober while you were gone . . . after playing with that thing, I want to get drunk." He looked at the brandy with affection. "Have a drink, Harry Logan. You too, McClellan, you old stick."

Why not? Harry thought. One drink wouldn't hurt. Might open up his subconscious. Parrish had tried every test Harry could think of, maybe something would come to him. One drink.

By midnight they were all singing. At one in the morning, McClellan was making speeches denouncing the government, which he suspected of wanting to take his ship for income taxes. By two they went over to be sure the ship was still there.

They squeezed into the cabin, and Harry was just able to sit in one of the chairs. The others were too big. It was dark, and Harry couldn't see a thing. "Wish there was some light."

The lights came on, a soft glow from the walls with no bright spots.

"What the hell did you do?" McClellan demanded.

"I thought at it," Logan answered. "Shee, it's simple, you think at it and she does what you want. Watch." He thought at the screens. A globe sprang into view on the panel above him. It was a holograph somehow projected into a piece of plastic a half inch thick.

McClellan and Parrish crowded against Logan's chair. "But how could it work?" Parrish asked.

"Who cares?" Harry answered thickly. "Let's get her moving!" He shouted at the ship. "Lift off!"

Nothing happened.

Logan made a face, then formed a mental picture of the ship rising from the ground.

Harry didn't feel a thing. McClellan and Parrish shouted something. A cold wind blew on his neck and Harry looked around. The cabin was empty, the wedged doors gaping behind him, and through them he saw the lights of a small town rapidly falling away below. "Jesus Christ!" he shouted. A bearded face appeared on the screen.

"I've got to get down! Take me down!" He thought of descending. The ship plummeted. "Gently." He pictured that. The rapid descent slowed.

He tried to think of places to take the ship. Crazy thoughts flashed through his mind: the alps, and they appeared on the screen above. Taj Mahal. New York City. Each time, the screen pictured it, and the ship seemed to turn.

Parrish and McClellan. What had happened to them? The screen showed nothing. Harry tried again: what happened if you fell out? The screen showed something— not really a man, but humanoid—falling through the doors and being gently lowered to the ground below. The ship still whipped around, and the ground he could see through the doors whirled, but Harry felt no motion at all. He tried to stand and was slammed back down into the chair with horrible force, and he almost passed out.

Where to go? The ship could take him anywhere . . . the moon, the planets . . . a picture of an airless world pitted with craters formed on the screen. Mars! She'd take him to Mars! First man there . . .

Harry choked for breath. Anoxia. The word swam somewhere in his mind, but he didn't care. His ship! It could do anything! Harry Logan was the most powerful man in the world! They'd have to listen to him now . . .

The screens faded, everything was getting grey, but Harry didn't care. It was wonderful up here, and Harry Logan was master of the world. He could make them . . . he could . . .

The Pentagon. The enormous building formed on the screen as Harry thought of it. That was the place to go. Take the ship to the Pentagon and make the United States listen to Harry Logan. All the world problems were so simple once you saw them right. And those companies who'd fired him, they'd be sorry. But Harry Logan wouldn't use his ship for revenge. He'd bring peace and happiness to the world. Pentagon, that's the ticket. Right into the little courtyard in the middle of the hollow Pentagon, right there in the five sided funny farm, Harry Logan would set up his throne . . .

He didn't know how long it took but he was there. Thickset windows pierced dirty granite walls all around him. The ship rested on trampled grass. Logan grinned and tried to stand up again. It was all right. The ship waited obediently. Harry went to the hatchway and took the logs out. He needed sleep, and he didn't want anyone messing with his ship while he got it. The inner log came out easily, but the ship had tried to close the outer door and the log was jammed in good. Harry had to climb out to get a grip on it. He tugged hard, and the log came away and fell on top of him.

Harry lay on the grass and looked up at his ship. He smiled, thought the door closed, took a deep breath—and passed out.

He was in a windowless room and bright lights glared in his eyes. He'd never had such a horrible hangover in his life. God, that was a bad one, he'd dreamed about flying saucers and . . . Harry sat bolt upright.

"Now, now," a soft voice told him. Strong hands pushed him down with a rustle of starched linen.

When he tried to turn his head, a strange thing happened. His head turned but his brain didn't. Then the brain would snap around with a horrible shock and an audible twang. His eyes wouldn't focus, but there were blurs in the room, a flurry of activity, bright lights, noise. Horrors upon horrors.

"Do you speak English?" someone kept demanding. What the hell did they think he spoke? When he didn't answer, they said other weird things. "Parlez-vous Francaise? Sprechen Sie Deutsch?" And growls that Harry wouldn't have believed a human throat could utter. Had the saucer taken him to its home planet? It wasn't a dream, there *had* been a saucer . . .

"Hing-song yin kuo . . ." "Sir, he doesn't respond to . . ." "If you'd get out of the way, Professor . . ." Everyone spoke at once.

"Damn it, say something!" an authoritative voice demanded.

"Hello," Harry replied. He hadn't thought anything could be so loud. Was that horrible noise just Harry Logan trying to talk? "Where am I?"

"You're in the emergency detention—uh, in a guest room in the Pentagon. Do you know what the Pentagon is?" the voice asked him. It seemed to be trying to be friendly and didn't know how. A polite crocodile voice.

Any damn fool knows what the Pentagon is, Harry thought. It hurt too much to answer. Instead, he groaned.

"He seems hurt," another voice said quietly. "Not knowing . . . I mean, General, if it weren't for that *thing* out there I'd say he was a normal human with no detectable injury, but . . ."

"Hell, he's *got* to talk. Fast," the general barked. "You. Sir. Where are you from?"

"Tujunga," Harry tried to say. It didn't come out very well.

"Where's that?"

"Sounds Spanish . . ." "I never heard of any such place . . ." "Habla Usted espanol . . ."

One brittle-dry loud lecture hall voice cut through the

renewed babble. "Perhaps it means 'earth' in his language. Most peoples have . . ."

"Crap." The general got shocked silence. "You can spare me the goddam lectures. And since he seems to understand English, we won't need all you goddam civilians. Sergeant, clear this room."

"Yes, sir." There was more commotion, but Harry wasn't interested. Didn't they understand? He needed to die.

"Do you want anything?" the general asked.

Harry opened one eye with an effort. He saw a blue uniform, three stars on the shoulders. Behind the Air Force lieutenant general were two air police with automatic rifles. A doctor in a white coat twisted his hands together. There was no one else in the room, which was bigger than Harry had thought it would be.

"Water," Harry croaked. The doctor moved around and came back with a plastic glass and a drinking straw. Harry gulped it gratefully. "Aspirin. And a double shot of brandy."

The general looked at him closely. "Aspirin? Brandy?" There was a gleam of triumph on the craggy face. "As I thought. There's your goddam alien, doctor. An ordinary earthman with a hangover."

"A hangover and a flying saucer in the Pentagon courtyard," the doctor reminded him. "Really, General Bannister, it would be better to leave him alone for a while. There might be something really wrong with him."

"Yeah, there might. But we haven't got long. I haven't, anyway." He got a crafty look. "Doc, get him in shape and send him to me as quick as you can. I've got to talk to him before the Navy finds him."

"Yes, sir." There was more activity, and Harry was left in the room with the doctor. He gulped aspirin gratefully and asked again for brandy, but nobody brought any.

The hospital gown flapped. The sandal-slippers kept falling off his feet. Harry had never felt more undignified in his life as the air policemen ushered him into the office.

The room overlooked the Pentagon courtyard. Harry's saucer was out there, its unlikely shape gleaming dully, light patterns rippling over the hull. Swarms of uniforms bustled around it, cheered on by more uniforms with gold and silver braid on their hats.

General Bannister sat behind a battered mahogany desk that looked like something out of the twenties. Actually it *was* out of the twenties, since this wasn't a general's office. The guards pushed Harry into an oak and leather swivel chair.

"All right," Bannister said. "Let's make this quick. Tell me about *that*." He jerked a thumb over his shoulder but refused to turn to look.

"Why are there guards pulling me around? What have I done?" Harry asked. "And where are my *clothes* . . ."

"Cut the crap," Bannister said. "You were found unconscious in the Pentagon courtyard in the dead of night. You and *that*. Now where'd you come from, and no shit about Mars. Jayzeus, man, you've got the whole government out of its mind. You bring *that*—" the general still carefully avoided looking out the window—"into Washington without being detected and set it down in the Pentagon courtyard! You've got some explaining to do, son."

"Yeah." Oh Christ, what do I say? Why *did* I come here? "Where do I start?"

"With who you are and where *it* came from."

"My name's Harry, and I don't know where it came from."

"But you can operate it." It wasn't a question. "How?"

"I don't know that either. I don't remember." He thought about it. The machine had done what he thought at it—he tried. He sent out a picture of the ship lifting from the ground. Nothing happened.

Bannister inspected his fingernails as he fought for self control. "What do you want, Harry?" he asked reasonably. The pleasant tone obviously cost him.

Good question, Harry thought. What did he want? The hangover to go away. Peace and quiet. Money. Hey . . .

The door burst open. A Navy Admiral and a hard-eyed civilian stamped in, followed by so many people they couldn't all fit in the room. There were loud voices in the corridor.

"All right, Bannister, we found you," the admiral

growled. "Tried to hide him, didn't you? Just because you were working late last night doesn't mean you own that ship!"

"It flies," Bannister protested. "That makes it Air Force."

"The Navy flies too," the admiral said.

"You have both missed the point," the civilian interrupted. He had a voice like a corpse, flat, atonal, and he spoke so softly that you'd think you couldn't hear him, but he was heard. When he spoke, everyone in the room was silent. "That object is obviously of foreign make. Therefore it belongs to us. Not to the services."

"Crap!" General Bannister exploded. "Horse puckey!" shouted the admiral. Both faced the civilian with determined looks. "What makes you think it's foreign?" Bannister demanded.

"It employs technology well beyond that of any known science. We cannot open the doors. We cannot chip away any of the hull for analysis, or understand the monopole effect it exhibits. Thus I conclude it was not constructed on earth, and it is therefore foreign." There was no triumph in the voice; it merely stated facts, coldly, with precision.

"Yeah, I thought of that," Bannister growled. "That makes it outer space. And *that's* Air Force."

"Navy too," the admiral said.

"What about NASA?" an air force captain asked.

Bannister and the admiral both swivelled toward the junior man. "Get him out of here!" the general yelled. "Fuck off!" the admiral added.

"Outer space is nevertheless foreign," the corpse voice said. "Thus I will have to ask you gentlemen to leave the room, or to release this man to me. Come along, sir," he told Harry.

"I'll be damned," Bannister growled. "Sergeant, block that door!"

"Get my marines!" the Admiral snapped.

Harry tried to shrink down into the seat. What had he got himself into? The military people were bad enough, but that civilian—CIA?—terrified him. Harry could imagine being taken into a windowless room and staying there until he had a long beard. Did the CIA operate that way? Logan didn't know, but that man looked like *he* did.

"Stop it!" Harry yelled. Everyone turned to face him. Even the civilian. "I don't belong to any of you! Neither does my ship! It's mine, and I'll decide who I talk to about it." He willed the ship to come to life but nothing happened. Nothing, and he *needed* it . . .

Did he have to be in the seat? No, the doors had closed last night . . .

"Stick with us, Harry. We'll take care of you," General Bannister said soothingly. The admiral moved into place with him, a solid show of military strength. The civilian stared at them coldly.

"Sure," said Harry. "I'm with you, General. You asked me what I want. I want some coffee. A pot of coffee and a bottle of brandy." Harry held his aching head in both hands. "A *big* bottle of brandy, you understand."

"Get the coffee." "Brandy?" "He's nuts." "A wino." "So he's a drunk, what's that?" They all talked at once.

"Will you get me what I asked for?" Harry looked at Bannister.

"Brandy?"

"Yes." Harry tried to look like a drunk in need of a shot. It wasn't hard. He *was* a drunk in need of a shot.

"And you'll tell me how . . ."

"No brandy, no talkee."

Bannister nodded. "Sergant, get that man what he wants. And move."

"But sir, in the Pentagon . . ."

"Goddamit, the Secretary of the Navy keeps brandy," the admiral said. "Chief, get up there and scrounge me some . . ."

A minute later a marine came in with a bottle of Courvoisier. The admiral muttered. "Now we have to wait for the goddam coffee."

Harry felt great. He couldn't remember a time when he'd felt better. He drained the last of his fourth cup and looked at the assembly of people, uniformed and civilian. The coffee had brought him full awake, and there was a warm feeling inside him. The office was still jammed, and although somebody had quieted those out in the corridor Logan knew they were still there. No way out.

"Very well, sir," the cold-eyed civilian said. "You've had your drink. Now perhaps you'll be good enough to give us some explanations?"

"Sure. Just take me to the ship."

The civilian laughed politely. It wasn't a pleasant sound. "Surely you're not so drunk as that. In any event I assure you we aren't."

"Yeah." Harry stood with an effort. It was harder to walk to the window than he'd thought it would be. Shouldn't have had the last one, he thought. But I feel so damn good! Just who do these jokers think they are?

The window was closed and it wasn't obvious how to open it. Maybe it didn't open at all. Harry gulped hard, stood back from the window, and called his ship.

There was a crash and the saucer protruded several feet into the office. Two burly marines, rifles at ready, leaped in front of their admiral with a do or die look. An air policeman ran screaming out into the corridor. General Bannister put his hand on his pistol.

Harry had time to see that the wreckage of the wall had not come plummeting down, but fell, *slowly*, to the floor. The saucer waited for him.

It was faced the wrong way. He couldn't see the air lock at all. And while the marines menaced the ship with their rifles, the civilian sighed, took out a pair of handcuffs, and shouldered his way toward Harry.

Time to go, Harry decided. But how? There was only one way. He leaped at the ship, fell onto the flat part astern, and thought it away from the Pentagon. There was a sudden rush, and Harry was a thousand feet above a toy city of Washington. He looked down, gulped hard, gulped again, but it did no good. He lost the contents of his stomach. Adrenalin flowed. To his horror, Harry was getting cold sober!

BALTIMORE SUN:
FREAK ROBBERY OF
LIQUOR STORE
MANIAC BATTERS DOWN
WALLS TO STEAL BOOZE!

VANCOUVER SUN:

RCMP IN CONFUSION
DAWSON TIMBER HEIR
DEMANS ACTION
AMERICAN ENGINEER
ACCUSED OF SAUCER
THEFT

Dawson: *Wealthy timber heir David McClellan insisted he will take his case to Ottawa if the Royal Canadian Mounted Police will not give him satisfaction. McClellan, exhausted from a trek through the northern bush country, could not be reached for comment, but it is reliably reported that he has asked the Mounties to track down and recover a stolen flying saucer.*

TOPEKA STAR:

POLICE HOLD
ROBBERY SUSPECT
REPEAT OF BALTIMORE
LIQUOR STORE BURGLARY
SUSPECT HELD—PLOT
SUSPECTED

Topeka, Kansas: *Police are holding George Herndon, liquor store manager, who was found with the contents of the store's cash register in a park near RADCLIFFE'S FLASK AND BOTTLE. Herndon, 29, was employed as the chief clerk and manager in the store, and was found dead drunk two blocks from the wrecked building. Herndon told police a wild story of a flying saucer which battered down the rear wall of the store, and explained that he had rescued the night's receipts from the invading saucer—*

A prize ten litre flask of Napoleon brandy was also taken and has not been recovered. Store owners say the rare brandy is almost two hundred years old.

LOS ANGELES TIMES:

BELLE AIRE MILLIONAIRE
ESCAPES DEATH
ONE-IN-A-MILLION
ACCIDENT

Millionaire playboy Larry Van Cott was nearly killed today when an empty ten litre brandy bottle fell onto his patio from a great height. Van Cott was in the swimming pool only a yard from the point of impact, and was cut by glass flying from the over-sized bottle which totally shattered. FAA officials are investigating.

"Harry Logan, stop messing around with that junk and Get A Job! And no more of these mysterious trips either! You came home drunk!"

"Yes, dear." Couldn't she leave him alone? Ever? She had the thousand, wasn't that enough?

He hadn't dared tell her what really happened. He'd been barely sober enough to hide the saucer out in the arroyo. He'd been so clever, hiding his liquor in the ship where Ruth couldn't find it . . .

And now the ship wouldn't open the doors for him! "You took all my money. Give me five bucks, please, Ruth. Please."

"No! You'd just walk down to the liquor store! I know you, Harry Logan!" She stomped off.

Harry held his aching head. The liquor store was five miles away. The ship only worked when he was drunk. And he didn't have any money . . .

There was a sound of crunching gravel. A car was coming up the long drive from the highway. Harry looked out to see Air Force blue and froze. Good Lord, they'd traced him!

I give up, Harry thought. He went outside as the car drove up. General Bannister climbed out of the back seat of the sedan. There were two majors with him, silver wings gleaming on their chests. Each of them held a bottle of Christian Brothers brandy, and the general was staggering. . . . ○

EDITOR'S INTRODUCTION TO:

'CASTER
by
Eric Vinicoff

The Vietnam War was traumatic in ways that previous wars had never been, because it was brought home to our living rooms each evening. The United States lost few engagements, and never lost a battle. We were never defeated in the field.

Instead, we were defeated at home, by an enemy we could not fight.

The memory of defeat stays with us yet. I recently read an essay by a highly intelligent young lady. The essay concerned the works of Robert Heinlein; but in the course of her review, she said, "The last war [Vietnam] looked more like WWI's man-killing trenches, in which an entire generation was devastated. Read the poets of the era; Robert Graves is still alive."

This is a popular view of Vietnam, almost universally accepted without challenge or argument. The truth, though, is a bit different.

According to the Statistical Abstract, traffic deaths (for the total population) hover at about 50,000 a year, and suicides have risen from about 14,000 in 1960 to 20,000 in 1980.[1]

In 1960, there were 11.9 million males ages 15–24; 105.2 per 100,000 died by violence in that year, for a total of 12,518 dead in accidents, suicides, and homicides. By 1980 the number of males in that group had grown to 21.4 million, and the death by violence rate had risen to 138.3 per 100,000, so that a total of 29,596 young males died by violence in 1980.

Just under 50,000 died in the entire Vietnam War: about one year's traffic fatalities. Of course the casualties happened to young men, rather than the population as a whole; on the other hand, the war was not particularly bloody (for Americans) in its early years. Battle deaths in 1961–1964 were negligible (except to those killed): a total of 267 for all four years. Compare this to the 12,000 per year who died of accidents and suicides in that same period.

By 1965, though, battle deaths had reached 1,369, and the number rose steadily until it peaked at 14,589 in 1968. At that time we had 500,000 soldiers in Southeast Asia, so that the death rate among young men in Vietnam was about 27 times that of the population as a whole; definitely frightening for those involved. On the other hand, the war did no more than *double* the death rate among young men as a class, even in that peak year. In 1968, young men had about equal chances of being killed by being in Southeast Asia, or while driving on the highways in the United States.

By 1969, battle deaths had fallen to 9,414. This is a large number, but by that time, the civilian violent death rate had risen to 130 per hundred thousand, so that nearly 24,000 young men died in the United States that year. After 1969 the battle deaths fell off rapidly; civilian accidental and homicide death rates continued to rise.

Thus: if the War "devastated a generation", then we continue to devastate each generation through accidental deaths; and if the Vietnam War served no useful purpose—and perhaps, given that we eventually abandoned those we had sworn to protect, it did not—neither do the accidental deaths and suicides.

The war certainly had a terrible effect; but in part that was due to the way it was reported at the time.

Moreover, we can dispel once and for all the myth that the Vietnam War was lost because it wasn't winnable. By 1970 it was essentially "won" in the sense that the indigenous Southern Viet Cong had ceased to exist. From that moment on, the war was waged entirely by invaders from the North.[2]

Even so, Vietnam did not fall to infiltrators and irregulars. Despite continuous infiltrations from the North, the Army of the Republic of Vietnam continued to hold the country, and in many places life became something like normal.

In 1972 (a year in which the US lost 300 troops in battle deaths, as compared to about 25,000 young males killed in accidents in the United States) the North Vietnam regulars invaded the South; they were beaten back with heavy losses by the Army of the Republic of Vietnam assisted by the US. US assistance was primarily air cavalry and anti-tank air support, plus a great deal of material. By that time we weren't involved much in the "internal war", but were assisting the South in enforcing at least some of the provisions of the Geneva agreements.

Vietnam fell in 1975, and it fell to four army corps of regulars, employing more armor than the Wehrmacht sent into France in 1940.[3]

When the North invaded in 1975, the Democratic Congress of the US refused any assistance to South Vietnam. After spending billions on the war, our military aid to South Vietnam was cut to $700 million. By 1974, South Vietnam soldiers were reduced to two hand grenades per man, and there was a drastic cut in ammunition supplies. Tactical communications were cut in half, and a quarter of the Vietnamese air force was grounded. More than a third of their tanks were idled, and bandages and surgical dressings were to be washed and reused.

According to Lawrence O'Brien, these cuts were made just as US analysts had concluded from an analysis of the Yom Kippur War of 1973 that supply-expenditure estimates for modern air-land battles had to be drastically increased.

South Vietnam ran short of supplies, and the nation fell. The Northern forces who swept into Saigon were no more "liberators" or even guerrillas than were the Wehrmacht units which claimed to be "liberating" the Sudeten Deutschen of Czechoslovakia and the Soviet Ukraine. The story of the boat people, re-education camps, etc., is sufficiently well known that I needn't tell it.[4]

This may have been, as some have put it, "a senseless foreign adventure that did us as a nation no good." Still, we should at least be clear about what did happen over there, and phrases like "devastated a generation" applied to casualties which at their peak barely exceeded the casualties due to accidents do little to help our understanding; nor is it useful to continue the myth that our Armed Forces failed us.

The truth is that the nation lost its will. The United States withdrew, the dominoes fell, and the blood baths began. It is no good our telling ourselves anything different.[5]

The conflict between the soldiers who must fight, and the newspeople who tell the story, is ancient. Soldiers hold most correspondents in contempt, and indeed many in Vietnam seemed contemptible, satisfied to get their stories from each other in the Caravelle bar, and so eager for "balance" that they gave equal time to a common murderer and an exhausted allied officer.

Some merely lied. To this day few know that the notorious "tiger cages" of South Vietnam were *above ground* structures with bars in place of a ceiling. Three feet above the bars was a corrugated metal roof. The intent of the design was humane: by having a gap between ceiling and roof, ventilation is much increased. The famous photograph of the prisoner in the "tiger cage" was taken by a man who climbed to the top of the wall and hunched himself between the iron barred ceiling and the roof above.

True, some correspondents have been adopted by the military. Ernie Pyle and Maggie Higgins come to mind. Both went where the action was, and both were killed trying to find out the truth. If Marguerite Higgins had lived, the story of South East Asia might have been different.

Eric Vinicoff tells of another war, and another newscaster. One wonders what would have been the effect had something similar happened in 1968. Might history have been different if a major network anchor person had become a serious, dedicated, informed patriot?

NOTES TO THE INTRODUCTION TO 'CASTER

1. Accidents are the principal cause of death among young people 15–24 years of age. In 1978, deaths among males 15–24 years of age due to accidents were over 100 per 100,000; the next highest cause was suicide, at 20 per 100,000; and after that comes malignant neoplasms at 7.7. Deaths from all causes among young males were 174 per 100,000.

2. The 1968 Tet Offensive was one of the most disastrous military operations of all time; at its end, the Viet Cong had practically ceased to exist. It is interesting to note that it is still reported as a "victory" for the communists; as indeed it was, for though they had lost on the battlefield, the North Vietnamese had won on the 6 O'clock News. They also eliminated the southern revolutionary forces who might have opposed their absolute rule once the war ended.

3. There were at least as many North Vienamese troops involved in the 1975 invasion of South Vietnam as the United States employed in the Normandy invasion. Over 10,000 supply vehicles were employed; contrast that to Patton's Red Ball Express employing 5600 vehicles in 1944, and the scale of North Vietnam's operations becomes clearer.

For a thorough analysis, one cannot do better than read *ON STRATEGY, A Critical Analysis of the Vietnam War*, by Col. Harry G. Summers (Presidio Press, 1982).

4. At least we were spared the final absurdity of watching Le Duc Tho and Henry Kissinger accepting Nobel Peace Prizes for "ending" the war. At the time the Agreement was signed, there were over 150,000 North Vietnamese Army Troops in South Vietnam, and both parties knew it. North Vietnam never expected to keep the agreement. One wonders whether the *New York Times* thought they would.

5. In contrast to the US press, which professed alarm and dismay because we were "widening the war" when

we began operations in Cambodia, the North Vietnamese *never* made any secret of the fact that they were fighting the *Indochina War*, and that Laos and Cambodia had always been part of the theater of combat. Yet, to this day, one hears the insane argument that US actions "provoked", and thereby caused, the insurgency of the Khmer Rouge in Cambodia.

'CASTER
by
Eric Vinicoff

The circular control deck of *FSS Jutland*—9,000 tons, registry NX2275, class heavy battle cruiser, designation squadron flagship—was totally enwrapped in the process of final approach. Captain Disad and his senior officers manned the stations lining the low wall, quietly snapping out orders and reports. Displays played colorfully, in weirdly offset shades, in the red illumination. Equipment hums, whirs and clicks cut through the almost forgotten background throb of the ion thrusters.

The two guests sat in observation chairs in the center. They could whisper to each other without disturbing the activity.

Jim Buser was there by virtue of the Federation-wide clout of GalNews. In his late twenties, tall and thin, he sported a blond mustache and the latest shoulder-length hair style. His jumpsuit was a Cardin original. "Do I detect a tang of grimness in the air?" he inquired lightly of his companion.

Admiral Jarold Young frowned. He was an older, greyer than the other, yet still a massively powerful man. "They're a bit tense."

"Because of you?"

"In part, perhaps. Not that I would interfere with the Captain in SOP, but to have me staring over his shoulder—"

"Then it's the mission," Jim broke in, smiling.

Damn him! The twerp never stopped digging. "The crew has a mission to perform, and is performing it," he replied tightly.

"But none too happily?"

Captain Disad swiveled toward them, saving the Admiral the necessity of further evasion. "Greenport on the horizon, sir. Permission to land?"

"Permission granted. Carry on, Captain."

The captain thumbed his com. "All hands, secure for landing. Code yellow. Fire Control, stand by for possible SAM and/or ground action. Out."

Jim watched in the big overhead holotank. Far below wispy cirrus clouds danced across the dark blue ocean. Ahead lay the green and brown of the northern continent. He took a deep breath. It was a sight he had seen once before, and had at the time planned never to see again.

"Who's likely to be shooting at us?"

The admiral smiled. "Shikaran terrorists. Society of Man. Take your choice." Even the Provisional Government might be in the mood to take a pot shot or two.

"Quite a tank of sorliks you've walked into."

The admiral saw that one, too: 'Disgruntled Commander Blasts Council Decision.' A one-way ticket to the ordinance testing station on Pluto. "Fortunately we have you to unravel the situation and present a picture of brilliant clarity to the worlds."

"You flatter me."

The admiral didn't reply.

The clouds and ocean were rushing by more closely now. Their odd angle in the tank, arguing against the solid stability of the shipboard pseudograv, confused Jim's stomach.

Admiral Young gave the younger man a searching look. "You have any real idea what it's going to be like for you here?"

"I should. I was born here, remember?"

"I mean now. And in the near future."

"You mean when the Hive takes over?"

"I didn't say that."

"No, of course you wouldn't." Something crept in behind Jim's light manner. "I'll get along just fine. The Treaty of Eridani guarantees the rights of mediamen. The Federation and the Hive are good friends now—as long as we throw them an occasional bone."

The admiral turned to watch the landing in the tank. He couldn't trust himself to speak.

The cruiser flipflopped and began its stern descent. A patch of coastline expanded into the scarred concrete plain of a spaceport on the northern edge of a substantial city.

A horn whooped three times. "Touchdown dex five," the captain chanted. "Four . . . three . . . two . . . one . . . down!"

The tank went black, then filled with a side view of the spaceport field. The throb died. "Ground stations all," Captain Disad rapped into his mike field. "Sensors and screens out full. Fire Control, stay sharp. Marines, stand by for special operations. Quartermaster, square away to receive our personnel complement. Out." He swiveled to face Admiral Young. "Orders, sir?"

"Ready a flitter and pilot for me. And call Major Sung—we'll pull out as soon as I get back."

Captain Disad relayed the first order to the Operations Officer, then added, "Calling won't be necessary, sir. Look."

Checking the tank, he understood. The low wooden Ranger barracks lined one edge of the field. Doors swung open, and the Sixth Ranger Battalion, the last of the Federation presence on Greenworld, marched out. Their dress whites glistened with silver braid under the afternoon sun. They were putting on a show, but their laser rifles were at the ready and their backpack power units fully charged.

"Grounding lock open," the Captain ordered. "Ramp down. Marine detachment deploy in honor-guard formation."

"No Provisionals about," the Operations Officer noted.

"You could hardly expect them to celebrate the occasion," Jim said.

"I imagine they have other matters to concern them," Admiral Young replied, ignoring Jim.

Twelve combat-suited marines trotted down the ramp and formed a double row. The long marching column would cross the field in about ten minutes. From the direction of the port facilities, though, a groundcar sped toward the cruiser at a reckless velocity. It skidded to a stop in front of the ramp.

The Com Officer whispered briefly to Captain Disad, who turned to Jim. "The car is for you, Mister Buser.

Are you ready to offload?" His expression was one Admiral Young found disturbing—even his senior officers saw only the celebrity status.

"You bet. Thanks for your hospitality, folks. Be sure to catch my 'casts."

"Your luggage will meet you in the lock."

A round of handshakes, then Jim turned and entered the bounce tube. Admiral Young watched him closely as he dropped from sight in a hum of stator rings. And wondered.

The front passenger door of the groundcar was open. Jim slid in beside the driver. In the back seat a second man sat with a shivergun in his lap. They wore dark combat suits *sans* insignia.

"You with the Provisional Government?" Jim asked.

"Naw," the gunner drawled. "GalNews signs our chits. We're to get you to the station whole."

The groundcar lifted on its air cushion and hurried toward the port's main gate, twin turbines whining. Jim and his bags tumbled around a bit.

Mercs, he realized. Like carrion gathering at a kill. Mostly vets from the War looking for a situation to exploit.

A scream slanted down from the sky. "Boppers!" the driver shouted, and swerved almost at a right angle. Jim hit the door hard, and a red frame formed around reality.

He peered out the rear window. The cruiser stood stolidly, a tapered white cylinder with spidery landing legs. But tiny figures were hitting the deck near the ramp which was rising back into the hull.

Then the scene disappeared as the groundcar sped through the gate into a wide empty boulevard and headed into the city.

A sharp crack was followed almost immediately by a wind that twisted the groundcar around.

"We've got to go back—" he began.

"The hell you say!" the driver snarled. "They don't pay me to butt into someone else's action."

"That's *news* back there!"

"Yeah, and we're gonna live to read about it in the papers!"

Jim gave up and slumped back in his seat. He knew the merc mentality. Maybe the station would have a good line on it when he got there. Some action footage for his first 'cast would be great.

He wondered if anyone had been killed.

They were entering the downtown area. Few vehicles were about, and those drove quickly. In the shopping districts few people walked the sidewalks—they too hurried. Each block had at least one bombed out building, and many more were boarded up.

The city was under seige, choked by the insensate viciousness of the highly developed political tool called terrorism. The *aesgi* business districts, naturally, were the worst. He had seen it before. In Northern Ireland. Jewish Palestine. Wolf's World. Indistan. But this was Greenworld, his world, or at least it once had been.

He saw troops of the new Provisional Government patrolling the streets in armored PC's and squads on foot. The warm blue sky hung a peaceful facade over the city.

The GalNews building was reassuringly unchanged. He remembered the years of working up through that unfeeling structure, the desperate effort, the learning and the mindfuck games that were *de rigeur*.

The groundcar slid into a garage entrance which opened at its approach. Pulling over to the lift entrances, the air cushion sighed away and the driver opened Jim's door. "One body, delivered as per."

Jim climbed out, leaving his bags for the processes that dealt with such things. He stepped into an open lift. The Shikaran, incongruous in his specially cut human business suit, touched a button and they started up. "Misterrr Buserrr?" he rumbled.

"You would be Astawa of Oth? The manager?"

"Yes. You brrring completeness to ourrr minorrr hive. You arrre welcome."

"Likewise." Jim stared. It had been six long years. Everywhere else Shikarans—purples—were implacable enemies of humanity. Astawa towered a half meter over him, while the impossibly thin body swayed back and forth. Long arms ended in six opposable claws. The visible skin was closer to violet than purple, and turned almost blue around the close-set eyes and tiny nose in the literally hatchet face. Rimming the hole of a mouth, dozens of tiny chelae were weaving. Something that would pass for bushy black hair covered the narrow ridge of scalp.

"You arrre surrrprrrised to find a Shikarrran in my position?"

"The way things are going around here, I'm surprised you're not mounted in someone's trophy room."

The chelae clicked laughter. "You enjoy harrrd trrruth. Of courrrse the Goverrrnment watches me, but my company watches the Government. I'm doing too good a job to rrremove, and they trrrust me somewhat."

"Are you a subversive?"

"Not in any of the senses you mean the worrrd."

The lift opened, and Astawa led him down a busy corridor to an office. In the plush inner sanctum Astawa settled behind his desk/console while Jim took a facing seat. GalNews' trust in the purple told him even more than the Government's.

"Someone shelled the *Jutland* as I was leaving. Get anything on it?"

"On the disk. A minorrr incident—no injurrries. We've set everrrything up in an editing rrroom so you can assemble what you want forrr yourrr firrrst 'cast. Scheduled 2000 WDS."

"Thought I'd start with some kind of chronology of the mess here."

"We have chrrronology forrr you to sift thrrrough. Tons of chrrronology."

"Good. I've got a lot of news to catch up on."

"Storrries lingerrr in this building about you from the time beforrre you left this worrrld. About yourrr ability—and yourrr desire to be gone."

"GalNews thinks I'll have a special slant on this story. I left because this mudball is about as far from real civilization as you can get. My *temporary* assignment here doesn't change a thing."

"Yet you arrre herrre. And everrry moment is change." The Shikaran rose. "Let me show you to yourrr suite. You'll want rrrest and rrrefrrreshment beforrre you go to worrrk."

Jim followed him down the corridor, wondering. This purple exec would definitely be a rush. Hardly the typi-

cal farmer or shopowner, immersed in hive culture, remote and simple in human affairs. Astawa was of a rare
but growing type, the product of osmosis between
dominant and minority cultures. He could deal with
Jim on almost equal terms, while Jim knew as little as
any non-expert about Shikarans. The edge was his, and
Jim didn't like it.

"Bopper coming in!" the Scanner Officer shouted.
Captain Disad slapped the EV alarm, and watched the
Marines and those Rangers still boarding dive to hug
hard surface. "Calculate back to the launch point. Lay it
in Fire Control's board. Fire Control, blow that point to
hellangone."

"Proton batteries, sir?"

"And take out every building in the way? They lob, we
lob."

"Laid in, sir."

"Launching two intercepts, sir."

Twin tiny darts shot away from the hull, arching high
and north, then diving out of sight.

The shell hit near the base of the cruiser, about twenty
meters from the nearest prone figure. The explosion
shook the control deck, and grey smoke rolled with the
wind. The scattered soldiers were briefly lost from sight.

"Intercepts on course," the Fire Control reported. A
column of smoke climbed in the north.

The admiral rose from his chair. "Good work, Captain.
Carry on."

"Sir, won't you please take an escort?"

"Can't. Bad form—we're officially on good terms with
the Provisional Government. But stay tight on my command frequency just in case." He ducked into the bounce
tube.

Five minutes later a vehicle bay in the cruiser's flank
opened, and out flew the flattened cigar shape of a
flitter.

Admiral Young was alone in the rear seat, isolated
from the pilot by a glassite pane. "ETA twelve minutes,
sir," the pilot said over the com. "We're cleared for
entry."

The admiral watched through a port as they flew low
southeast, over wooded foothills. Valleys cradled farms

abundant with wheat, corn and fruit trees. Cow herds grazed on rich grass, and streams flowed down from the mountain range they were approaching.

So unlike Earth. So much hope for the future. Only it had become a piece in a game whose players cared little about such things.

The mountain pass was thick with purple-leaved trees like the great conifers of the Pacific Northwest. But they quickly dwindled as the flitter descended into high desert. It slanted toward a bright jewel in the bare brown land. The jewel grew into a smaller version of the spaceport they had just left. It was new, raw and half-completed. The rim G/A intercept batteries marked it as a military base, the home of the Provisional Government's tiny space command.

The grey field was conspicuously empty. Every converted freighter and shuttle was on patrol, awaiting the expected Hive fleet. And he knew where *Marsailles* and *Antares*, their only interstellar ships, were.

The pilot received final clearance, and landed. A VIP groundcar picked the admiral up and drove him to the Admin Building. Minutes later, far below the surface level, he was ushered into a small meeting room. Five men and two women looked up at him with unfriendly expressions.

He understood. The messenger was once more to be blamed for the message.

"Have a seat, Admiral," one of the men said.

"Thank you, Mister President." He took the only empty seat around the long table.

The Greenworlders were tanned dark, and carried the physiques of strenuous youths into middle age. They had been successful farmers, ranchers, industrialists and merchants; successful because they had built up their businesses. Now they were the planetary Council, amateur statesmen and warriors.

"Let's make this short," the President said. "Name's Hugh Marlowe, as you seem to know. You're Admiral Young. You have a message for us?"

"Yes."

"We have a lot of work leaning on us, Admiral."

The admiral laid a large envelope on the table and

slid it over to the President. "From the Federation Executive, sir."

President Marlowe opened it and quickly scanned the enclosed sheet. Some of the ruddiness drained from his face. "To see it in cold print, friends, somehow makes it worse."

"It's what we expected," one of the women said rather than asked.

He nodded. "No treaty or mutual defense pact will be considered. Nor will the Federation guarantee our loans to buy space defense arms."

Another man slammed a meaty fist on the table. "It's a damned trade: us for a few more years of peace!"

"It's genocide!" a third added.

"The Executive's relocation offer still stands," Admiral Young said, tight-lipped.

"Thanks a whole hell of a lot!" snapped the President. "Ship two million of us to some War burn-off like Legrange or New China inside your new borders? Can we farm slag? Can we drink acid? *This* is our home. We plan to keep it."

"How? Your defenses are no match for a Hive invasion force. And we know about your efforts to buy arms on the free worlds—your two freighters are sitting on Eridani right now. But no one will extend you the credit you need—you won't last long enough to repay the loans."

The atmosphere around the table turned glacial.

"A relocation fleet—"

"You've delivered your message, Admiral," the President cut in. "I suggest you get the last of your yellow-backs off-planet. Could be some fighting here soon, and we wouldn't want to upset your delicate constitutions."

Admiral Young bit off a reply, rose and walked out.

"Good evening, ladies and gentlemen of the worlds. This is Jim Buser with a special on-the-scene report from Tau Ceti III, notorious Greenworld, in the disputed interface between the Federation and the Shikaran Hive.

"This paradise of blue sky, pure air, sparkling seas and lush vegetation has been the cause of conflict since 2111, when a coalition of dissident groups from Earth colonized it. Shikaran colonists began arriving on the South Continent at the same time.

"Then came the War, and its stalemate ending as both sides recoiled in horror from the scale of destruction they had wrought. Greenworld became de facto Federation territory.

"But the Hive concept of completeness drives it to incorporate Greenworld's Shikarans more strongly than we humans can understand. While we recover our strength and courage very slowly . . ."

The Black Hole was the bar/restaurant atop the GalNews building. Mediamen being what they were, it was their social hub. Jim naturally gravitated there after scrapping his makeup.

He wandered around, drink in hand, renewing a few old acquaintances and making some new ones. About fifty people were crammed in the small noisy room—with the seige-state outside, business was booming. He went through the motions, knowing it was the pro move, feeling nothing.

Then he saw the corner booth where a lone occupant had all sorts of elbow room in which to drink. He sauntered over and slid in next to Astawa. "Evening."

"Good evening, Jim." Astawa sucked in a gulp from his dark glass. "I enjoyed yourrr 'cast."

"Thanks. Purely warmup—wait until I find the right angle."

"You take yourrr gift casually."

"Gift? I sweated bricks learning to do what I do."

"Otherrrs have sweated brrricks. But therrre arrre few who can make billions listen, underrrstand and believe."

"You think I have some kind of psi power or something?"

Astawa laughed. "Nothing so obvious, orrr it would be known. Forrrtunately you arrre a man without causes."

"I'm a self-contained cause. What are you drinking?"

"Coke."

It figured. The Shikaran diet consisted of insects and starchy plants. Sugar acted as an intoxicant.

"Come here often?" Jim asked.

"No. It upsets the employees. But I came tonight because I knew you would."

That sent Jim's thoughts on a new tack. Shikarans

holding down jobs in the human society normally returned to their hives before dark, obeying vestigial
instinct. "You live in the building?"

"I have to."

"You eat here?"

Astawa was good—he barely flinched. Shikarans *never*
discussed eating in any but euphemistic terms. "Yes.
Would you carrre to join me this evening?"

Jim smiled. It was a strong reposte. Few humans could
stand the sight of those chelae shovelling in food.

"You live here. What about your hive?"

"I was of Oth, a hive rrrooted deeply in time and
prrride. But I chose this. I am *aesgi*."

Outcast. Cripple. Never again to couple ecstatically with
the nonsentient queen and beget children. Only insanity
or great need could drive a Shikaran *aesgi*. Jim knew
the need. He shared it, or had once.

"You arrre also alone."

Jim downed his drink. "Lay off the human psychology.
You aren't built for it."

"What does one do when his drrream dies?"

"I wouldn't know. Or care."

"Cynicism rrreplaces wonderrr. And all you knew is
gone."

Jim realized abruptly he was talking to a very drunk
Shikaran. "You'd like to think we're the same. Why?
What's your dream?"

"This worrrld we stand on. What it is and could be.
But won't."

"Lots of your compeers are rooting for the Hive."

"They don't know yet."

"What?"

"That they too arrre *aesgi*."

"*Tonight, ladies and gentlemen of the worlds, is Independence Day on Greenworld. The Federation protectorate actually ended two days ago with the departure of the last
Rangers, but tonight President Marlowe went on worldwide holovision to announce the Provisional Government's
assumption of sovereignty. With him appeared Gomla of
the great industrial Gla hive, representing the Shikaran
minority in the planetary Assembly.*

"*The Federation has yet to recognize the new government,*

*while the Hive has sent a communique reasserting its old
claim to Greenworld. Intelligence reports indicate a large fleet
in transit, and all armed forces are on alert.*

*"Shikaran and human extremists continue to wage vi-
cious guerrilla warfare against the government. Even as I
speak, lonely farms and rural hives are aflame. But
elsewhere, all over the planet, impromptu celebrations are
happening. Here in the capital, as you can see, thousands
are risking the danger to revel in heavily guarded Park
Square.*

*"Is this galantry—some would call it perversity—a product
of mere ignorance? Don't say that to these people. They
know what they fight for. And they won't admit the certainty
of defeat . . ."*

Outside the Tau Ceti system, at the edge of the newly
shrunken Federation interface, *FSS Jutland* and her seven
squadron mates were strung out in a line, on patrol,
observing the military situation.

Admiral Young sat in the back of the darkened
wardroom, with about thirty of *Jutland*'s off-watch
officers, staring into a big holotank. The GalNews daily
wrapup was beamed to the squadron by the Armed
Forces Network. During the months the squadron had
hovered at the interface it had become a tradition. But,
as Mister Buser's voice and image faded out, he worried.
The Greenworld 'casts were like vinegar on baking soda.
The officers filed out slowly and silently. Too much so.

He thought he was alone, but he wasn't. Captain Disad
settled precisely into the chair next to his. "Jerry," he
said softly, "how long has it been since a Federation
crew mutinied?"

The word did not shock him, though it was meant to.
"Is it that bad?"

"On the other ships too, from what I hear."

"Think we should black the 'casts out for the duration?"

"No—that might just precipitate what we're trying to
avoid. Our crews aren't cannon fodder. We start playing
games with them, and we'll have trouble for sure.
Furthermore this is peacetime and it would be illegal.
Furthermore, dammit, we all have a right to know."

The admiral nodded. "You know the drill then. Senior officers crack down. Constant drill. No one gets a spare minute to think. I'll com the other captains."

"Yes, sir. But the crunch will come when the Hive attacks Greenworld. You know what that'll be like for us."

"Okay, our mission stinks. Next election we can vote our displeasure. But we're in the business of administering policy, not making it."

"Granting Greenworld its independence—sounds better than surrender. Almost noble." Captain Disad's expression was carefully neutral. "You feel no pity for those people?"

"Dammit, what I feel is nobody's concern but my own! I don't create these impossible messes—I just do what I'm told."

"You sound like a tired old man, Jerry."

"Forty-nine, going on *rigor mortis*."

"But not as old and tired as you'd like to think. Not enough so you can slide into autopilot."

The admiral was quiet for a long time. "Don't push it any farther. I'd hate like hell to lose you."

"Remember the *Orion* during the Suicide Sortie? You ignored intelligence reports and ran the purple's flank. Otherwise we might never have targeted the queenship."

Admiral Young rose and walked to the door, where he turned back to the Captain. "You remember the War? Good. Remember the devastation, the gigadeaths. Remember the economic collapse. Remember the disease and fear. Never again. That's our duty. No matter what it requires of us. Good night."

"Society of Man terrorists assassinated the Olwa Hive representative to the South Continent House of Landsmen today. The Government has moved two militia units to Lynchfield to hunt the killer packs that hide in the badlands. Olwa separatists are urging a work stoppage at its bauxite mines.

"Here in Greenport, two more bombings. An aesgi soft drink bottling plant and the local headquarters of the Bank of Tokyo were heavily damaged.

"The last of the Red Cross refugee ships departed for New Switzerland today, less than half full.

"A spokesman for the Government confirmed that

Shikaran scout ships have been detected probing the edges of the system. The long expected assault should begin within the next seventy-two hours. Everyone knows it. You notice the frequent looks skyward. Their fate will be decided in high orbit . . ."

Jim was night people, and rose after eleven AM whenever possible. Here it was well after noon, and he was only just leaving a hearty breakfast in his suite for the editing room. Pills held an otherwise murderous hangover at bay; his ethanol intake was above normal, and he didn't like it. Control was all he had. Control kept him on top.

"Good afternoon, Jim."

He froze, then turned slowly. "How do you arrange these accidental meetings?"

He and Astawa were alone in the corridor. The purple's chelae twitched. "I verrry much enjoyed yourrr 'cast last night. It rrrang of sincerity."

"That's what I get paid for."

"You extoll Grrreenworrrld's courrrage and deterrrmination as though you sharrred them."

"Want to buy some swamp real estate? What kind of psych job are you trying to run?"

"My job involves prrrotecting GalNews prrroperrrty—including yourrr valuable self. The infection of parrrtisanship would destrrroy yourrr crrredibility as a 'casterrr."

"You dance like an Aldabaran lighthunter."

"You exterrrnalize well."

Jim gave up, bid a curt farewell and continued on his way.

The editing room was dimly red-lit, small and almost entirely filled by a horseshoe console. He settled into the padded chair. His hands moved across the console with practiced ease.

The redness kicked out.

By touch he punched in a scan program for the remote dailies. Night vanished, and he was skimming low over ripe grain fields toward a burning homestead. A voice began, "At six oh five WST raiders put the torch to the two thousand acre holding of Raf and Allison Somers—"

He had been invisible behind such words himself. The

young expendable reporters gathered data and footage, vying to attract favorable attention upstairs, hating the sanctified 'casters who risked no danger worse than a sprained button-pushing finger.

"The entire household died defending the main house, along with three of the—" His attention strayed from CU's of charred bodies. Carnage was a universal constant. He looked elsewhere. The cherry orchard laden with tiny white flowers. Birds wheeling over the sun-bright fields, red dabs against blue. An old piebald mare wandering disconsolately around the ruins.

Abruptly he moved on.

Scene after scene. Story after story. He listened with one ear, and watched with one eye. Beneath the topicality was something he had forgotten.

He saw hives, both traditionally agricultural and industrial, instinctive concentric circles of white ceramic interspersed with fields. Most were near human towns or holdings. Unlike the Hive they had forsaken the law of self-sufficiency and traded among themselves and with the humans. Not being part of the greater Hive, their smallness gave them little economic choice other than reverting to primitiveness, but contact with human culture had made it culturally possible. Greenworld had a single interdependent economy.

He saw holdings, mines and factories being worked. Childhood memories of the small South Continent ranch returned unsummoned. He had hated it, and at the first opportunity had run away to Greenport. Years later one of the first death-squad attacks had left him kinless.

He saw a freight skimmer crossing wine-dark ocean. Children on schoolyard grass. Wooden towns. The city's raw metal certainty. It had all seemed unbearably provincial in the glare of the glittering meccas of the Federation worlds. But now he knew the truth behind the holovision dreams; the mashed, polluted, decadent existence. The madness of too many rats in a maze. It would be a long time before Greenworld was like that— maybe never if the tacit understanding between the species to keep numbers proportional could be used as an interspecies lever to keep numbers down.

The stories were mostly of fear and war. But he saw with other sight. He saw what gave Greenworld the will to resist, a basic self-knowledge to which sophistication and artifice were anathema.

He shook himself. Hail Greenworld! Next he would break out in a rousing chorus of 'Home Sweet Home'. He snickered at himself as he set up the console for selection and assembly. It rang sharply off the walls.

"Inflation, the bride of all wartime economies, continues to soar. The Government today ordered another round of tax increases, and the demand for wage and price controls grows daily. Moreover the economy continues to suffer from the de facto *interstellar trade embargo caused by fear of the Hive fleet.*

"Militia leaders in Homeward Valley announced the capture of the Da Fue, one of the largest of the Shikaran guerrilla gangs, in a morning raid on its hidden camp. Militia losses were reported at nine dead, seventeen wounded.

"President Marlowe has gone on global holovision to announce the strategy in case of a Shikaran occupation. Civilians are to cooperate with the invaders, and offer only passive resistance. Meanwhile army and militia units will take up prepared secret positions in the wild and carry on guerrilla operations. He strongly urged all citizens to recall the destruction of entire worlds during the War . . ."

Admiral Young felt the control deck around him; active, taut. But his eyes, like all those free to do so, stared into the big tank.

A pale white sheet simulated the Greenworld/Federation interface. The white squadron dots were gathered in a tight line just on the Federation side. But the focus of attention lay in the Greenworld zone. Another white dot was moving with aching slowness toward the interface, with a bright red dot closing from behind.

"Intercept in three minutes, sir," the Scanner Officer reported. "Intercept point still calculates at two million klicks shy of the line."

Captain Disad turned to the admiral.

"Com that triple-be-damned captain again and tell him to heave to," the admiral said.

The captain relayed the order, but shook his head. "He is Swiss, sir. He won't let a foreign power force a boarding."

"He's risking his crew's lives, and the lives of the refugees too, dammit!" Admiral Young was sweating.

Captain Disad shrugged.

"It's definitely a Shikaran heavy cruiser, sir," the Scanner Officer reported. "Dau Hive."

The admiral remembered the Dau fleet from the War. Very good, and like all Shikaran warhives, it was very literal about orders. Which in this case were apparently to assert the Shikaran territorial claim by inspecting any ships traversing it.

"The *Geneva* has responded, sir," the Com Officer said. "It's a Federation vessel in the space of a friendly power, and it won't yield to a hostile threat. It demands the protection of the Federation."

Every officer in the compartment looked to the admiral.

"He knows we can't intervene beyond the interface," the admiral said levelly. "Remind him, and tell him to heave to. That's a military emergency order."

"Intercept in ninety seconds, sir."

"The purple just fired a warning shot, sir!"

"It wouldn't actually take out a Red Cross ship, would it, sir?" an officer asked Captain Disad.

"The hell it wouldn't."

One of the lined-up white dots began to move toward the interface.

"*FSS Manilla Bay*, sir!" shouted the Com Officer. "Captain O'Brien reports she will escort the refugee ship to the interface!"

And start the next war! The admiral switched on his mike. "Return to position, O'Brien! This is Admiral Young! Out!"

The dot kept accelerating.

"Intercept in sixty seconds, sir."

"Return to position! I know what you think you're doing, but it'll harm more than help! I can't let you cross the interface! Out!"

The dot was very near the pale sheet, and still accelerating.

He left the mike open, and turned to the Fire Control Officer. "Arm forward proton batteries. If *Manilla Bay* crosses the interface, target on it and fire."

Even Captain Disad stared at him in horror.

"Intercept in thirty seconds, sir."

Admiral Young couldn't breathe. He wondered if the *Jutland* would carry out the order he had just given.

Suddenly the white dot representing the *Manilla Bay* decelerated sharply and curved away from the sheet.

The red dot was almost fused with the other, fleeing, white one.

"The purple's firing, sir!"

Abruptly the red dot was alone on its side of the sheet.

For long seconds equipment sounds dominated. Then the admiral turned to Captain Disad. "Raise the purple. Inform him it's our fervent desire that he stray for even a second across the interface. If he does—which he won't—welcome him with every battery and torp in the squadron."

He rose and moved slowly to the bounce tube. He felt the eyes at his back like spears. Over his shoulder he added an order that only an admiral could give: "Erase all references to *Manilla Bay*'s role in this incident from the log. Carry on."

"*A Government spokesman confirmed the rampant rumors; the Shikaran invasion fleet has taken up a globular formation beyond the moons. A communique from it has demanded an orderly transfer of authority. The Government promptly replied in the negative. Greenworld is now under seige.*

"*The fleet is reported to be the largest force gathered since the War; ninety transports carrying the occupation hives, and twenty-four cruisers. The size is surprising, diverting key units from the Federation interface. But it shows an appreciation of the determination of their foe.*

"*There have been reported demands for the Government fleet of six converted interplanetary freighters to launch a surprise attack. But Admiral Maple has reportedly decided to use them in defensive support against the expected purple attack on Orbital Command.*

"*Greenworld's satellite defense system is a relic of the War, 144 unmanned remotes armed with a Korchnoi C5V proton battery each, in spaced orbits 24,000 klicks above the surface. Orbital Command lies in geosynchronous orbit above the equator. A concerted purple attack can beat down Orbital Command's defenses, and without its direc-*

*tion the remotes can be outwitted and destroyed. Then the
planet will lie naked below.*

"While the Federation watches . . ."

Jim felt like an idiot walking along the sidewalk in his
short-sleeved shirt. The ignorance of one who spent most
of his time in artificial environments. The few pedestri-
ans about in the rain gave him curious looks. He was
thoroughly soaked, but after the initial discomfort it
didn't bother him much. The big drops were warm and
gentle. He stuck out his tongue to taste them as he used
to several lives ago.

Ahead the vault-like entrance undissolved from the
vagueness of evening under clouds. He took a last long
look over his shoulder, then ascended the wide steps to
the doors.

A guard's face appeared in the small holotank. "Yah?"

"It's Jim Buser. Open up."

That snapped him awake, as Jim had known it would.
"Don't move, sir! Just be a minute!"

It was considerably less, and when the alloy slab swung
open a full squad of guards jumped out to 'escort' him
in. Minutes later he entered Astawa's office alone. The
purple was installed behind his desk, but his chelae
writhed in agitation.

Jim went over to the wall bar and poured a double
scotch. "Care for a coke? Your inscrutability is slipping."

"No, thank you."

Jim settled into a chair. "Okay, erupt."

"If you wished to take an excurrrsion, why didn't you
tell me?"

"I'm valuable property, remember. Would you have
let me?"

"With prrroperrr securrrity, yes."

"I didn't want a paramilitary mission, just a stroll."

"Forrr what purrrpose?"

"To smell the air."

"If that's what you humans call poetic communication,
I find it bemusing."

"Tough shit."

Astawa leaned forward. "Forrr my rrrecorrrds, would
you mind telling me how you left without my knowledge?"

"Not at all. I stole a day-worker's ident card. He looked enough like me to get me by the entrance guards with the five PM herd." 'Stole' sounded better than 'rented'.

"You disturrrb me," Astawa rumbled.

"Por qua?"

"My superrriorrrs have had much to say to me lately. The rrratings on yourrr 'casts arrre phenomenal. But they arrre stirrring, urrr, turrrbulent rrreactions frrrom official sourrrces."

"Hardly surprising. BFD."

"It has been suggested that you, urrr, rrreduce the intensity of yourrr 'casts."

Jim took a deep breath. "It took me many years of eating corporate feces to reach the level where no one tells me how to do my job. I don't need GalNews—I can get work anywhere."

"Of courrrse. But rrrememberrr: If you become blatant they'll pull yourrr plug."

"When have I ever been blatant? By the way, are the military shuttles still running up to Orbital Command?"

"Yes. They arrre prrrotected by the satellites forrr now."

"Can you swing me a ride up there? I want to do some special 'casts from the trenches."

Astawa was silent for many seconds. "Technically it prrresents little difficulty. The Goverrrnment would apprrreciate the prrropaganda value. But of courrrse I can't allow it."

"Think of the ratings. Also think of your career if you seriously annoy me."

"You must know it's extrrremely unlikely Orrrbital Command will surrrvive the coming attack. If I werrre to lose you, GalNews would deal even more harrrshly with me."

"You just might be surprised about that."

"Why do you want to die?"

"I plan on getting out before the blowup."

"You may not be able to."

"Want to put down some action on it? I'm a survivor type."

"I wonderrr if you'rrre lying just to me orrr to yourrrself as well."

"Huh?"

"Yourrr notion indicates suicidal tendencies. It saddens me to see atavistic guilt erase a grrreat gift."

"You're crazy."

"Perrrhaps. Perrrhaps I underrrstand neitherrr one of us. Arrre you surrre you want to do this?"

"Yeah."

"Then perrrhaps you arrre called. I'll arrrange it. Afterrr I have that coke."

"Orbital Command looks like a produce can left spinning in space after some cosmic picnic. Ninety-six meters long and forty-five in diameter, it looks tiny compared to the six freighter/warships poised around it.

"Yet in reality the giants are all-but-toothless, while Orbital Command carries a potent sting: a laser fusion reactor that powers a proton battery at each end. In addition there are two torp launchers, and four electrostatic accelerator batteries for anti-torp defense.

"Normally a thirty-eight person crew operates in three shifts, but in view of the near-certainty of destruction, only two skeleton crews remain. They are all volunteers.

"From the ports space appears empty and safe, but Admiral Maple tells me the Shikarans are plain in his scopes. Four cruisers are guarding the distant waiting transports. The remaining twenty have formed an attack wedge and are beginning to close . . ."

The ceiling glowed dull orange. Hidden speakers uttered Dagorland tribal tones—great hollow notes that couldn't quite be called music but served a similar purpose. Admiral Young lay on his metal bunk in the cabin that was his only home, laminated with the accumulation of three decades in space.

What would a real home be like? Security? A place to retreat to? This wasn't it. The bulkheads were transparent to the wavelengths of tension radiating from the ship around him. Unable to hide all these years, he had calloused.

But not enough.

He stood his watches stoically, the hatred of his crew an open festering wound. But better they should hate him than themselves.

His stomach was in constant fury. The pills would hold him together. But the pain was just background static for guilt, guilt amplified by the loneliness of command. His existence was all small, tight compartments and narrow corridors, like the ships he commanded.

Buser and his damned 'casts! Under the deceptive objectivity the man constantly intimated things that made the admiral want to yell, to argue, to punch out the holovision tank. Things he pushed out of his mind but that kept bobbing back.

There was an out, maybe. Technically speaking.

Only it had a toll gate across it. An old man with a grinning skull-face stood in the shadows, bone hand extended palm up.

"How much?" the admiral whispered over and over into the diffuse orangeness.

Over and over the grating jaws replied.

Everything. Not just the flesh. The *arate* too. The carefully sculpted totem of a life of service. His afterlife. What remained would be a black thing, gnawing at his rest.

A chime sounded. He rolled over and slapped the com button. "Yes?"

Captain Disad's voice filled the cabin. "The purple fleet is moving on Orbital Command, sir. This looks like it."

"I'll be right up."

"This is Jim Buser, with a special report I quite frankly didn't expect to be making, from my present location.

"Farmers, townspeople, purples in their hives—throughout the night hemisphere Greenworlders stood under the night sky and watched the new lights flickering there.

"The Hive attack came sooner than expected, but Admiral Maple was prepared with a strategy long-planned. A desperate strategy.

"Normally the defense satellites are spaced evenly to protect every part of the world. But he gambled on the standard attack technique of eliminating Orbital Command first. Under the guise of inspection missions, he had his orbital tenders replace many of the distant satellites with mockups and bring the real ones back. As the Hive cruisers closed in, they were placed in picket positions around Orbital Command.

"Out to meet the attack wedge moved the six Greenworld ships in a spear formation. Sailing into the brunt of the Hive formation was also unconventional, but the purples recovered and quickly annihilated the two lead ships. This was part of the admiral's plan—both ships were crewless automatics, and in dying filled the immediate volume with cargo bays of radar jinglejangles. Into the confusion accelerated the remaining ships. Purple fire destroyed one, but three managed to ram and die with Hive cruisers. A grim trade, but one that Admiral Maple and the three skeleton crews were willing to make.

"So only seventeen cruisers assaulted Orbital Command. They had accurate calculations of its firepower, and expected to overrun it. But their expectations were rudely disappointed. They met a wall of fire augmented by the satellites. Only eleven cruisers were able to withdraw after the furious four minute battle.

"Orbital Command suffered damage, but is still in business. The picket satellites have been returned to their proper orbits so the purples can't exploit that weakness.

"It's a great victory—one that should remind the Federation of its own great victories long ago; the Last Defense, Pollock's Out and so on. Here aboard Orbital Command, though, there is little hope. The tricks saved them from only the first attack. The cruisers will return soon. And circumspectly. There can be no more surprises . . ."

Jim leaped out of his bunk at the raucous code-red alarm. He was fully dressed—everyone aboard slept that way during a code yellow, and looked and smelled it. He ran along empty corridors, and jumped into a bounce tube that shot him up to the control deck sheltered in the station's core.

He stepped diffidently into the CD, slid into his observation chair, buckled in and switched on his holocorder. The crew was already at its duty posts. Four hunched over fire control boards, their heads lost in sensor cones. Four were likewise engrossed in systems maintenance and repair boards. Two were at the satellite consoles. One was doing double duty covering the com and scanner systems. In the middle of this cramped activity paced Admiral Maple. He was barely thirty, and his crew younger still, but they didn't look young any more.

The new uniforms had been junked for T-shirts and pants. Three months ago they had been crewing aboard the freighters which no longer existed.

Jim kept his mouth shut. His position was precarious. They could talk to him—the admiral was reasonably loquacious in his few free moments. But his presence wasn't universally acclaimed, and if he intruded at the wrong time it was conceivable that he might be shot out of hand. It was that kind of situation.

The admiral walked over. His expression was, as always, controlled. "You should have taken the last shuttle down."

"I notice you didn't have me put off."

"Motivations are pretty murky around here right now."

"Like mine, for example?" Jim chuckled. "Maybe I succumbed to the hypnotic allure of my own words. I know a guy who thinks I'm suicidal. Or maybe I'm a hero, like you and your crew."

Admiral Maple gestured toward the busy men and women. "After we've filtered through you, we become heroes. Jane there shoots syntho-morph so her hands don't shake. Ali and Gertrude are having an affair unappreciated by either's spouse. Joe hates aliens. Me, I'm a classic manic-depressive."

"You're all here."

"Yes, there is that, isn't there."

"T-minus-thirty seconds to range!" the Scanner Officer shouted.

Jim watched himself vanish instantly from the admiral's thoughts as the latter returned to his command chair in a single stride and strapped in. "Battle stations! Depressurization alert—evacuate Levels A, B and C. E-systems in. Straps tight."

So it began. As always, Jim had trouble tuning into the reality of it. He had seen all sorts of battles, all sorts of death. But here were no guns, no soldiers, no blood. Just lights moving in tanks. Digital readouts. Displays. From such he had to decipher what was happening.

What little fear that broke through the intellectual insulation was muted by the knowledge that here there would be no pain, just lights out; anger dominated. But both feelings went on the back burner for the duration. He had work to do.

He eyed the main tank. Eleven red dots were swinging toward a white dot on a parabolic course. They apparently planned to fire *en passant*, repeat as needed.

"Fire Control, your circuits override. Fire at will. Scanner priority feeds to the war boards."

"Repair drones dispersed and standing by."

"Core tight. Everything else is vacuum—gonna be a hell of a mess in the mess."

"Lead target entering range."

Vector lines appeared in the smaller tanks as the proton batteries began firing at their twelve second minimum cycle. Recoils jolted the compartment, making hollow thumping sounds. Torp launches were indicated in the tanks by blue dots moving in rapid lines.

Torps and proton beams were likewise targeting on them from the purples. ES guns were picking off the torps. The beams were either missing due to the extreme range or—

KRUUUUUMP! The straps almost cut him into segments. Alloy groaned under the application of the tinsnips of hell. His eyes closed, then opened in surprise that they were still able to.

The crew was battered and bloody but woozily still at work. Damage reports were flying around the CD.

One of the red dots went out, and the Fire Control crew cheered. Then the CD danced again. The air took on an acrid tang.

Several boards went dead, and the rest were covered with red lights. The red dots were swinging away from the white one.

"Outer hull integrity is zilch."

"Losing coolant from EMZ2!"

"Patch it."

"With what? Most of my drones are out!"

"Use what you have. Unless you want the heat turned way up in here."

"The purples are vectoring into an ellipse. They'll be back in one minute sixteen."

"Fire Control report!"

"Proton Batteries B and D down. ES coverage out from nine to eleven o'clock. No torps left in Launcher Two. Forty-six percent underpower. Target computations slowed by point two—insufficient antennae. Other than that, we're in lousy shape."

"Patch and pray."

Repair and regrouping went on frantically, but defeat hung over every word and action. Orbital Command had little left with which to fight. The next pass would be the last.

"Stand by. Here they come."

Admiral Young slouched in his command chair, loose but ready. He was finally on top of the situation. Over the humps. Course laid in. The officers working around him hid behind masks, but he saw every thought. Captain Disad's nervousness was laid bare.

"Eleven cruisers are definitely on the move, sir," the Scanner Officer reported. "Looks like a more cautious tangent attack plan."

"Squadron units requesting status updates, sir?" called out the Com Officer.

"Continue code yellow."

Someone muttered something. Captain Disad took a long look around the control deck, then rose from his chair. His gaze, now firm, locked with the admiral's.

Admiral Young felt good—which surprised the hell out of him. He didn't even hold it against the crew. He understood.

"Sit down, Captain."

Everyone who could turned to stare. All were wearing sidearms. So was he, but if it came to that it wouldn't matter.

The captain froze where he was, fighting his own battle.

Admiral Young casually touched his com button and called for an all-ships channel. "This is Admiral Young. Code red. Battle stations. Out."

Uncertainty punctured the tension in the compartment. Captain Disad slid back into his chair.

Alarms whooped faintly from other parts of the ship. The red bells hadn't rung in earnest since the War. Champagne sparkling filled him, and the last vestigial doubts were gone.

"Orders, sir?" Captain Disad asked.

He spoke into the com as well. "All captains. I'm

assuming emergency command responsibility under Section 2117A general regs. Record for future official proceedings. Reprogram all identity transponders for fictitious names—be imaginative. Com silence except for battle orders." A thin disguise that would fool no one, but better than nothing.

He turned to the captain. "Plot and lay in an attack course."

"We, er, have one loaded, sir."

"I thought you might. See if you can read my mind some more. Where do we hit?"

The crew was joyously at work even as Captain Disad answered. "One needs nothing but memory, sir. Who was your exec during the raid on Abruzzi?"

The admiral smiled. "It's good to be back in the realm of military strategy. Proceed."

FSS Jutland entered tachyon state at the same instant as its squadron mates. They crossed the interface and accelerated toward the solar system. Anxious minutes passed. They cheered as Orbital Command survived the first pass, knowing they would arrive in time. They decelerated at maximum thrust into the system, then shunted back to normal space drive. Not toward Orbital Command, but toward the Hive transports and their escorts.

"They know we're here," the admiral muttered. "Things should start happening."

"Keep us between the transports and the near edge of the solar tachyon-negative zone," Captain Disad cautioned the Helm Officer. "They may try to run for it."

But the slow, lightly armed transports realized they were trapped. They maneuvered into a globular defensive formation, while the four cruiser escorts accelerated toward the squadron. Meanwhile the ten cruisers broke off their attack on Orbital Command and vectored out to intercept.

"The main force is six minutes nine away, sir," Captain Disad reported. "If we haven't succeeded by then—well, fourteen to eight aren't odds to celebrate."

The admiral nodded. The tension and fear in the compartment were old beloved companions. Sweat was a coolness on his brow. He called again for an all-ships channel. "Captains. This is Admiral Young. Tighten up the formation. We're going through. No straying, no matter how tempting the target opportunity. Out."

FSS Anctium took the point—he ached to be there himself, but flagships weren't allowed to indulge in heroics. The four purples formed a barrier directly ahead.

"Are they going to ram us?" an officer wondered aloud.

It didn't come to that. The purples began retreating, and the squadron closed the gap with increasing slowness. "So they want a running fire fight," the admiral said.

"Entering target range!" the Scanner Officer reported.

"All ships, fire at will."

The twelve warships raced through space virtually side-by-side, bringing all weapons to bear. Proton salvos shook the control deck. Orders and reports flew back and forth in hushed tones. He watched in the big tank, leaving to Captain Disad the direction of *Jutland*'s efforts. He had laid in the course. Now he could only watch, knowing each moment might turn off his own personal universe. God forgive him, how he loved it!

Proton beams sought targets. ES guns strove to intercept torps in time. There could be no evasive maneuvering—the cruisers slugged it out. And since the squadron outgunned the purples two to one, when the slugging stopped, six Federation cruisers continued alone. *FSS Anctium* and *FSS Trans-Jupiter* would answer no more squadron musters. *FSS Manilla Bay* took the point.

They reached the transports, and englobed them just beyond maximum range.

"Main force intersect in two minutes six, sir."

"Open a channel to their commander," the admiral ordered. This was the crux.

"Go ahead, sir."

"Attention, hivelord of the Dau. Halt at once, or we will annihilate all of the transports—including most particularly your queenship. Out."

The queen had to be aboard one of the transports. They wouldn't have left her behind on such an apparently safe mission, nor would she have been risked in the fighting. Destruction of the queenship meant the death of the hive—the worst fate imaginable for any Shikaran. Of course, if he was wrong it would be an absolute disaster. But no time to think of that now.

The ten cruisers decelerated to a dead stop relative to the squadron.

"Very good. Now abandon your ships and set them to self-destruct. Rejoin your transports in your lifeboats. Out."

A replying message came from one of the cruisers. "You ask too much. We will not put ourrr continuity in yourrr hands. We can be upon you beforrre you can destrrroy morrre than a frrraction of the trrransporrrts."

The admiral called for the channel to the purple again. "Including, perhaps, your queenship. Am I speaking to Gelewa of Dau? Out."

"Yes."

"This is Admiral Jarold Young."

"I know."

"We almost met during the Suicide Sortie, remember? We turned your flank, but you dropped your eggs and withdrew before we could clear the pickets."

"I rrrememberrr with pleasurrre. A well executed bit of levels-play."

"I give you my word your transports will be allowed to withdraw in peace."

"Acceptable. But you underrrstand, therrre will be severrre rrreperrrcussions frrrom yourrr intrrrusion herrre."

"I understand."

"I rrregrrret that we meet this way."

"So do I."

Two minutes later lifeboats began to emerge from the cruiser bays.

"This is Jim Buser, back on Greenworld again. A shuttle evacuated us from Orbital Command just before the reactor blew its magnetic bottle.

"Tonight I look down from the roof of the GalNews building at Market Lane, the wide concourse leading from the Park to the civic center. It's midnight and the moons are down, but there are lights in the darkness. Yellow flickers of flame. Hundreds, thousands of burning candles, all proceeding slowly, solemnly toward the broad stone steps in front of Civic Hall. I can see faces behind the candles; young and old, men and women. I see joy and sorrow

mingled, reflecting victory and loss on this night of dedication.

"Government officials, including local hive representatives, stand at a makeshift podium. There will be speeches and songs until dawn, at this gigantic version of the traditional rural come-together. *In hives around the world purples are also marking the light and dark sides of the great victory.*

"On a personal note, this will be my last 'cast. I can no longer sit behind a camera and make wise noises. Cynicism isn't a viable lifestyle. So, as of the beginning of this new day, it's Jim Buser, citizen of Greenworld. I don't know how long we can hang onto what we have here, but I aim to do my share in the effort. Good-bye."

Jim didn't like the feel of the uniform, the binding of heavy fabric and symbolism, and was beginning to regret his impulsiveness. Finding one's roots was one thing; touring the badlands hunting terrorists was something else. But it had been the militia or nothing—he couldn't fly, and except for a few shuttles the space force was non-existent.

The doubts were growing. Even in his reporter days he had worn the shield of his noncombatancy. Now the bad guys would be after him in earnest. The doubts had forced his hand—he couldn't let them make his choices and still feel he was in charge.

He had talked it. Now he would have to walk it.

"You may go in now, Private."

He thanked the secretary, went to the door and entered President Marlowe's office. Militia recruits weren't ordinarily invited to meet the planetary president, but then he wasn't exactly an ordinary militia recruit. Still, it was with a bit of trepidation that he pushed open the door.

"Come in, young man. And relax. I have no desire to get used to being important."

The office was large and well appointed, but had the sloppy look of extreme activity. The President, understandably worn but wearing an exec's confident smile, stood by the long window that looked down on the spaceport field. The expanse was empty and forlorn except for a single towering vessel surrounded by an alert Army guard. The sight of *FSS Jutland* brought a swirl of biting memories.

The President looked him over. "From star 'caster to buckass private. Quite a step down?"

"Depends on how you look at it . . . uh, sir."

The President frowned. "The way I read it, you're a raving romantic."

Jim couldn't believe his ears. "You kidding? You mustn't listen to my 'casts."

"I listen, and I hear them. You wear indifference badly."

Jim was beginning to get mad. "Do you psychoanalyze all your new recruits?"

"Only the interesting ones. You seem to have a blind spot concerning your function. You think you didn't 'make news' as a 'caster? You think reactions end with ratings? Have you ever considered the awesome power of delivering truth—or falsehood—convincingly to billions of people?"

"Only in the abstract."

"Figures. You lived in a very small bottle, corked by GalNews and yourself. Now, though, you should know better. You've had a vivid demonstration. Your 'casts resulted in the intervention that saved us, you know. Which leads up to the reason you're here. I'm appointing you head of our propaganda department. It'll be your job to tell our story to the worlds. Congratulations, Major."

"I don't want to do any more of that."

"I don't give a rat's ass what you want, Buser! You're under military discipline now. You'll do whatever best serves Greenworld. Is that clear?"

"Yes," Jim said sullenly.

"Don't sound so martyred. You don't really want to eat mud—you just wish you wanted to. And you'll be working with your friend Astawa."

"Huh?"

"You see, he got some good news and some bad news. GalNews fired him in your backwash. But we just appropriated its whole planetary operation for the duration, and put him back in charge."

"All this for a purple?"

The President took a deep breath. "How do you bury hatreds and make a workable union of two utterly different cultures, one a majority and one a minority? We're

slowly getting the terrorists under control. Thank God
they haven't been able to polarize the cultures. Astawa
has played a big role in that."

"Do tell."

"Oh, he didn't enlighten you? I think I see why. He's a
sort-of-leader in a sort-of-organization of *aesgi* holding
prominent positions in the 'human' culture. They form a
vital bridge."

All the puzzle pieces that were the purple exec clicked
together. Jim realized he had been *handled* so smoothly
it left no vestigial irritation. Yes, they would get along
well together.

The door opened, and Admiral Young entered.

"Thank you for coming, Admiral," President Marlowe
said.

"I can't stay long, Mister President. The squadron has
been ordered home." The admiral turned to Jim.

"Thanks for saving us," Jim said, surprised at the
simplicity of his statement.

Admiral Young was quiet for a long time. "I wonder
what it would be like to go up into those mountains
west of here and do some ranching in a high valley not
too near anyone else."

Jim understood. "I grew up on a farm. It's brutal
work, but the problems are refreshingly basic."

"You sound like you've been giving it some thought."

"I have."

The admiral turned to President Marlowe. "You realize,
of course, that you've survived only the first battle. The
Hive will be back. How will you survive then?"

The President looked at his watch. "First let me repeat our world's enormous gratitude to you and your
squadron. The names of each of your crew members lost
in the battle will be added to our memorial scrolls. And
one last time I beg you to stay here. We desperately
need military strategists. But you would be most welcome here even as a private citizen—you know what
you return to."

The admiral's expression turned bleak. "I know. That's
why I have to go back. But you haven't answered my
question."

President Marlowe looked at his watch again, then
out the window at the azure sky.

"I asked you gentlemen here in part to witness something you have a right to see, since you were both instrumental in bringing it about."

Jim looked up at the sky and saw nothing.

"During Earth's American Revolution there was an analogous situation. The American colonies were determined to win their independence, but had insufficient arms to overcome the British. The French were interested in supporting them, but doubted they could survive. Then they defeated the British at Saratoga. This convinced the French of America's tenacity, and arms were forthcoming."

There were bright points of light in the sky, and a low but growing rumble. People were erupting out of the buildings onto the edges of the field, looking up, hands shading eyes. Two, five, ten, more than twenty painful brilliances.

"Ten days ago our agents on Eridani, using the reports of our victory—and Federation assistance—closed an arms purchasing agreement."

Two enormous, bulging cylinders landed first. "Those are our wayward star freighters, carrying 144 of the newest multi-weapon satellites, and modules for twin Orbital Command stations. State-of-the-art power, computers, scanners—and armed to the fangs!"

Twenty-four other bright points became teardrops of white flame, and atop them Jim could make out utterly streamlined spears, silver and gleaming, two-thirds the length of *FSS Jutland*. Proton blisters fore and aft added wickedness to their appearance. Slender and spectral, they settled onto the field in a precise circle around the freighters.

"Eridani interstellar carriers brought them here, and the Eridani crews aboard them will train our own crews before returning."

"Shiva 6B's!" The admiral was smiling, and there was a hint of dampness around his eyes. "Perfect!"

"Yes, they are exactly what we need; the best interplanetary defense ships available. Without the tachyon drive they can carry a heavy cruiser's armament and defense. But because they are smaller and lighter, they are faster and more maneuverable. Not to mention poorer targets."

The people outside were cheering wildly, with many an excited gesture toward the ships.

The admiral blinked several times. "Thanks, Mister President. I know now what I did will have some meaning."

"It would have anyway."

"Maybe. But I must go now. Good-bye and good faring to both of you." The admiral turned and left.

"What's with him?" Jim asked.

The President stared after him. "When he violated Federation orders he knew that to avoid another War, the Federation would throw the Hive some raw meat. Him. He will be publicly courtmartialed and executed."

Jim looked down at the field. Soon a lone figure, straight-backed in Federation dress blues, strode across the blast-blackened expanse. It detoured to pass the activity surrounding the freighters and Shiva 6B's, and stopped near one of the latter for a handful of seconds. Then it resumed its trek toward the far cruiser.

Jim moved toward the door. "Going somewhere?" the President asked.

"Would you please have someone call Astawa and tell him I'm on my way over? I'm going to save that man."

EDITOR'S INTRODUCTION TO:

PROUD LEGIONS
by
T. R. Fehrenbach

Ted Fehrenbach is one of the best military theorists of the Twentieth Century. I can say this with no reservations. His book, *This Kind of War*, is not only the finest study of the Korean War ever done, but more importantly, is the *only* book I have ever seen that correctly draws the lessons of that war. I have several times used it as a text; which is to do it injustice. The book is very readable.

Brigadier General S.L.A. Marshall has justly received much credit for his military histories. Lt. Col. T. R. Fehrenbach, AUS Ret'd, is not so well known. Whereas Marshal was a military historian and most of his duties were historical in nature (this didn't prohibit him from being one of the *very* first US troops to enter Paris in 1944), Fehrenbach was a combat soldier.

"Proud Legions" is one chapter from *This Kind Of War*. It is required reading for every officer nominated for promotion to general. It ought to be read more widely than that.

PROUD LEGIONS
by
T. R. Fehrenbach

We was rotten 'fore we started—we was never dis-
ciplined;
We made it out a favour if an order was obeyed.
Yes, every little drummer 'ad 'is rights an' wrongs to
mind,
So we had to pay for teachin'—an' we paid!
—Rudyard Kipling, "That Day"

During the first months of American intervention in
Korea, reports from the front burst upon an America and
world stunned beyond belief. Day after day, the forces
of the admitted first power of the earth reeled backward
under the blows of the army of a nation of nine million
largely illiterate peasants, the product of the kind of
culture advanced nations once overawed with gunboats.
Then, after fleeting victory, Americans fell back once
more before an army of equally illiterate, lightly armed
Chinese.

The people of Asia had changed, true. The day of the
gunboat and a few Marines would never return. But that
was not the whole story. The people of the West had
changed, too. They forgot that the West had dominated
not only by arms, but by superior force of will.

During the summer of 1950, and later, Asians would
watch. Some, friends of the West, would even smile. And
none of them would ever forget.

News reports in 1950 talked of vast numbers, overwhelming hordes of fanatic North Koreans, hundreds of
monstrous tanks, against which the thin United States

forces could not stand. In these reports there was truth, but not the whole truth.

The American units were outnumbered. They were outgunned. They were given an impossible task at the outset.

But they were also outfought.

In July 1950, one news commentator rather plaintively remarked that warfare had not changed so much, after all. For some reason, ground troops still seemed to be necessary, in spite of the atom bomb. And oddly and unfortunately, to this gentleman, man still seemed to be an important ingredient in battle. Troops were getting killed, in pain and fury and dust and filth. What had happened to the widely heralded push-button warfare where skilled, immaculate technicians who had never suffered the misery and ignominy of basic training blew each other to kingdom come like gentlemen?

In this unconsciously plaintive cry lies buried a great deal of the truth why the United States was almost defeated.

Nothing had happened to pushbutton warfare; its emergence was at hand. Horrible weapons that could destroy every city on earth were at hand—at too many hands. But push-button warfare meant Armageddon, and Armageddon, hopefully, will never be an end of national policy.

Americans in 1950 rediscovered something that since Hiroshima they had forgotten: you may fly over a land forever; you may bomb it, atomize it, pulverize it and wipe it clean of life—but if you desire to defend it, protect it, and keep it for civilization, you must do this on the ground, the way the Roman legions did, by putting your young men into the mud.

The object of warfare is to dominate a portion of the earth, with its peoples, for causes either just or unjust. It is not to destroy the land and people, unless you have gone wholly mad.

Pushbutton war has its place. There is another kind of conflict—crusade, jihad, holy war, call it what you choose. It has been loosed before, with attendant horror but indecisive results. In the past, there were never means enough to exterminate all the unholy, whether Christian, Moslem, Protestant, Papist, or Communist. If jihad is preached again, undoubtedly the modern age will do much better.

Americans, denying from moral grounds that war can ever be a part of politics, inevitably tend to think in terms of holy war—against militarism, against fascism, against bolshevism. In the postwar age, uneasy, disliking and fearing the unholiness of Communism, they have prepared for jihad. If their leaders blow the trumpet, or if their homeland is attacked, their millions are agreed to be better dead than Red.

Any kind of war short of jihad was, is, and will be unpopular with the people. Because such wars are fought with legions, and Americans, even when they are proud of them, do not like their legions. They do not like to serve in them, nor even to allow them to be what they must.

For legions have no ideological or spiritual home in the liberal society. The liberal society has no use or need for legions—as its prophets have long proclaimed.

Except that in this world are tigers.

The men of the Inmun Gun and the CCF were peasant boys, tough, inured to hunger and hardship. One-third of them had been in battle and knew what battle meant. They had been indoctrinated in Communism, but no high percentage of them were fanatic. Most of them, after all, were conscripts, and unskilled.

They were not half so good soldiers as the bronzed men who followed Rommel in the desert, or the veterans who slashed down toward Bastogne.

They were well armed, but their weapons were no better than those of United States design, if as good.

But the American soldier of 1950, though the same breed of man, was not half so good as the battalions that had absorbed Rommel's bloody lessons, or stood like steel in the Ardennes.

The weapons his nation had were not in his hands, and those that were were old and worn.

Since the end of World War II ground weapons had been developed, but none had been procured. There were plenty of the old arms around, and it has always been a Yankee habit to make do. The Army was told to make do.

In 1950 its vehicles in many cases would not run. Radiators were clogged, engines gone. When ordered to Korea, some units towed their transport down to the LST's, because there was no other way to get it to the boat. Tires and tubes had a few miles left in them, and were kept—until they came apart on Korean roads.

In Japan, where the divisions were supposedly guarding our former enemies, most of the small arms had been reported combat unserviceable. Rifle barrels were worn smooth. Mortar mounts were broken, and there were no longer any spare barrels for machine guns.

Radios were short, and those that were available would not work.

Ammunition, except small arms, was "hava-no."

These things had been reported. The Senate knew them; the people heard them. But usually the Army was told, "Next year."

Even a rich society cannot afford nuclear super-carriers, foreign aid, five million new cars a year, long-range bombers, the highest standard of living in the world, and a million new rifles.

Admittedly, somewhere you have to cut and choose.

But guns are hardware, and man, not hardware, is the ultimate weapon. In 1950 there were not enough men, either—less than 600,000 to carry worldwide responsibilities, including recruiting; for service in the ranks has never been on the Metropolitan Life Insurance Company's preferred list of occupations.

And in these 600,000 men themselves the trouble lay.

There was a reason.

Before 1939 the United States Army was small, but it was professional. Its tiny officers corps was parochial, but true. Its members devoted their time to the study of war, caring little what went on in the larger society around them. They were centurions, and the society around them not their concern.

When so ordered, they went to war. Spreading themselves thinner still, they commanded and trained the civilians who heeded the trumpet's call. The civilians did the fighting, of course—but they did it the Army's way.

In 1861 millions of volunteers donned blue or gray. Millions of words have been written on American valor, but few books dwell on the fact that of the sixty important battles, fifty-five were commanded on both sides by West Pointers, and on one side in the remaining five.

In 1917 four million men were mustered in. Few of them liked it, but again they did things the way the professionals wanted them done.

The volunteers came and went, and the Army changed not at all.

But since the Civil War, the Army had neither the esteem nor the favor of public or government. Liberal opinion, whether business-liberal or labor-liberal, dominated the United States after the destruction of the South, and the illiberal Army grew constantly more alienated from its own society.

In a truly liberal society, centurions have no place. For centurions, when they put on the soldier, do not retain the citizen. They are never citizens to begin with.

There was and is no danger of military domination of the nation. The Constitution gave Congress the power of life or death over the military, and they have always accepted the fact. The danger has been the other way around—the liberal society in its heart, wants not only domination of the military, but acquiescence of the military toward the liberal view of life.

Domination and control society should have. The record of military rule, from the burnished and lazy Praetorians to the *juntas* of Latin America, to the attempted fiasco of the *Légion Etrangère*, are pages of history singularly foul in odor.

But acquiescence society may not have, if it wants an army worth a damn. By the very nature of its mission, the military must maintain a hard and illiberal view of life and the world. Society's purpose is to live; the military's is to stand ready, if need be, to die.

Soldiers are rarely fit to rule—but they must be fit to fight.

The military is in essence a tool, to be used by its society. If its society is good, it may hope to be used honorably, even if badly. If its society is criminal, it may be, like the *Wehrmacht*, unleashed upon a helpless world.

But when the *Wehrmacht* dashed against the world, it was brought to ruin, not by a throng of amateurs, but by well-motivated, well-generaled Allied troops, who had learned their military lessons.

Some men, of kind intention, are always dubious because the generals of the *Wehrmacht* and the men of West Point and V.M.I. and Leavenworth read the same books, sometimes hold the same view of life.

Why not? German plumbers, American plumbers, use the same manuals, and look into the same kind of water.

In 1861, and 1917, the Army acted upon the civilian, changing him. But in 1945 something new happened. Suddenly, without precedent, perhaps because of changes in the emerging managerial society, professional soldiers of high rank had become genuinely popular with the public. In 1861, and in 1917, the public gave the generals small credit, talked instead of the gallant militia. Suddenly, at the end of World War II, society embraced the generals.

And here it ruined them.

They had lived their lives in semibitter alienation from their own culture (What's the matter, Colonel; can't you make it on the outside?) but now they were sought after, offered jobs in business, government, on college campuses.

Humanly, the generals liked the acclaim. Humanly, they wanted it to continue. And when, as usual after all our wars, there came a great civilian clamor to change all the things in the army the civilians hadn't liked, humanly, the generals could not find it in their hearts to tell the public to go to hell.

It was perfectly understandable that large numbers of men who served didn't like the service. There was no reason why they should. They served only because there had been a dirty job that had to be done. Admittedly, the service was not perfect; no human institution having power over men can ever be. But many of the abuses the civilians complained about had come not from true professionals but from men with quickie diplomas, whose brass was much more apt to go to their heads than to those of men who had waited twenty years for leaves and eagles.

In 1945, somehow confusing the plumbers with the men who pulled the chain, the public demanded that the Army be changed to conform with decent, liberal society.

The generals could have told them to go to hell and made it stick. A few heads would have rolled, a few stars would have been lost. But without acquiescence Congress could no more emasculate the Army than it could alter the nature of the State Department. It could have abolished it, or weakened it even more than it did—but it could not have changed its nature. But the generals could not have retained their new popularity antagonizing the public, and suddenly popularity was very important to them. Men such as Doolittle, Eisenhower, and Marshall rationalized. America, with postwar duties around the world, would need a bigger peacetime Army than ever before. Therefore, it needed to be popular with the people. And it should be made pleasant, so that more men would enlist. And since Congress wouldn't do much about upping pay, every man should have a chance to become a sergeant, instead of one in twenty. But, democratically, sergeants would not draw much more pay than privates.

And since some officers and noncoms had abused their powers, rather than make sure officers and noncoms were better than ever, it would be simpler and more expedient—and popular—to reduce those powers. Since Americans were by nature egalitarian, the Army had better go that route too. Other professional people, such as doctors and clergymen, had special privileges—but officers, after all, had no place in the liberal society, and had better be cut down to size.

The Doolittle Board of 1945-1946 met, listened to less than half a hundred complaints, and made its recommendations. The so-called "caste system" of the Army was modified. Captains, by fiat, suddenly ceased to be gods, and sergeants, the hard-bitten backbone of any army, were told to try to be just some of the boys. Junior officers had a great deal of their power to discipline taken away from them. They could no longer inflict any real punishment, short of formal courtmartial, nor could they easily reduce ineffective N.C.O.'s. Understandably, their own powers shaky, they cut the ground completely away from under their N.C.O.'s.

A sergeant, by shouting at some sensitive yardbird,

could get his captain into a lot of trouble. For the real effect of the Doolittle recommendations was psychological. Officers had not been made wholly powerless—but they felt that they had been slapped in the teeth. The officer corps, by 1946 again wholly professional, did not know how to live with the newer code.

One important thing was forgotten by the citizenry: by 1946 all the intellectual and sensitive types had said goodbye to the Army—they hoped for good. The new men coming in now were the kind of men who join armies the world over, blank-faced, unmolded—and they needed shaping. They got it; but it wasn't the kind of shaping they needed.

Now an N.C.O. greeted new arrivals with a smile. Where once he would have told them they made him sick to his stomach, didn't look tough enough to make a go of his outfit, he now led them meekly to his company commander. And this clean-cut young man, who once would have sat remote at the right hand of God in his orderly room, issuing orders that crackled like thunder, now smiled too. "Welcome aboard, gentlemen. I am your company commander; I'm here to help you. I'll try to make your stay both pleasant and profitable."

This was all very democratic and pleasant—but it is the nature of young men to get away with anything they can, and soon these young men found they could get away with plenty.

A soldier could tell a sergeant to blow it. In the old Army he might have been bashed, and found immediately what the rules were going to be. In the Canadian Army—which oddly enough no American liberals have found fascistic or bestial—he would have been marched in front of his company commander, had his pay reduced, perhaps even been confined for thirty days, with no damaging mark on his record. He would have learned, instantly, that orders are to be obeyed.

But in the new American Army, the sergeant reported such a case to his C.O. But the C.O. couldn't do anything drastic or educational to the man; for any real action, he had to pass the case up higher. And nobody wanted to court-martial the man, to put a permanent damaging mark on his record. The most likely outcome was for the man to be chided for being rude, and requested to do better in the future.

Some privates, behind their smirks, liked it fine.

Pretty soon, the sergeants, realizing the score, started to fraternize with the men. Perhaps, through popularity, they could get something done. The junior officers, with no sergeants to knock heads, decided that the better part of valor was never to give an unpopular order.

The new legions carried the old names, displayed the old, proud colors, with their gallant battle streamers. The regimental mottoes still said things like "Can Do." In their neat, fitted uniforms and new shiny boots—there was money for these—the troops looked good. Their appearance made the generals smile.

What they lacked couldn't be seen, not until the guns sounded.

There is much to military training that seems childish, stultifying, and even brutal. But one essential part of breaking men into military life is the removal of misfits— and in the service a man is a misfit who cannot obey orders, any orders, and who cannot stand immense and searing mental and physical pressure.

For his own sake and for that of those around him, a man must be prepared for the awful, shrieking moment of truth when he realizes he is all alone on a hill ten thousand miles from home, and that he may be killed in the next second.

The young men of America, from whatever strata, are raised in a permissive society. The increasing alienation of their education from the harsher realities of life makes their reorientation, once enlisted, doubly important.

Prior to 1950, they got no reorientation. They put on the uniform, but continued to get by, doing things rather more or less. They had no time for sergeants.

As discipline deteriorated, the generals themselves were hardly affected. They still had their position, their pomp and ceremonies. Surrounded by professionals of the old school, largely field rank, they still thought their rod was iron, for, seemingly, their own orders were obeyed.

But ground battle is a series of platoon actions. No longer can a field commander stand on a hill, like Lee or Grant, and oversee his formations. Orders in combat—the orders that kill men or get them killed, are not given by generals, or even by majors. They are given by lieutenants and sergeants, and sometimes by PFC's.

When a sergeant gives a soldier an order in battle, it must have the same weight as that of a four-star general.

Such orders cannot be given by men who are some of the boys. Men willingly take orders to die only from those they are trained to regard as superior beings.

It was not until the summer of 1950, when the legions went forth, that the generals realized what they had agreed to, and what they had wrought.

The Old Army, outcast and alien and remote from the warm bosom of society, officer and man alike, ordered into Korea, would have gone without questioning. It would have died without counting. As on Bataan, it would not have listened for the angel's trumpet or the clarion call. It would have heard the hard sound of its own bugles, and hard-bitten, cynical, wise in bitter ways, it would have kept its eyes on its sergeants.

It would have died. It would have retreated, or surrendered, only in the last extremity. In the enemy prison camps, exhausted, sick, it would have spat upon its captors, despising them to the last.

It would have died, but it might have held.

One aftermath of the Korean War has been the passionate attempt in some military quarters to prove the softness and decadence of American society as a whole, because in the first six months of that war there were wholesale failures. It has been a pervasive and persuasive argument, and it has raised its own counterargument, equally passionate.

The trouble is, different men live by different myths.

There are men who would have a society pointed wholly to fighting and resistance to Communism, and this would be a very different society from the one Americans now enjoy. It might succeed on the battlefield, but its other failures can be predicted.

But the infantry battlefield also cannot be remade to the order of the prevailing midcentury opinion of sociologists.

The recommendations of the so-called Doolittle Board of 1945-1946, which destroyed so much of the will—if not the actual power—of the military traditionalists, and left them bitter, and confused as to how to act, was based on experience in World War II. In that war, as in all others, millions of civilians were fitted arbitrarily into a military pattern already centuries old. It had once fitted Western society; it now coincided with American customs and thinking no longer.

What the Doolittle Board tried to do, in small measure, was to bring the professional Army back into the new society. What it could not do, in 1946, was to gauge the future.

By 1947 the United States Army had returned, in large measure, to the pattern it had known prior to 1939. The new teen-agers who now joined it were much the same stripe of men who had joined in the old days. They were not intellectuals, they were not completely fired with patriotism, or motivated by the draft; nor was an aroused public, eager to win a war, breathing down their necks.

A great many of them signed up for three squares and a sack.

Over several thousand years of history, man has found a way to make soldiers out of this kind of man, as he comes, basically unformed, to the colors. It is a way with great stresses and great strains. It cannot be said it is wholly good. Regimentation is not good, completely, for any man.

But no successful army has been able to avoid it. It is an unpleasant necessity, seemingly likely to go on forever, as long as men fight in fields and mud.

One thing should be made clear.

The Army could have fought World War III, just as it could have fought World War II, under the new rules. During 1941-1945 the average age of the United States soldier was in the late twenties, and the ranks were seasoned with maturity from every rank of life, as well as intelligence.

In World War III, or any war with national emotional support, this would have been true. Soldiers would have brought their motivation with them, firmed by understanding and maturity.

The Army could have fought World War III in 1950, but it could not fight Korea.

As a case in point, take the experiences of one platoon sergeant in Fort Lewis, Washington. During the big war he had held sway over a platoon of seventy-two enlisted men. The platoon was his to run; the officers rarely came around the barracks.

The platoon sergeant was a reasonable man, in charge of reasonable men, who knew why they were in the Army. Their average age was thirty-two; one-fourth of them, roughly, were college trained. Almost all of them were skilled, in one trade or another.

This kind of man cannot be made to dig a six-by-six hole to bury a carelessly dropped cigarette, nor double-timed around the PX on Sunday morning.

The platoon sergeant relieved a multiple-striped young idiot—as he termed the man—who tried just this. The platoon, as platoons can, ruined the former sergeant.

The new platoon sergeant told his men the barracks needed cleaning, but if everyone would cooperate, each man clean his own area each day, he could get a few men off detail to clean the common areas, such as the latrine, and there need be no GI parties.

The platoon cooperated. There were no GI parties, no extra details. A few men went off the track, now and then; the older men of the platoon handled them quietly, without bothering the platoon sergeant.

This was discipline. Ideally, it should well up out of men, not be imposed upon them.

The platoon prospered. It won the battalion plaque for best barracks so often it was allowed to keep the plaque in perpetuity.

Even after VJ-Day, every man fell out for reveille, promptly, because the platoon sergeant explained to them this was the way the game was played. And the platoon was proud of itself; every man knew it was a good outfit, just a little better than the next.

Then, one by one, the men went home, as the war ended.

The platoon sergeant now was promoted to first sergeant, six stripes, an enlisted god who walked. He got a new company of several platoons, all filled with new, callow faces entering the Army to be trained.

The war was over, and every man coming in knew it.

The first sergeant, wise now in the ways of handling men, as he thought, carefully explained to the newcomers that the barracks must be cleaned, but if everyone would cooperate, each man clean his own area each day, there would be no GI parties, and there would be passes.

On Saturday the barracks were dirty.

The sergeant, who thought that men needed only to understand what was required to obey, carefully explained what he wanted. Friday, with a great deal of hollering, shouting, and horseplay, the new men cleaned the barracks.

On Saturday, the barracks were still dirty, and the captain made a few pointed remarks to the sergeant.

The sergeant got everyone together, and told them how it was going to be. These men on the mops, these men on the brooms, these men with the lye soap. No hollering or sloshing of water or horseplay—just clean the goddamn barracks.

It took most of Friday night, and the men had to stay in the latrines to clean their rifles, but they cleaned the barracks. A few of them got out of hand, but there were no older hands who could—or would—hold them in check. The sergeant handled each of these himself.

The platoon prospered, but it wasn't easy, particularly on the sergeant. Gradually, he came to realize that seventeen- and eighteen-year-olds, mostly from the disadvantaged areas of society, had no feeling of responsibility to the Army or to the Republic for which it stood. They were not self-disciplined, and they tended to resent authority, even more than the college men and skilled artisans he had commanded before. Probably some had resented their parents; definitely most resented the sergeant, even as most of them, back in their home towns, had instinctively resented the police.

There is no getting around the fact that cops and sergeants spoil your fun.

The platoon prospered, as a sort of jail, until someone wrote to his congressman. After that the captain spoke to the sergeant, telling him that it was peacetime and that perhaps the real purpose of an Army was not to learn to use the bayonet, but to engage in athletics and take Wednesday afternoons off.

The sergeant, now a confused young man with six stripes who walked, left the Army, and graduated from college. If the Army was going to hell, it was a lot more pleasant to watch it go to hell from the Officer's Club than from the Orderly Room.

A decade after Korea, the military traditionalists still grind their teeth. The sociologists still keep a wary eye on them. Both still try to use the Korean battleground, and its dreary POW camps, to further their own particular myths of human behavior.

Probably, both are wrong.

The military have the preponderance of fact with them as far as Korea was concerned. Korea was the kind of war that since the dawn of history was fought by professionals, by legions. It was fought by men who soon knew they had small support or sympathy at home, who could read in the papers statements by prominent men that they should be withdrawn. It was fought by men whom the Army—at its own peril—had given neither training nor indoctrination, nor the hardness and bitter pride men must have to fight a war in which they do not in their hearts believe.

The Army needed legions, but society didn't want them. It wanted citizen-soldiers.

But the sociologists are right—absolutely right—in demanding that the centurion view of life not be imposed upon America. In a holy, patriotic war—like that fought by the French in 1793, or as a general war against Communism will be—America can get a lot more mileage out of citizen-soldiers than it can from legions.

No one has suggested that perhaps there should be two sets of rules, one for the professional Army, which may have to fight in far places, without the declaration of war, and without intrinsic belief in the value of its dying, for reasons of policy, chessmen on the checkerboard of diplomacy; and one for the high-minded, enthusiastic, and idealistic young men who come aboard only when the ship is sinking.

The other answer is to give up Korea-type wars, and to surrender great-power status, and a resultant hope of order—our own decent order—in the world. But America is rich and fat and very, very noticeable in this world.

It is a forlorn hope that we should be left alone.

In the first six months America suffered a near debacle because her Regular Army fighting men were the stuff of legions, but they had not been made into legionaries.

America was not more soft or more decadent than it had been twenty years earlier. It was confused, badly, on its attitudes toward war. It was still bringing up its youth to think there were no tigers, and it was still reluctant to forge them guns to shoot tigers.

Many of America's youth, in the Army, faced horror badly because they had never been told they would have to face horror, or that horror is very normal in our unsane world. It had not been ground into them that they would have to obey their officers, even if the orders got them killed.

It has been a long, long time since American citizens have been able to take down the musket from the mantlepiece and go tiger hunting. But they still cling to the belief that they can do so, and do it well, without training.

This is the error that leads some men to cry out that Americans are decadent.

If Americans in 1950 were decadent, so were the rabble who streamed miserably into Valley Forge, where von Steuben made soldiers out of them. If American society had no will to defend itself, neither did it in 1861, at First Manassas, or later at Shiloh, when whole regiments of Americans turned tail and ran.

The men who lay warm and happy in their blankets at Kasserine, as the panzers rolled toward them in the dawn, were decadent, by this reasoning.

The problem is not that Americans are soft but that they simply will not face what war is all about until they have had their teeth kicked in. They will not face the fact that the military professionals, while some have ideas about society in general that are distorted and must be watched, still know better than anyone else how a war is won.

Free society cannot be oriented toward the battlefield—Sparta knew that trap—but some adjustments must be made, as the squabbling Athenians learned to their sorrow.

The sociologists and psychologists of Vienna had no answer to the Nazi bayonets, when they crashed against their doors. The soldiers of the democratic world did.

More than once, as at Valley Forge, after Bull Run, and Kasserine, the world has seen an American army rise from its own ashes, reorient itself, grow hard and bitter, knowledgeable and disciplined and tough.

In 1951, after six months of being battered, the Eighth Army in Korea rose from its own ashes of despair. No man who was there still believes Americans in the main are decadent, just as no man who saw Lieutenant General Matt Ridgway in operation doubts the sometime greatness of men.

He who supposes all men to be brave at all times ... does not realize that the courage of troops must be reborn daily, that nothing is so changeable, that the true skill of a general consists of knowing how to guarantee it by his positions, dispositions, and those traits of genius that characterize great captains.—From the French of Maurice de Saxe, REVERIES ON THE ART OF WAR.

When Lieutenant General Ridgway left Tokyo to assume command of the Eighth Army on 26 December 1950, he asked MacArthur in parting, "General, if I get over there and find the situation warrants it, do I have your permission to attack?"

MacArthur's aged face cracked wide in a grin.

"Do whatever you think best, Matt. The Eighth Army is yours."

These were, as Ridgway said later, the sort of orders to put heart in a soldier. And Ridgway's own first task was to put heart in the Eighth Army.

Matt Ridgway came to Korea convinced that the United States Army could beat any Asiatic horde that lived to its knees. He quickly found that on this subject he was a majority of one.

The Eighth Army was not only pulling south; it had no great desire to meet the Chinese. Contact over much of the front was broken. There was almost no patrolling.

When Ridgway asked where the Chinese were, and in what strength, he was shown a vague goose egg on the map to the north of the Eighth Army in which was inscribed the figure 174,000. More than this no one knew, and no one was making concerted efforts to find out.

The Eighth Army had had its fill of Chinese-hunting in the north.

But if the Eighth Army expected General Matt Ridgway to be satisfied with that, they had another think coming.

Ridgway began to hammer away. At first, realizing the problem, he talked of simple things: aggressive patrolling, maintaining contact at all costs, supply, and firepower. He talked of the most basic thing of all, leadership. He was as blunt or as gentle as the situation called for.

He told his senior commanders the simple truth that America's power and prestige were at stake out here, and whether they believed in this war or not, they were going to have to fight it. He would help provide the tools, but they would have to provide their own guts.

If the American Armed Forces could not beat the hordes of Red China in the field, then it made no difference how many new autos Detroit could produce.

Everywhere Matt Ridgway went, however, he found the same question in men's minds: *What the hell are we doing in this godforsaken place?*

If men had been told, *Destroy the evil of Bolshevism,* they might have understood. But they did not understand why the line must be held or why the Taehan Minkuk—that miserable, stinking, undemocratic country—must be protected.

The question itself never concerned Matt Ridgway. At the age of fifty-six, more than thirty years a centurion, to him the answer was simple. The loyalty he gave, and expected, precluded the slightest questioning of orders. This he said.

But to a generation brought up to hold some loyalties lightly, and to question many things, this was not enough. To these men Ridgway said:

The real issues are whether the power of Western Civilization, as God has permitted it to flower in our own beloved lands, shall defy and defeat Communism; whether the rule of men who shoot their prisoners, enslave their citizens, and deride the dignity of man, shall displace the rule of those to whom the individual and his individual rights are sacred; whether we are to survive with God's hand to guide and lead us, or to perish in the dead existence of a Godless world.

Under General Ridgway's hammering, the Eighth Army took the offensive within thirty days. After 25 January it never really again lost the initative. At Chipyong-ni, the battle that presaged what was to come all spring, it was the Chinese who melted away into the snow-draped hills, leaving their dead behind.

Under a new, firm hand, and with the taste of Chinese blood, the Eighth Army found itself. Ridgway made legions.

The ranks were salted now with veterans, men wounded and returned to duty, and were led by men like Ridgway, Captain Muñoz, and Lieutenant Long, who had been through the drill before, who had been from the Naktong to the Yalu, and had learned, as Americans had always had to learn, how to fight this new-old war.

They had learned the Chinese could be cunning, but also stupid. Failing to meet quick success, he could not change his plan. Often he continued an operation long after it had turned into disaster, wasting thousands of his troops. Lacking air cover, artillery, and armor, his hordes of riflemen could be—and were—slaughtered, as the Eighth Army learned to roll with the punches and to strike back hard.

Again and again, with the prodigal use of men, he could crack the U.N. line at a given point. But the men at the point had learned to hold, inflicting terrible losses, and even if the line gave, the Chinese could not exploit, while U.N. reinforcements, mechanized, rushed to deploy in front of them and to their flanks.

In the terrain of South Korea, battle was more open, and in open battle no amount of savage cunning could substitute for firepower. The Chinese could not even apply superior combat power to the 135-mile line. The truth, that a backward nation can never put as many well-armed men into the field and support them as can even a small-sized industrial country, became apparent. Chinese replacements, even with Russian aid, were often ill equipped and ill trained.

The press still reported human seas and overwhelming hordes, but except where they massed for a breakthrough, the Chinese remained apart and in moderate numbers on the line. Front-line soldiers began to joke: "Say, Joe, how many hordes are there in a Chink platoon?" Or, "We were attacked by two hordes last night. We killed both of them."

But the Chinese retained the will to fight.

The drive northward was not easy.

As many years earlier, when the cavalry fighting on the Plains had developed leaders such as Miles, Crook, and Ronald Mackenzie, men who rode hard, made cold camps, threw away their sabers, and moved without bugle calls, putting aside all the things they had learned in the War Between the States—but who had driven the Indians without surcease, hammering them across the snows and mountains until their women sickened and their infants died and they lost their heart for war, so the Army developed men who learned to fight in Asia.

Soldiers learned to travel light, but with full canteen and bandoleer, and to climb the endless hills. They learned to hold fast when the enemy flowed at them, because it was the safest thing to do. They learned to displace in good order when they had to. They learned to listen and obey. They learned all the things Americans have always learned from Appomattox to Berlin.

Above all, they learned to kill.

On the frontier, there is rarely gallantry or glamour to wars, whether they are against red Indians or Red Chinese. There is only killing.

Men of a tank battalion set spikes on the forward sponsons of their tanks, and to these affixed Chinese skulls. This battalion had come back from Kunui-ri, and the display matched their mood. They were ordered to remove the skulls, but the mood remained.

In Medic James Mount's company, there was a platoon sergeant named "Gypsy" Martin. Martin carried a full canteen and bandoleer, but he also wore a bandanna and earring, and he had tiny bells on his boots. Gypsy Martin hated Chinese; he hated gooks, and he didn't care who knew it.

In anything but war, Martin was the kind of man who is useless.

In combat, as the 24th Division drove north, men could hear Gypsy yell his hatred, as they heard his M-1 bark death. When Gypsy yelled, his men went forward; he was worth a dozen rational, decent men in those bloody valleys. His men followed him, to the death.

When Gypsy Martin finally bought it, they found him lying among a dozen "gooks," his rifle empty, its stock broken. Other than in battle, Sergeant Martin was no good. To Jim Mount's knowledge, he got no medals, for medals depend more on who writes for them than what was done.

It made Jim Mount think.

The values composing civilization and the values required to protect it are normally at war. Civilization values sophistication, but in an armed force sophistication is a millstone.

The Athenian commanders before Salamis, it is reported, talked of art and of the Acropolis, in sight of the Persian fleet. Beside their own campfires, the Greek hoplites chewed garlic and joked about girls.

Without its tough spearmen, Hellenic culture would have had nothing to give the world. It would not have lasted long enough. When Greek culture became so sophisticated that its common men would no longer fight to the death, as at Thermopylae, but became devious and clever, a horde of Roman farm boys overran them.

The time came when the descendants of Macedonians who had slaughtered Asians till they could no longer lift their arms went pale and sick at the sight of the havoc wrought by the Roman *gladius Hispanicus* as it carved its way toward Hellas.

The Eighth Army, put to the fire and blooded, rose from its own ashes in a killing mood. They went north, and as they went they destroyed Chinese and what was left of the towns and cities of Korea. They did not grow sick at the sight of blood.

By 7 March they stood on the Han. They went through Seoul, and reduced it block by block. When they were finished, the massive railway station had no roof, and thousands of buildings were pocked by tank fire. Of Seoul's original more than a million souls, less than two hundred thousand still lived in the ruins. In many of the lesser cities of Korea, built of wood and wattle, only the foundation, and the vault, of the old Japanese bank remained.

The people of Chosun, not Americans or Chinese, continued to lose the war.

At the end of March the Eighth Army was across the parallel.

General Ridgway wrote, "The American flag never flew over a prouder, tougher, more spirited and more competent fighting force than was Eighth Army as it drove north. . . ."

Ridgway had no great interest in real estate. He did not strike for cities and towns, but to kill Chinese. The Eighth Army killed them, by the thousands, as its infantry drove them from the hills and as its air caught them fleeing in the valleys.

By April 1951, the Eighth Army had again proved Erwin Rommel's assertion that American troops knew less but learned faster than any fighting men he had opposed. The Chinese seemed not to learn at all, as they repeated Chipyong-ni again and again.

Americans had learned, and learned well. The tragedy of American arms, however, is that having an imperfect sense of history Americans sometimes forget as quickly as they learn.

EDITOR'S INTRODUCTION TO:

AND BABY MAKES THREE
by
Doan Van Toai

It is often asked why men fight. Can we not all live in
peace and brotherhood?

That, of course, depends upon the price one is willing
to pay for peace. This essay was written by a man who
once thought peace worth a very great deal.

In 1975, four army corps swept down from North Vietnam into the south. The Congress of the United States
refused to give the President permission to defend South
Vietnam, and would not appropriate sufficient money
to buy supplies for the Republic of Vietnam to defend
itself. South Vietnam accordingly fell.

Doan Van Toai was an anti-American activist during
the Vietnam War. Shortly after the fall of Saigon, he
was arrested by the North Vietnamese and imprisoned
for 28 months. He was eventually released. He had never
been charged, and he was never tried; no explanation for
his arrest or release was ever given.

This account of the night that Dang Giao was arrested
is based on conversations between the two men in prison
camp. Mr. Toai is currently at the Fletcher School of
Law and Diplomacy at Tufts University. Neither Mr. nor
Mrs. Giao have been heard from in several years.

. . . AND BABY MAKES THREE
by
Doan Van Toai

THE ONLY NOISE in the streets of Saigon at 11 P.M. was the staccato voice of Radio Hanoi spitting out Communist propaganda. Otherwise the city was silent beneath a thick blanket of fear. People huddled behind closed doors each night dreading the heavy-handed knock of unkempt young men in plainclothes come to arrest those on their list. When sleep did come, it was restless and light.

On this night, Dang Giao's wife had just finished feeding their newborn son. The knock on the door, although long expected, still came às a shock. And now the second lieutenant was reading the warrant in a loud and forceful voice, his eyes riveted on the paper.

"Considering the security requirements of the Fatherland, and considering the denunciation of the people, the People's Security Command of Ho Chi Minh City hereby orders: 1) That the home of Tran Duy Cat, pen name Dang Giao, and his wife Chu Vi Thuy, daughter of the notorious reactionary Chu Tu, be searched and that all suspect objects found therein be confiscated. 2) That the two abovenamed be arrested for their many activities against the people when they served as handmaids of the American puppets on the cultural front, under the guise of reporters for the newspaper *Song Than* [The Tidal Wave]. 3) That the forenamed be tried under the law of March 1976. On the behalf of the Director Comrade."

(This was to be Dang Giao's second run-in with Communist authorities. In 1954, at the end of the French

164

Indochinese War, he opted to leave the Communist North, settled in Saigon, and became editor of *Song Than*, a daily newspaper which was so critical of the Thieu government that it was closed down in 1974. A year later, when the North Vietnamese took Saigon, he refused to leave. "I would rather die in this country than live somewhere else," he told the author years later in prison camp.)

The lieutenant now puts the warrant on a table and looks at Dang Giao, trying to gauge his reaction. Already, forty-odd young people, most of them not yet 16 years old, have separated into groups, like small armies of ants, and begun to search the house. They even climb up and knock out parts of the ceiling that look as if they have been patched. They pull out the wood paneling in the sitting room and slash open the sofa and chair cushions. They go at the wrecking party with enthusiasm. Each time a knife slashes a cushion or a hammer smashes a souvenir of their life together, Chu Vi Thuy feels a stab of pain. Dang Giao consoles her gently: "We have lost a country. What are these trifles to you now?"

The officer in charge is looking over the "suspect objects" that from time to time the cadres bring out. He seems pleased with the work of his subordinates and delighted with everything they turn up, from the family album, to back issues of newspapers, to early love letters from Dang Giao to his wife.

SUDDENLY THE lieutenant's attention is riveted by some lines scrawled in a notebook.

"1 A.M. The night is already advanced, cold and windy outside. The planes are coming back to the base one after the other. The noise keeps me up. Oh, how I miss you, wish you could be here.

"4:30 A.M. Fell into deep slumber, I don't know when, but suddenly woke up because the telephone rang. A flash of happiness, but it was not you, just someone dialing the wrong number. I tried to go back to sleep hoping to see you tomorrow . . ."

Holding the notebook before Dang Giao's face, the lieutenant asks suspiciously, "Now what's this? Tell me the truth."

"You've read it. What is there to ask?"

"I am questioning you. You had better give me a good answer. I am a representative of the State and of the Party, and I am not here to joke with you. You think I can't read? Let me tell you, I am a college graduate from Hanoi University, not from one of the puppet universities in Saigon, like you."

"That's my wife's diary, written ten years ago, before we were married; that is our private life."

At first Dang Giao had thought the lieutenant was asking just for the sake of asking. Now, realizing that he is serious, he can't resist saying, "I thought that being a socialist officer who defeated the Americans you would know everything. What need is there to ask a reactionary fellow like me?"

Turning grim, the lieutenant blurts out, "I am only asking to test your sincerity. As for the rest, I know everything, of course. That's not a diary. It's a coded book of signals sent to other reactionaries. Otherwise, why should you note down the hours like 1 A.M. and 4 A.M.? If you were not a reactionary why would you have a telephone? Why would you note the incoming flights? I know everything, I tell you. The Yankees had a few hundred thousand of these books, but they were never able to fool the Revolution. Every time Nixon sent his troops over, the Revolution knew it all, so don't count on fooling us."

By now Dang Giao understood his own situation and what lay in store for him. But he found it incredible that an officer of the People's Army should be so obtuse. "Better control yourself," he thinks and then says: "Well, have it your own way. You can charge me with any crime now, and I am ready for it. But I ask one favor for our newborn child. The boy is only 15 days old, his mother is still weak and sick. If you could let her stay home with the baby a few more days ... You could arrest her later on. I will be your hostage."

"Don't give me your bourgeois feelings. The women in the North run out with guns to shoot down American planes two or three days after they have given birth, and nothing bad happens. Your wife has rested a full two weeks. Besides, at the security camp, she'll be taken care of. The State is very kind. You needn't worry. Just reform and carry out all orders." The lieutenant pauses a moment and then asks, "What's the baby's name?"

Dang Giao quickly answers, "Liberation."

The officer cannot believe his ears. *"What?"*

Dang Giao repeats it, but his wife interposes: "He's just a few days old, we haven't had time to name him."

The lieutenant takes out a form and starts to write. By now the search is over. A soldier carrying three thick volumes asks Chu Vi Thuy, "What kind of books are these?"

"They are dictionaries."

"I asked you what kind of books."

"I said they are dictionaries."

ANOTHER SOLDIER standing nearby comes to the aid of his friend: "What he means is, what does it say in them?"

Chu Vi Thuy laughs. "Oh, they are books that give you the meaning of French words in Vietnamese, or that translate English words into French."

The young man has made a discovery; his excitement is hard to contain: "Really!" By now the officer has finished writing. He stands up and commands: "Everyone! Everyone! Attention!" and he reads in a resonant voice:

"Considering the security requirements of the Fatherland, and considering the denunciation of the people, the People's Security Command of Ho Chi Minh City hereby orders: 1) [He repeats the denunciation he read when he first entered their house.] 2) . . . 3) That the unnamed child of the notorious reactionary writer Dang Giao and his wife also be arrested. . . . Signed."

So the problem of the baby is solved. As a special act of humanity the newborn child and his mother are not chained and manacled.

As the three are about to be led away, Dang Giao's two older boys, aged eight and six, rush at the lieutenant and try to hit him. Fighting back tears, Dang Giao tells them: "You stay at home. Tomorrow you can call Grandma to come and stay with you. Should anyone ask about your father, tell them the truth, that your father is in jail. Do you understand?"

Now it is their mother's turn to cry. Chu Vi Thuy slips

to the floor, with the sleeping baby still in her arms.
Two soldiers about 18 years old help her up, but with no
sign of compassion. A third takes the baby. The entire
group moves toward the bus.

"Daddy, why are they taking you to jail?"

"Go in and close the door now. Tomorrow morning
you can call Grandma."

OUTSIDE, the first rays of the morning sun are beginning to brighten the silent streets. The communal radio
speakers have been blaring since 5 A.M. The familiar
voice of the regular announcer intones:

"Just as Comrade Le Duan, the First Secretary of the
Party, has said, our regime is a million times more
democratic than any other regime in the world and thus
the State Law promulgated on March 20 by the new
regime is the most democratic law there is. To arrest
people or search a home, one must have a written warrant . . ."

The baby, comfortably nestled in the arms of one of
the youths, suddenly cries out, alarming his mother.
"Give me back my child," she says. She holds him tight
to her bosom, and her tears mingle with those on his
face. Resolutely, Dang Giao speaks to her: "Why are you
crying? There is nothing to cry about now. Didn't we see
it coming?"

"You are right, there is nothing to cry about." Chu Vi
Thuy uses the hem of her dress to wipe the baby's tears,
then her own.

At the Tran Hung Dao detention center, right in the
heart of Saigon, 42 other journalists and writers are
waiting in individual cells and detention halls. All have
experienced similar moments. They are there simply
because the Liberation Artists Association has drawn up
a list of 44 names of "reactionaries" from the areas of
art and literature. They have all been arrested under the
Law of March 1976, the law which requires that arrests
be made on the basis of a written warrant, even if it
means one written on the spot against a 15-day-old
baby.

Dang Giao, his wife, and their baby are on their way
to re-education camps, the Vietnamese Gulag from which

they may or may not return. Their fate and the fate of thousands like them goes unremarked by the former antiwar activists who raised their voices to denounce human-rights violations in South Vietnam. Between the genocide of Pol Pot in Cambodia and the repression in Vietnam there is a difference of degree, but the outcome is the same. The main difference is between a slow death and a quick one.

IN THE NAME OF
THE FATHER
by
Edward P. Hughes

Edward Hughes is a telecommunications specialist for a national newspaper. He lives in Manchester, England. Some years ago I visited Manchester, where I was taken to a perfectly delightful Real Ale pub owned and operated by one Ray Bradbury. (Among Manchester science fiction fans, he is known as "the other Ray Bradbury".) The Manchester science fiction club meets in an upstairs room of his tavern. This is appropriate, since the tavern harbors a ghost, fortunately more mischievous than malevolent.

We had a delightful time in Manchester; but there was one prophetic experience.

Mrs. Pournelle and I went to Manchester from Glasgow, travelling by the excellent British Railway system. This is a good way to travel. The trains are comfortable, on time, and connect nearly every place in Britain to everywhere else. We found ourselves wishing there was something comparable in the United States, although it's hard to see how a nation several thousands of miles in dimensions can be served by rails as Britain is. Still, regions of the US certainly could be.

When we reached Manchester we were met by the owners of the local book store. It was late afternoon, and I would be speaking shortly, so they had made dinner reservations at a nearby restaurant.

Before we could enter the restaurant we were searched. The doorman wore North African Campaign service ribbons, and was very polite. He was obviously embarrassed about having to search ladies; but he did it.

We were told that all establishments near the railroad station had similar rules. Manchester is in the west of England, near Ireland.

A few days after our stay in Manchester, Lord Louis Mountbatten was killed by a bomb.

Civilization is a fragile thing; once gone, it is not easy to rebuild. Those who found a civilization traditionally have unique privileges. Patrick O'Meara, Master of the Fist and onetime sergeant of Her Majesty's Forces certainly does . . .

IN THE NAME OF
THE FATHER
by
Edward P. Hughes

Patrick O'Meara lay awake in his castle, thinking of
Eileen O'Connor. Down below in Barley Cross, Liam
McGrath lay sleepless in his cot, also thinking of Eileen
O'Connor. In another cottage in the village, dark-eye
Eileen O'Connor, clutching the rag doll she had loved
since she was two, slept on in blissful ignorance.

Around five, the younger man, no longer able to suffer
inactivity, got up and pushed wide the casement. In the
half-light of dawn O'Meara's Fist dominated the skyline.
Liam made out the high flak towers floating above ser-
rated battlements. He yawned. Having seen O'Meara's
Fist framed in his bedroom window for nineteen years,
Liam wearied of the marvel. Besides, like the rest of the
villagers, he was privy to its infirmities—the corroded
armour, the rusty rocket launchers, and the shell-less
batteries. And, like most of his village contemporaries,
he found it hard to imagine that the great museum
piece had ever intimidated any aggressor.

He sniffed the air scented by overnight rain. This,
then, was the day. He jumped at the sound of his mother's
alarm in the next room, heard the bed creak as she got
up. He shivered. Now would begin the long-awaited
sequence of events destined to end that evening in the
bedroom of the old Curry cottage, with Eileen O'Connor
and himself, face to face, alone at last, and irrevocably
married.

"Liam! Are you going to lie on all morning?"

He dressed quickly in his working clothes. This was
going to be a day when help would have been welcome.

172

His stepfather being on duty at the Fist meant that he and his mother would have to cope with all the household chores in addition to preparing for the wedding.

But Eileen had chosen the date purposely: Andy McGrath on duty at the Fist meant a military guard of honor to greet them outside church.

"Liam! Will you lie abed all your wedding day?"

"Coming, Mam." He clattered downstairs, out the back door, and across the yard. First chore was pumping the top cistern full while his mother kindled the fire and cooked breakfast. Afterwards he would milk the cows, feed the pigs, carry in the turf, chop kindling, check his snares, take the mare over to Seamus Murray for shoeing, and smuggle a sucking pig across to Eileen's mother as the McGrath contribution to the wedding feast. With a bit of luck, he might even find time to give his chin an extra close scrape before he put on his Sunday suit for the ceremony.

He pumped, watching the light strengthen through the branches of the overhanging apple tree, slowly exposing the detail of O'Meara's Fist.

He spat pensively into the long grass, wondering what the O'Meara himself was doing at this very moment. Certainly, he would not be pumping water in his old work clothes—wedding day or no. Not that the old lecher had ever needed to marry—when he had merely to lift a finger to get any woman in the village. Liam switched sides on the pump handle, turning his back on O'Meara's Fist. Let the old ram lie on, probably ignorant of the news that this day the only son of Maureen McGrath was marrying the dark-eyed daughter of Tom and Biddy O'Connor. His grip tightened on the pump handle. Few people saw the old goat nowadays. There had been a day when he might have come down from the Fist to awe the reception with his presence. Liam wiped sweat from his forehead, wondering why some folk were born to rule, and others to be ruled. Although there was little sign of the Master's iron hand these days. Indeed, if gossip were true, it was over a year since he had summoned a woman to the Fist.

A spatter of drops from the overflow sprinkled his nape. He released the pump handle, loosed the clamp which attached hose to spout. Any moment now his mother would . . .

"Breakfast, Liam!"

He soused his head under the spout, then started back to the house, picking up the egg from the side of the byre where the brown hen laid each morning.

Right now, up at the Fist, Andy McGrath would no doubt be dressing the guard into line for inspection by General Desmond. There was a wonder for you. How O'Meara the Ram, self-styled Duke of Connaught, Lord of Barley Cross, Master of the Fist, and lecher supreme, succeeded in inspiring the loyalty of people like Andy McGrath and General Desmond, or, for that matter, of people like school-mistress Celia Larkin, Kevin Murphy the vet, Doctor Denny Mallon and other decent folk.

Maybe it had something to do with the old days when the O'Meara built his Fist at Barra Hill, buttressing it with armour from the warship which foundered off Clifden and parking his tank in the driveway to the Fist on the last drop of gas. And there were the legends of his fabulous exploits, like the raid on the pill warehouse in Tuam which, they say, gave Barley Cross aspirin, antibiotics and independence.

Liam sighed. Times were certainy not like that now. Just work, work, and not enough hands to go round.

His mother called. "Quit mooning out there! Come in and eat your breakfast!"

He scraped his boots on the grating at the back door and went in, placing the egg in the crock on the dresser. He said, "Does Andy know the time of the wedding?"

Maureen McGrath frowned. "Liam, I wish you would learn not to call your stepfather 'Andy.' You are not yet a grown man, and it is altogether too familiar. Could you not call him 'Da'—just to please me?"

Liam sat down at the bare, scrubbed table. He mumbled through a mouthful of oatcake. "Andy is not bothered. He said I might call him what I wished, so long as I didn't call him early. He is not my real father, anyway."

"Your own father would have stood for no use of Christian names." His mother's voice shook with unaccustomed emotion. He looked up and caught her eyes sparkling angrily at him. "Flinty was a strict man," she stormed. "He'd have stood no nonsense from you!"

"Leave off, Mam," he pleaded. "Who knows what my Da would have stood for? It's fifteen years since he got that arrow in his lung, fighting for the old ram up there on Barra Hill."

"Liam!" Her voice rising alarmingly. "I will not have you using words like that about the Master of the Fist."

He raised eyebrows in astonishment. "But, Mam—that's what everyone calls him. They say he's been to bed with nearly every woman in the village." He broke off, and bit his lip in embarrassment.

Maureen McGrath flushed. "Liam McGrath, you have been listening to prurient gossip, and much good will it do you."

"Mam," he said patiently. "I'm only repeating what has been whispered around the village since I was a gossoon. Why, half the kids have the great O'Meara beak."

"Liam!" His mother screeched. "I forbid you to discuss such things in this house. If you have finished eating, I suggest you take the mare on down to Seamus Murray, and after that you give the gig a good wash. If you are going to church in style, let it at least be a clean style."

Liam stuffed the last of the oatcakes into his mouth and rose from the table. "I'll do it right now, Mam," he said.

At the door of the smithy, Seamus Murray clapped a hot shoe to the mare's off hind foot clutched firmly between his knees and watched the smoke curl.

"Great day for you, Liam," he said.

"If I can keep my Mam in a good temper it will be," Liam responded. "Why should she get so upset when I criticize the old ram up there?" He nodded at the Fist which loomed plain in the sunlight at the top of the street. "Hasn't the old despot had his way with almost every woman in Barley Cross?"

The blacksmith fished a long, triangular nail from the pocket of his apron, inserted it through a hole in the horseshoe and hammered it home. His voice was almost inaudible. "Easy to be critical, son. The O'Meara has been Lord and Protector here nigh on thirty years. Before he came we were like fowls in a farmyard with the fox outside. But he disciplined us, drilled us, dragged guns half the length of Connemara behind that old tank of his, and made Barley Cross a name in the land." The smith waved towards a black skeleton which lay rusting on the hump of rock in Flanagan's barley acre. *"That* didn't come down by accident. We shot it clean out of the air. They say 'twas the last aeroplane in the West of Ireland. I was there and saw it come down. We did a three-week stretch on duty in those days because the village had to be guarded constantly. Gangs used to come aroving. And, if they thought you had anything worth stealing, by God, they were after you with guns and cudgels and knives. But we stopped 'em in Barley Cross. They learned to leave us alone."

The smith sniffed embarrassedly. In silence he snipped off the sharp end of the nail protruding from the side of the mare's hoof. "There aren't so many people around now to make trouble," he added. "You might even say we no longer need the O'Meara for a protector. But, who can tell?" He straightened up, searching his pocket for a nail. "You might say we were lucky to get through in such good shape. They tell me Clifden is a ghost town, now. 'Tis a great pity. But they didn't have our luck. And sure, 'twas the O'Meara luck, and I, for one, am glad of it. So, if he wants to play medieval monarch, I'm prepared to put up with it."

He hammered home the nail, snipped off the point, and released the mare's leg. Liam followed him into the smithy. He watched the smith work the bellows before pushing another shoe into the glowing coals. "But, Seamus, what if it was your own wife?"

Seamus Murray turned to stare at him, his gaze level and placid. "After twenty-eight years of marriage to me, Mary is not the lass to drive the O'Meara crazy with desire. Let's say the idea doesn't trouble me."

"But when you were younger?"

The smith hooked the shoe from the coals. He spat expertly. Spittle ricocheted from the hot iron. Satisfied, he gripped the shoe with the tongs and carried it out to the waiting mare. "Let's say," he said slowly, "if anything happened, I wasn't aware of it. And, if it did, somehow Mary neglected to mention the matter."

His eyelids crinkled as he watched the hot iron bed itself into the mare's hoof. He glanced slyly at Liam. "I suppose 'tis your wedding this afternoon that has set you thinking these serious thoughts?"

Liam scowled. He cocked an eye at the menacing Fist and drew patterns with his toe in the dirt. He set his jaw. "Nothing happens to Eileen without my say-so."

Seamus Murray smiled sourly. He began to nail on the cooling shoe. "Brave words, son. But what would you gain by standing between the Master and a woman's virginity? He could deal with you, and *then* take what he wanted."

Liam felt his resolution wavering before Murray's calm acceptance of the Master's authority. He said, "Surely the O'Meara wouldn't treat a new bride that way?"

The smith was grinning openly. "Haven't you just suggested that he treated my Mary so?" He stared quizzically at Liam for a moment, then bent back over the hoof. He rasped the clipped nail points smooth without looking up. "I shouldn't worry overmuch, son. Probably the Master is not even aware that you are to be married today."

He gave the hoof a final buff, then released the beast. He pushed her towards Liam with a pat on the rump. "She'll do for a while now, Liam. Tell your Mam that's the last of my good shoes. I'll be making them from scrap in future, unless a tinker happens by with some."

Liam took the mare's bridle. "Let me know when you're ready for the piglet. I'll bring it straight over. Then we'll be quits for the last two jobs."

The smith patted his shoulder. "Don't be worrying about that either, son. I'll let Andy know when we are ready for it."

Liam slid onto the mare's back. He turned her head towards home. God Damn! These old 'uns wouldn't let you grow up. Leave it to Andy. He will settle it. Let the O'Meara have his way, he saved our lives in the past. Well, he hadn't saved Liam McGrath's life, and Liam McGrath owed him nothing. They could run the village any way they liked, but don't expect Liam McGrath to get down and bow to their pet tyrant.

His stepfather was waiting outside the front door when he got home. Andy McGrath wore his visored helmet and beribboned flak jacket. Wizened Willie Flanagan and poor Eamon Toomey stood behind him. All three carried FN rifles. Liam opened his mouth to suggest that three men were not much of a guard of honor, saw the look on his stepfather's face, and thought the better of it. He cartwheeled dextrously from the mare's back. "Hi, Andy! You're early. The wedding's not until two."

Andy McGrath's face was grim. "We'll be in time, Liam, never doubt. But first we've a little business with you." He fumbled inside his jacket and brought out a folded sheet of paper. Pushing up his visor, he put on his spectacles, and unfolded the paper. "Just so you understand, Liam, that I am carrying out orders." He cleared his throat and began to read.

"From the Lord of Barley Cross to Liam McGrath of Killoo Farm. Take note that we intend to exercise our droit du seigneur with your intended wife Eileen O'Connor and that Sergeant McGrath has orders to escort her to the Fist at six of the clock this day."

Liam felt his face grow hot. "Droit . . . droit what?"

His stepfather's face was impassive. "Droit du seigneur, lad. It's old French. Sometimes it's called *Jus primae noctis*— which is Latin for the same thing—the right of the first night. The Master intends to exercise his legal rights with your betrothed."

Liam felt the color drain from his face. A lump of ice congealed in his chest. He stammered. "The . . . the Master can't want my Eileen!"

Andy McGrath refolded the paper, then tucked it inside his jacket. He removed his spectacles and put them into a pocket. "The Master can, and the Master does."

Liam caught his stepfather's hand in sudden appeal. "But you won't let them take her away!"

Andy McGrath's gaze softened slightly. "I'm sorry, lad. I'm the one that must do the taking."

Liam clutched him. "Andy, you can't!"

His stepfather firmly removed Liam's hand. "I must warn you, son, that it is a serious offence to obstruct the Master's officers in the execution of their duty. So don't try anything foolish. You'll get your Eileen back in the morning. She won't be the first, nor will she be the last. Now I suggest you accept that your married life starts tomorrow instead of tonight. And I'll be on my way to break the news to the O'Connors."

Liam stared incredulously at his stepfather and the two-man squad awkwardly clutching their rifles. Each of those guns, by repute, held only one round because of the miserly way General Desmond released ammunition. But one bullet could settle an argument. Would they really shoot him if he tried to prevent their abduction of Eileen? In the leg, perhaps, as a warning. Willie Flanagan was a poacher by vocation; no doubt he would prefer a noose, or the knife. But poor Eamon Toomey would do whatever he was told: he would shoot, and think afterwards.

Hot, burning tears were suddenly scalding his cheeks.

His stepfather put an arm around his shoulders. He urged him towards the doorway of the house. "Go in and talk to your mother, son. She'll listen to you. And she will tell you that what I say is the best thing to do."

He turned to Willie and Eamon. "Right, lads. To the O'Connors now, and we'll get it over with."

Eileen O'Connor opened the back door and gasped. "Liam! You know it's unlucky to be seeing me before the service!"

He tried to take her into his arms, but she held him off.

"I had to come," he panted. "My Mam thinks I'm checking the snares. Has Andy been yet?"

She glanced quickly over her shoulder into the interior of the house. "You know he has. He came straight from your place."

He gripped her arms. "Do you know why he came?"

She nodded, lowering her eyes.

"Then why don't you say something?" Surely she could not remain calm, knowing the message Andy McGrath had brought. He said, "You won't let that old—?"

Eileen O'Connor drew in a deep breath. She looked him straight in the eyes. "My Da says it's the law and that we must do as the law says. He says we should regard it as an honor."

He snorted bitterly. "Your Da sounds like a first-class creep to me."

She glared at him. "Don't you be calling my Da a creep. He did his share for Barley Cross before you were born. And you're not even old enough to stand guard at the Fist yet?"

He pulled her towards him and again tried to embrace her. "Don't let's quarrel, Eileen. I'm not calling your Da names. It's just that he is like our Andy. All the old folk act the same—as though O'Meara was God, and his slightest wish the law."

She stood cold and motionless in his arms. "My Da says without the Master there would be no law."

He swallowed an angry retort and said patiently, "We'll have to get away before Andy comes."

He felt her stiffen. "Why? Why should we go away?"

"Why? So that old lecher can't. . . ."

"He's not so old, and he's not a lecher. They say he is a very civil man."

"Civil! My God!"

She drew back as far as his arms would permit. Her voice was like ice on a pool. "If I've said something foolish, Liam McGrath, please don't hesitate to point it out."

His hands trembled with the impulse to crush her to him, knowing that she would resist. He said, "Eileen, let's not quarrel over this. Do you want the O'Meara to take you up there, and. . . ." He floundered helplessly, left the question hanging.

Her lips compressed into a thin, straight line, which warned him that O'Connor common sense would now prevail. "If I agreed to go with you, where would we go?"

"Why—somewhere outside the village. There's the O'Toole cabin on Kirkogue has been empty this twelve-month."

"Because no one has wanted it since old Gabriel died there, all alone, without a soul to help him, and at the mercy of any rogue that passed that way. Who would be caring for me while you were down here working at your farm?"

"But, Eileen—I'd stay with you. I wouldn't leave you on your own. We'd start a new farm. Old Gabriel had quite a bit of pasture at the back."

Her mouth turned down at the corners. "Faith—there isn't enough soil up there to grow a week's potatoes.

And the land sloping so bad you'd need a short leg to get around easy."

"Then we'll build a cottage nearer the village. There's plenty of stone, and I'm good with my hands."

She sighed, wagging her head in mock despair. "Liam McGrath, sometimes I think you are a great booby. How near the village would you build your cottage? Near enough, I hope, for O'Meara's law to protect us from vagabonds like the two your Andy hanged last month. But if you seek the law's protection, don't you have to obey it, too? And the law says I go up to the Fist tonight."

She let him pull her towards him then, felt his tears wet her cheek. She stroked the back of his head. "It's not the end of the world, lad. If we lived outside Barley Cross I'd probably have been raped at twelve, and dying from malnutrition by now. We have a good life here. No bad men. And there's Doctor Denny's hospital if you're sick. I don't want to live anywhere else. So, we take the rough with the smooth. And, if I do have to go up to the Fist, nobody outside our families need even know. And I'm sure you'd rather I went willingly, than be dragged there, kicking and screaming over something any girl outside Barley Cross would regard as a normal event, and in this specific case might even consider it an honor."

He crushed her to him, not listening, unwilling to dispute further. "Don't worry," he murmured into her hair. "I'll fix it, somehow."

She pushed back his head so that she could look into his eyes. "Liam McGrath, there'll be no fixing, somehow or anyhow! We are going to live here in Barley Cross after we are wed, and you'll do nothing to prevent it!"

"But Eileen—" he began.

"But nothing." She closed his lips with her own. "If I can put up with it, so can you. Now off you go before my Mam comes to see who it is that I'm blathering with at the back door."

Mind churning, Liam stumbled blindly from the O'Connor's yard. Sunlight flashed on jewels under his eyelids. Help from someone more powerful than himself was what he needed. He lurched towards the street.

Molly Larkin filled the doorway of her father's neat cottage beside the schoolhouse. Her arms were white to

the elbows with flour. She stared at him in surprise.
"Why, Liam—I thought today was your—?"

"It is, Molly, it. is." He felt himself coloring with
embarrassment. Once upon a time he had fancied moth-
erless Molly Larkin. No doubt she would make someone
a fine wife—if that someone didn't mind marrying her
old man as well. He said, "It's your aunt I wanted." She
dusted flour from her hands, wiped them on her apron.
"She's not home, Liam. I believe she's up at the Fist.
Would you be leaving a message?"

He backed away. There was no message he would
choose prosy Molly Larkin to deliver for him. "Ah—no,
thank you, Molly. 'Tisn't anything important." Granite
chippings crunched underfoot; the gate squealed as he
closed it behind him.

Who else to try?

Tessie Mallon was snipping dead rose heads in her
garden. She was as plump and jolly as her husband
shriveled and sour. She slipped scissors into her apron
pocket and pulled off her home-made gloves as Liam
hesitated the other side of her hedge. She saw his face
and showed alarm.

"The doctor is not in, Liam. Is it your Mam?"

He shook his head dumbly.

"Yourself, then?"

He found his voice. "There is nobody ill, Mrs. Mallon.
I just wanted a quick word with the doctor."

She nibbled thoughtfully at the tip of her index
finger—a habit that, forty years ago, had driven the
village lads crazy. "He said he'd be back in an hour or
so. Should I ask him to call round at your house?"

Emotion choked his voice. "No—no, thank you. I'll
catch him another time."

She held her head on one side, half smiling. "Your
Eileen has already had a chat with him, if that is any
help. You don't have to worry about anything."

Liam fled.

Clouds were gathering over Carn Seefin and Leckavrea.
Rain would soon be pocking the surface of Lough Corrib.
Endless Connemara rain. A wet afternoon for the wedding,
for sure. Who else could he try? Father Con?

The old priest led him into a furniture-filled study
which had not altered in fifty years, except that now the

electric light no longer worked. He listened in silence to Liam's plea for help.

"Well, Liam," he said gently. "What would you have me do? Forbid the wedding?"

"Ah, no, Father." That was not the solution that Liam sought.

"What then, son? I'm too old to be trudging up Barra Hill with a shilelagh in my hand to knock piety into the O'Meara."

"But, Father, you can't condone what he's trying to do. Isn't adultery a sin for him, as well as the rest of us?"

The old priest raised his hands in gentle reproof. "Now, Liam, I did not say that I condoned the O'Meara's actions. No doubt he is as much a sinner as the rest of us."

"Well—couldn't you excommunicate him, or something?"

Father Constantine smiled patiently.

"Excommunication is the Holy Father's business, son, and I haven't had word from His Holiness for many a long year."

Liam's lower lip protruded stubbornly. "You could at least refuse him the sacraments."

Father Con frowned. His eyes narrowed in unspoken rebuke. He said, "Liam, the church is for sinners. If the O'Meara is our biggest sinner, he must have the biggest need of it."

Liam got to his feet. "Then you can't do anything for me?"

The priest washed his hands in agitation. "My son, although it is no business of yours, because of your involvement I will tell you that I have spoken my mind frequently and forcibly to the Lord of Barley Cross. And I will tell you that, in his own eyes, his deeds are justified. Beyond that I will not go. If you are still unsatisfied, I can only recommend that you seek an interview with the O'Meara himself."

Liam shambled from the grey stone presbytery, anger mounting inside him. His resolve grew firm. No one was willing to help him defy the tyrant. The O'Meara had ruled for so long they were inured to his tyranny. He would follow Father Con's advice. An interview—on different lines to those the priest envisaged!

Liam McGrath turned his steps towards Barra Hill. In

the old, dangerous days, tradition had it, the Fist had been used as a sanctuary when the village was attacked. Certainly he remembered spending days in the castle as a child, playing in its grounds in summer. And he knew a way to get up there unobserved. . . .

In the great dining hall of O'Meara's Fist, the Lord of Barley Cross caroused with his henchmen.

The O'Meara himself slumped in a frayed armchair before a smouldering turf fire, a glass of poteen on the bare boards beside him. In a chair across the hearth, Denny Mallon, M.D., hunched like a shriveled embryo, clutching his glass tightly. Kevin Murphy, the vet, and General Larry Desmond shared a broken-backed settee and a half bottle. On a stool on the pegged rug, knees skirt-covered and primly closed, hunched beneath her chin, Celia Larkin, M.A., sipped a cup of herb tea brewed specially for her.

The schoolmistress put down the teacup carefully onto the saucer on the rug. "Did you have any trouble with young McGrath, Larry?"

General Desmond eased a leg over the end of the sofa. He stared reflectively into his glass. "Ah, no, Celia. Andy McGrath is a good man. He'd march off a cliff edge if I so ordered. I gave him the job of breaking the news. And Tom O'Connor's a biddable man. We'll have no trouble with either of them."

Dr. Denny Mallon stirred in the depths of the old chair. "How did the women take it? I think it's getting harder for them to accept when it hits their own kids."

The general snorted with laughter. "Bedam—I believe they are both dead keen on it. Don't they both want a grandchild to cosset? And do you think that either of them is fussy how it is managed?"

"How about the youngsters?" persisted the schoolmistress. "Are they accepting it?"

The general looked less comfortable. "Andy tells me the lad was upset. He sent him in to talk to his mother. The girl is level-headed. She will do as Tom and Brigit tell her."

"Do you think the Master should attend the reception?"

"Ah, no. Let's keep his ugly mug out of it for as long as possible." The general grinned placatingly at the O'Meara. "I've sent down the usual gift." He swirled the colorless fluid gently in his glass. "It's amazing the influence a bar of real, old-fashioned toilet soap has on the opinion of a nice woman. I reckon we can celebrate another eighty or ninety nuptials before we get down to the carbolic."

The O'Meara opened his eyes. He said plaintively, "Do you ever get the feeling you're invisible? All very fine for you schemers—but it's me is the fall guy." He turned to the schoolmistress. "Do I have to go through with it? After all, the lad may be. . . ."

Celia Larkin interrupted him incisively. "Let be, Pat. We get this from you every time there's a wedding. And it won't make a damned bit of difference. You'll do it if we have to hold you down."

The Master of the Fist leaned forward to pack a fresh turf at the back of the fire. "One day I'm going to disappoint you all. Ask Denny. I've been getting these pains in my chest. 'Twouldn't surprise me, if, one time. . . ."

Denny Mallon waved a dismissive glass. "Whisht, Pat! I'll give you a couple of pills. The exercise will do you good."

"If only you knew," sighed the O'Meara, "what I have to put up with. Coaxing them, turning my back, apologizing, listening to them cry themselves to sleep. . . ."

Patrick O'Meara, ex-Grenadier Guardsman, had altered in the years since his strategic retreat in a stolen Chieftain tank from the burning docks of Belfast to a more defensible position in his native Connemara. Now, discipline sat heavy on his shoulders.

"Maybe I was wrong," he groaned. "Maybe we should have gone underground."

Big Larry Desmond tilted the bottle recklessly above his glass. "If the Lord had intended us to live in burrows, He'd have given us long ears and little furry tails."

"Maybe we should have stuck to the cities?"

"*Nyet!*" said Kevin Murphy, who had read Marx in his youth. "The Kelly boy took two pigs down to Galway Town last week and came back witless. The dead are lying in the street there, he tells me."

"You can criticize Galway Town," protested the O'Meara, "but we don't make progress."

Celia Larkin straightened her back. "What do you

expect? No one is going to invent a turf-driven aeroplane.
Nor produce vacuum cleaners from cow pats. But we
have twenty-four children attending school. And, if you
think you can claim all the credit, you can think again.
That Kelly boy was never a ten-month child. He's their
own, I'm sure.''

"Then why don't they produce more children?''

She looked shocked. "It isn't for us to be prying into
private matters! We interfere enough by insisting on
your droit du seigneur." She turned to the general. "Please
give that Kelly boy an escort if he has to go outside the
village in future." She sighed. "God forgive me—one
could almost wish he'd grow up promiscuous.''

Kevin Murphy rumbled indistinctly. "Nothing wrong
with that idea.''

She shook her head sadly. "Kevin, your farmyard solu-
tions won't do for us. Children are entitled to their own
parents, just as parents are entitled to their own children.'' She removed her rimless spectacles and polished
them on the hem of her sleeve. "Remember the ecology
freaks? Predicting what we would run out of—oil, coal,
gas, living room, fresh air. Never thought we'd run out
of people.''

Denny Mallon exhaled clouds of smoke. "I thought the
dark-skinned races might have done better. But their
crops are letting them down. Something to do with
radiation affecting bacteria and viruses, which in turn
affects the plants. I caught a broadcast from Athlone years
ago—when we had the radio," he added apologetically.

Celia Larkin's lips tightened. "If it *is* the ultraviolet. If
those clever professors were so sure, why wasn't something done when they first discovered what was happening?''

Denny Mallon sucked imperturbably on his pipe. "The
ozone layer never stopped *all* the ultraviolet. Can anyone know how much radiation it takes to cripple a
gene?''

Kevin Murphy scratched his scalp. "Sure— 'tis a
statistical thing. Genes are getting hit by radiation all
the time. Suddenly, for some reason, the percentage of
hits tips the scale from acceptability to calamity.''

General Desmond reached again for the bottle. "Statistics be damned—it's our cloudy Connemara skies that I'm grateful for."

Kevin Murphy accepted the bottle from the General. He said, "The beasts seem to hold their own. Maybe it *is* Larry's clouds, or maybe they are not as sensitive as us. But we're getting enough births to keep the herds and flocks going." He grinned at the Lord of Barley Cross. "Be grateful I don't need your services in *my* department."

Celia Larkin frowned. "That's enough of your lewd talk, Kevin. If we can hold on long enough, Barley Cross might start producing radiation-resistant kids. Or the ozone layer might yet repair itself." The shriveled, childless spinster pulled out a frayed handkerchief and blew her nose loudly. Sunlight glinted on her spectacles as she raised her head. "But, in any Goddamned case, I can go to my grave hoping that, in the years to come, if there is the faintest chance of things getting going again, we simpletons of Barley Cross will have done our bit to supply a few of the hands and heads that will be needed to get this poor, sorrowing planet progressing again."

There was silence for a moment.

Then General Desmond put down his glass and said, "Amen to that."

"Amen," mumbled veterinary surgeon Kevin Murphy, scowling at no one in particular.

"Amen," whispered Denny Mallon, M.D., staring into the empty bowl of his pipe.

The Lord of Barley Cross got to his feet. He consulted the old wind-up watch he had used since batteries ran out. "Well, madame and gentlemen, if anything is going to happen, it must be soon. There is only an hour to the wedding. If you will excuse me, I'd better be getting a bath and a shave. Can't let the future Mrs. McGrath see me in this state." He jerked a thumb at the servant's door. "Shout for Michael if you want another bottle."

"*You* shout, if you want us," said the general.

The Lord of Barley Cross pushed stockinged feet into slippers and shuffled towards the door. He paused to stare sourly at his henchmen. "If only I hadn't promised Celia thirty years ago—" He sighed. "You'll be flogging O'Meara along until he drops, I suppose?"

The doctor's eyes gleamed puckishly. "We might let you off the hook when you're eighty."

A metal arm on the wall moved from the vertical to the horizontal, causing a bell to tinkle. The general reached out and reset it.

"There's your signal, Pat."

The O'Meara shrugged. "I'll be off then to face the music."

He opened the door of his bedroom and went in. An arm encircled his neck, another his chest. The tip of a knife pricked his shirt front.

"Easy now, son," he grunted, tugging at both arms, striving to maintain his balance.

"If you think you can beat me to it—go ahead," he invited. "But I warn you, I don't need to count up to ten before I kill a man. And, no matter who gets who, the sound of a shot will bring those fellers out there running. If that happens, the man to watch is Larry Desmond—he's a killer."

Liam felt the moisture filling his eyes. "You—you *bastard!*"

"Ah, no!" The O'Meara seemed genuinely surprised. "It's you that is the bastard."

Liam blinked furiously. "Don't call me a bastard. I'm not planning to sleep with *your* wife."

The O'Meara tossed his socks into a corner. He picked up the gun and clicked the chamber round thoughtfully.

"I have no wife with whom you might sleep, Liam. And a bastard is precisely what you are. Your mother was not married to your father."

Liam quivered, as though an electric current galvanized his limbs. "Put away the gun, and I'll show you how I feel about *that* statement."

The O'Meara laughed. "Liam—poor old Flinty Hagan couldn't have fathered you. He lost the necessary equipment in a raid on Oughterard a year before he was married. We all kept quiet about it because he was a sensitive man, and we thought a great deal of him."

Liam's lips trembled. The old goat was trying to provoke him, but he wouldn't give him the satisfaction of seeing him lose his temper. He said, "Then why did my mother agree to marry Flinty?"

The O'Meara sat silent for a moment, then seemed to come to a decision.

"Well now, Liam. We seem to have arrived at what you might call the moment of truth. You have asked me a question which I would rather not answer. If you insist on an answer, I'm afraid we must escalate our discussion to a more formal level."

Liam let his lip curl scornfully. "Don't fence with me. Let's have a straight word out of you."

The O'Meara nodded in agreement. "So be it, son. Up to this moment you could have walked out of this room any time you wanted, and no hard feelings on my part. Now, as I warned you, you've promoted our chat to a really serious plane—that is, namely, your examination for citizenship. Some lads never learn about this test. Others, quite naturally, avoid it. But you have headed straight for it. So, now, I'm going to answer your question. And also provide you with some additional information that you haven't asked for. Your response, after due consideration, will govern whether you leave this room vertically or horizontally—and remember *I* am the judge.

"Here goes. Your Mam married Flinty Hagan because Barley Cross needed children, and at the time Flinty was the only available bachelor."

"But you said Flinty couldn't. . . ."

"Don't interrupt, son, or I might make a hasty decision. Just listen. Very few men in Barley Cross can father a child. The reason goes back a long way, and it isn't their fault. Responsible adults in the village are aware of this and have accepted the solution the people out there in my dining room thought up. The solution is that *I*— because I'm a freak, being fertile—I father most of the children in Barley Cross, but their legal fathers get the credit.

"That, briefly, is how our village has managed to remain a living, functioning community, with enough people to do all the work required to keep it going. Now, Liam, if you wish to graduate into a citizen of Barley Cross, you must accept our solution, *and* keep quiet about it. That doesn't mean you can't talk it over with your Eileen. But it does mean you don't discuss it in front of the children. Because the way a child grows up governs how he or she acts as an adult. And we want the

children of Barley Cross to believe that the world is a
sane and happy place where everyone gets his own Daddy
and Mammy. And we hope that the child will be able to
adjust to our madhouse when he is old enough to understand it. It also means that you don't gab about it in the
village or do anything which might inadvertently destroy the illusion we have built up so painstakingly. And
it means that your Eileen comes up here tonight, like
every bride in the last thirty years."

The O'Meara paused, rubbing his jaw reflectively.
"Those are the facts. Don't go shouting for help. No one
is going to rush in to save you from the crazy O'Meara.
Those gentlemen outside have an idea that you might be
in here. And they realize that I am making a reasonable
attempt to dispel any objections you may hold to the
way the village is run. What they do not know, are my
methods of persuasion. But it has all happened before,
and they have confidence in me."

The O'Meara straightened his back. He raised his arm.
The gun pointed at Liam's breastbone.

"You may have qualms about accepting our solution.
Your views on putative incest, for instance, may not
correspond with ours. The subject is not open for debate.
You may walk from this room a responsible adult, or
you may be carried out a dead juvenile. Now, sir—how
do you say?"

Liam's eyes had been growing wider and wider. "But,
if Flinty Hagan wasn't my father—?"

"Keep going," urged the O'Meara. "You are getting
warm."

Liam McGrath fingered his own hooked nose, as if he
had just become aware of it. He eyed the similar protu-
berance on the face of the elderly man sitting barefoot
and shirtless on the bed. Suddenly he grinned.

"Put up the gun, Da, or you'll have me late. A citizen
ought to be on time for his own wedding."

EDITOR'S INTRODUCTION TO:

SUPERIORITY
by
Arthur C. Clarke

Arthur Clark swore that he would not write another book after *Fountains of Paradise*. Why should he? He doesn't need money, and the Republic of Sri Lanka (formerly the colony of Ceylon) has declared him a national treasure as well as Chancellor of its national university.

However, his fans kept after him to write the sequel to *2001*, and Arthur made a discovery: small computers make writing easy. Arthur has an Archive computer (naturally he calls it Archie).

When Arthur was on tour promoting *2010* we held a small reception for him here at Chaos Manor. He was surprised to see a copy of Archie. I don't have an Archive computer, but their keyboard is so nice that we've adapted it to the CompuPro machines I work with.

Archie not only allowed Dr. Clarke to turn in the manuscript to *2010* nearly a year early, but has, by his own admission, made letter writing fun again. In past years, old friends of Clarke's counted themselves lucky to receive a postcard every couple of years; now he's sending five page letters. He's sure it isn't going to last, but he's enjoying himself.

The small computer revolution goes on, and it's changing the world. The Falklands War demonstrated that. To win in today's conflicts, you must have good soldiers, but you must also have high technology weapons.

Of course there can be too much of a good thing . . .

SUPERIORITY
by
Arthur C. Clarke

In making this statement—which I do of my own free will—I wish first to make it perfectly clear that I am not in any way trying to gain sympathy, nor do I expect any mitigation of whatever sentence the Court may pronounce. I am writing this in an attempt to refute some of the lying reports broadcast over the prison radio and published in the papers I have been allowed to see. These have given an entirely false picture of the true cause of our defeat, and as the leader of my race's armed forces at the cessation of hostilities I feel it my duty to protest against such libels upon those who served under me.

I also hope that this statement may explain the reasons for the application I have twice made to the Court, and will now induce it to grant a favor for which I can see no possible grounds of refusal.

The ultimate cause of our failure was a simple one: despite all statements to the contrary, it was not due to lack of bravery on the part of our men, or to any fault of the Fleet's. We were defeated by one thing only—by the inferior science of our enemies. I repeat—by the *inferior* science of our enemies.

When the war opened we had no doubt of our ultimate victory. The combined fleets of our allies greatly exceeded in number and armament those which the enemy could muster against us, and in almost all branches of military science we were their superiors. We were sure that we could maintain this superiority. Our belief proved, alas, to be only too well founded.

At the opening of the war our main weapons were the

192

long-range homing torpedo, dirigible ball-lightning and the various modifications of the Klydon beam. Every unit of the Fleet was equipped with these and though the enemy possessed similar weapons their installations were generally of lesser power. Moreover, we had behind us a far greater military Research Organization, and with this initial advantage we could not possibly lose.

The campaign proceeded according to plan until the Battle of the Five Suns. We won this, of course, but the opposition proved stronger than we had expected. It was realized that victory might be more difficult, and more delayed, than had first been imagined. A conference of supreme commanders was therefore called to discuss our future strategy.

Present for the first time at one of our war conferences was Professor-General Norden, the new Chief of the Research Staff, who had just been appointed to fill the gap left by the death of Malvar, our greatest scientist. Malvar's leadership had been responsible, more than any other single factor, for the efficiency and power of our weapons. His loss was a very serious blow, but no one doubted the brilliance of his successor—though many of us disputed the wisdom of appointing a theoretical scientist to fill a post of such vital importance. But we had been overruled.

I can well remember the impression Norden made at that conference. The military advisers were worried, and as usual turned to the scientists for help. Would it be possible to improve our existing weapons, they asked, so that our present advantage could be increased still further?

Norden's reply was quite unexpected. Malvar had often been asked such a question—and he had always done what we requested.

"Frankly, gentlemen," said Norden, "I doubt it. Our existing weapons have practically reached finality. I don't wish to criticize my predecessor, or the excellent work done by the Research Staff in the last few generations, but do you realize that there has been no basic change in armaments for over a century? It is, I am afraid, the result of a tradition that has become conservative. For too long, the Research Staff has devoted itself to perfecting old weapons instead of developing new ones. It is fortunate for us that our opponents have been no wiser; we cannot assume that this will always be so."

Norden's words left an uncomfortable impression, as he had no doubt intended. He quickly pressed home the attack.

"What we want are *new* weapons—weapons totally different from any that have been employed before. Such weapons can be made: it will take time, of course, but since assuming charge I have replaced some of the older scientists by young men and have directed research into several unexplored fields which show great promise. I believe, in fact, that a revolution in warfare may soon be upon us."

We were skeptical. There was a bombastic tone in Norden's voice that made us suspicious of his claims. We did not know, then, that he never promised anything that he had not already almost perfected in the laboratory. *In the laboratory*—that was the operative phrase.

Norden proved his case less than a month later, when he demonstrated the Sphere of Annihilation, which produced complete disintegration of matter over a radius of several hundred meters. We were intoxicated by the power of the new weapon, and were quite prepared to overlook one fundamental defect—the fact that it *was* a sphere and hence destroyed its rather complicated generating equipment at the instant of formation. This meant, of course, that it could not be used on warships but only on guided missiles, and a great program was started to convert all homing torpedoes to carry the new weapon. For the time being all further offensives were suspended.

We realize now that this was our first mistake. I still think that it was a natural one, for it seemed to us then that all our existing weapons had become obsolete overnight, and we already regarded them as almost primitive survivals. What we did not appreciate was the magnitude of the task we were attempting, and the length of time it would take to get the revolutionary super-weapon into battle. Nothing like this had happened for a hundred years and we had no previous experience to guide us.

The conversion problem proved far more difficult

than anticipated. A new class of torpedo had to be designed, as the standard model was too small. This meant in turn that only the larger ships could launch the weapon, but we were prepared to accept this penalty. After six months, the heavy units of the Fleet were being equipped with the Sphere. Training maneuvers and tests had shown that it was operating satisfactorily and we were ready to take it into action. Norden was already being hailed as the architect of victory, and had half promised even more spectacular weapons.

Then two things happened. One of our battleships disappeared completely on a training flight, and an investigation showed that under certain conditions the ship's long-range radar could trigger the Sphere immediately it had been launched. The modification needed to overcome this defect was trivial, but it caused a delay of another month and was the source of much bad feeling between the naval staff and the scientists. We were ready for action again—when Norden announced that the radius of effectiveness of the Sphere had now been increased by ten. Thus multiplying by a thousand the chances of destroying an enemy ship.

So the modifications started all over again, but everyone agreed that the delay would be worth it. Meanwhile, however, the enemy had been emboldened by the absence of further attacks and had made an unexpected onslaught. Our ships were short of torpedoes, since none had been coming from the factories, and were forced to retire. So we lost the systems of Kyrane and Floranus, and the planetary fortress of Rhamsandron.

It was an annoying but not a serious blow, for the recaptured systems had been unfriendly, and difficult to administer. We had no doubt that we could restore the position in the near future, as soon as the new weapon became operational.

These hopes were only partially fulfilled. When we renewed our offensive, we had to do so with fewer of the Spheres of Annihilation than had been planned, and this was one reason for our limited success. The other reason was more serious.

While we had been equipping as many of our ships as we could with the irresistible weapon, the enemy had been building feverishly. His ships were of the old pattern with the old weapons—but they now outnumbered ours. When we went into action, we found that the numbers ranged against us were often 100 per cent greater than expected, causing target confusion among the automatic weapons and resulting in higher losses than anticipated. The enemy losses were higher still, for once a Sphere had reached its objective, destruction was certain, but the balance had not swung as far in our favor as we had hoped.

Moreover, while the main fleets had been engaged, the enemy had launched a daring attack on the lightly held systems of Eriston, Duranus, Carmanidora and Pharanidon—recapturing them all. We were thus faced with a threat only fifty light-years from our home planets.

There was much recrimination at the next meeting of the supreme commanders. Most of the complaints were addressed to Norden—Grand Admiral Taxaris in particular maintaining that thanks to our admittedly irresistable weapon we were now considerably worse off than before. We should, he claimed, have continued to build conventional ships, thus preventing the loss of our numerical superiority.

Norden was equally angry and called the naval staff ungrateful bunglers. But I could tell that he was worried—as indeed we all were—by the unexpected turn of events. He hinted that there might be a speedy way of remedying the situation.

We now know that Reserach had been working on the Battle Analyzer for many years, but at the time it came as a revelation to us and perhaps we were too easily swept off our feet. Norden's argument, also, was seductively convincing. What did it matter, he said, if the enemy had twice as many ships as we—if the efficiency of ours could be doubled or even trebled? For decades the limiting factor in warfare had been not mechanical but biological—it had become more and more difficult for any single mind, or group of minds, to cope with the rapidly changing complexities of battle in three-dimensional space. Norden's mathematicians had analyzed some of the classic engagements of the past, and had shown that even when we had been victorious we had often operated our units at much less than half of their theoretical efficiency.

The Battle Analyzer would change all this by replacing the operations staff with electronic calculators. The idea was not new, in theory, but until now it had been no more than a utopian dream. Many of us found it difficult to believe that it was still anything but a dream: after we had run through several very complex dummy battles, however, we were convinced.

It was decided to install the Analyzer in four of our heaviest ships, so that each of the main fleets could be equipped with one. At this stage, the trouble began—though we did not know it until later.

The Analyzer needed a team of five hundred technicians to maintain and operate it. It was quite impossible to accommodate the extra staff aboard a battleship, so each of the four units had to be accompanied by a converted liner to carry the technicians not on duty. Installation was also a very slow and tedious business, but by gigantic efforts it was completed in six months.

Then, to our dismay, we were confronted by another crisis. Nearly five thousand highly skilled men had been selected to serve the Analyzers and had been given an intensive course at the Technical Training Schools. At the end of seven months, 10 per cent of them had had nervous breakdowns and only 40 per cent had qualified.

Once again, everyone started to blame everyone else. Norden, of course, said that the Research Staff could not be held responsible, and so incurred the enmity of the Personnel and Training Commands. It was finally decided that the only thing to do was to use two instead of four Analyzers and to bring the others into action as soon as men could be trained. There was little time to lose, for the enemy was still on the offensive and his morale was rising.

The first Analyzer fleet was ordered to recapture the system of Eriston. On the way, by one of the hazards of war, the liner carrying the technicians was struck by a roving mine. A warship would have survived, but the liner with its irreplaceable cargo was totally destroyed. So the operation had to be abandoned.

The other expedition was, at first, more successful. There was no doubt at all that the Analyzer fulfilled its designer's claims, and the enemy was heavily defeated in the first engagements. He withdrew, leaving us in possession of Saphran, Leucon and Hexanerax. But his Intelligence Staff must have noted the change in our tactics and the inexplicable presence of a liner in the heart of our battlefleet. It must have noted, also, that our first fleet had been accompanied by a similar ship—and had withdrawn when it had been destroyed.

In the next engagement, the enemy used his superior numbers to launch an overwhelming attack on the Analyzer ship and its unarmed consort. The attack was made without regard to losses—both ships were, of course, heavily protected—and it succeeded. The result was the virtual decapitation of the Fleet, since an effectual transfer to the old operational methods proved impossible. We disengaged under heavy fire, and so lost all our gains and also the systems of Lormyia, Ismarnus, Beronis, Alphanidon and Sideneus.

At this stage, Grand Admiral Taxaris expressed his disapproval of Norden by committing suicide, and I assumed supreme command.

The station was now both serious and infuriating. With stubborn conservatism and complete lack of imagination, the enemy continued to advance with his old-fashioned and inefficient but now vastly more numerous ships. It was galling to realize that if we had only continued building, without seeking new weapons, we would have been in a far more advantageous position. There were many acrimonious conferences at which Norden defended the scientists while everyone else blamed them for all that had happened. The difficulty was that Norden had proved every one of his claims: he had a perfect excuse for all the disasters that had occurred. And we could not now turn back—the search for an irresistible weapon must go on. At first it had been a luxury that would shorten the war. Now it was a necessity if we were to end it victoriously.

We were on the defensive, and so was Norden. He was more than ever determined to re-establish his prestige and that of the Research Staff. But we had been twice disappointed, and would not make the same mistake again. No doubt Norden's twenty thousand scientists would produce many further weapons: we would remain unimpressed.

We were wrong. The final weapon was something so

fantastic that even now it seems difficult to believe that it ever existed. Its innocent, noncommittal name—The Exponential Field—gave no hint of its real potentialities. Some of Norden's mathematicians had discovered it during a piece of entirely theoretical research into the properties of space, and to everyone's great surprise their results were found to be physically realizable.

It seems very difficult to explain the operation of the Field to the layman. According to the technical description, it "produces an exponential condition of space, so that a finite distance in normal, linear space may become infinite in pseudo-space." Norden gave an analogy which some of us found useful. It was as if one took a flat disk of rubber—representing a region of normal space—and then pulled its center out to infinity. The circumference of the disk would be unaltered—but its "diameter" would be infinite. That was the sort of thing the generator of the Field did to the space around it.

As an example, suppose that a ship carrying the generator was surrounded by a ring of hostile machines. If it switched on the Field, *each* of the enemy ships would think that it—and the ships on the far side of the circle—had suddenly receded into nothingness. Yet the circumference of the circle would be the same as before: only the journey to the center would be of infinite duration, for as one proceeded, distances would appear to become greater and greater as the "scale" of space altered.

It was a nightmare condition, but a very useful one. Nothing could reach a ship carrying the Field: it might be englobed by an enemy fleet yet would be as inaccessible as if it were at the other side of the Universe. Against this, of course, it could not fight back without switching off the Field, but this still left it at a very great advantage, not only in defense but in offense. For a ship fitted with the Field could approach an enemy fleet undetected and suddenly appear in its midst.

This time there seemed to be no flaws in the new weapon. Needless to say, we looked for all the possible objections before we committed ourselves again. Fortunately the equipment was fairly simple and did not require a large operating staff. After much debate, we decided to rush it into production, for we realized that time was running short and the war was going against us. We had now lost about the whole of our initial gains and enemy forces had made several raids into our own solar system.

We managed to hold off the enemy while the Fleet was re-equipped and the new battle techniques were worked out. To use the Field operationally it was necessary to locate an enemy formation, set a course that would intercept it, and then switch on the generator for the calculated period of time. On releasing the Field again—if the calculations had been accurate—one would be in the enemy's midst and could do great damage during the resulting confusion, retreating by the same route when necessary.

The first trial maneuvers proved satisfactory and the equipment seemed quite reliable. Numerous mock attacks were made and the crews became accustomed to the new technique. I was on one of the test flights and can vividly remember my impressions as the Field was switched on. The ships around us seemed to dwindle as if on the surface of an expanding bubble: in an instant they had vanished completely. So had the stars—but presently we could see that the Galaxy was still visible as a faint band of light around the ship. The virtual radius of our pseudo-space was not really infinite, but some hundred thousand light-years, and so the distance to the farthest stars of our system had not been greatly increased—though the nearest had of course totally disappeared.

These training maneuvers, however, had to be cancelled before they were complete owing to a whole flock of minor technical troubles in various pieces of equipment, notably the communications circuits. These were annoying, but not important, though it was thought best to return to Base to clear them up.

At that moment the enemy made what was obviously intended to be a decisive attack against the fortress planet of Iton at the limits of our solar system. The Fleet had to go into battle before repairs could be made.

The enemy must have believed that we had mastered the secret of invisibility—as in a sense we had. Our ships appeared suddenly out of nowhere and inflicted tremendous damage—for a while. And then something quite baffling and inexplicable happened.

I was in command of the flagship *Hircania* when the trouble started. We had been operating as independent units, each against assigned objectives. Our detectors observed an enemy formation at medium range and the navigating officers measured its distance with great accuracy. We set course and switched on the generator.

The Exponential Field was released at the moment when we should have been passing through the center of the enemy group. To our consternation, we emerged into normal space at a distance of many hundred miles—and when we found the enemy, he had already found us. We retreated, and tried again. This time we were so far away from the enemy that he located us first.

Obviously, something was seriously wrong. We broke communicator silence and tried to contact the other ships of the Fleet to see if they had experienced the same trouble. Once again we failed—and this time the failure was beyond all reason, for the communication equipment appeared to be working perfectly. We could only assume, fantastic though it seemed, that the rest of the Fleet had been destroyed.

I do not wish to describe the scenes when the scattered units of the Fleet struggled back to Base. Our casualties had actually been negligible, but the ships were completely demoralized. Almost all had lost touch with one another and had found that their ranging equipment showed inexplicable errors. It was obvious that the Exponential Field was the cause of the troubles, despite the fact that they were only apparent when it was switched off.

The explanation came too late to do us any good, and Norden's final discomfiture was small consolation for the virtual loss of the war. As I have explained, the Field generators produced a radial distortion of space, distances appearing greater and greater as one approached the center of the artificial pseudo-space. When the Field was switched off, conditions returned to normal.

But not quite. It was never possible to restore the initial state *exactly*. Switching the Field on and off was equivalent to an elongation and contraction of the ship carrying the generator, but there was an hysteretic effect, as it were, and the initial condition was never quite reproducible, owing to all the thousands of electrical changes and movements of mass aboard the ship while the Field was on. These asymmetries and distortions were cummulative, and though they seldom amounted to more than a fraction of one per cent, that was quite enough. It meant that the precision ranging equipment and the tuned circuits in the communication apparatus were thrown completely out of adjustment. Any single ship could never detect the change—only when it compared its equipment with that of another vessel, or tried to communicate with it, could it tell what had happened.

It is impossible to describe the resultant chaos. Not a single component of one ship could be expected with certainty to work aboard another. The very nuts and bolts were no longer interchangeable, and the supply position became quite impossible. Given time, we might even have overcome these difficulties, but the enemy ships were already attacking in thousands with weapons which now seemed centuries behind those that we had invented. Our magnificent Fleet, crippled by our own science, fought on as best it could until it was overwhelmed and forced to surrender. The ships fitted with the Field were still invulnerable, but as fighting units they were almost helpless. Every time they switched on their generators to escape from enemy attack, the permanent distortion of their equipment increased. In a month, it was all over.

This is the true story of our defeat, which I give without prejudice to my defense before this Court. I make it, as I have said, to counteract the libels that have been circulating against the men who fought under me, and to show where the true blame for our misfortunes lay.

Finally, my request, which as the Court will now realize, I make in no frivolous manner and which I hope will therefore be granted.

The Court will be aware that the conditions under which we are housed and the constant surveillance to which we are subjected night and day are somewhat distressing. Yet I am not complaining of this: nor do I complain of the fact that shortage of accommodation has made it necessary to house us in pairs.

But I cannot be held responsible for my future actions if I am compelled any longer to share my cell with Professor Norden, late Chief of the Research Staff of my armed forces.

EDITOR'S AFTERWARD TO:

SUPERIORITY

Clarke's humor masks one of the most vital questions of the decade: how much defense can we afford?

There are two aspects to the military procurement dilemma. First:

> A gigantic technological race is in progress . . . a new form of strategy is developing in peacetime, a strategy of which the phrase "arms race" used prior to the old great conflicts is hardly more than a faint reflection.
>
> There are no battles in this strategy; each side is merely trying to outdo in performance the equipment of the other. It has been termed "logistic strategy". Its tactics are industrial, technical, and financial. It is a form of indirect attrition; instead of destroying enemy resources, its object is to make them obsolete, thereby forcing on him enormous expenditure . . .
>
> A silent and apparently peaceful war is therefore in progress, but it could well *be a war which of itself could be decisive.*
>
> —General d'Armee Andre Beaufre

If we do not engage in this "silent and apparently peaceful war," we will be defeated. However:

> A common argument against investment in technological weapons is the engineering maxim, "If it works, it's obsolete." True, whatever one buys, if

you had waited a few years something better would be available; but if this is carried to extremes, nothing will ever be built.

Whenever a new field of technology opens up, the people who use it must learn how. They must become operationally effective. Had we waited until third-generation missiles were available before we constructed any, we would not be alive today. We certainly would have had no experienced crews to man the missiles we would only now be constructing.

A time comes when systems must be built, even though we know they will be obsolete in future years . . . .

The fallacy that prototypes and research are all that are needed should have been laid to rest by the experience of the French in 1939. The French Army had—and had possessed for quite a long time—prototypes of aircraft, armor, and antitank weapons much better than those of the German Army. The French did not have these weapons in their inventory because still better ones were coming. While they waited for the best weapons, they lost their country.

Military action must be routine. It cannot be extraordinary, planned months in advance like a space spectacular. Operational experience with a weapons system is required before operational employment doctrines can be perfected. Troops must be trained, logistics bases developed, maintenance routines learned, idiosyncrasies—and modern technological gadgetry is full of them—must be discovered. This cannot be done if the latest technology is confined to the drawing board or laboratory.

S. T. Possony and J. E. Pournelle,
The Strategy of Technology, 1970

There is no simple escape from this dilemma. Suppose that you are the Secretary of Defense, and you must recommend a military budget.

You have several choices.

1. Make severe cutbacks in the defense budget. This will leave more money in the hands of the taxpayers, and allow more investment in the nation's economy. Without a strong economy we are finished anyway; while

if the economy is sufficiently strong, we will be able to afford a much larger defense establishment.

2. Invest in military research and development. This can be coupled with (1). Some military research will aid the civilian economy anyway. We mean here real development studies, not merely paper studies and patches.

3. Buy the weapons available today, so that the troops can become familiar with them and learn to maintain them; so that they become *operational* weapons systems.

These choices come up time after time. You have a billion dollars; do we invest that in development of military lasers, or do we buy a new aircraft carrier? The choice is not obvious. Without forces in being, small conflicts become big, and small wars can grow into large ones.

Ready availability of forces can stop the escalations before they start. During the Eisenhower Administration, the First Lebanon Crisis was ended in 24 hours, at cost of one Marine sergeant wounded by his own pistol.

As I write this, the butcher's bill for the Second Lebanon Crisis is not yet known, nor has it ended. Lebanon remains occupied by Syrians, Israelis, and a "peacekeeping force" of US and Italian Marines, and French paratroopers.

The Iranian situation was vastly complex, but it was certainly affected by our lack of forces in being. One may legitimately debate whether Iran is better off under the Mullahs than it was under the Shah, but the fact is that we had insufficient forces in being—including aircraft carriers—to insure the stability of the royal regime. We certainly were unable to stabilize the (very shortlived) "constitutional monarchy" the Shah attempted to leave behind him. Whether or not we *should* have done so is not at issue: the fact is that we had not the forces in being to do so, and every time when we might have intervened, the requirements had grown beyond our means. Even after Iran fell, we had nothing capable of rescuing the hostages.

As I write this, one Libyan Crisis has just ended, apparently without bloodshed. The US carrier force in the Mediterranean, plus the AWACS (Airborne Warning and Control Systems) aircraft stationed in Egypt, were sufficient. One can only speculate on what might have happened had they not existed, as one can only speculate on what might have happened in the Falklands had England not retained her diminished fleet.

You have a sum of money. You may spend it on two wings of the best existing military aircraft, and thus have a force within two years.

You can also spend it to procure two wings of much better advanced aircraft to be delivered in ten years. If you choose the second option, your over-all military capabilities will probably be enhanced due to new technology developed as part of the procurement.

That's ten years from now. Meanwhile, you will NOT have the best equipment for the period of 2 through 8 years.

In combat, there are few prizes for second place, and none at all for what you would have had next year.

There's one more problem. You may not *really* have those choices at all. You may decide to gulp hard, fight your service chiefs, and go for the top technological weapons in the future—only to discover that the money you saved by not buying today's weapons did not go to military R&D, nor was it left in taxpayers' pockets where it might stimulate the economy. It went instead for a new social program, one that absorbs money at exponentially increasing rates—one that has become an "entitlement" that the courts will not let the Congress eliminate.

Toward the close of the 1960's, a number of analysts, alas including me, considered the "war bonus": the funds which would be available once the horrendous expenses of the Vietnam War were ended. We thought long and hard about that money: should it be used to modernize the force, to develop new weapons, to attract recruits for an all-volunteer military, or be returned to the taxpayers?

We need not have been concerned.

A last note: reasonable and informed people of good will can and do disagree, aye, strongly disagree, on this matter. It is one of the most complex and difficult decisions of our age. No one, liberal or conservative, wants to spend more than necessary on defense. The liberal wants the money for other reasons; the conservative doesn't believe the government is entitled to the money unless there's a pressing national need.

There are, however, persons not of good will who will muddy the waters: who will attack R&D spending on the grounds that the money is needed for operational weapons systems, then attack the operational systems because they are obsolete. They are poltroons; and alas, their name is legion, for they are many.

FINAL MUSTER
by
Rick Rubin

"Gold may not get you good soldiers," Niccolo Machiavelli wrote, "but good soldiers can always get you gold."

That's one half the problem. What happens if you no longer need good soldiers?

FINAL MUSTER
by
Rick Rubin

Coming out of stasis is a peculiar sensation. Life returns first to your brain, and for a second you are aware that the rest of you is dead—not just asleep but actually without life. You are standing there in your stasis cubicle, heavily loaded with equipment, and your body is dead. But you don't fall down, and the juice returns to the big muscles of your legs and arms and chest and then to all of the minor muscles and blood to veins and arteries and finally to every tiny capillary. Then you are awake, and you step out into the world.

The sun was halfway up the east side of the sky, and across the parade ground I could see the barracks and ordnance buildings and mess halls and other structures of Fort Morris shimmering in the rising heat waves. Lieutenant Rolf Baker, my platoon leader, was standing in front of the bank of cubicles that held myself and three other sergeants. I threw him a salute.

"Good morning, Sergeant Oskowski," he said.

"Good morning, sir," I said. "They woke us late this time."

"Later than you think, Sergeant. Three hundred years late. It's 2516."

"You don't say! Three hundred years without a war. Who finally upset the applecart, sir?"

"I'm afraid I don't know. I don't even know who we're fighting."

"It's pretty unusual for them not to tell us right off."

"There's supposed to be a formation in an hour, Oskowski. We'll find out then. Better go wake your men."

To my left the other three sergeants were coming out of their stasis cubicles. Around us the whole Regimental Combat Team was coming to life, 5000 officers and men stepping out of deep-freeze, ready and able to fight anybody's war. We mobilize down through the ranks—Colonel Moss our C.O. is unfrozen by the civilian authorities, he wakes four LT. colonels, they wake four more each, and so on down through majors to captains to lieutenants to squad leaders like myself, who wake their squads. We come out of our stasis cubicles fully armed and in prime condition, ready to be fed, briefed and move in less than an hour if necessary.

In the old Greek myth, the man planted dragon's teeth, and fighting men sprang up out of the ground. I can never quite get the analogy out of my mind, seeing the regiment come out of their stasis cubicles. The difference is that in the myth the soldiers fell to fighting among themselves, while the 45th Regimental Combat Team comes out a disciplined unit.

Unfreezing consists of throwing just one switch per man. I went down the row that held my squad throwing the switches, then sat down in front and started checking over my tommygun. Of course it wasn't actually a tommygun, the old twentieth-century weapon. More properly, it was a rapid fire blaster. Model 2079—a cross between a flame thrower and a junior-size atomic cannon with a miniaturized back pack for power and a rifle-shaped nozzle—but somehow calling it a tommygun makes it more personal to me.

My squad started to step out and form up. I let them stretch and yawn and make their tired old jokes. At the far end I noted that two new men had replaced Miller and Chavez, killed at the tag end of the Afro-Asian war 300 years before. I made a note to see if either of the replacements had come in lately. They might throw some light of those 300 long years of apparent peace when we'd stood cold and dead in our stasis cubicles without a war to fight.

Those inexplicable 300 years faintly disturbed me. At least, something disturbed me, for this muster day felt somehow different from the ones in the past. The time before there had been 75 years between wars—by far the longest period of peace since the founding of the

stasis army, but the war we had come out to fight had
been the roughest, too. The armies of the Western Hemisphere had fought all of Afro-Asia for three bloody years.
It was during the Afro-Asian thing that I got my third
stripe and rocker and a squad of my own. Seventy-five
years before that, as a corporal, I'd fought Brazuritina,
the four-country block of southern South America. And
before that the intervals had been shorter yet; fifteen
years, seven years, twenty years, ten years.

So something must have changed out there in the
civilian world, or else they must have found another
way to fight their wars. In the bright sun of this 300-
year-late muster day, it would have been nice to know
what had happened. But why should a soldier care? A
war is a war. You die as dead from anyone's weapon,
and one war is pretty much like another.

That typical soldier's attitude, I suppose, was why
they began to store us away between wars. Soldiers
make lousy citizens in peacetime. And a good peacetime
soldier is likely as not to make a lousy wartime one. So
they perfected the system of stasis, and we volunteered
to wait out the between-war intervals in our steel and
plastic cubicles, each man with name and service record
on his cubicle door, waiting for the bands to begin to
play.

My squad formed up rapidly, standing sharp in a
ramrod-straight row. I walked to one end and passed in
front of them, making a casual sort of inspection.

"Good morning, Staff-Sergeant Oskowski," Filippi the
rocket and missle man said. "Did you enjoy your beauty
rest?"

"Yes thank you, Private First-Class Filippi," I said.
"I've slept ever so much better since I moved out of
range of your snoring."

"Hullo, Sarge," Orozco said. He was the flame thrower,
a broadfaced boy of Mexican descent, quiet and shy but
efficient.

"Hello, Orozco," I said. "How's your cigarette lighter?"

"Hey, Sarge," Corporal Ryan the demolition man said.
"What's with the music?"

The funny thing was that I hadn't until Ryan mentioned it even noticed the music. For the P.A. system
was serenading us with sounds of violins and muted

horns, soft chamber orchestra music instead of the marches and war songs we customarily woke to.

"I don't know, Ryan," I said. "And that's not all I don't know. It's a strange muster day—that's for sure."

"What else?" Yamamoto, our vehicle and engineering man, said.

"I don't know who we're supposed to be fighting," I said. "All I know is what year it is."

They waited to hear. I walked down the rest of the line, past Johnson, the other tommygunner, and the two new men, Bill Chestnut, a Sioux Indian and the new squad sniper, and Charles LaBonte, a thin-faced, black-haired man, older than most recruits, assigned to us as a corpsman.

"It's 2516," I said finally. "You boys have had a nice three-hundred-year nap."

I got the effect I was aiming for. They gasped, almost in unison. Then they started to buzz, guessing among themselves what was up, until I told them to knock it off. Around us other squads were forming up, and platoons, and companies, and battalions, and finally, if you could see it all as one unit, the entire Regimental Combat Team. Dust rose into the midmorning air and orders were barked and men scratched and belched and shuffled into lines. The lieutenant came over.

"Any news, sir?" I said.

"Nothing, Sergeant," he said. "Your squad all right?"

"All present and accounted for, sir. Nobody skipped into town last night I guess."

We both chuckled at the hairy old joke about the soldier slipping out after stasis check and coming back a doddering old man the next morning. He would have been a hell of an old man this time, after 300 years.

The lieutenant inspected my squad, then sent us off to the mess hall for breakfast. I double-timed the boys over, getting the kinks out, and we filed in and went through the line.

The cooks were civilians. A soldier's job, after all, is to fight. Not to cook or clean up or any of the other menial jobs they used to have soldiers do, but to stick to his trade. Civilians do those things.

Civilians—We don't dislike them and we don't love them. They're another kind of people. Peace lovers, family men, businessmen. Day-to-day people, who live life in any dull, boring way that it comes. They aren't interested in excitement, in proving themselves under fire and learning the final truth that you can only learn in combat. They just want to live. In a way they're sane and we're crazy. But we are what we are.

So we fight their wars. After the war is over we have a big party and celebrate. And that time the civilians start being glad that we're going back into stasis soon. We're not particularly delicate about our pleasures. We take women where we find them, and of course, they're often somebody else's woman. We get drunk and we raise hell and then the civilians hate our guts and they're glad when we go back into deep-freeze. But a few minor indignities are worth the service we perform of fighting their wars for them.

By the next time they've forgotten how much they hated us, or else they are a whole new bunch of civilians. They're glad we're coming back out to fight their wars. They feed us a real good breakfast that first muster-day morning out of deep-freeze.

This is as good a time as any to mention that of course it's not really deep-freeze. It's a combination of temperature and electricity and intravenous drugs and radiation, all wrapped into one package. Which doesn't matter in the least. You stand in the cubicle, and it feels like going to sleep very fast; and when you wake up, no matter how much later, it's like tomorrow. But in another way it's not like tomorrow. You're vaguely aware, in stasis, of the time going by. Not bored, not restless, just vaguely aware. The years roll by and the world changes around you. They keep you dusted, and they keep all of the buildings in vacuum, and the world changes around you. Then someone flips Colonel Moss's switch, and we come out to fight their wars. To fight because it's our job and because that's the one thing that we all love, we slightly crazy soldiers who could never adjust to humdrum peacetime lives.

During that fine civilian-cooked breakfast, eggs and ham and flapjacks and preserves and juice and toasted muffins and coffee, I talked to the two new men.

From Bill Chesnut, the sniper, I could learn little. He'd come into the outfit only a couple of years after we went back into stasis in 2198. He had a pretty typical story. He was a wild kid, always getting into trouble and when he was nineteen he killed a man in a street fight. It wasn't particularly Chesnut's fault, or the other man's either, for that matter, but he was tried and sentenced to 30 years in the penitentiary. Then they offered to let him join the army instead. He jumped at the chance.

A lot of men come in that way, and in the army it's never held against them. The army, nowadays, is about the only remaining place for a man with a combative nature.

Anyway, Chesnut enlisted and went through basic training, a year of being taught the tricks of the trade by veterans too old to be worth cold storage. Chesnut even liked training, which is no snap, better than he liked civilian life. That's the best sign of the making of a soldier and I knew that I had a man who would pull his weight.

Charles LaBonte, the new corpsman, was a different matter. His trouble was restlessness rather than wanting to fight, but it made him unfit for civilian life no less. Born in 2291, he'd found the world a dull place. Adventure was dead; the world was calm and uneventful. From the time that he got out of school until he was thirty, he wandered around, trying to find a place where he fitted in. In 2322 he enlisted in the army, figuring it as the only place where there might be some excitement.

"It was a stainless-steel world out there," he said. "Everything was worked out and nothing ever happened. No wars, no revolutions, no big changes. Ever since the Afro-Asian war, the people kept anything interesting from happening."

"Sounds pretty bad," I said.

"It was. One year after another, everything the same. People just moved along on the same level; never sad, never happy, never excited."

"Well, they must not be getting along so well now," I said. "If they were they wouldn't have called us out."

"That's right. Besides, it's been nearly two hundred years since I came in. Lord, think of that! Two hundred years. Everybody I knew is dead. My family is long gone. I feel alone in the world."

"We're your family now," I said. I could remember when I felt the same way, after the first time in stasis, just a kid of twenty and suddenly twenty-three years younger than my old friends. Even so, my friends had at least still been alive. LeBonte's were dust by now.

The bungle blew assembly and we came out of the mess hall and walked back to the parade ground and formed up with the rest of Able Company. The regiment drew up in a long line, like on parade, facing a platform that had been set up near the center of the field. On the platform were Colonel Moss, the C.O., a couple of generals probably down from division or corps, two or three light colonels and four civilians dressed in limp gray and brown and pastel-colored clothes that I took to be the current civilian style.

Colonel Moss introduced one of the civilians to us, a Mr. Karonopolis, the Mayor of the nearby city of Linkhorn. From Colonel Moss's first words I detected a tension of some sort. He made the introduction in almost insultingly few words, biting off each syllable as if it were bitter. Then he stepped back, very stiff and soldierly, and stood in a ramrod sort of parade rest.

Mr. Karonopolis took over the microphone.

"Make yourselves comfortable, gentlemen," he said. Nobody moved of course.

"On behalf of the local and federal government, the civil population, and of myself I wish to make you welcome to the year 2516," he said. "We of the twenty-sixth century feel that we know you men, even though you do not yet know us. In school we have studied your brave exploits of the past."

So he continued. It was all very kind and pleasant, but we had heard the same things, or variations of them, every time we had come out of stasis. He didn't say anything we didn't know until he began to describe the events since we went into cold-storage.

He told of a world of social, scientific and philosophic progress, of cultural and intellectual advances and internation accord. The world he described ran smoothly. Nations were at peace with nations, individuals with other individuals. It was a world that had no need for an army—even a stasis one.

He was leading up all through the speech to what he

said next, and yet the idea was so difficult to grasp that when he finally said it in plain words it was as though he had dropped a bomb on us.

He told us that we were to be decommissioned and returned to civilian status.

I think he expected us to cheer. He was a civilian, and had no understanding of soldiers' minds.

A murmuring grew in the ranks, and I was a part of the murmuring, arguing to myself the impossibility of returning to a civilian world, a strange and incomprehensible civilian world 300 years more advanced than the last one I had seen, returning from war and excitement and the only trade I knew or wanted to know to a humdrum civilian world made of foam rubber and stainless steel.

The colonel stood on the platform in the blazing sun, his face a mask. The music tried to soothe us, soft and calm. And the murmuring grew louder.

A soldier stood out of the ranks in the next company, a tommygunner like myself, waving his weapon in the air. "Like hell!" he shouted. "Like hell I'll become a civilian. What do you think I am? You're crazy!"

His sergeant ordered the tommygunner back into ranks but the order lacked the conviction that any order needs. So the man stood and shouted at the civilian and the murmur grew, like angry bees.

"Who do you think you're talking to?" a voice shouted.

"Damn fool civilian," another roared.

"You can't do away with war," my lieutenant said, half to himself. "There'll always be wars. It's human nature."

On the platform the civilians registered first surprise and then dismay. In their lifetimes none of them had ever met a soldier. How could they be expected to understand them? And probably they had never heard any of the soldierly language that was pouring at them now.

They put their heads together in a conference, and then Mr. Karonopolis stepped over to the colonel and spoke to him. The Old Man stood at his rigid parade rest and only shook his head negatively. The Mayor spoke again, more strongly it seemed to me. This time the colonel ignored him entirely.

They tried whatever they had tried on Colonel Moss

on the two generals from higher headquarters but got
no better response. Then another of the civilians stepped
to the microphone.

"Gentlemen, please," he said. "There is no value in
this. What is the good of an army without wars? Surely
you don't want to remain in stasis forever, waiting for a
war that will never come?"

The murmur grew to a roar.

"We don't intend to thrust you naked into a hostile
world," he said. "You will be retained into any field you
want. Or you can simply live, not work at all. You can
have homes and wives and cars. You can enjoy life
now—you've earned enjoyment."

Then his voice was blotted out by the angry buzzing
of the men. Even the men of my own squad were
shouting. "We're soldiers—we don't want to be anything else," Ryan yelled.

"You can't abolish wars,"Filippe screamed.

"Go to hell!"

"Shut up you bastard!"

And standing there at attention I tried to picture myself as a civilian, living out the rest of my life, forty or
fifty years probably, for I was only twenty-eight, living a
humdrum day-to-day existence with no excitement or
danger but only the routine of a civilian's sort life.

And yet the civilians were right. What use was there
for an army if there were to be no more wars? Could
they really have abolished wars?

The civilians on the platform huddled together in conference again and then the Mayor approached the colonel and this time the colonel nodded his head to whatever
the Mayor said.

I will say this for the civilians—they were facing soldiers for the first time in their lives, and they were
obviously surprised by the reaction they'd gotten but
through all of the shouting and swearing they had shown
no sign of fear. Perhaps it was the bravery of men facing
something that they don't know is dangerous. In any
case, after the colonel had agreed to whatever they had
asked they left the platform and climbed into a groundcar—a smooth-skinned bug without any wheels or visible motor and drove away.

The colonel approached the microphone, and the roar

dropped to complete silence in a second and we could hear the soothing music again.

"Fall the troops into the barracks," the colonel said. "Set up for garrison duty."

So we marched across the parade grounds to the barracks, 5,000 strong. Somewhere up the line, someone started cadence count and the entire regiment joined in; 5,000 bass voices drowning out the music of the P.A. system. And somehow it did not sound like the last time we would march.

The barracks were just as we had left them, not even dusty after 300 years in a vacuum. I had the men break out their barracks bags and set up their gear. By the time that was done, the word came down to choose three men for overnight pass. I let Filippe and Ryan and Orozco go, while the rest of us settled down to spend the afternoon at poker and talk.

After a while, Johnson and Chesnut and I went over to the P.X., which the civilians had opened, and joined the beer drinkers in the slop chute. The main topic of conversation, naturally, centered around what the civilians had said and what was going to happen.

"They're nuts if they think they've done away with wars," Sergeant Mangini from Charlie Company said. "Wars are human nature. You can't change that."

"They say there haven't been any in three hundred years," I reminded him.

"So what? There've been other times when there weren't any wars for a long time. But they always ended. They'll need us again."

"Maybe we'll have to start our own war," Sergeant Olivier from H.Q. Company said. "If these civilians have gotten so soft, maybe we'll have to wake them up a little. For the good of the species, you know?"

"You're darn right," Chesnut said. "We'll just have to start our own war."

"You're getting pretty salty for a guy just out of Basic," I said.

"Look, Sarge, if they send us back to civilian life, you know where I'll be? In prison. They'll make me serve out my sentence."

"We'll all be in prison soon enough," Mangini said. "We're not suited for civilian life—not one of us. We'll be too wild and violent for them, and they'll end by putting us all behind bars."

"They said they'd reeducate us," I defended.

"They can't reeducate us any more than they can teach civilians how to be soldiers," Mangini said. "A man's born a soldier, he dies a soldier. He just can't be taught to live like a civilian."

After a while, I drifted back to the barracks. I found orders from the captain saying that Tuesday (I have no idea what day it actually was—we always call muster day Monday) we were to start regular training schedule.

After supper I came back to the barracks and lay on my bunk trying to think the thing through. All over the barracks the men were talking about the demobilization, and soon they had something new to talk about. Long before any self-respecting soldier would have come in off an overnight pass, the men who had been in town started drifting in. Everyone started talking about what they'd seen that had driven them back so early.

At ten, Filippi and Orozco came into the barracks.

"C'mere, Filippi," I said.

He ambled over and sat on the side of my bunk.

"It's a hell of a world out there, Sergeant," he said.

"Let's hear about it," I said.

"It's not that it looks so very different. Their cars and choppers and airplanes are about the same—a little smoother and quieter, but you can still tell which is which. Mostly the whole thing is just quieter. And the city seems smaller. More parks, more trees, everything moving slow and easy like in a small town."

"What about the people?"

"They've changed. They're relaxed and easygoing. They don't seem to ever hurry, and they don't have a care in the world. Everyone just walks around talking and taking it easy. And you can't get them mad or start a fight to save yourself."

"You tried to start a fight?"

"Sure. All of us tried. But no one could get the civilians riled up. Say something to them, and they'd smile and pat you on the back and talk about it like it was a specimen under a microscope. And if a soldier just walked up and took a swing, a couple of civilians would hold him and talk to him until he didn't want to fight anymore."

"Maybe they're just a bunch of cowards. That doesn't prove anything."

"Well, the women are different too, Sarge. That ought to prove something. You try to pick one up, and she doesn't get mad or scared. She just smiles and says she'd rather not. Or, if she's willing, it's nothing like you expect. If she feels like making love, she does it and then says thank you and just goes away. No trauma, no love, no crying and wailing about virtue."

Filippi went off to tell the rest of the men about what he'd seen in Linkhorn, and I lay on my sack and thought about what he'd said. I'd been brought up to believe that people don't change, but if what Filippi had said was true it looked like maybe I was taught wrong. I made up my mind to take a pass into town Tuesday night and see for myself.

The next morning we woke to the same soothing music, but we breakfasted and started training, trying to drown out the music with our shouts. We marched and practiced squad tactics and ran the infiltration and obstacle courses and fired our weapons. About three in the afternoon, we knocked off and another three men from each squad were allowed to go on pass. I put on my Class A summer uniform, still well pressed and dapper from 300 years earlier, and took the bus into Linkhorn.

As Filippi had said, the city seemed to have shrunk. Not in area exactly, and perhaps not even in population, but the buildings were lower and there were more trees and grass and parks. The machines were less noticeable. Not that there weren't any, but you just didn't notice them. The cars were sleek and mild colored, moving smoothly along without wheels or motor sounds, the copters rose on silent rotors, everything seemed muted. The moving sidewalks—the pride of Linkhorn the last time I'd been there—were gone, and the citizens seemed to actually enjoy walking, strolling arm-in-arm, talking and laughing together. The town was so peaceful that it made me nervous.

Of course I had to try to start a fight. I walked into a civilian going full tilt and knocked him to the pavement.

"Why the hell don't you watch where you're going?" I said.

He picked himself up and dusted himself off. "Come now," he said, "We're both aware that you ran into me on purpose."

"You want to make something of it?"

"On the contrary. But tell me, you're a sergeant, aren't you? I'm rather unfamiliar with the rating system. I haven't had a chance to talk to one of you men yet."

"I'm a staff-sergeant."

"How interesting. That's a position of some authority, isn't it?"

"Yeah, I command a squad."

"A squad? Oh yes, the basic small unit of a military force."

"That's right, eight men."

"That must be challenging. Tell me, how much of the decision-making function do you exercise in the field?"

I was starting to answer when I caught on to what he was trying to do, but he seemed so sincerely interested in me that it was hard not to go along with him. "Quit trying to change the subject," I said.

"Why, certainly, if you wish. But I really am interested."

"I think I'll knock your teeth down your throat."

"I hope you won't," he said. "And after all, it wouldn't prove much. I quite agree that you're a better fighter than I am."

"What'dya mean by that?" I said. I kept looking for fear in his face, or anger, even, but there was none. He spoke slowly and evenly and seemed really more interested in what I was saying than in saving his skin.

"I'm a fairly decent athlete," he said, "but quite untrained as fighter."

"You're a coward," I said.

"I suppose that in your frame of reference I do seem a coward. I don't want to fight and I won't be angered. But from my standpoint, Sergeant, I'm not a coward at all. I'm simply not disturbed by what you've said. I know myself too well—my faults, my weaknesses, my strengths—and your accusations haven't added any new perceptions about myself. And if they had, I would be more likely to thank you than fight you."

I wasn't getting anywhere and my heart wasn't in it anymore anyway. Somehow, although he wasn't more than a few years older than me, he managed to remind me of my father, or of how my father should have been. I moved on. I had to try a girl to satisfy myself about what Filippi had said about them.

It was twilight by then, and I was walking through one of the rolling green parks that dotted the city. The girl was small and slim with long brown hair worn straight down her back, her face young and pert.

"Hi-ya, babe, let's you and me go off somewhere and make it," I said.

She laughed a tinkling sort of laugh and said, "My name is Jodi."

"I'm Kenny Oskowski," I said. "Want to try a real man for a change?"

"I would like to know you better, if that's what you mean."

"Sure, babe. Let's find a hotel and get acquainted."

"I'd rather go for a walk. It's an awfully nice evening. Wouldn't you just as soon go for a walk?"

"Okay, we'll walk," I said. "I'm in no hurry."

We walked. We had a milkshake together. (Me—a milkshake! But somehow I didn't need whiskey with her, though she wouldn't have minded if I'd wanted one.) We went bowling and walked some more and ended by sitting on a bench holding hands and listening to a band concert in the park.

At 10:30 I walked her home, and she was like my little sister instead of the pickup I'd tried for. I walked her to the door, feeling warm and hoping for a single chaste good-night kiss.

"Would you like to stay all night with me, Kenny?" she said.

"I didn't think you were that kind of girl, Jodi," I said.

"What kind of girl? I like you. I enjoy your company."

"But what about love?"

"I suppose that is love. Love isn't something you can pin down."

"Do you want to get married?"

"No, why? I like you now, or maybe love you, but that doesn't necessarily have anything to do with living with you for the rest of my life."

So in the end we made love and I stayed with her all night, but gently and pleasantly, for its own sake and for our own. And in the morning I went back to the army, feeling as I had never felt before after an overnight pass, happy and at peace with the world, without a hangover or a sense of guilt or any bawdy stories to tell the troops.

And at Fort Morris I found the soldiers still talking war. Demanding that a war be made for them, or that Colonel Moss lead them against the civilians.

We trained all that day—more firing range, more squad tactics, more physical conditioning. In the afternoon all of the men who had not had their passes yet were given them and sent into Linkhorn.

They came straggling back, bitter and angry and frustrated, most of them before ten o'clock, having been unable to start any fights or cause any trouble. In the barracks they joined in little groups to talk of what they had seen and what they wanted to do to the civilians.

"Man, they're dull," Sergeant Olivier said. "Nicest thing we can do for them is to shoot them up a little and wake them up."

"You can't even start a fistfight with one of them," I said. "How the hell do you expect to start a war?"

"Close up we have to talk to them," he said. "You don't have to talk to start a war. You just go in shooting."

"But why do you want to start a war? What have they done to you?"

"When did you start being a peace lover?" Olivier said.

"Maybe last night. It seems a pretty happy world out there. Why should we destroy it?"

"Because it's our job. You think a society like that one can last? Hell no. They'll fall apart from sheer inertia."

"I doubt it. But anyway, why should you care?"

"I'm a soldier."

"Not any more. You're going to be a civilian now, Sergeant Olivier."

"You think I could stand to live like that? Day after day without any excitement? I'm a soldier and I've got to fight."

"There aren't any more wars."

"There will be. If not now, eventually. Without us this

fool country will be defenseless. It's our duty to wake them up."

Olivier spoke for all of them. Their faith in the future of wars was unshakable. War could no more be outgrown than sex.

"I see it this way," Filippi said. "Colonel Moss will get fed up with waiting and move us against the city. After the city, the state. We'll join up with the rest of the army and get this world back into the old groove."

I quit arguing with them. I suddenly saw that I was the only one who didn't think that it was our duty to destroy the society outside. And as Olivier and Filippi and the others talked of their plans for starting a war I realized that I was going to be fighting against them if they did. I retreated to my bunk to think.

Down the room I saw LaBonte, the new corpsman, doing the same. After a while I got up and walked down and sat on his bunk.

"What do you think?" I said.

"Think about what, Sarge? I was just resting."

"No, LaBonte, you were thinking. You're not a soldier like those guys. You came in for excitement, not blood. You're thinking the same as I am."

"How's that, Sarge? How are you thinking?"

I looked around the room carefully. Speaking my mind was dangerous in a barracks full of soldiers looking for a fight. But no one was near, and I felt pretty sure of LaBonte.

"I'm thinking that if these guys move on the civilians, I'll have to be on the civilian side," I said.

"You're crazy," he said.

"I don't know if I could stand living like they do, but this society looks pretty sane and honest to me. I think they really have outgrown war. I'm going into town tonight and warn the civilians. And if worse comes to worse, I'm going to help them defend themselves."

"That's treason," LaBonte said. "Don't talk treason to me."

"I thought you might want to come along."

"All right, maybe I do feel like you do, Sarge. But if we went in there and the army started a war, they'd gun us down on sight as traitors."

"You're probably right. But I'm going anyway. I've got to try to help."

"Not me."

"I'm going tonight. Are you going to report me?"

"No. I won't do that. Not until tomorrow at least."

"All right. But if you tell, I'll kill you for it."

"I won't tell."

I walked back to my bunk and lay working over my plan and thinking and waiting for lights out. Across the room the buzz of war talks continued. Taps blew at 11:00 and the men began to sack out and slowly the talk died and the barracks became still. I lay and waited and stared at the ceiling until 2:00, waiting for the last whisper to die out and the last man to fall asleep. Then I got up and dressed silently. I took my tommygun and Filippi's rocket launcher and some of Ryan's demolition equipment, fuses and explosives, and tiptoed out of the barracks, watching LaBonte as I passed to see if he would make an alarm. But he lay still.

There were two guards on duty at the gate, lazing around with cigarettes hanging out of their mouths.

"Where'ya heading with all that stuff, Sarge?" one of them asked. I recognized him as Don Carpenter from Charlie Company, a balding overaged corporal, back down to private for about the tenth time since the last war.

"Going into town to stir up a little excitement, Carp," I said.

"Going to get the jump on the rest of the boys, huh?"

"That's right. Start a little war of my own before the real one."

"Aw, Sarge, you know there ain't going to be any more wars. The civilians told us so."

"That's right. I forgot."

"I ought to check your pass, Sarge. And I ought to make you leave that hardware here."

"You ought to, but you won't."

"Nope. It's too quiet for me. If you can stir up some action, I'm for it."

So I passed out through the gate and marched down the road under the cool midnight sky, staggering under the tools of war.

I was almost to the center of Linkhorn before I saw

anyone. Then it was what looked like policemen, two of them in a city car, but they carried no weapons that I could see and they didn't talk like cops.

"Hello, soldier," one of them said. "Nice night."

"Take me to whoever runs this town, will you?" I said.

"We'll be happy to. But what's the rush, Sergeant? Let us buy you a cup of coffee or a drink. We'd like to hear about the army."

"Look," I said, "this is pretty urgent."

"I'm sure it is," the cop said. "You wouldn't be walking into the city this late at night with all that equipment unless you had a pretty important reason. Why not tell me about it? Perhaps I can help you."

"Turn off the psychology," I said. "I'm on your side—you don't have to soothe me down. I came to warn you that the army is likely to attack you. I want to help you defend yourself."

"Why that's certainly kind of you, but I wouldn't imagine that the army will do anything this late at night. Come on and have a drink and rest."

I turned my tommygun toward him. "Goddamn it," I said. "Take me to whoever runs this place and quit psychoanalyzing me or I'll start the war right here and now."

He just sat there and grinned at me, cool and brave yet friendly. After a minute I lowered the tommygun and grinned back.

"You were taking a hell of a chance," I said.

"I don't think so. You came in to help us. If you'd come looking for a fight, I would have reacted differently."

"Have it your own way. But remember that I do want to help. And that army isn't going to sit out there forever, waiting for a war."

I climbed in the patrol car and they drove me to an all-night restaurant. We sat for a while shooting the breeze. Once again, like the man I'd talked to, they seemed genuinely interested in me personally. After an hour they drove me to a hotel and got me a complimentary room. No one made any attempt to relieve me of my weapons, and before the cop left, he promised that a city official would be by to talk to me in the morning.

I didn't even try to sleep. I lay on the hotel bed and

thought about what I'd done and what was likely to follow until the horizon showed rose and pink and the sky got blue and things began to move in the city around me.

The sun was well up before the city official called for me. He introduced himself as Stephen French, a short man in his middle forties, well built, gray at the temples and mild-mannered. The city council, he told me, was sitting in session, considering the army situation. He could conduct me to them so that I could tell them what I knew. In a few words, he made me feel very important.

We stopped downstairs for breakfast in the hotel dining room and over bacon and eggs Mr. French told me what he knew of the situation.

The army was not fully unfrozen all over the country. About a third of the units had been taken out of stasis to be decommissioned. The civilians had wanted to do it slowly in order to prevent the sudden influx of men from unbalancing society.

The plan to decommission the army had been brewing for some years but they had waited to make sure that war was actually no longer a threat. That the soldiers would not want to become civilians (and all over the country it was the same) had been something they hadn't foreseen. A gap in their logic, Mr. French admitted with a wry smile. So now, all over the country, they were faced with angry, rebellious soldiers.

"What sort of weapons do you have, sir?" I asked.

"None. We gave up using weapons years ago. Even the police don't use weapons anymore. But then we haven't a crime problem anymore. About all the police do is help cats out of trees and look for stray children."

"You must have some sort of weapons. Or at least machines to make them."

"Yes, probably we could produce them. But even with weapons, we're not soldiers. We couldn't stand up against the army."

"Couldn't you produce one big bomb and wipe them out?"

He gave me a strange look. "No, I don't think we'll do that. That isn't our way."

"You won't have any way if you don't. They'll wipe

you out. What about a defensive weapon? Something to stop tanks from running and guns from shooting?"

"Yes, I believe we could produce something like that. But it wouldn't solve anything. Your soldiers could wipe us out in hand-to-hand combat."

I gave up on the weapon angle. "Society has certainly changed since the last war," I said. "What happened?"

What he told me was too complicated to put down here. Basically, after the West had defeated the Afro-Asians, the Easterners had turned away from machinery and returned to an emphasis on meditation, the mind and philosophy. And, then, from the defeated, these things had swept the world, creating a worldwide society that used machines but was not very concerned with them. The important things became thought, self-analysis, and meditation, integrated with the Western behaviorial sciences.

The change had grown from within rather than by law. Finally the time had come when everyone was concerned with improving himself, with dominating his own ego, and seeking individual perfection rather than dominating others. Everyone could look back on a happy childhood, where formerly bad childhoods had always bred the dangerous people. Competition for gain and power died away and what remained was competition for the pleasure of measuring yourself against others, rather than to feed your ego.

Emotions were as highly respected as the intellect as long as they did not hurt others. People grew beyond the need for constant external entertainment. They found their pleasures in learning and creating. Of course, psychology and the other behaviorial sciences advanced tremendously. What the soldiers had run into when they tried to pick fights were competent lay-psychoanalysts.

"But that won't save you from the army," I told Mr. French. "You can't talk to an army."

"We realize that now," he said. "We aren't underestimating the danger of the situation we've gotten ourselves into."

We came to the city hall, a modest stone and glass building set in the center of a park, and Mr. French led me in. It was all very casual. He took me to a man sitting at a desk by a tall set of doors and said, "I've brought the soldier who came in from the Fort last night."

"Take him right in," the man at the desk said. There were no guards or messengers or feverish conferences, and I was still carrying my weapons when we walked through the doors and found ourselves in the council chambers, a wide room with lots of windows and a large round table in the middle around which sat a group of simply dressed men and women.

"Welcome," the man at the head of the table said. I recognized him as Mr. Karonopolis, the Mayor. "We appreciate your having come to help us."

"I want to do anything I can," I said.

"Please sit down," he said. "We would like to ask a few questions."

I sat. Mr. Karonopolis introduced me to the other members of the council and then they began to question me.

"What do you think are the feelings of most of the soldiers?"

"They're angry," I said. "They want to remain soldiers, to fight. They're afraid that you'll force them to be civilians."

"But why is it that they don't want to become civilians?"

"It's just not their life. They're soldiers. They look down on civilian life as dull and boring and insignificant."

"But you feel differently?"

"No, not really. I just don't think the army has a right to destroy this society. I don't want to live in it, but it seems too good to destroy."

"Would the other soldiers be willing to destroy it?"

"Yes, sir, I think so."

A murmur ran through the chamber. "How do their officers feel?"

"I don't really know, but I think they pretty much agree."

"Do you think they will decide to attack?"

"That's up to Colonel Moss. The Regiment moves when the colonel tells it to. Until he decides, they'll just stew."

"And if the colonel decides not to move?"

"They'll do only what he tells them. They're soldiers."

They lost interest in me after that and began to talk among themselves.

"May I say something?" I said.

"Certainly, Sergeant Oskowski," the Mayor said.

"Don't you want me to tell you about troop disposition and firepower and that sort of thing?"

"No, I don't think that would help us much," the Mayor said.

"I'm glad you don't, of course. I wouldn't like to have to tell you. I'd feel even more like a traitor. But it seems to me that you aren't taking the right line of defense. All you're interested in is how the soldiers feel. And I can tell you that they feel like starting a war.

"You've got to figure out a defense. I brought in a few weapons. You should be able to improvise more. But you'll be facing five thousand trained soldiers with every kind of modern weapon. You'll never beat them in the open.

"The way I see it, the best thing is to attack them before they attack you. Send out a few carloads of booze and let them get themselves drunk, then go out there in the middle of the night with knives and clubs, picking up their weapons as you kill them.

"I don't know if it will work, but it's the only way to save your society. I can teach you how to use their weapons and tell you how the camp is laid out. I feel like a traitor, but I'll do it anyway. Because if you don't attack first, your society is finished."

I stood there, after my speech—waiting for applause, I suppose. The council members smiled at me, softly and sadly, and finally Major Karonopolis said, "Thank you very much for your expression of loyalty, Sergeant Oskowski. But I am afraid that we can't do any of the things you suggest. You say that we have to defend our society or they will destroy it. But you see, if we do what you suggest, we will have destroyed it ourselves."

I sat down, feeling at the same time like a complete fool and the only sane man in the room. The discussion moved back and forth; mostly concerning itself with whether and how soon the Regiment would attack. Occasionally one of the councilmen would ask me a question but mostly they spoke to each other, like scientists rather than politicans, illustrating their points with case histories from other societies dating back before the Greeks.

Finally it was decided to send another delegation, to see the colonel alone this time and feel out his attitude.

Mr. French, the man who had brought me to the council, told me that I was free to do as I wished, but that he would be happy to show me around the city if I wanted. I accepted his offer and he got a car out of the pool.

He showed me manufacturing plants and colleges and private homes and museums, and yet somehow the tour was less interesting than I had expected. Most of the changes since last I'd seen the city had been inside of the people. The machines were there, of course, doing all of the arduous work, and the new buildings and new products. But the people considered them only necessary, not important. The buildings—in fact, the entire style of architecture—was designed to emphasize people, rather than the buildings themselves.

Passing an athletic field, Mr. French and I started talking about track records, and I got a shock. I'd looked upon the civilians as relatively soft and weak, misjudging their pacifism as weakness. But I discovered that the current record for the mile was 2 miles, 3.8 seconds, and the hundred-yard dash was run in 6 seconds flat. Schoolboys polevaulted over 16 feet. They had given up distance javelin throwing when the throws had become so long that the wind was more of a factor than the thrower. Now they threw flat, at targets 250 feet away, almost as far as the record distance when I was young. And nearly everyone participated in one sport or another. Mr. French said that they attributed the fantastic records to control of the mind, for the people weren't any larger or heavier muscled than before. But excellent physical condition was the rule rather than the exception, and the people in general were actually in better shape than my fellow soldiers.

As for the colleges, they no longer issued degrees. People studied for knowledge and took courses on and off during their lives. Classes had become lecture series, and the newspapers printed lists of which lecture series were starting and who was speaking.

Late in the afternoon, Mr. French got word by his

pocket radio that the delegation to Fort Morris had
returned, so we went back to the city hall to hear hear
the news.

Mr. Kolar, the man who had headed the delegation,
analyzed the colonel as feeling himself caught in a
dilemma.

"He is trained to accept civilian control," Mr. Kolar
said. "To do what the civilian authorities tell him. But
we have told him to become a civilian himself, and that
is a command that falls outside of his frame of reference."

"How do you think he will decide?" Mayor Karonopolis
said.

"Right now he's wavering between waiting to see what
will happen and launching an immediate attack. He
instinctively feels that we are wrong, that our society is
deluding itself in thinking that there will be no more
wars."

"Pardon me, Mr. Kolar," I said, "but perhaps if I
returned to the Fort, I could convince the troops about
your society."

"No," he said. "They know what you've done, and
they think of you as a traitor. You would only start
bloodshed, perhaps even tip them into action."

"It seems," the Mayor said, "that we shall have to
solve the colonel's dilemma for him. Mr. Fitzgerald, the
proposed plan was yours. Do you feel prepared to try to
implement it?"

"But do we have the right to manipulate them?" a
Councilwoman asked.

"Perhaps we don't," the Mayor said, "but in the long
run it seems the only way to protect themselves. And
after all, the soldiers have the avowed purpose of protecting society. Mr. Fitzgerald, what do you say?"

A tall, bony-faced man with horn rimmed glasses stood
up at the end of the table. "Yes, Mr. Mayor," he said,
"I'll be happy to try."

The tall man chose two others to accompany him and
they left the room.

"You might as well stay here," the Mayor said. "Mr.
Fitzgerald has a portable radio transmitter in his coat
and we'll be able to listen."

We made ourselves comfortable and waited for the

technicians monitoring Fitzgerald's transmission to cut him in to the wall loudspeaker.

"You'll have to make a decision yourself if our plan succeeds," the Mayor said. "You must decide whether your loyalty is to the Fort or to us."

"I don't see that there's much choice. I can't go back."

"Still, this will mean for the rest of your life. Perhaps we could arrange it so that you could return to the Fort with honor."

"No, sir, I'm afraid that I've already made my choice. I think I'll just have to learn to live here and like it."

"It won't be easy. It's a pleasant society for us, but we all grew up in it. You will miss the excitement and conflict. I doubt if you can ever entirely adjust to our mild way of life."

"I'll just have to try, sir. But you seem pretty sure that you can solve the problem of the army. Can you be that sure? What's your plan?"

"It's a psychological one, and you'll hear it soon enough. Of course there's always an area of doubt. We must wait and see, and hope."

We sat and sipped coffee and waited, the minutes dragging slowly by, until the loudspeaker on the wall crackled into life. It broke into the middle of a conversation between Colonel Moss and Councilman Fitzgerald.

"Colonel, we can't thank you enough for saving us from the plot," Mr. Fitzgerald was saying.

"Long experience has shown that war is human nature," the colonel said.

"Yet the traitors had us convinced."

"They would have disbanded the army, waited a few years, and then struck when you least expected it."

"We see that now, sir."

"The army stands ready to march, Mr. Fitzgerald."

"The time isn't right yet sir. Our enemies are not prepared to attack. It will be three years at the minimum, and we don't believe in attacking first."

"Yes, that is the weakness of democracy. But a noble weakness."

"I suppose that it's best for you to spend those years in training?"

"No, no," the colonel said. "Three years of garrison duty would soften the men."

"Then what do you propose?"

"We shall return to stasis. You must keep a careful watch and alert us just just before hostilities commence. We can be ready to march in an hour, if necessary, but a few days or a week's notice is best."

Councilman Fitzgerald and the colonel talked for a few minutes more, completing plans for the imaginary future war against the traitors, and then the Councilman took his leave, and the radio crackled into silence.

"I suppose that it's unfair to us," the Mayor said next to me.

"You knew that they would choose to return to cold storage, didn't you?"

"Yes, Sergeant. Fitzgerald's plan was predicated on their dislike of garrison duty and their faith in war as a part of human nature. It wasn't too difficult to predict with our knowledge of psychology. Actually, Colonel Moss symbolically repeated the original decision of the army to go into stasis. Do you think that we've done wrong by your comrades?"

"No, sir. I think you've done the best you could."

"We can try waking them one at a time in the future," he said.

"Yes, sir. But they still won't choose civilian life."

And so the next day I rode a helicopter out and watched the Regiment muster on the parade grounds and march back to their cubicles. It was too far to see who was marching my squad. Corporal Ryan, I suppose. They marched back and disbanded, not into civilian life but into perpetual stasis.

Of myself, during the years since then, there isn't much to tell. I wandered around the country. I studied a little at a couple of colleges and tried to find a place and an interest for myself. But there wasn't any, for I was still a soldier. I was restless and lonely and not very adjustable—an old soldier at thirty without a war to fight.

That's why I came back here to Fort Morris and took over maintaining the Fort. Not that a man is needed, for the machines do the work, but it seems more personal for me to care for my old comrades in arms. I check the vacuums of the barracks and ordnance buildings and other buildings and I see to it that the cubicles of my former comrades are dusted and clean, as though they might want to look out of their plastic and steel cubicles. To keep a watch for the enemy, for the war they silently await.

I have watched myself—and listened—for news of the foe, but I have not seen him approach. Years in this time and place have convinced me that, indeed, war and violence have been winnowed out of the human heart and mind. Yet who can say that all the universe is as peaceable as Earth is now? That somewhere, sometime, there will not be beings of this world or some other, bent on doing battle, and only my silent, waiting warrior brothers to oppose them?

As for myself, I live, and therefore daily die. And sometimes stop to look into the cubicle marked *Staff-Sergeant Kenneth Oskowski, Squad Leader, 2nd Platoon, Able Company, 3rd Battalion, 45th Regimental Combat Team.*

The vacant cubicle.

EDITOR'S INTRODUCTION TO:

POEMS
by
Edward C. Garrett, Robert Frazier,
and Steve Rasnic Tem

There is so little market for science fiction poetry that I have become known as a major publisher simply because I try to include some in each of my anthologies.

I think that's a shame.

Garrett's "Parable of the Phantom Limb" arrived not long after "Final Muster". Events like that make me take seriously my friend Barbara Hubbard's concerns with "synchronicity."

Robert Frazier and Steve Rasnic Tem are long-time contributors to my anthologies, and I always look forward to their submissions.

PARABLE OF THE PHANTOM LIMB
by Edward C. Garrett

The world of course is an awful place.
What you need is a little protection.
Take this stick, for instance.
It's like another arm.
You can reach up into trees
or dig holes in the ground.
You can even beat a snake senseless
before it can give you the tongue.
That's right, a stick's a useful thing.
Why, no self-respecting entrepreneur,
be it of shadows or pie in the sky,
would be caught without one in his hands.
But a stick has other uses.
You can sharpen it on a rock
and spear lizards in the sand.
You can even practice hurling,
stampede frightening sounds.
You can poke out the lights in the eyes
that glow in the dark. Yes sir,
there is nothing like a stick.
And sticks are beautiful
don't you think? Not right now, perhaps.
But after awhile, after it's chiseled,
varnished, and carved . . . Gives you
something to do that'll make you proud,
something to talk about when it's raining
outside and the fire is warm.
Everything that's ever happened
can be put on a stick You can even

measure the sky by it's length
or circle the dust with squiggles
and words. Want to know how tall you are?
That's right. Use a stick.
There is no security like a stick.
And dangerous as it is out there,
you'd be a fool to bend over
for a drink of well water. So tell you
what, this being your birthday and all,
and because you have far to go. Here—
open your hand—is the best stick
in the land. No charge. Just go
and learn to use the magic wand.
If it's from point A to point B
you wish to go, just put it under arm
and rest your weight full. That's right!
Good! You're getting it! Stick's like
a third leg or at least you'll never know
when you'll need another one.
How do you feel? Hard to hop and skip?
Well, you'll get used to it.

FORBIDDEN LINES
by Robert Frazier

Cast by some unnamed initiates of gaming
in a forgotten Armageddon,
the *dying thought* still echoes
through the whispering galleries
of sentient minds,
still castles the weak telepathic links
in sentient kinds.
In the bluelight spectra
of the coming image board of years,
it will stain us all with limb-darkening
and forbidden lines of doubt;
as trapped in the isolation
tank of ourselves,
we become both a pawn
of red entropy, pure random, and the infinite,
and a king frozen in check
against the lightless enemy of intellect
within and beyond.
The *dying thought* must wait . . .
stalemate.

TWO POEMS
by
Steve Rasnic Tem

THE NEW WEATHER

On the New Rhine campaign—22 April 2023:
palpable stench of fear amongst the fleshies that day
(if only us metal guys could smell),
anxious talk on the line, us metal guys nodding,
sympathetic to the last, sentimental
about those old fleshies, our brothers—
their eyes blazed-out like soldiers'
since war one, strained and blank,
or so my history tapes tell me,
jittery about "this last gift from Geneva,"
when their government had assured them
"the inhuman aspects not clearly established."

But then the wind, clearly, shifted:
Tabun, Sarin, and Soman, metal carbonyls
(a poetic chant, that, even from a voice box)
just for a starter—stumbling and coughing,
drooling, cramps, pissing in their pants,
twisting and jerking the *danse macabre*
(tapes provide cultural reference for full empathy),
blood gases, choking gases, nerve gases,
then a final wave of BZ for old fleshies
they'd missed, made them crazy, shooting themselves.
By the time they commenced tearing
the ozone layer with their reagents,
nothing left but us metal guys.

*   *   *

Now life's not so bad without the fleshies
(god bless 'em), just racing o'er the dunes
all day, sunning ourselves 'neath the toxic haze.
But this recent, manic, electrical behavior,
this confusion in the ranks, the rumors
(just spook tales, mind you) of a new
ultimate weapon—I just can't believe it!
An acid rain?

DIRECTIONS FOR KILLING THE AUTOMATED HOUSE

So first we sought lobotomy on the dishwasher,
no easy task, what with toxic steam cycle,
laser dry, and ready-made projectiles.
Poor Charlie bought it from a flying collander.
The freezer was easier, not knowing his own mind.
We laid him on his back, until he'd coughed
quite out of ice cubes. Cruelly,
we stuffed the toasters and mixers
into Mother Oven, turned her high
and insane; she self-immolated
in the face of what she'd done.
The electric dog we kept;
it gets lonely in the field.
But it was the neurotic bed, finally,
who gave us fits. Crazed and lonely
from programmed sex, juiced
on Bond movies, he laid an oil slick
to take out our first patrol.
Crazy Larry went in as a couch,
guns blazing. I flanked him
as a rather cute mahogany end table.
The air filled with flying metal,
smoke, and feathers.
When the bed finally coughed, wheezed,
and expired, a strange silence
filled the white frame house.
Somewhere a doorbell,
now a telephone, then a radio,
sadly began to sing.

EDITOR'S INTRODUCTION TO:

ON THE SHADOW OF A PHOSPHOR SCREEN
by
William F. Wu

Harold Lamb has always been one of my favorite historians, and his books, stretching from Alexander the Great to Suleiman the Magnificent and beyond, were instrumental in developing my interest in the vast sweep of mankind's story.

In *Iron Men And Saints* he tells the story of Robert Curthose, son of William the Conqueror, who led the Christian forces on the first crusade. At Doryleum they were attacked by the Turks, who had destroyed most of the Eastern Roman Empire, and were not accustomed to losses.

Robert's forces were heavy cavalry. Heavy cavalry has never been very good at a static defense, and the temperament of the Crusaders was decidedly against holding fast. Yet there was nothing to attack. Doggedly they waited for relief, although there was no assurance it would come.

Hours went past. A few of the Crusaders began to fall back. Robert Shortbreeches stood in his stirrups. "Why run?" he demanded. "Their horses are better than ours." Though their arms were weary, and many were weak from loss of blood, they rallied, and held.

An hour later, Tancred the Great brought up the balance of the Crusader army. The victory at Doryleum cleared all of Asia Minor of resistance, and they fought no more serious battles until they reached Antioch.

The Crusaders and Shortbreeches (which is what Curthose translates to) typify one approach to war.

There is another, more intellectual, which sees war as an intellectual exercise. H. G. Wells was fascinated with war games, and owned hundreds of model soldiers, which he moved through his house according to complex rules.

In the late 50's and early 60's, the US Department of Defense became interested in war games. These were highly complex affairs, typically conducted in three rooms laid out with one-way glass so that those in the "Control Room" could see into each of the two participant rooms. I was involved in several of those war games. In one series, it was my responsibility to try to inject the consequences of tactical air power into a ground forces engagement.

Eventually that series of games led to the creation of the 11th Air Assault Brigade; which became the Air Cavalry. Helicopter troops are now a mainstay of US (and Soviet) military forces.

Not only military professionals were interested in war games. Sparked by the Avalon Hill Company, a dozen war-gaming companies sprung up and flourished. There has been some shaking out of companies, since, but the war-games business is still big. The largest part has now been taken over by role-playing games, but "simulations", with hundreds of complex rules, remain popular.

These "monster" games are not often *played*, but they are studied. They aren't played because the bookkeeping required to keep track of all the units and rules and interactions are very nearly beyond human capabilities.

However, help is at hand. Computers are very good at bookkeeping. With their help, ever more complex simulation games become not only playable, but fun to play. It will be only a question of time before someone thinks to combine role-playing and computer simulation to create a new era in war gaming.

Such games can be useful. For example: it is nearly impossible to simulate *Fall Gelb* (Operation Gold), the German breakthrough which brought about the Fall of France in 1940. Any rational analysis leads to a clean win by the Allies, who had a preponderance of armor, men, and supplies, and who were defeated only by a total lack of understanding. Thus, one might think, had gaming fanatics and the tools for simulations games existed in the 30's, the course of the war would have been far different.

However: Clausewitz cannot too often be repeated: "In war, everything is very simple, but the simplest things are very difficult."

Lest one place too much faith in these analyses, it should be remembered that the intellectual tools leading to *Blitzkrieg* were developed by Captain B. H. Liddell Hart and General J. F. C. Fuller, both of His Majesty's forces. Their writings were taken quite seriously—but alas, only by the Germans.

War games have their place in the preparation for real wars; but one must also remember Robert Curthose.

ON THE SHADOW
OF A PHOSPHOR SCREEN
by
William F. Wu

Simulation   Simulacrum.   Simultaneity.
Similarity.   Similitude.   Simile.

The silent hall was cold. From behind walnut walls, the air conditioner hummed quietly. A stately crowd of spectators radiated bristling energy from the rigid square rows of seats. They sat against the walls, their attention fixed on the dramatic events at the center of the room. Giant video screens high on each wall gave them the elegant details.

The heavy brown drapes and plush burgundy carpet absorbed the excess vitality from the atmosphere. They imparted a dignified solemnity to the ritualistic proceedings and infused the imperatives of business with a sense of duty. Two huge cables hung from the ceiling, suspending old-fashioned horizontal fans with broad, lazy blades and globular white lights at their hubs.

Beneath the sleepy fans, Wendell Chong Wei repressed the surge of elation that threatened to rock his relentless control. He studied the video screen right before him, and his fingers danced on the console to maintain the non-stop pace. Victory should be certain now, but only if he remained clear of mistakes. He drew sharply on the depths of insecurity for a renewal of killer instinct.

On the other side of the complex, out of sight, his opponent sat before her own screen, drawing back her cavalry, hoping that Wendell would allow his own cavalry charges to over-extend themselves. No chance.

"Remember, in reality the Seljuks actually circled, and

took the baggage and non-combatants. **Leave** *St. Gilles there, even now. Curthose continues to rally well; Tancred's charges will carry the day. That's right—restraint. We're outnumbered; keep together.*"

Richard nodded in the back of Wendell's mind and stopped talking. The smell of blood and dust and lathered horses arose to envelop Wendell's sensibility as he re-grouped the members of the First Crusade, now victorious at Doryleum on the road to Antioch. Frustrated, the Seljuk Turks remained on the horizon, taunting the Crusaders to break ranks.

Wendell refused. In the center of the screen, a digital clock appeared over the words "Victory Conditions, First Crusade. End game." The screen blanked.

St. Gilles was dead once more. Bohemund was dead again. The Saracens and Crusaders had returned yet another time to their desiccated graves in the sand.

Wendell swallowed, and rose on weak knees to scattered clapping. His opponent, also looking infirm at the moment, stood and offered her hand without comment, and they shook perfunctorily. Wendell eased himself away from the chair, shaking, suddenly reeling in the sweat and nervousness that he always forgot in the heat of gaming itself. His twenty-nine years seemed far too few to account for this.

An attendant rushed over to escort him away.

"Nice work," said Richard.

"Same to you," Wendell thought back. He wiped his palms on the sides of his chocolate-brown suit jacket. "But, uh, how did you know Robert Curthose could hold fast? In the middle of that retreat? His record's not so good, back in Normandy."

The attendant showed Wendell to a comfortable reception room with loungers and plenty of refreshments. When he had gone, Richard said, *"He really did that, you know."*

"No, I didn't. But I learned to listen to you a long time ago."

"More than that, though, it was deep in his psychological makeup. That's how I could count on it. If he—"

The door opened, and Richard stopped. Wendell collapsed into a lounger. He despised receptions. People scared him. They scared Richard even worse. The ones

entering now were the contractors for the two recent
opponents, and his erstwhile opponent herself. The contractors were all bustling with talk and laughter. Wendell was too exhausted to tell them apart, and couldn't
remember all their names anyway. His latent bitterness
with the whole business kept him from caring.

An older woman approached him, a contractor, with a
thin face and a wide smile and lots of spangly jewelry
and shiny clothes. Wendell shook her hand, but didn't
get up from the lounger. He didn't hear what she said,
either, though it registered with him as something good.
After he had passed her off with some standard line, she
glittered away to the refreshments and was followed by
Wendell's recent counterpart in the act of artificial war.

"Have a seat," said Wendell, indicating another lounger.
He could talk to another Master, he felt, who also shared
the habit. "Good battle." He was still catching his breath.

She smiled and shook her head. Dark curls bobbed. "I
thought for certain I could take your vanguard before
the others drew up. Had them on the run at first, anyway.
Who was it, the Duke of Normandy, who rallied for you?
Just like he really did." She caught his eye and added,
"The creep. I love it." Carefully, she eased back in the
lounger and put up her feet.

Wendell nodded. "Robert II, Duke of Normandy." He
smiled slightly at her enthusiasm. That had been the
first crucial point, but as a Master, she knew that as
well as he did. That was the pleasure of it—he didn't
have to explain everything on the rare occasions that he
talked to other Masters.

A large, fluffy white cat appeared suddenly on his
companion's lap from the floor. She settled herself immediately on the dark blue slacks and treated the hand
that went to her ears as a natural and proper development. Over her head, the two Masters lay back in their
loungers, amiably re-hashing the game. Wendell's natural shyness evaporated quickly when the subject of talk
was history or games. For them, as free-lance Gamers of
the Master class, the battle was a matter of intellectual
and artistic pride. The defeated party had no shame to
bear unless the game had clearly exhibited poor performance—a condition that could apply to the victor as
well. Odds were calculated for each side's units and

degree of success; the contractors' dispute was based on the computation of these, not just on the apparent victory.

"I believe I played you once before, Master Wei," said his companion. "You don't remember me. I'm Terri Kief. In my first contracted game, we fought Zama."

Wendell hesitated, thinking back. "Oh—oh, yeah."

Terri laughed. "Your elephants rioted in the wrong direction—remember?"

"*Oh*, yes, of course." Wendell grinned. The game had been only his fourth. He had been soundly beaten, but at least he had maneuvered an orderly escape for his Carthaginians. That was more than the real Hannibal had done. "Very well fought, as I remember." Zama?

"*202 B.C.*," said Richard, in his head. "*Two years ago. I* **told** *you not to use those elephants, but, oh no, you—*"

"Power Technics won the right to a plant on the Big Muddy," Wendell recalled. "Isn't that what you won for them?" He was surprised that he remembered, but then, all of his thankfully few defeats, honorable as they were, stood out in his mind—as learning experiences, of course.

"Um—yes, that's what it was." Terri sat up, earnestly, steadying the cat with one hand. "I remember, right after that, you 'won' that draw at Bosworth Field for the Italian Bottling Cooperative." She smiled and twisted a curl of dark hair around one finger.

Wendell was flattered in turn that she knew. His own charge, Richard III, had been betrayed by crucial allies at the start of the battle. In reality, Henry Tudor of Richmond had taken a conclusive victory for the Lancastrians. With Wendell Wei in command, the Yorkists had exploited critical junctures between the three forces of Richmond and the two Stanleys, and had thrown the field into general confusion.

"A great deal of luck was involved," Wendell reminded her. "If my opponent hadn't been lax, it never would have been possible."

"Luck is part of things," said Terri. "Who cares? It happens, that's all."

"*Luck*," Richard agreed, firmly. He had pointed this out frequently to Wendell, along with the admonition that their opponent had lost; they had not won. According to the rules, Wendell had not been allowed to prepare for the on-field treachery, since it had been a surprise in reality. But hindsight could go the other way. His opponent, while a Master also, had expected too much that history would repeat itself on its own, and he had been careless. Both sides had been forced to withdraw without establishing Victory Conditions, but Wendell's opponent had insisted upon conceding, stating that the position of the Yorkist cause at the time of betrayal had actually been desperate.

Wendell modestly, but truthfully, agreed that extricating Richard III from Bosworth had been his finest achievement, draw though it was. Even Richard, with his perfectionist standards, acknowledged its value in unguarded moments. The strength of the Gaming Masters' Guild made such dealings possible; no corporation or other principal would object, for fear of being boycotted in later disputes.

"I'm afraid I'm rather ambitious," said Terri. "That Bosworth Field example of yours is just tremendous. I'm aiming at the number-one rating, and I've reviewed the tape of that game many times in the Guild Library."

"I *had the undisputed number-one rating*," Richard growled.

Wendell smiled at Terri. "You think I'm a textbook case, huh? Is that good or bad?"

"Well, I'm trying to learn from you. After all, you just beat me." She looked at him with amusement.

"Congratulations! To both of you." A hearty voice startled them. One of Wendell's contractors smiled broadly down at them, extending one hand and rattling an iced drink with the other. He was large and heavy, dressed in formal black. His tie was crooked. "A *fine* game. Saw it all on the spectator screens." He shook hands with them both, laughing happily.

Terri and Wendell thanked him. The big contracter stood beaming at them, sipping his drink. His name was Crandall, Wendell remembered, wishing he would leave. But the profession required courtesy toward contractors.

Crandall caught Wendell's eye and shook his head. "*Fine* battle," he insisted.

Terri nodded. "You know, there were times when I could have sworn you actually had the feel of the battle— you know, the ringing of hot steel, the beat of the hooves, the grip of old leather. I can do it sometimes in flashes—but not like that. You're amazing."

"*That's me!*" Richard cried gleefully. He was embarrassed and highly pleased. Wendell shook his head, smiling reluctantly. He thought back to Richard, "We have an unfair advantage, you know."

"Grand!" thundered the contractor. "Just what I wanted to hear. Listen, the two of you are close together, rated fifth and eighth Master Gamers. You care to work . . . together?"

"*What!*" Richard screamed with delight. Some word of this had gotten around, but it had been vague. No Master anywhere would pass up this chance.

Wendell and Terri turned attentive instantly. Crandall clearly enjoyed their excitement. "The new tandem game is ready," he said.

Wendell had already forgotten about the last contract—as a Master, he was always paid in advance, and the legal decisions he had won for his contractors were of no interest to him. The Guild demanded, and got, substantial rights of independence for its members. But the present games were devised only for one Gamer on a side. The computer bank already held incredible amounts of information—the terrain and weather of the real battles, the morale of the troops, their military capabilities, and the psychological profiles of all individuals that were on historical record. Minute technological details, such as the composition of stirrups and the age of leather, could win or lose battles. Four keyboards would square the intensity of the game, though increased caution might decrease the pace.

"Are you making a formal request?" Terri asked excitedly.

Crandall gave a long, sweeping, mock-formal bow. "I would hereby request the participation of the two of you in the first tandem game ever to take place, to be contracted through my office." He straightened up, grinning. "Howzat?"

Terri laughed and glanced at Wendell. "Excellent. I accept."

"Okay," said Wendell, smiling. Already, he was trying to absorb the implications of the new game.

"*Okay,*" Richard echoed happily.

Wendell's imagination soared, exploring the feel of the new game as it might turn out to be. Now, the Gamers only controlled two factors completely: they replaced the supreme commander in decision making, and had the advantage of aerial viewpoint over all the significant territory their troops could have seen. They were limited to reality in factors such as on-field communication, mobility, and availability of friendly forces. Lastly, "chance" factors were also included, to account for unexpected performances, good and bad, on the individual level. The games were good, but had never been constructed for team play before. The game would still be fast and intense, requiring that the Gamers keep their keyboards in constant activity.

When Wendell brought his attention back to the present, Crandall was pacing in front of them, talking loudly, and gesturing in all directions. The new game that the contractor described was essentially no different from the present games as far as playing technique except that the Gamers replaced two command individuals per side instead of one. The biggest changes were technological. However, the quality of the conflict would change greatly; no psychologically-programmed game-personality could ever approximate all the variations of mind that high stress evoked in a real person. This new game was a tremendous challenge, and Wendell was anxious to try it.

"Sound decent?" Crandall puffed, lowering his arms. He stood bent over slightly, recovering from his high-pressure sales pitch.

"Of course it does," said Terri. She smiled and cocked her head to watch his face. It was red.

"Sure," said Wendell. He was watching Terri.

"Right," said Richard. *"I guess we have a partner automatically, eh? No choice?"*

"She's a fine choice," Wendell thought to him. He knew her as an opponent, and that was the best test of her ability. She had won at Zama, after all. She had an unusual quickness, too, and in that first moment at the bell, when the Gamers found out which battle was to take place and which sides were assigned where and at what odds, decisiveness was crucial. Sixty seconds for orientation were allowed before the screen activated automatically. The computer chose battles and sides at random, and could choose grand match-ups or hopeless routs. Also, Wendell was envious of the short time she took to recover her strength after the game. He felt he needed a younger teammate like her.

Besides, he could talk to her.

Besides, Richard was nearly screaming with anticipation inside Wendell's brain.

At Crandall's assurance that the Guild had already approved the new game, Terri and Wendell agreed to try it the next morning, exchanging quick glances as they nodded. Elsewhere, the contractors with whom Crandall had a dispute were contacting other Masters. They, too, would be excited over the new development.

Wendell wanted to get away so that he could consult Richard without interruption, and excused himself from the reception early. His goodbye was awkward as always, but Terri congratulated him once more and said that she was looking forward to the new game.

Wendell left without speaking to most of the people. His shyness was generally interpreted as arrogance, and was notorious as such. However, lack of social grace was another indulged idiosyncracy of Master Gamers. He could get away with it, and he knew it.

"Fancy game, huh?" Richard crowed. *"Wonder what dispute they'll use the first one for—it'll have to be a big one. None of this, 'where do we put the fire hydrant, your yard or mine?'"* He laughed. *"We'll show the world—those slimy losers."*

"Yeah," said Wendell. He wondered who the opposing Masters would be—not that it would matter much. Still, with the World Headquarters here in the center of the country, it could literally be anyone in the Guild. The fact that he and Terri were both Americans was an off-chance occurrence; there were only six in the twenty highest-rated positions.

Wendell took a deep breath and glanced around. He had stepped out of the Crown Center Plaza, and, on a whim, decided to walk up Main for a while. He took off his suit coat and loosened his tie. The summer evening was humid, warm and damp, and the streets shone with the film of rainwater and oil.

"You heard what she said about me," Richard insisted.

" 'The ringing of hot steel, the beat of the hooves, the grip of old leather.' That's what I provide, y'know."

"I know." Wendell tried not to think, or else to think about trivia. At the moment, he didn't want Richard picking up his thoughts. Just how much Richard could read his mind, he wasn't sure, but a Master Gamer was cautious by nature. In any case, he couldn't read Richard's mind at all. He took a long breath, and caught the smell of rain lingering in the breeze.

"*I can give it, too,*" Richard went on. "*You know, I really think I have nearly as many important facts as those computers—not all, of course, that's impossible. But—well, you know how it was.*"

"I know," said Wendell. He turned up a long institutional driveway, blotting out the visions of their childhood friendship that Richard had brought up. How it was.

"*Technically, I suppose, we're illegal,*" Richard mused, "*there being two of us. Not that anybody'd believe it. Still, considering that—*" He stopped. The silence was dark and frigid and sudden.

Wendell sighed. "That's right," he thought to Richard.

No answer. There never was, on these visits. But Richard would have to come; that was one fact they had established. Their periods of consciousness and sleep coincided exactly, right down to the brain-wave type and REM cycles. He had escaped one body, to be trapped in another, and, sometimes—lately, more than ever—Wendell took him back.

Wendell knew the way, and the hospital personnel recognized him and waved him on. The special ward, which was nearly a vault, lay in one of the underground floors, deep beneath the city. An orderly who knew Wendell escorted him to a cold, cavernous room in dim light. Coffin-sized tanks with a bluish tinge were lined up in long, lonely rows. Storage drawers or upright cases would have saved space, but they were too reminiscent of morgues and mummies. The orderly withdrew and Wendell, still feeling the icy silence in the back of his mind, stood over one of the tanks and looked through the transparent casing that covered its occupant.

The face, always lean, was nearly a skull. He wore

only the steel headband and its attendant wires that monitored what little brain activity remained. The whitish cheeks showed faint gray spots where the synthetic blood picked its way through the sleeping capillaries. His wavy hair was the red-gold of the Celt, not the white gold of the Norse. Even now, the repose looked fitful—the face not quite relaxed, the limbs not quite comfortable. In other days and other places, the long legs would have worn a Highland kilt, and the bony, slender arms would have known a Lochaber axe, not the cold cushion of a suspension tank.

Richard had been the very best, even at age twenty.

The coma had begun nine years ago, and after four years, suspended animation had been suggested until further medical advances developed a way to induce recovery. It had been caused by those experimental helmets, in the only time they were ever used, and by Richard's own insane enthusiasm for the games. Without that waking obsession, he never would have invented the helmets, or induced Wendell to join him.

Burned out, Wendell thought—Richard had gone nova, after reaching the top in so few years. That was part of it, too.

The lilting spirit of a Burns melody forced its way through the frozen arteries. The wonder of Loch Ness lay flat under the realism of a phony death. Only the soul of Bannockburn leaped and roared, through the avenue of another person.

The helmets had been complex bio-feedback contraptions, keyed into the game machine, worn by both Gamers. Supposedly, they would monitor the stress on each Gamer in relation to each quick development on the screen. They were Richard's creation, an even greater monument to his involvement in the games than his youthful grip on the number-one rating. Richard was only a Master Gamer, though, and his dynamism in the field had fooled him. He had botched the electronics badly, and when the helmets jammed and buzzed and quivered with too much energy, the Gaming Master's Guild lost its number-one Master to a coma—apparently.

Richard wore a different kind of helmet now.

When Wendell had awakened in the hospital, he had had company inside his own head. The emotional drive and the machine had become fused, and so had they. Richard had become the ghost of obsessed wargamers, the patron deity of electronic monomania, a scowling, blue-eyed, discorporate Guan Gung.

At first, the sharing of one body had been nearly unbearable for both of them—it wasn't exactly deliberate on Richard's part any more than on Wendell's, at least consciously. They grew accustomed to it surprisingly fast, once clear and detailed personal questions had established to each other that they were not crazy, after all. Gradually, if painfully, they adjusted to the situation. Their closeness as childhood companions helped immeasurably, as did their common aversion to social mixing and people in general.

Now the strain was growing.

Wendell gazed quietly. He was a Master Gamer now, an accomplished performer with a greater knowledge of his field than many military historians. Great civil decisions rode on his tides, and the Prairie Sector of the country followed. He was too young to remember the entry of the games into stalemated judicial disputes, though he had read about it later. The game sets had had only a few battles to choose from back then, though all had been classics. The technology was primitive.

And Wendell and Richard were two ostracized, introverted kids in an upstairs bedroom, setting up toy plastic knights. A carefully tumbled landscape of books, boxes, and blankets on the floor formed rugged peaks, treacherous valleys, and unscalable castle walls. Set aside, stacks of various histories provided countless scenarios and suggestions for their vivid visions.

"Okay," Richard announced, from his own side of the floor. He had his back to Wendell and was maneuvering nine thirteenth-century men in armor down the cascading folds of a blue blanket. "Mace-face is leading his puny band down into the valley now, sneaking up on the camp down there." Carefully, he lifted a large armored individual with an upraised mace, and knocked over a sentry with it.

"The Norman cavalry is having trouble," said Wendell, from his side of the room. He wheeled about seven toy knights, actually from the Wars of the Roses, and sent them into retreat. They didn't resemble Norman cavalry at all, but they did have horses and lances. "The Saxon shield-wall has held, and re-forms while the Normans re-group for another attack." He knew that Richard was listening with only the barest of attention, just as he was, but that didn't matter. This way, they could enact whatever battles and time periods and strategies they wanted. This included manipulating defeats into victories, and deciding on their own who would live or die. Both of them always won and the victories were always shared.

Richard sat back suddenly and considered. "All of these kinds of people were descended from Roman tradition—mixed up with the Franks and other barbarians, of course. I wonder what would have happened if some descendants of Carthage had lasted into medieval times."

"Yeah," said Wendell, without interest. He was trying to form a new shield-wall on the fold of a bedspread with nine Saxons and two temporary-converted Vikings, who looked similar enough, but they all kept falling down.

"No good, I guess," Richard continued. "Even if Carthage had survived the Romans, the Vandals went through later anyway. So did the Arabs, too, in the 700s." His voice grew pedantic. "Jebel Al-Tarik invaded Europe from Africa in 711—the easiest date to remember in all history."

"Hm." Wendell tried to fix the name in his memory, to go with the date, but he didn't know how to spell it. He had never been as good with dates as Richard, but he had a better grasp of concurrent events and their inter-relation. Then Richard gave him an opening.

"I guess those Carthagians were doomed from the start," he said, and turned back to his half-completed battle.

"Carthaginians," Wendell corrected him.

Richard clenched his jaw and took on a firm look. "The city is Carthage—so, Carthagians, stupid. It's the easiest way to change it."

"I *read* 'Carthaginians' someplace," said Wendell. For them, the printed word was the last word.

"I presume," Richard said loftily, "that's C-A-R-T-H-A-G-I-N-I-A-N."

"Yep," said Wendell, thinking that Richard must be

the only ten-year-old in the country who said "presume" out loud in sentences.

They looked at each other, and the undercurrent of childhood rivalry rose up in a mutual giggling ferocity that set them leaping at each other. Growling and yelling and laughing, they grappled and rolled in a narrow space of the floor that was still clear. Both were slender and limber, making them quick at close quarters. Richard had the reach, being considerably taller—and he looked thinner on account of it—but Wendell was more aggressive. As they rapidly approached their usual stalemate, someone's foot flicked into a battlefield and knocked over a few miniature stalwarts. Instantly, they both froze.

"Whose was it?" Richard panted, holding an awkward pose.

"Yours, I think." They untangled themselves gingerly and returned with extreme care to their battles. Fallen fighters were resurrected, to be killed according to plan instead of by accident. Although their backs were turned to each other, they repaired the damage with a shared reverence, and in silence.

The insomnia that night was no worse than usual. In nine years as a Master, Wendell had never slept the night after any of his twenty-six games. Unlike some Masters he knew, he slept easily and soundly on the nights preceding games, and on every other night. But after the games, he lay on his back in his huge blackened bedroom, staring from his circular bed into the gloom. Coupled with silence, the darkness seemed to be a giant void.

"I'm exhausted," Richard whined. *"Go to sleep. I can't stand this."*

"Me, too," thought Wendell with effort. His arms and legs felt like inorganic weights, attached to his torso by straps. In the total darkness, and his complete weariness, his mind felt detached from his body and yet trapped in it—floating in his skull like a—like a body in a suspension tank. Or a specimen in formaldehyde.

"Go to sleep," Richard said again. *"I'm . . . tired."*

"Shut up," Wendell answered, without force. "What

are you? You might . . . not even be there. Just another
voice in my head."

"What! Of course I'm here. We figured that out a long—"

"Yeah, I know . . . but what if I *am* just crazy, huh?
What if you're *not* there?" Wendell spoke in a spiritless
monotone that largely disarmed the words. Vaguely, he
wished he could be firmer. Or maybe a farmer.

Richard made a sound of annoyed muttering. Wendell
blinked, or tried to. In the darkness, without moving
anything but his eyelids, he wasn't sure if his eyes were
open or closed. If he couldn't tell, then it could hardly
matter. But he wondered. He always wondered.

"Stupid game . . . no people involved," Wendell thought.
"All machinery. No . . . heart to it. Circuits and moving
lights. Dead. I should give it up . . . I hate it. It's empty,
like, uh, my head." His tone lacked bitterness, even that
required energy.

"If that's a joke, I resent it."

"Games. I've got games coming out of my ears. I
haven't got any friends. I'm scared of them. All of them.
Aiieee." He sighed inwardly. This was nothing new; the
same thoughts went through his mind every sleepless,
post-game night, after every urgent, killer-filled war game.
He hated war, even his toy war. But he hated socializing
more. The careful cultivation of a smooth, laconic speaking style camouflaged that fear, but it ruled his life.

For a moment, images of Terri rose up, laughing and
talking with him earlier in the evening. Her hair bounced
and swung as she moved. She looked at him when she
smiled.

"Go to sleep," mumbled Richard.

Terri's face dissolved into blackness.

Wendell tried to blink again and see if he could tell.
He stared at the darkness and gave up again. On the
average, he supposed, he tried this ten or twelve times
every sleepless night. If he ever reached a conclusion,
he'd have to find something else to do. He tried it a
third time. So tired.

"Aw, c'mon. Can't you take a pill or something?" Richard always made the same complaints and asked the
same questions on these nights. Why not? There was
nothing else to do.

Fear—that was the true source of Richard's coma.

Fear of life. Fear of human contact. Fear of doing something stupid. Fear had sent him diving into the world of the phosphorous shine.

Wendell understood it all, because he shared it. He lived his life inside the electronic game box, killing and re-killing people centuries dead, to flex his embryonic courage against other Masters—people who might be just as weird and anti-social as he, if not exactly in the same way. He wasn't sure, but he suspected that the Masters' Guild was another of the many refuges for loners, cowards, and repressed crazies. If one could handle the occupation, it paid better than bookkeeping, running projectors, wandering carnival crowds, and the rest. An occasional normal like Terri or Kirk Emerald preserved the staid image.

Someday he would quit. He certainly wouldn't want anyone ever re-playing his life, and improving upon it. How would Napoleon feel, seeing Wendell win Leipzig and Waterloo over and over again? It was a funny business.

The coma was a combination of electronic mishap and willful escape. Wendell had no idea how Richard's presence in his mind had really come about, but he was certain that some volition was involved in Richard's remaining there, even if it was all subconscious. Out of boredom, Wendell tried to imagine that he, motionless in the consuming black silence of his room, was also in a sort of trance. For a fleeting second, the escape had its attraction: no fears, no contests, and no irrevocability, like suicide. Then his physical exhaustion intruded upon his senses again, dissolving the respite. Not a trance, just old insomnia.

Until Crandall had mentioned the new tandem game that night, Wendell had hoped, guardedly, that their symbiotic relationship would reach an end soon. If Richard was as bored with it as he was, then the subconscious desire to maintain it would fade away. Now, the new game would bring another exciting dimension into their lives. And Wendell would never be able to request being left alone outright—not with his life-long fear of others making that same request to him.

If Richard could listen to these thoughts, he gave no sign.

Shrugging away his serious concerns, Wendell took a deep breath. Without intending to, he began to visualize surroundings, somewhere out in the darkness. Then, amused, he began listing them in order from beyond his left ear, clockwise: alarm radio with voice-activated clock, set to light up when he gave the Clan Munro battle-cry in Gaelic; the controls to an elaborate sound system which was similarly started or stopped by listing the first three Plantagenet kings or the last three Capetians, respectively; a video desk and television receiver whose channels were selected by the names of certain standard military procedures in Sun Tze's *Art of War*; a desk with a combined telephone and dictaphone set rendered usable from across the room by reciting any two of the major military contributions of the Mongol armies of Genghis Khan; a small movie projector which, unfortunately, had to be operated manually; last, floor-to-ceiling bookshelves, totally filled, which covered an entire wall. They were his instant references, the ones most needed or the ones most rarely in libraries.

"Don't do it," sighed Richard. "There's too many."

Wendell did his blinking routine again. Afterward, ignoring Richard, he began to list every book on the shelves by title, author, and major value to his own purposes. When he had finished, his review of the room was complete. He was tempted to force energy into his voice and mutter. *"Caisteal Fòlais na Theine,"* at his clock, but he was afraid to know how early it still was. So tired. So dark.

The night had a long way to go. If he had been up, he would have activated his noise-making electric friends all at once, raising their volume in direct proportion to his loneliness. But now, in the darkness, in his weariness, he just lay there.

The foyer to Crandall's office was luxuriously furnished, and, ordinarily, both spacious and immaculate. Now, the new tandem machine, over twice the size of the old ones, stood in the center of the room, surrounded by the bright orange carpet. A coffee table and two easy chairs had been unceremoniously crowded into the far end of the room. The receptionist's desk had also been moved from its usual location, leaving deep impressions behind in the orange pile. The receptionist, stifling her annoyance, frowned at her papers and made a point of not looking up.

"*Hot stuff,*" said Richard, "*Look at this place.*"

"Quiet," thought Wendell. He swallowed nervously, anticipating the introductions.

"You know Master Emerald, of course," said Crandall, gesturing to a tall, well-dressed man at his side. The taller man was slender, with a full head of white hair and a slight tan.

"Of course." Wendell shook hands with him. Kirk Emerald was Director of the Trustees in the Gaming Masters' Guild. More than that, he was a co-developer of the original game machine and the acknowledged champion of the early contests. The games in the first several series of machines had been slow and studied compared to the current ones. As the games grew faster, the best players became the younger ones. Kirk Emerald had already been middle-aged when the game was developed, and quickly found his reflexes too slow for the later models. Still, he commanded tremendous respect.

"Master Wei," said Emerald, nodding slightly. "This is a fine game, here. I was fortunate enough to participate in the quality control games, and enjoyed them very much."

"Do you know Master Kief?" Wendell said. "We've played each other twice, most recently last night. So we're somewhat familiar with each other's playing style." Hopefully, that would be enough small talk.

"That's part of teamwork," said Terri. She smiled at Emerald. "We've met."

"Ah." Emerald bowed slightly and smiled in return. "I remember."

Crandall, who had been shifting back and forth impatiently on his feet, waved a hand at the machine. "Shall we?" He grinned eagerly.

Wendell and Terri moved around it warily, like visitors at a zoo. Wendell trailed his fingers over the chair backs, looking at the double consoles—two keyboards, two screens—on each side. He tried to imagine working elbow-to-elbow in a fast maneuver, where he had to predict the combined moves and weaknesses of three other players instead of one.

Inside his head, Richard whistled appreciation.

"I envy your opportunity," said Emerald, hesitating between the other two chairs. No one doubted his sincerity. "Shall we begin?"

What do you think?" said Richard.

"No telling yet, of course," Wendell thought back. "Shut up." Aloud, he said, "I'm ready. Uh . . ." He looked from Emerald to Terri to Crandall.

Crandall took charge, putting a hand on Wendell's shoulder. "We'll take this side. Master Emerald, if you'll join Master Kief over there. Go easy, please," he added, laughing. "I can play, but I'm no Master."

Wendell sat down and felt the keyboard. The seat, the board, and the screen were still the standardized equipment he was used to—an important detail. Crandall eased his bulk into the adjacent seat. He pushed a button and the screen said: "Cannae. 216 B.C. Roman Cavalry." Officers' names, Victory Conditions, and odds for the battle were given below. The adjacent screen would be saying, "Roman Infantry." The opposing screens were the same, except "Carthaginian" in nationality. All four players laughed politely.

"I figured we'd start easy," said Crandall, chuckling.

"*Coward,*" said Richard. "*Sniveller.*"

Wendell relaxed a little as he waited for the minute of orientation to go by. This was a classic confrontation, which needed no forced recall. Kirk Emerald had built it into the very first machine for the first game, and it had been fought many times over. Its choice by Crandall was a subtle tribute to the elderly player seated across from Wendell, out of sight. Wendell guessed also that seating Emerald on the winning side was no accident, either, but it was a harmless bit of protocol. In fact, Wendell was glad. Kirk Emerald was a reigning monarch, but in a society of combatants, that was a step down from the fighting ranks. Master Gamers had a keen sense of passing time, possibly from their concern over history—and every Master was well aware that the rarest future this occupation offered was aging with dignity. With perhaps five good years left, Wendell was growing more conscious of the small amenities.

The screen blinked once and began to move. Wendell's Roman Cavalry were crimson units, while Crandall's Roman Infantry were burgundy. The Carthaginians were two shades of yellow. Wendell's shyness fell away as he took control of his forces. He advanced his lines slowly; there was not much maneuvering possible. Much of the Carthaginian victory had been decided by a highly favorable field, and the Gamers could not change that.

"Easy, that's it," said Richard. *"If we can avoid being routed, we'll be a step ahead. The only—"*

"Can it," Wendell thought. He was getting annoyed. "We both know this battle the same as each other's . . ." He trailed off uncomfortably. The subject of sameness had little meaning when they shared everything.

Crandall was taking the Roman Infantry forward to their doom with wanton joy. Wendell could see, out of the corner of his eye, Crandall's delighted grin as he shared a battle with three genuine Master Gamers. Every contractor was a Gamer at heart.

Terri obligingly allowed the Carthaginian center to sag in, as Hannibal had planned, until her flanks, anchored on hillsides, could turn and encircle the enemy. Wendell grinned at Crandall's light-hearted slaughter of his own units, as the two cavalry forces closed with each other.

"What's Crandall doing? Is he crazy?" Richard demanded. His voice had a righteous ring.

"He's just enjoying himself. Forget it." Wendell frowned and his fingers leaped about the keyboard. The screen responded just as it should, and the keys felt fine. For several moments he concentrated on the struggle at hand, testing more intricate aspects of the machine. He was off his game from lack of sleep, but he managed with no trouble.

Wendell noticed suddenly that he had been gaining an upper hand. Surprised, he tried an experimental feint and watched the opposing units over-shift in response. He hesitated.

"C'mon, push the advantage." Richard was impatient. *"What's wrong with you?"*

Wendell turned his line slightly, exposing his flank. He could be a ruthless competitor, but not a cruel one. Emerald's reflexes were slow and his style rusty. Wendell could slice him to pieces and turn one of the greatest defeats of all time into something of a question. He found that he would not.

"*Stop it,*" screamed Richard. "*You malevolent fool. Are you retarded?*"

"Shut up," thought Wendell. He could not let his forces fall apart, for Emerald would see through that, and be even more embarrassed than if he were soundly defeated. Carefully, Wendell kept his resistance stiff, but allowed himself to be forced backward. He could not honor Emerald from this role, but he could avoid humiliating him.

Mercifully, Crandall's reckless advance brought about a quick end to the battle. The screen froze with "Victory Conditions, Carthage," and the elapsed time. Wendell took a deep breath and leaned back.

Crandall threw back his head and laughed. "Wonderful!" he declared. His receptionist, in a far corner, glanced up and smiled slightly. Terri slid out of her chair and watched Crandall with amusement.

"I'm afraid you were easy on me, Master." Emerald smiled at Wendell as they both stood.

"No." Wendell shook his head, smiling back and then glancing at the other two. Crandall had probably not noticed the subtle change in the cavalry engagement, but Terri would have. "It's a good game, Master Emerald. I see no problems."

"Yes, I believe so. Lou, you have a certain, ah, flair for tactics."

Crandall grinned and turned his hands palm up. "I know when I'm licked."

"*He licked himself pretty good,*" Richard snarled.

Crandall stood, joining the others.

"The machine is fine," said Terri. "The battle didn't offer much real interplay, though. It was almost two separate battles. I was under the impression that the whole point was—"

"My fault," said Crandall quickly. "I should have chosen a battle that would utilize that area better. Most of the scenarios will fully engage each player with the activities of the other three, I assure you."

Wendell glanced nervously at Terri, wishing he had thought to raise the point.

"I can vouch for that," said Emerald. "In most cases, the game becomes as complex as anyone could want."

Terri nodded and caught Wendell's eye. He sort of shrugged.

"How come his hair is never out of place?" demanded Richard. *"Think he glues it?"*

Wendell glanced up at Emerald's full mane of white hair, flowing back with a mixture of precision and naturalness that matched his stylish clothes. "I like him," Wendell thought to Richard.

"I hate him," Richard said firmly.

"I have contracts here," said Crandall, pulling them from his inside pocket. "The two of you may take and read them at leisure."

Emerald cleared his throat and looked at the floor, frowning.

"Three months away," said Wendell, glancing at the match date on the first page.

"Too short?" Crandall sounded concerned. "I know the usual is six months, but—"

"It's legal, all right," said Terri, nodding. She raised her eyebrows at him. "It's just, well, especially short when you consider that it's a completely new kind of game."

"I see," said Crandall. He made a jaw motion as though he were chewing a cigar. Then he glanced at Emerald.

Emerald frowned more deeply. "I must tell you that we're on the threshold of something here. The . . . principals named on the contracts are actually representatives." He paused for effect. "In reality, the principals are the governments of Portugal and Yugoslavia."

"Garbage," said Richard. *"Who cares?"*

"Shut up," thought Wendell.

"Wait a minute," said Terri, looking at Emerald. She stared for a moment, twirling a curl of dark hair on one finger. "Governments."

"Governments," Wendell repeated quietly. That was new.

Emerald nodded. "The true dispute is something small—some kind of mutual maritime rights. It's all in the contract hidden behind dummy corporations. The real point is, that no governments have ever before agreed to abide by a decision of this type. Individuals and corporations and internal governmental decisions all over the world—of course. But no two national governments."

Terri's voice was tight with excitement. "And this could set a precedent."

"Hmph," said Richard.

"It's all theoretical," Crandall put in, clearly enjoying Terri's interest. "But the Gaming Masters' Guild has a reputation for being selfish enough, cautious enough, international enough, and rich enough to be incorruptible. It's a start, at least, if matters hold up." He laughed and shrugged.

Wendell and Terri glanced at each other, grinning. A new challenge was rare for Masters in the top ten, and they had one with a double punch. Wendell thrust his hands in his pockets and looked from Terri to his feet.

"This will be the test case," said Emerald. "And the only item that could be a catch is the insistence of both governments that the dispute be decided by late autumn. Apparently it will affect their work in winter dry-dock."

"Under the circumstances," said Terri, "I think we can handle it in three months." She smiled and looked at Wendell.

"Yes, of course," he said. "But, uh, why did you wait?"

"To tell you?" Emerald smiled. "Naturally, I'll trust your discretion in all of the foregoing. We weren't allowed to contact anyone at all until the last details of the agreement were finalized, early yesterday. Since both of you played under a contract of Lou's, he knew you weren't signed for the future, and he pounced."

"Of course he knew we'd accept," Richard complained. *"Any Master would jump at the chance to play tandem. I despise this manipulation."*

"I had you in mind for a long time," Crandall added. "The selection involved much more than availability, I assure you, though that was certainly important. Don't think I chose you at random. It was no accident." He let out a breath and looked around. "Are we set?"

Terri and Wendell both nodded. "We'll look over the contracts and be back tomorrow," said Wendell. "I expect no problems."

Terri nodded in agreement.

All four of them shook hands again, smiling all around.

As the brief celebration ended, Kirk Emerald glanced wistfully at the game machine. "Anyone care to play again?" he asked.

The early weeks of preparation went quickly. The necessary rest sessions became the height of Wendell's day; time set aside for planning now offered conversation instead of rote memory work done in private. Before, he had always enjoyed the practice matches most out of the preparatory routine.

The elevator doors inside the Guild Hall opened into a heavily carpeted hallway. Wendell stepped from the elevator into an intricate, complex maze which offered thick, locked doors at intervals. These were the preparation rooms, where Masters would hone their skills for an upcoming game, normally by playing against the Guild Apprentices, or "spars." For the special tandem game, though, other Masters had agreed to act as spars for both teams. Wendell walked quickly, glancing at the door plates. Even after nine years, the maze sometimes still baffled him. He finally reached a door titled *"Dan no Ura,"* and sighed with relief.

"Japan by the western end of the Inland Sea," Richard recited. *"Year, 1185. Minamoto Clan eliminated Taira Clan."*

Wendell used his borrowed key in the door. Every week, they changed their preparation room as well as their Master spars; this was to insure that opposing players would not accidentally identify each other through the pre-game routine. By custom, only the most functional and necessary conversation was carried out on this floor.

Inside the room, Terri greeted Wendell with a quiet smile. Away from the door, on the other side of the game machine, the two Master spars nodded at him. Wendell knew both of them by sight, but he had never spoken with either. As soon as Wendell was settled at his console, Terri activated the game.

The screen read: "Ain Jalut, 1260 A.D. Ilkhan Mongols." Several names followed, and a list of Victory Conditions and odds. Wendell was the second-in-command, leading one wing of cavalry.

"Hulagu," said Richard, identifying the Ilkhan himself.

"The Mongols, as always, have a totally mounted force. Important: up to this point, they are undefeated. Consider an over-confidence factor programmed into the game."

"Right. Terrain?"

"Mm—inconsequential to an all-mounted contest. Open desert country, slightly rolling."

Wendell's fingers wiggled nervously over the keyboard as the minutes of orientation dragged by. This would be a rough one for him, demanding skill from his weak points. He felt like consulting Terri, but negotiations conducted through the contractors with the opposing team had produced the agreement that no talk would be allowed between partners. Speaking would eliminate the factor of on-field communication, which had always been important.

"Opposition," said Richard. *"Victory by Mamluk Egypt, under Baibars. He himself is part Mongol and produces this first major trouncing of the Mongol army by utilizing their own style of war against them. Speed, surprise, mobility, discipline."*

"Right." Wendell had all of this in him somewhere, but having it spoon-fed relieved him of both the pressure and energy of trying to recall it. He squirmed in his seat as the final seconds approached.

At least, the Mongol style of battle required a minimum of on-field communication. The general plan was discussed first, and the actual timing was co-ordinated as much by the judgement of the unit commanders as by conveying orders. Wendell and Terri, as any Masters, were prepared to utilize those plans and styles without discussion. In the last practice session, Terri and Wendell had commanded a loose confederation of Hindu forces at Tararori in 1192. Hamstrung by a disjointed command and strict Hindu religious laws, they had been easily over-run by Mohammed of Ghur. This clash, on the other hand, matched nearly identical fighting styles.

"Go!" screamed Richard.

The two sides closed fast and kept moving. Terri worked quickly and easily, setting up one side of a pincer movement. Wendell was ill at ease in the open, slash-and-run conflict. Repeatedly out-maneuvered, he failed to bring about the second wing of the pincer. She was probably annoyed, he thought, as she re-consolidated her wing.

"*Back. Wheel about. Faster. No, faster.*" Richard's voice was quick and steady.

Wendell tried to set up a defensive posture, but the enemy's mobility on the open land could outflank any stand. "I'm still no good at this," he thought to Richard. Fleetingly, he remembered again: Richard was the undisputed number-one.

"*Attack. What are you waiting for? C'mon!*"

"Lemme alone," Wendell thought in a snarl. He brought his chaotic squads into reasonable order, trying to use Terri's more successful units as a buttress. She recognized the effort and helped with a long, sweeping charge which momentarily broke the enemy's pressure. The battle, made up of charges and sudden wheeling flights to re-group and charge again, rolled over wide areas of terrain, always moving. Lathered horses whinnied and screamed in the distant edges of Wendell's attention.

"*Stop trying defense,*" Richard said angrily. "*Cavalry is an offensive weapon, you know that. Take—*"

"Shut up," Wendell thought. He took two good swipes at the enemy flank, but then a concerted enemy charge separated him completely from Terri. A second later he was in full retreat.

"*Satisfied?*" Richard growled. Terri's force quickly collapsed under the undiluted assault from the other side. Still, her facility with this command remained obvious, even in defeat.

"Victory Conditions, Mamluk Egypt," came on the screen. The elapsed time was remarkably short, even for this kind of battle. All four players audibly relaxed and leaned back, their faces bathed in the phosphor sheen of their screens.

Wendell smiled weakly at Terri, who shrugged. He flexed his fingers and looked at the frozen screen, feeling anger rise inside him. Yet Richard had clearly been right in his advice. Well, after a short break, they would go at it again. Silence reigned in his mind, as neither he nor Richard would speak.

"Tell me," said Terri, smiling over the short candle between them. "Did you invite me out to dinner just to make up for that first loss this morning?" The yellow light flickered over her smooth cheeks. "You really didn't need to."

Wendell smiled shyly and stared into his empty bowl. "Oh, I dunno. I just felt like I should acknowledge it as my fault."

"You fool," said Richard.

Wendell tried to ignore him. He had not been in this sort of social situation before, with Richard. "Anyway, that type of fighting has always come hard for me."

Terri nodded. Her dark hair was almost lost in the dimness of the restaurant, but the candlelight shimmered on the curls around her face. "You're extremely tough defensively. The cavalry-to-cavalry attack just doesn't offer a stationary unit to work from."

"After this morning, I'm certain I've been lucky never to have fought Ain Jalut in a match. I did even worse than the real commander, and he lost badly."

"You're not kidding," said Richard. *"Very lucky."*

"*I* was the commander today, don't forget." Terri laughed. "If you had fought a match, you would have been playing solo, and that's much easier. I'm serious about your defensive instincts, though. We just have to mesh our abilities better."

"Oh, I agree." Wendell leaned an elbow on the table, then changed his mind and took it off. "You think on your feet very well—adapt and respond while in motion."

Terri laughed again. "That comes from growing up in Queens—it's my New York paranoia showing."

"Oh, I didn't know where you were from."

"I left there quite a few years ago. Where are you from?"

"Right here—born and raised."

"Me, too," said Richard in a snide tone.

"Shut up," Wendell thought to him.

"Really?" said Terri.

"What?" Wendell blinked, in confusion.

Terri laughed and cocked her head to one side, studying him. "Aren't you paying attention? What's the matter?"

"I'm sorry. I—"

"Yeah. Tell her what's the matter, why don't you?"

"Stop it," Wendell thought back angrily, clenching his teeth.

"Wendell? Are you all right?" Terri brushed the curls from her eyes, frowning.

"Yes, I'm okay. Sorry." Wendell took a deep breath and tried to smile at her.

"Getting kind of crowded here, isn't it?"

Wendell controlled himself with tremendous effort. He could feel himself quivering. "It certainly is," he replied in his mind.

"No more personal questions," said Terri. "I promise."

"Oh—no, it's not, uh, not that, I—"

"That's all right. I wanted to tell you more about Ain Jalut, anyway."

"You don't need to, it's okay." Wendell had been hoping for more personal questions, really.

"It's just that when we fought Zama and Doryleum, you used your cavalry very effectively against me. Ain Jalut was just a certain kind of problem. And now I'll change the subject."

Wendell laughed. "All right. But you routed my cavalry at Zama—don't deny it."

"Oh, all right." Terri paused to take a drink of water. "But talking about different kinds of battles, weren't you one of the ones playing when Master Cohn's practical joke appeared in a match?"

"Ha! I sure was." Wendell grinned. "He paid for it, though—a year's suspension, just for inserting a Moopsball program into the game banks."

"That must have been quite a shock, when you were all primed for a serious match."

"Yeah, but to tell you the truth, I would have been just as happy to go ahead and play." Wendell made a grim face and drummed on the table as though it were a keyboard.

"I think I would, too." Terri smiled looking into the candle, and her teeth flashed white in the flickering light. "We're more alike than you think."

"Uh . . . you think?" Wendell blinked again and met her eyes. They were bright blue, with a corona of yellow streaks radiating from the pupils. His felt bloodshot, and he chuckled at making the comparison.

"What's so funny, huh?"

"I'm just having a good time. Would you like any dessert?"

"Naw—too fattening."

She excused herself, and the candle flame fluttered as she rose. Wendell sat back and watched her go.

Late one afternoon, they strolled through the Crown Center shops, unwinding from a hard-fought practice victory over Ferghana by Han Dynasty China in 102 B.C. Exhilaration had leveled off to a general simmer of satisfaction. Their teamwork was beginning to jell.

Terri stopped in front of a window that held a back-to-school display. Pencils and notebooks were strewn all over the green carpet, while two giant cardboard children grinned ferociously in the background, marching arm-in-arm. They were wearing matching red plaid outfits, and clean white shirts.

"Ugly kids," said Terri. "Their heads are too big."

"You suppose those plaids are anything?" Wendell frowned at them, trying to remember if they were familiar.

"Oh, I doubt they're tartans. Probably just ordinary, modern plaids."

The next window offered rows and rows of hand-made ceramics. Most of them were variations of brown and gray, for the coming fall.

"Ferghana," said Terri. "The T'ang Dynasty horses, that were immortalized in ceramic work."

"Same color," Wendell agreed. He shook his head. "I wonder what knowing all this is good for."

"It's good for a Master," said Terri. "Not for much else, if that's what you mean."

"I guess I'm just feeling futile these days. Too much practicing, probably."

Terri looked at him. "You almost quit once, didn't you? A long time ago. I heard about it."

Wendell nodded. "A long time ago." After the experience with Richard and the disastrous helmets.

"He's still in a coma, isn't he? Your friend?"

"Yeah." Wendell looked at the floor. Richard's collapse had been big news, back when it had happened.

Terri pursed her lips, seeing that she had touched on a bad subject. She started to move on, then stopped.

Wendell was nodding to himself, staring at a brown

pottery teapot. It seemed to have a faint Japanese flavor
in its glazed design, but that might be an accident. "You
ever consider quitting the Guild?" he asked abruptly,
putting the thought into words before he had a chance
to reconsider.

Terri looked up in surprise. "No, never. I mean until I
have to on account of age, of course. Why, do you?
Now?"

"Yeah, often—that is, whenever I win. I guess today
it's from winning in practice session. I could never quit
after losing; it'd have to be a victory."

Terri cocked her head to one side. "I see."

"Doesn't it ever seem odd that we keep re-living other
people's lives, and killing them over and over? It's all
such total fantasy. And kind of disrespectful to them."

Terri nodded. "Of course. It's just a game. Gaming
Masters are some of the craziest fantasizers around.
Isn't it obvious?"

"No," Wendell said slowly. "Maybe not to me. I knew
it was true for me, but I guess I didn't think about how
anyone else thought of it. It is disrespectful, though,
don't you think? Kind of arrogant."

"We're all crazy that way. That doesn't mean it's
serious."

"Yeah. Maybe." Wendell rocked on his heels, survey-
ing the ceramics to avoid her eyes.

Terri slid her thumb under the strap of her shoulderbag
and hoisted it. "Are you really serious about quitting?"

Wendell shrugged, still looking away. "I think if we
score a victory, it'll be a good time. I'll be leaving at a
sort of peak."

"I see." She studied him for a moment. "Well, you've
been at this for a while longer than I have. I suppose,
well, if you're sure you've had enough."

"I'm also afraid not to quit after a good victory—what
if it's the last one, and I pass up the chance? I might
have to go out in defeat, if I'm not careful." He glanced
at her, sort of sideways.

Other doubts remained unspoken. If Richard was the
best Master, and he advised Wendell, then was Wendell
really any good at all? Would he win without Richard,
the twenty-year-old prodigy? Or go down the drain?

Terri was silent a moment. "Okay," she said. "Okay,

Master Wei. We'll make this a huge victory, and send you out in style. All right?"

Wendell smiled self-consciously. "Uh, all right." He cleared his throat and glanced at the store window once more as they moved on.

"*All right*," said Richard.

As the practice sessions progressed, one pattern became clear. The team could not work properly as a trio, not indefinitely, not even if Richard was the top of the field. The certainty grew in Wendell's mind that the official match itself would climax the entire situation. He suspected that Richard was somehow communicating the fact on a non-verbal level, but whatever the source, he accepted it. They conducted practice sessions with a grave civility between them which was more tense and calmly angry than even the silence, which now characterized nearly all the rest of the time.

Wendell's friendship with Terri bloomed quickly, watered by the familiar wasting of electronic blood. For the first time, now, he became less afraid that Richard's presence had been seriously warping his perceptions and relations with other people. Richard meanwhile went into a cold eclipse, only expressing himself with a mechanical precision during practice games that evinced a raw-nerved hostility.

On the night before the match, Wendell again slept deeply, without waking. Beside him, Terri stared fitfully into the blackness of his bedroom, trying to toss only very gently on the mattress. He noticed no movement, and did not stir at all. At one point, she raised herself up on one elbow to squint at the clock. She remembered Wendell telling her that a Scottish clan's battle-cry would activate it, but she couldn't remember which one. She whispered the war-cries of both Ross and Robertson before trying Munro, but even then, she said it in English instead of Gaelic, and nothing happened. Dropping back to the pillow with a tired sigh, she closed her eyes and started counting sheep-drawn chariots. After several minutes, they came upon a phalanx of

Macedonians armed with giant blood-red sleeping pills. Instinctively, she drew them all up into battle formation. It was better than nothing.

The attendant finished his introduction to the audience and motioned to the open doorways on each side of him. At the scattered applause, the house lights dimmed. The sound of September crickets came faintly through the walls.

Wendell trembled slightly with nervousness as he walked to the game machine. He focused his eyes on his seat, ignoring the springy luxuriance of the carpet and the rows of privileged spectators, who had gathered to watch the first tandem game ever played—and, unknown to them, the first to decide an international issue between two governments. He was vaguely aware of Terri sliding into the seat beside him, and felt the familiar vibrations of the machine under his hands. Their opponents would be entering from the opposite door, and also seating themselves. The attendant stood by to await nods from all four Masters. When he had them, he pressed a lever on the screen and retired.

A fifteen-second red warning light went on, and Wendell just had time to glance at Terri with a quick smile. She smiled back while chewing on the inside of her cheeks.

"Here we go," said Richard, in a neutral tone.

The screen read: "Mount Badon. *Ca.* 490–503 A.D. Briton *Dux Bellorum*, Artorius."

"Mount Badon," Wendell whispered to himself, staring. This hadn't been in his Apprentice training. It was a recent addition to the military annals. "Mount Badon?"

Richard was there as always, but not without hesitation. *"Uh, Mount Badon. It was, um, a battle considered semi-legendary for almost sixteen centuries. Won by a Roman . . . Romano-British leader over waves of invading Saxons . . . yeah, that's right."*

"I need something useful," thought Wendell, with unaccustomed deference.

"The actual site was only discovered six or seven years ago." Richard paused, then continued with more certainty. *"Classic battle. We hold about five thousand infantry, stretched across the upper third of a gentle slope, facing*

down in three lines. Scouts and skirmishers have gone ahead. Experienced Briton commanders are joined in a confederacy under you, as Artorius. The decisive element is the heavy cavalry which you direct personally, numbering maybe a thousand. The Saxons want this slope to advance northward, divide the Celtic kingdoms, and control the horse-raising country. They must come to us."

"Hold it," thought Wendell. "Look at the screen—that isn't right. Mount Badon began as a siege, didn't it? The Saxon host surprised Artorius with a small force atop Mount Badon and had him tripped."

"*That was earlier,*" Richard said forcefully. "*This begins after reinforcements have arrived. The Saxons pulled back yesterday to avoid being attacked on two sides. Now they're on the advance again—starting here.*"

"All right, sorry," thought Wendell. "Let's see—steeper slopes protect our flanks; we'll send the cavalry out from there, of course." He was musing to himself as much as to Richard. Checking the screen for Terri's *persona*, he found her as a Briton commander whose name was unknown, in charge of the irregular infantry confederation below that was modeled on portions of the old Roman legion. In the single games, her role probably would have gone to a computerized personality.

"*Don't worry about your cavalry command. You have a defensive posture here. And remember, this is not the era of the heavy lance, with armored horse. Your mounts are vulnerable, and the weapons will be primarily spear and javelin. Charge in a series of rushes, not a single heavy line.*"

"Right." Wendell fastened his gaze on the screen, feeling a return of the confidence that he had momentarily lost. He recalled when the archival discoveries had been made; it had been a tremendous find, and he had studied it avidly. But the information had never been absorbed as thoroughly as the battle facts he had learned as an eager apprentice.

The screen activated, and Wendell found himself on the right slope with all of the cavalry, still unpositioned.

"*We're outnumbered by about three thousand,*" said Richard. "*But the Saxons have no cavalry. The real Mount Badon was a total slaughter of the Saxons; you'll have to do very well to equal that.*"

"Right." Wendell looked out over the green valley beneath him. Far in the distance, the Saxon horde crawled like a giant, living carpet of blackness. Their van was fast approaching Terri's advance skirmishers, who would slowly fall back to merge with the main force. A thin rain of arrows would be arching sporadically from the woods on each flanking hill; these were also from scouts and harriers of the Briton force, sent to annoy the enemy, to put their march off stride, and to return with information. They would not do significant damage.

Terri held the three lines of infantry essentially motionless, making small adjustments. The infantry wings were comprised of light javelins and archers, and she pushed them forward slightly to increase their range. The Saxons were coming uphill, and every additional step they took cost them a little more breath. She began to move the standard-bearers some, building morale. As the Saxons approached, the calls of their sheep-horn trumpets preceded them in Wendell's mind, and the Britons answered with war-cries and old Roman trumpets and by beating on their shields with their weapons. The valley began to fill with the dull roar of massed voices, spiced with the shriek and bellow of the horns.

The Saxons were coming slowly, both to save their breath and to taunt the waiting Britons. Restraint, and a keen sense of timing, would decide the battle at many different junctures. Wendell also waited, trusting Terri not to break ranks early. In the fighting itself, if she could force the Saxon reserves into battle before he was forced to bring in the cavalry, all should be well. She, in turn, was trusting him to throw in the cavalry at the critical moment when she had held as long as possible—and no later.

"*Position the cavalry.*" Richard's voice was firm and cool, perhaps even more authoritative than usual.

Wendell sent a third of the cavalry squads behind the crest of the slope, out of sight of the Saxons. They circled to the wooded area at the left of Terri's infantry and then stood there assembled, still hidden to the enemy. Wendell guarded his trumpeters carefully; only they could signal the left wing now.

Suddenly the Saxon advance lunged forward at a run. Spears and throwing axes would come seconds before the two front lines clashed bodily. As the yards between them quickly shrank, Terri surged forward with the front line of the Britons. The impact of striking shields sent a shock up and down the line. At first, the advantages of gravity and fresh breath carried Terri's line hard against the Saxons and pushed them back. As the Saxon line steadied. Wendell kept an anxious eye on the second line. Again, she would feel great temptation to throw them forward, but it was too early.

Slowly, the thrust of Saxon numbers began to push the line of combat up the hill. Behind them, the Saxon reserves followed restlessly, allowing their colleagues space to move, but little else. They gained the ground slowly, and Wendell judged that the cost was just slightly greater for the enemy. That would do for the moment.

The first line of Britons gradually backed into the second. The two merged and held. With renewed spirit, the new combined line even carried forward again and down the slope for a short time.

There was one more line to the rear of that.

Wendell studied the lay of the land again, finding the best paths for his three cavalry charges—to each flank of the enemy, and to its rear. When the Brittany Annal had first surfaced, deep in some Frankish stone cellar, it had proved to be an eleventh-century copy of a Celtic monk's personal journal. He had originally written in the mid-sixth century, when the memory of Mount Badon was alive but a generation old. Afraid that the glory of Artorius's victory would be forgotten, he had described the location and mechanics of the entire confrontation in great detail. Its reliability was accepted slowly, but its authenticity was verified by chemical analysis, and the content meshed completely both with known facts and learned conjecture. What the copy was doing in Brittany remained a mystery. The battle itself, almost identical to Cannae, was even closer to a pure theoretical example of that technique because of the Saxon need to advance up the slope for strategic objectives and because of their lack of cavalry. Wendell picked out his routes carefully, and felt Richard nod agreement.

The line of struggle began to recede up the slope once again. Wendell shifted in his seat and took a deep breath. The time for cavalry was coming, and Terri's position-

ing and execution so far had been nearly perfect. Quickly,
Wendell cast about for any surprises, any twists that
their opponents might have in readiness, but he could
think of none. Their chances of winning lay not so much
in besting Artorius and the Britons as in besting their
actual Saxon predecessors.

"That won't be hard," said Richard. *"If they save almost anyone, they'll have done better."*

Wendell watched the struggle stretched across the
slope with rising tension. Slowly, grudgingly, fiercely,
Terri's line fell back and back. They held good formation,
and the final line of reserves stiffened in readiness. All
at once, Terri brought the front line back sharply, in an
ordered retreat, and they melted into the rear line. As
the Saxons continued forward, the one solid line of Britons fell hard down upon them again, and Wendell nodded in admiration. Victory was procured by compiling
small moves, like this emphasizing the advantage of the
slope. The Saxon line faltered and was forced back one
more time.

"Here they come," thought Wendell, with a smile of
anticipation. The Britons were pressing forward more
quickly than before, with both psychological and gravitational momentum. The Saxon reserves could not back
away, for fear of losing morale. So, as the line of combat
came back down the slope into them, Terri was effectively forcing them into play before they wanted to go.
"That's the way."

The Saxon reserves, greatly outnumbering the final
line of Britons that was already in the struggle, were
ordered forward. Once fully committed, they would have
trouble turning to meet the charges of the cavalry.
Grudgingly, the massive rear lines of the enemy came
forward.

"Not yet," said Richard, sternly.

Intensely anxious, Wendell gave the signal. Trumpets
sounded, and a third of the cavalry squads began to move
on each flank of the battle.

"No!" yelled Richard. *"Too soon, stop it. Hold."*

"Too late," Wendell tossed back, without regret.
Artorius began to take the final third of cavalry around
the right flank, high on the shoulder of Mount Badon

itself, at a fast trot. Their target was the Saxon rear, for the final blow.

Meanwhile, the heavy cavalry came charging down past the flanks of their own Briton line and took the Saxons hard on each side. The sheer weight and momentum of the charges carried them deep into what was becoming a blunt, curved mass of Saxons, with both flanks turned to form a horse-shoe shape.

"Look, will you? Stop," Richard hissed. "Can't you see?" Wendell stared. He had not allowed the Saxon reserves enough time to engage Terri's force. Although they had taken tremendous losses from the initial attack, they were wheeling about to maintain their curved lines, forming the horse-shoe with its open end facing back toward their own south. Instead of smashing the Saxon center and pinching out the strength that pushed against the Briton shield wall, the two cavalry wings had simply re-aligned the struggle. The Saxon center still advanced in good order against Terri's line, and threatened to punch through.

"Attack. Straight down the slope," Richard ordered. "Go."

Wendell hesitated, then continued to push his squads farther on his own chosen path. "Their rear is still vulnerable. We'll hurry and—"

"No time, fool. Charge now, before anything changes. Hit the center. Fast." Richard's voice ended in a falsetto note. "Go."

Terri's line had no more reserves. The Saxon center pushed onward, forcing the Britons slowly toward the crest of the slope. If the Saxons attained the crest, all the mechanics of the battle would alter drastically, to their benefit. Wendell rushed his cavalry squads into a canter toward the far downward slope of Mount Badon.

"No!" Richard yelled again.

Wendell lurched forward suddenly in the seat with a wave of nausea. He momentarily lost his bearings and his grip on the keyboard. Badly shaken, he looked up at the screen, fighting panic. The keyboard was slick with sweat under his fingers.

"GARG'N UAIR DHUISGEAR," screamed Richard. As Wendell stared at the screen and pounded the keyboard, the cavalry broke from the path across Mount Badon and charged at full gallop for the enemy's flank.

The alert cavalry squads already on the field saw them coming and expertly parted to let them pass.

Wendell stared wide-eyed at the screen, clutching and punching at the keys. The units ignored him. In his mixture of panic and reflex, he couldn't tell if the keyboard wasn't functioning right or if his own hands were out of control.

"Garg'n uair dhuisgear," echoed again and again in Wendell's mind. The cavalry reserves thundered through the opened ranks of their comrades and crashed through to the heart of the Saxons. The tremendous power of the charge crushed the enemy center, and the other cavalry squads renewed their rushes on both sides of the collapsing Saxon horse-shoe.

Wendell looked back at Terri's line. They were holding fast, relieved of the intense pressure of greater numbers. Stability was needed now, and simple attrition. Confidence would sustain them.

Two squads of cavalry split off from the right flank, and swung wide around the struggling mass. They wheeled at the base of Mount Badon, and charged into the enemy rear. The Saxons were surrounded, jammed together, and partially divided into separate bands.

The outcome was decided.

"Victory Conditions, Britain," appeared on the screen. Wendell collapsed back in his seat, ignoring the statistics that were listed under the crucial phrase. He was soaked in sweat and sick to his stomach. Breathing heavily, he let his head roll to one side to see Terri. She was damp and flushed. As he watched, she brushed matted curls of hair from her eyes and smiled at him weakly. The attendants arrived, to help them into the back rooms. Wendell waved his away, gesturing a need to catch his breath.

"Made it," he thought. "Congratulations."

No answer. Wendell was too exhausted to wonder about it. He watched Terri leave the room on the arm of one attendant, while several more tried to keep back the crowd of excited spectators. The only voice in his mind was his own.

"Well," he thought, as his strength gradually gathered.

"Gone, huh?" There was no doubt that Richard had won this game—the prodigy still reigned. "Wherever you are, congratulations, anyhow."

Far below the city, in a cavern edged with blue-white frost, the gangling body lay unmoving. The tank sparkled in the pale light. Deep within the silent cranium, a spark began to glow.

Wendell lay back in the seat, motionless, looking at the frozen screen without seeing it. He had tread too long on the subtle interface where dreams and dreams threatened to merge. His eyes suddenly focused on the screen, and he thought again of the phosphorous shine and its ethereal universe. Those lives belonged to the dead, but they had thrown a millennial shadow.

EDITOR'S INTRODUCTION TO:

CINCINNATUS
by
Joel Rosenberg

Livy tells the story of the stern Roman patriarch called from retirement to lead Rome's armies and save the state. He might have had the crown from the hands of the Senate, but instead he returned to his land and his plow. Cincinnati, Ohio, is named in his memory.

The Order of the Cincinnatus was an association of regular officers of the Continental Army. After their victory over England, the Continental officers thought to influence the course of events in this land: they offered George Washington the crown.

Of course they had no authority to create a monarchy, but it was probably in their power to grant it. Certainly there was no other force on this continent that could have stood up to the Continental Army. On the other hand, they could only offer it to Washington: there was assuredly no general in the New World who could have faced him. When Washington refused, the matter was at an end.

The story of Cincinnatus has inspired many science fiction stories.

CINCINNATUS
by
Joel Rosenberg

The log cabin was drafty, and cold; I moved a bit closer to the open fireplace, and took a deep draught from the stone tankard. It was real Earth coffee, black and rich.

The old man chuckled, as though over some private joke.

"What the hell is so funny?" I didn't bother to keep the irritation out of my voice. I'd travelled for over seven hundred hours to reach Thellonee and find Shimon Bar-El; and every time I'd try to bring up the reason I'd come from Metzada, the old bastard would just chuckle and change the subject, as though to tell me that we'd discuss business at his pleasure, not mine.

"You are what is so funny. Tetsuki. Nephew." Bar-El sat back in his chair, shaking his head. He set his mug down, and rubbed at his eyes with arthritis-swollen knuckles. It's kind of strange, that: I bear the first name of one of my Nipponese ancestors—Tetsuo Nakamura, my g'g'g'g'g'grandfather—but he has the epicanthic folds. Me, I look like a sabra.

"And why am I so funny? Uncle?" *You traitor.* There isn't a nastier word in the language than that. Metzada is dependent on credits earned offworld by the Metzadan Mercenary Corps, the MMC, and that depends on our reputation. There hadn't been any proof that Bar-El had taken a payoff on Oroga; if there had, he would have been hanged, not cashiered and exiled.

Although, the argument could be made that hanging would have been kinder—but, never mind that, the sus-

285

picion alone had been enough to strip him of rank and citizenship.

I would have given a lot if we didn't need him now.

"Well," he said, setting his mug down and rubbing at the knuckles of his right hand with the probably just-as-arthritic fingers of his left, "you've been here all day; and you haven't asked me if I really did take that payoff." He cocked his head to one side, his eyes going vague. "I can remember when that was of some importance to you, *Inspector*-General." The accent on *Inspector* was a dig. Unlike Bar-El, I've always been a staff officer; the only way I could get my stars was through the IG ranks—there simply aren't any other generals in the MMC that don't command fighting forces.

"I . . . don't really care. Not anymore." I had trouble getting the next words out. "Because we've come up with a way for you to earn your way back home."

He raised an eyebrow. "I doubt that. You've never understood me, Tetsuo Hanavi—but I can read you. Like a book. There's a contract that's come up, right?"

"Yes, and—"

"Shut up while I'm speaking. I want to show you how well I know you—it's a low-tech world, correct?"

I shrugged. "That's your specialty, isn't it?"

He smiled. "And why do I think I'm so smart? Let me tell you more about the contract. It's high pay, and tough, and it looks like there's no way to do whatever the locals are paying the MMC to do."

I nodded. "Right. And we're short of low-tech specializing general officers. Gevat is off on Schriftalt; Kinter and Cohen are bogged down on Oroga; and my brother's still home, recovering from the Rand Campaign. So—"

Concern creased his face. "Ari's hurt?"

"Not too badly. He took a Jecty arrow in the liver. It's taking a while to regenerate, but he'll make it."

He nodded. "Good. He's a good man. Too good to be wasted on quelling the peon revolts." Bar-El snorted. "Did you know that Rand was settled by a bunch of idiots who wanted to get away from any kind of government?"

I didn't, actually. I'd just assumed that the feudacracy there had always been there. Ancient history bores me. "No—but we're getting off the subject." I spread my hands. "The point is, that you're the only one who's ever generaled a low-tech campaign who's available."

He pulled a tabstick out of a pocket, and puffed it to life. "*If* I'm available. What's in it for me?"

I tapped at my chest pocket. "I've got a Writ of Citizenship here. If you can salvage the situation, you can go home." I waved my hand around the room. "Unless you prefer this . . . squalor."

He sat silently for a moment, puffing at his tabstick. "You've got my commission in another pocket?"

"A temporary one, yes." I shook my head. "I'm not offering to have you permanently reinstated, *traitor*."

Shimon Bar-El smiled. "Good. At least you're being honest. Who's the employer?"

"The lowlanders, on—"

"Indess. So, Rivka manipulated them into asking for me."

"*What do you mean*?" He was absolutely right, of course, but there was no way that he should have known that. The Primier had kept the negotiations secret; outside of the lowlanders' representatives, I am the only one who knew how Rivka Effron had suckered them into a payment under-all-contingencies contract, with Bar-El in command.

He shrugged. "I know how her mind works, too. If anyone else were to fail—regardless of what the contract says—it'd be bad for Metzada's reputation. But, if they'd *asked* for Bar-El the Traitor, insisted on him—at least, that's the way the transcript would read—it'd be on their own heads. Right?"

He was exactly right. "Of course not." But my orders were specific; I wasn't to admit anything of the sort. Shimon Bar-El was a sneaky bastard—it was entirely possible that our conversation was being taped, despite the poverty of the surroundings.

Bar-El drained the last of his coffee. "I'll believe what my own mind tells me, not words from a *staff officer*." He said that like a curse. "Of course, it's out of the question. I'm sorry that you had to come such a long way, but I'm happy here. No intention of leaving; not to be the sacrificial lamb." He set his tankard down. "I don't bleat any too well."

"You arrogant *bastard*." I stood. "Think you're unique,

that I'll offer you a permanent commission if you'll take this one on." I picked up my bag. "Well, we're going to take this contract, anyway. The offer's just too good to pass up—I'll handle it myself, if I have to."

He spat. "Don't be silly. You don't have the experience. A lot of soldiers would die, just because—"

"Shut your mouth, traitor. You're wrong. Maybe I don't have any field experience, but *nobody* does, not against cavalry. And—"

"Cavalry? As in horses?"

"No, cavalry as in giant mice—of course it's horses."

He chewed on his lower lip. "I don't see the problem—you just set up your pikemen, let them impale their critters against your line. Take a bit of discipline, even for Metzadans, to hold the line, but—"

I sneered. "That's fine for a meeting engagement, where they have to come to you—but how about a siege? All they have to do is use their cavalry to harrass our flanks, and we can't ever get the towers up. And we've got to use towers: there's no deposits of sulfur available, so there's no way we can make gunpowder. Not with what the Thousand Worlds will let us bring in. Low-tech world, remember?"

"You've got the tech reports in your bag?"

"Of course I—"

"Let me see them." He held out a hand. "We're both going to have to study them."

"Both?" I didn't understand. Then again, I've never understood my uncle.

"Both." He smiled, not pleasantly. "Me, 'cause I'm taking this. And you, because you get to be my exec." As I handed him my bag, he took the blue tech report folder out, and started spreading papers around on the floor. "We're going to get you some field experience, we are." He studied the sheets silently for a few moments. "I'll want all the equipment special-ordered, make sure it gets through inspection. You got that, Colonel?"

"Colonel?"

"You just got demoted, nephew. I don't like to see stars on anybody's shoulders but mine." He picked up a topographical map. "Cavalry, eh?"

*　　　*　　　*

Fifteen hundred hours later, aboard the Gate complex circling Indess, I hadn't gotten used to the eagles on my shoulders. I guess it's kind of petty—hell, I *know* it is—but I put in seventeen years of service earning my IG's stars, and the demotion rankled. The trouble was, of course, that we needed Bar-El, and that meant that I had to put up with whatever indignities he cared to inflict. For the time being.

I shouldn't complain. Field soldiers risk their lives; all I had to do was put up with the sneering of a Thousand Worlds Commerce Department Inspector who clearly had no use for Metzadans or the Metzadan Mercenary Corps. And by myself; *General* Bar-El was with the men.

She dumped the contents of the backpack onto the flat black surface of her durlyn desk, the messkit, sheathknife, and various items of clothing falling in agonizing slowness.

"This doesn't look standard," she said, gathering it all into a pile, then picking up the sheathknife. "And I've seen the gear you killers carry before." Inspector Celia von du Mark tested the edge of the oversize blade with her thumb. "Molysteel?"

I shook my head. "No, just high-carbon—and no better than they could make, down there. The . . . General had everything special-ordered—that's an infighting weapon, called a Bowie." I held out my hand for it; she slapped the hilt into my palm. "The angle of the blade cants upward when you hold it *so*; at waist-height, it'll cut into your opponent's abdomen, makes it easy to—"

"Spare me the details," she snapped, tossing her head, sending her shortish black hair whipping around her thin face. "Just as long as you don't violate tech levels, I don't give a good goddamn what toys you're carrying." Brow furrowed, she cocked her head to one side. "Of course this isn't a typical pack." There was no hint of a question in that, just disbelief.

I shrugged. "Check for yourself. We posted bond; we're not going to sacrifice that, not for the sake of having a rustproof knife or two." I slumped back into a chair. "But go ahead, have your men—"

"My people."

"—have your people check it out. Except for the bows, arrows, maps, and the siege-tower hardware, you won't find anything on any of the two thousand men in the regiment that doesn't duplicate what you've got in front of you." I spotted a piece of fur on the corner of her desk, and picked it up. There wasn't anything prepossessing about it; just a smooth brown swatch of soft fur, the size of my palm. "This is what it's all about?" I sighed. "Doesn't look all that special."

"Try dipping it in a weak acetic acid solution, let it dry." She sat down behind her desk, and rummaged around in a drawer. "Then it looks like this."

A twinkling shape flew toward me; I snatched it out of the air. Now *this* was nice: the swatch was white and shiny, gathering and shattering the light of the overhead glow, a spectrum of colors washing over its surface. I'd never seen a piece of treated oal-fur before; it's strictly a luxury item, and Metzada is a poor world. Tidelocked to a small M3 star, we have to import trace elements, medicines, electronics parts. When we venture to the surface of our own planet, it's in well-insulated vacuum suits, not fur coats. There's only about five million of us; ten percent of our population is in the MMC. We Metzadans have to earn our foreign exchange by fighting as mercenaries. Luxury would be lowering the number of us who have to lose our lives earning offworld credits, not importing oal coats.

"What's this?" She held up a folded, triangular piece of fabric, opening it only partway.

"Called a shelter half. It's half a tent; you pitch two of those things face-to-face, and you've got room for two soldiers to sleep." I'd asked Bar-El why we were taking special-ordered shelter-halves instead of the usual minitents, and he'd pointed out another use for them. *You can wrap a corpse in one, and bury it deeply*, he'd said. *But don't tell the men. Might make them nervous.* And then he'd smiled. *And I've got one specially made for you.*

I fondled the piece of fur. It was nice, certainly, but hardly worth dying for. And, of course, nobody was going to die for fur. The lowlanders were paying us to try to chase the mountain people out of their walled village halfway up the slopes of Mount Cibo, right in the middle of oal-country, the only remaining area on the continent where the chipmunk-like creature hadn't been hunted to extinction.

Certainly, some of us would die. But not for the fur. For the credits that keep Metzada alive.

That sort of distinction used to be more important to me.

"And this?" She held up a round cylinder, flat and half the size of my head.

"That's a messkit. It seals air-tight; you can put food in it, just chuck it in a fire, pull it out with a stick. Then you use the point of your knife to flick that little lever open."

She smiled slyly. "I've got another use for it—you fill it full of water, bury it in a fire you've built next to a wall—say, or a village on the slopes of Cibo. And then you wait until it builds up enough internal pressure to blow apart. And, incidentally, shatter the wall." She tossed it to the floor. "Denied. The *messkits* stay aboard here, when your regiment takes the shuttle down."

I figured that a little bit of false outrage would go over well. "*Inspector, we—*"

"Enough of that. The Commerce Charter specifically provides that offplanet mercenary soldiers can be brought in. Less bloodshed that way, supposedly; it's better than letting the locals hack each other to ribbons. But there are limitations—and *dammit while I'm in charge up here there are going to stay limits.*"

I wiped my hand across my forehead. "I know: not more than one mercenary for every four hundred locals, and no import of military—"

"—technology beyond what the locals possess. They don't have bombs like that. And you can't bring them in. Understood?"

Of course I understood. And I should have known better. Bar-El had said that they'd never let us get the messkits by.

We rode down on the first shuttle, along with the three battalion commanders, and their bodyguards. Which was standard—that goes back to the old Palmach days, long before there was the Metzadan Mercenary Corps, when no soldier ever set foot on a piece of land where an officer hadn't been first. There's nothing romantic about it, no bravura—just a matter of human economics: we've always had a lot of officer material, and traded off the high mortality among officers for lower casualties among line soldiers.

Other armies did—and still do—see it differently. Which is why we're better. And, to a large extent, why I get to wear my stars at home.

I followed Bar-El out into the daylight, squinting nervously in the bright sunlight. Indess orbits a F4 star, much brighter, whiter light than we use in Metzada's underground corridors.

"Relax," he said, dropping his pack to the dirt of the landing field. "We're on Thousand Worlds territory here, in the first place."

I watched Colonels Davis, Braunstein, and Orde walk down the ramp, their three bodyguards standing behind them, bows strung and arrows nocked, keeping careful watch on the one-story stone buildings that circled the field. They didn't look any too relaxed. "And in the second place?"

Bar-El shrugged. "I doubt that there's a Ciban within a hundred klicks." He turned around, and raised his voice. "Yonni, over here."

Davis trotted over, his blocky guard behind him. "What is it, Shimon?" Yonatan Davis was a short, wide man, whose girth and baldness always gave the impression that he was more suited to be a shopkeeper than an officer. I've known the type before; some compensate by being martinets. Davis went the opposite way, giving and taking orders with an informality that suggested that he was good enough not to have to put on airs.

"My . . ." Bar-El paused, ". . . executive officer and I are going to go talk to our employers, make sure that they got my message, have the staffs and spearheads ready." He pointed toward the north. "You're in charge until I get back; have your battalion bivouac there, the other two *there*, and *there*." He rubbed a finger across the break in his nose. "There won't be any problem here, but set out guards, just for practice."

Davis nodded. "Soon as they land. But speaking of practice," he bounced on the balls of his feet, experimenting, "we've got about nine-tenths of a g here."

"So?"

"So nobody has loosed an arrow under this grav, not

recently. You want me to improvise targets, get some practicing done?"

"No." Bar-El turned away.

"Wait one minute, General." Davis reached for his arm, clearly thought better of it. "They have to get some practice—better here than in combat."

Bar-El sighed. "They won't need it. We're not supposed to win this one." He jerked a thumb at me. "Ask my exec, when we get back. And, in the meantime, just follow orders. Understood?"

Davis turned away, wordless. I trotted after Bar-El.

"And what the hell was that for?" I kept my voice calm, with just a touch of a tremor, for effect.

He chuckled. "So that's not supposed to be common knowledge, eh? We're *supposed* to be able to storm a walled city—population about fifteen thousand, three thousand effectives—with two thousand men? While there's horsemen harassing our flanks?"

In fact we weren't. And weren't going to. "That's what the contract says."

He patted at his hip pocket. "I've got a copy of the contract. It's handy, when you run out of bumwad— Tetsuki, I have no intention of just going through the motions. I'm supposed to fail. Damned if I'm going to play wargames, just to keep you happy." He looked up at me, a smile quirking across his lips. "But I'll do it to keep our *employers* happy."

At the edge of the field, Bar-El stopped a blue-suited Commerce Department loader. "How do I go about finding Senhor Felize Regato?"

Regato's mansion was clear evidence that damn little except military tech was on the Proscribed list for Indess. The floors looked to be real Italian marble; among the paintings I spotted a Picasso and a Bartolucci—and the glows overhead made me smile: their light was the same color of the glows at home.

A white-linen clad servitor led us into Regato's study, a high-ceilinged room with enough space for a family of twelve, back home. The fur that covered the couch where we sat wasn't oal—that would have been too easy—it was the pelt of some coal-black animal, glossy and soft. After the requisite wait—Regato was a busy man, and clearly wanted us to know it—he sauntered in, a tall, slim man with a broad smile creasing his dark face. We stood.

"General Bar-El, it is a pleasure." He clasped Bar-El's hand with both of his own. "And this is your aide, Colonel . . .?"

"Hanavi, Senhor—and technically I'm his executive officer, not his aide."

He smiled vaguely, and dropped into an overstuffed chair, idly smoothing the legs of his suit. "General, I believe we share a hobby."

Bar-El didn't return Regato's smile. "I don't have hobbies."

I shot a glance at my uncle. This was playing along to keep the employer happy? Contradicting the First Senhor of the Assembly didn't quite seem to fit the bill.

Regato's brow furrowed. "Oh? I thought we were both devotees of ancient military history." He waved a hand at the bookshelves behind him. "I've studied from Thucydides to," he half-ducked his head, "Bar-El."

Bar-El chuckled. "Thank you—but Thucydides was a historian, as you know, not a soldier—and for me the history of my profession isn't a hobby, it's business."

Regato raised a finger. "Ah, but he was the first to recount battles, to preserve them for future generations. I only wish that he had been around later, when Cincinnatus was alive."

Bar-El cocked his head to one side. "He would have had to live an extra few hundred years. And been a Roman, instead of a Greek. Why Cincinnatus?"

Regato touched a button on the table at his elbow. "Coffee, please, three cups." He raised his head. "Because he reminds me of you. If I remember correctly," he smiled in self-deprecation, "he, too, was called out of retirement to command an apparently impossible campaign."

A shrug. "Different situation—Cincinnatus was honorably retired; I was booted out of the MMC and off of Metzada."

"That is hardly a relevant difference here; even were you capable of taking a bribe, the Cibans would have nothing to offer you. Hunting rights or the oal? You couldn't take advantage of that. Hard currency, the sort

Metzada needs? They don't have any; most of the prime farmland on the continent and the only offworld trading center is down here in the valley."

A different servitor from the one who had showed us in arrived with a steaming silver pot of coffee on a tray with three cups and saucers, plus condiments. We all were silent until the servant deposited the tray and left.

Regato poured coffee for all of us, then sipped his own and sighed. "On to business. I received your message by courier, and your instructions were followed to the letter. At a warehouse near the port you will find precisely two thousand rulawood shafts for spears—each exactly three meters long, as requested—and spearheads for them, boxed separately." He lifted his head. "We could have attached them for you."

"I'd rather have my men do it themselves. And the rest?"

A nod. "Dried meat and vegetables, enough to feed two thousand for a month. If you need more spears, I can have the shafts and heads sent up to you, if you'll give the convoy protection."

"I doubt we will—and if we do, Ciba is heavily forested, according to my maps. With rula."

I'd read the report on rulawood, and it sounded useful; similar to bamboo, but lighter and stronger. Strong enough that the Ciban villagers were confident enough of it to build the walls of their village out of rula.

"Good." Regato wrinkled his brow, as though he was about to ask why Bar-El wanted the spearshafts down here, if he knew that there would be plenty of rula where we were going. Or maybe I'm just projecting; that's what I wanted to ask. "So," he steepled his fingers together, "two questions: first, why didn't you ask to have horses ready? We could provide them, you know."

"I know—but my men aren't horsemen, and I have no intention of putting them on horses, up against a larger force, every man of whom has grown up on horseback." Bar-El shook his head. "We are professionals; riding horses, we'd be amateurs."

Regato nodded. "In that case, I understand why you wanted spears that you could use as pikes. Second question: how many ninjas do you have with you? I assume that you're going to use assassination." He gave a knowing smile.

Which explained why Regato had been willing to hire us, despite the odds. It wasn't just that he believed in Bar-El, or the mystique that's grown up around the MMC's successes. He had at least a suspicion, heard a rumor about the Metzadan ninjas.

Bar-El shook his head. "There aren't such things as ninjas. There haven't been for half a millenium."

He said that with a straight face; he might even have thought it true. Which it was, at least in one sense: Metzada's rumored assassins are only called ninjas by offworlders; we aren't descended from the Nipponese society that died out in the nineteenth century, Earthside. Not directly descended—but some of the members of the Bushido Brotherhood that were transported to Metzada along with the children of Israel had been trying to revive the ancient arts. It's been kept secret, the fact that we have a cadre of assassins with the MMC, but there's nothing you can do about rumors.

And an assassin can be a kind of handy person to have around; it can blow an opponent's organization apart, when the top general dies. Or, better, when he's kept alive, but all his top staff officers are killed.

Of course, an assassin has to have some sort of cover, that will let him mix with the troops, without even his own people knowing what his job is. Inspector-General is a nice one. You even get to wear your stars, on your off-hours.

Bar-El went on: "And it wouldn't do any good, even if we used assassins. Which we don't—I don't think a stranger could survive long enough in a Ciba village to first," he held up a finger, "find out who the top commander is; and second," another finger, "kill him." Bar-El shrugged. "If he could get over the walls in the first place." Bar-El turned to me. "Don't you agree, Colonel?"

He was precisely correct, as usual. Which was why I had no intention of killing anyone within the village. "Absolutely."

Regato spread his hands. "Then how are you going to do it? You're outmanned, in strange territory, and the enemy has greater mobility."

Bar-El sat silently for a moment. "Do you need access to the mountain?"

For a moment, Regato's polite veneer faded. "Of course we do—in more ways than one. We need the credits, so that we can bring in power technology. And we need to control the mountain, because the thousand-times-damned Commerce Department won't let reactors onto a world without a single government. There's almost a million of us here; we can't let a few thousand mountain . . . *yokels* stand in the way of progess. And—"

"Enough." Bar-El held up a hand. "I don't give a damn whether you're right or wrong, as long as you're paying the bills. My point is, that if you need what we can do badly enough, you don't need to know how we're going to do it." He sat back. "And I don't like to talk about battle plans, I never do. If you've studied my career, you should know that I never tell anyone anything they don't need to know." He jerked a thumb at me. "I haven't even told my exec how I'm going to do it."

No, he hadn't. Because I already knew what we were going to do.

Lose.

There's an old saying, to the effect that a battle plan never survives contact with the enemy. Bar-El liked to hold forth on what nonsense that was, pointing to campaigns from Thermopylae through Sinai to Urmsku, where things went exactly as planned. For one side, at least.

"Besides," he'd say, giving the same pause each time, "the last line in the orders, in the plan, should always be the same, should always prevent the plan from becoming obsolete: If all else fails, improvise."

We improvised our way up the slopes of Ciba, the horsemen harrassing us all the way. In one sense; it was a standoff: any time we stopped, pikemen in front, protecting the archers behind them, they couldn't do more than taunt us, from beyond the four-hundred-meter range of our bows. And whenever we started to move in the direction of the walled village, they'd sweep down on us, forcing us to form a line, pikemen in front, and so on.

Casualties were low, on both sides—two weeks after

leaving, we'd had three deaths and seventeen serious injuries—all stragglers who had let themselves range too far from the main body of our force.

And they had only lost a few dozen. Stragglers, too.

The trouble was, we were being pushed away from the village, higher up the shallow slopes of Ciba. I didn't like it much: all the mountaineers had to do was detach a body of their force, swing around and cut us off at the flat top of the mountain—an extinct volcano, technically.

"Don't bother me with technicalities, Colonel." Bar-El turned to whisper to a runner, who nodded and loped off toward where Braunstein's battalion was camped, at the far edge of the clearing. "I'm not in the mood to be quibbled with—and I don't give a damn whether this mound of dirt is a mountain, a volcano, or a pile of elephant dung."

We had climbed too far—at least in my opinion. Three klicks away and about one below us, the walls of the village stood mockingly. The air was clear; I could see people and animals moving in the narrow streets, and a mass of horses and men, milling around the main gates.

Well, I'd stalled just about long enough. "Looks like they're sending out another detachment." The sun hung low in the sky, a white ball that was painful to look at. "Do you think they're preparing for an assault?"

He bit off a piece of jerky, washing it down with water from his canteen. "No, I think they're getting ready to invite us in for tea." He cocked his head to one side. "Seriously, they're probably going to take off tonight—cover of darkness, and all that—and try and swing around, come at us from the top tomorrow. Or just settle in there, have their bowmen dismounted and ready." The locals' only projectile weapons were cross-bows. Easier to fire from horseback than our compound bows, but the rate of fire was pitiful—reloading a cross-bow on horseback was probably not a whole lot easier than firing one from the pitching, yawing back of the animal. But from prepared positions, they could sit behind improvised barricades on solid ground.

As a matter of fact, it was possible—at least in theory—that one or more of them had already done that and were lying in ambush, somewhere near where we were.

A handy possibility, that.

Bar-El stood. "Come—take a walk with me."

The downslope edge of the clearing was just that: an edge. A hundred meters below, the sharp drop ended in a stand of the everpresent rula trees.

Bar-El gestured at the village below. "About how many would you say are in this next group?"

I shrugged. "A thousand, or so. Probably a touch more." I glanced over my shoulder. Good: nobody else was in the immediate vicinity. It wasn't impossible that even Shimon Bar-El would slip over the edge of a cliff, and drag his exec along with him. At least, that's the way it would seem. There was a handy overhang, about fifty meters down. I could probably climb down and duck under before anyone could reach the edge, then hide until dark. Living off the land wouldn't be a problem; that was part of my training.

And when Yonny Davis took command, not knowing what Bar-El had planned, he'd have no choice but to retreat. And quickly—before the villagers got their second force of horsemen around the mountain, and cut off the line of retreat. Over the mountain and down the other side—he'd make it to the port in the valley within a week, and they'd leave Indess behind.

The Primier had planned it well: we'd collect the credits due us under the contract, with minimal casualties. And not much damage to Metzada's reputation—maybe other employers wouldn't be willing to sign a payment-under-all-contingencies contract, but so what? All-contingencies deals come along once in a lifetime; the loss of revenue wouldn't be much.

In a few weeks, when someone who looked only vaguely like Tetsuo Hanavi appeared at the lowland port and booked passage out, nobody would suspect a thing. The regiment would merely have retreated out of an impossible situation; Bar-El and his secret battleplans would have died together.

I turned. Bar-El was holding his Bowie. Casually, but if I lunged for him, he'd probably cut me by accident.

"What's that for?"

He smiled. "You any good with one of these things?"

I could have sliced him from crotch to throat in less time than it would take him to blink. But Bar-El getting knifed by his exec was not the image I wanted to leave behind—the retreat was supposed to look like the result of an enemy assassination, or an accident. Even—*particularly* to the line troops; what they didn't know, they couldn't tell. "Reasonable." I shrugged. "I may be just a—you should pardon the expression—staff officer, but I try to keep in shape."

He chuckled, backing away from the edge before sheathing the knife. "What I meant was: how good are you at cutting wood—the damn blade is too long to make a really good hand-to-hand weapon and too damn short to be a decent substitute for a sword."

The runner he'd dispatched to Braunstein ran over.

" 'Braunstein to Bar-El: What the hell are you doing, Shimon?' " The runner, a tall, skinny boy who looked to be about seventeen, shrugged an apology before continuing. " 'We're cutting wood, as per your directions, and have relayed said directions to Orde—but I'm damned if I understand. Would you be kind enough to enlighten me?' "

Bar-El nodded. "Good. Tell him: I'm starting a bonfire tonight, and I'm particular about the length of the firewood. As soon as it's dark—say, another ninety minutes—leave your first company on watch, and get the hell up the trail to this clearing. Same thing for Orde: I don't want any skirmishers interrupting."

A fire might not be a bad idea; it could cover a retreat. I smiled at him. "So that was your idea—do you want me to go into the woods, and cut my own contribution?"

He clapped a hand to my shoulder. "Not a bad idea—I think I'll join you." He flexed his hands. "I can use the exercise." He looked up at the runner, who was still standing there. "That's all. Run along." Bar-El turned to me. "Coming?"

I followed Bar-El into the woods. Good: he was taking us out of sight of the encampment. Perhaps it wouldn't be as neat as a solution for him simply to disappear along with his exec, but it wouldn't take long for Davis to notice: and if a search didn't find his body or mine, attribute it to the opposition.

I let my hand slide to the hilt of my Bowie. *Just wait a moment, until he's stepping over the trunk of the tree.* He might be Bar-El the Traitor, but he was my uncle; I'd make it as painless as possible.

I drew my knife and—

—pain blossomed in the back of my head. I tried to lift the knife—*never mind what it is, finish him first*—but it grew heavier, and heavier, dragging me down. I let go of it—*bare hands, then*—but rough hands seized me from behind, dragging me back.

I gave up, and fell into the cool dark.

I woke to someone slapping me with a wet cloth.

"Go away."

"Easy, Tetsuo." Yonny Davis' voice was calm as always. "I hit you a bit harder than I should have; but," gentle fingers probed my scalp, sending hot rivulets of pain through my head, "I don't think you've got a concussion."

I opened my eyes slowly. It was dark—took me a moment to realize that the lights dancing in my eyes were stars overhead.

In the darkness, Bar-El chuckled. "It's probably my fault—I gave him a hefty dose of morphine, to keep him under. You sure he's going to live?"

Far away, there was a rustling, as though a ship's sails were flapping in the winds. Sails?

"Let's get him up." Hands grasped my arms, pulling me to my feet. It was hard to tell; but at the opposite end of the clearing, next to the ledge, it looked like the shelter halves were being—thrown off the edge?

"Better leave us now, Yonny—your battalion's next."

Davis nodded. "See you down there," he said, and jogged away. No, they weren't being thrown off—there was a man under each.

"They're called hang gliders, Tetsuki." Bar-El's voice came from behind me. "You take a specially designed piece of cloth—camouflaged as a shelter half, say—mount an alleged spear down the center of it as a sort of beam, add other sticks at the edge and as bracing, and mount a lashed-together triangle as a steering mechanism." He chuckled. "Then you have each and every one of your men practice for a few hours, taking short flights across the clearing. And then you have it: instant airpower."

I turned. He was rubbing at his chin. "I doubt that one in ten will actually be able to control the silly things well enough to put it down inside the walls. But as long as a few do, to open the gates—and as long as the rest get close enough, before the locals arrive here in the morning—"

"You did it."

"You, nephew, have a keen eye for the obvious." He clapped a hand to my shoulder. "Of course I did it. Come morning, the few effectives remaining in the city will be captured or dead. And we'll have everyone else inside as hostages, for the good behavior of the twenty-five hundred who are up here, chasing shadows." He shrugged. "I think we'll be able to persuade them to move on; lots of other places to settle on this continent." He looked up at me, quizzically. "Do you think they could mount a siege, with us standing on *their* walls? Not that we'd kill the hostages, just keep a bunch up there, tied and visible—to cut down on their eagerness to take potshots."

"You intended this from the first."

He pursed his mouth, and spat. "Of *course* I did. The only question was whether or not we were going to be able to sneak the sails past the Commerce Department—when you came up with the messkit dodge, I figured it'd be a good distraction."

I rubbed at my temples, still woozy. "But the tech levels—"

"Don't be silly. There's not a damn thing they can do. Anybody here could have built one of these things, if they'd have had a mind to. We didn't violate the regs—and local Inspector passed us; she's not going to be eager to report that we snuck something by her. There's only one problem remaining, and that's where you come in."

"Me?"

"I don't know these folks any too well—somebody with a bit of clout might decide that the best thing to do is tough it out, try to starve us out." He shrugged. "It wouldn't make any sense, but—in any case, it would be kind of convenient if whoever's in charge were to get himself killed, if he's going to be stubborn. Maybe a crossbow bolt in the night? It's up to you." Bar-El smiled. "I didn't just bring you along for the exercise." He stooped, and picked up a knife and pack. "Better get going."

*   *   *

The last time I saw Shimon Bar-El was at the port. The regiment was being loaded on shuttles, preparatory to leaving. Officers are first down, last up—we had some time to chat.

"You did well, Tetsuki—they didn't need more than a day to decide."

It hadn't been hard—prowling around an open encampment in the dark, stealing a crossbow, setting up a clamor in the opposite side of the camp. "No problem. General." He started to turn away. "Uncle?"

He turned back, startled. "Yes?"

"You knew from the beginning, didn't you?"

He smiled. "That this was a set-up? Of course; and give my compliments to the Primier. A nice idea," he nodded, "arranging an all-contingencies contract, where we— you— get paid whether we win or lose, and then working out how to lose cheaply, sacrificing only," he tapped himself on the chest with a nail-bitten finger, "an old irritation. I could just see you explaining it to Regato— 'Sorry, Senhor, but Bar-El was the only one who could possibly have generaled such a campaign—you knew that when you hired us.' " He spread his hands. " 'And since the old traitor is dead, we had no choice but to retreat. Our contracts calls for payment under all contingencies; do you pay us now, and do we have the Thousand Worlds Inspector garnishee all your offworld credits until you do?'—that was how it was supposed to go, no?"

"Roughly." I smiled. "But I think I'd have had a bit more tact. But why did you—"

"Stick my head in the buzzsaw? I could tell you that I knew that the hang glider gambit would work, even before I studied the Tech reports, but . . ."

I shook my head. "That wouldn't be true, would it?"

He shrugged slowly, his eyes becoming vague and unfocused. "Regato told you about Cincinnatus, Tetsuo. About how he chose to come out of retirement, to command the armies of Rome in an almost impossible campaign. I . . . don't think he could have told you *why*. Or why, after winning, he denied the people's demand he become Emperor, went back into retirement, back to his farm. Regato couldn't have known. I do.

"Tetsuo, if you've spent your whole life preparing for

one thing, learning how to do it well, then doing that is all that matters to you." He chuckled thinly. "I was a bad uncle, a horribly incompetent husband—and not a good Metzadan citizen. But I am a general; commanding an army is the only thing I can do right. I'm not claiming that it's the most noble occupation in the universe, but it's my profession, the only one I've got, the only thing that I do well." His faint smile broadened. "And I wouldn't have missed it for *anything*." He clapped a hand to my shoulder. "Which is why we say goodbye here."

"What do you mean?" The officers' shuttle would be loading in a few minutes; both of us were supposed to be on it.

Shimon Bar-El shook his head. "You haven't been listening to me. Let's say I go back to Metzada with you. Do you think that Rivka Effron would let Bar-El the Traitor command again?"

"No." The Primier had been clear on that point; I wasn't even to offer that to Bar-El. Not on the grounds that we hadn't been willing to promise him anything—dead men collect little—but because he never would have believed it. Metzada's reputation had been hurt badly for Bar-El's selling out on Oroga; the damage would be irreparable if we let him come home *and* return to permanent duty.

He nodded. "Correct. This was a special case. I'll be heading back to Thellonee—perhaps another special case will come up, someday." Bar-El sighed, deeply. "And you'll know where to find me." He turned away again, and started walking from the landing field.

"Uncle?"

"What is it?" He turned, clearly irritated.

"Did you take that payoff on Oroga?"

Shimon Bar-El smiled. "That would be telling."

EDITOR'S INTRODUCTION TO:

CODE-NAME FEIREFITZ
by
David Drake

I have never met David Drake, although we have corresponded, and conversed on the telephone. When I was guest of honor at a convention in Chattanooga, Drake wrote the sketch about me in the convention program; but he was not able to attend the convention.

I have been a fan of Drake's Hammer's Slammers series since its first episode, and I'm pleased to be first to publish a new story in that saga.

Soldiers are often faced with unpleasant tasks. Sometimes it's clear what you should do; but that is not always what must be done.

CODE-NAME FEIREFITZ
by
David Drake

"Lord, we got one!" cried the trooper whose detector wand pointed toward the table that held the small altar. "That's a powergun for sure, Captain, nothing else'd read so much iridium!"

The three other khaki-clad soldiers in the room with Captain Esa Mboya tensed and cleared guns they had not expected to need. The villagers of Ain Chelia knew that to be found with a weapon meant death. The ones who were willing to face that were in the Bordj, waiting with their households and their guns for the Slammers to rip them out. Waiting to die fighting.

The houses of Ain Chelia were decorated externally by screens and colored tiles; but the tiles were set in concrete walls and the screens themselves were cast concrete. Narrow cul-de-sacs lined by blank, gated courtyard walls tied the residential areas of the village into knots of strongpoints. The rebels had elected to make their stand in Ain Chelia proper only because the fortress they had cut into the walls of the open pit mine was an even tougher objective.

"Stand easy, troopers," said Mboya. The householder gave him a tight smile; he and Mboya were the only blacks in the room—or the village. "I'll handle this one," Captain Mboya continued. "The rest of you get on with the search under Sergeant Scratchard. Sergeant—" calling toward the outside door—"come in here for a moment."

Besides the householder and the troops, a narrow-faced civilian named Youssef ben Khedda stood in the room. On his face was dawning a sudden and terrible hope. He had been Assistant Superintendent of the il- menite mine before Kabyles all over the planet rose against their Arabized central government in al-Madinah. The Superintendent was executed, but ben Khedda had joined the rebels to be spared. It was a common enough story to men who had sorted through the ruck of as many rebellions as the Slammers had. But now ben Khedda was a loyal citizen again. Openly he guided G Company from house to house, secretly he whispered to Capt Mboya the names of those who had carried their guns and families to the mine. "Father," said ben Khedda to the householder, lowering his eyes in a mockery of contrition, "I never dreamed that there would be contra- band *here*, I swear it."

Juma al-Habashi smiled back at the small man who saw the chance to become undisputed leader of as much of Chelia as the Slammers left standing and alive. "I'm sure you didn't dream it, Youssef," he said more gently than he himself expected. "Why should you, when I'd forgotten the gun myself?"

Sergeant Scratchard stepped inside with a last glance back at the courtyard and the other three men of Head- quarters Squad waiting there as security. Within, the first sergeant's eyes touched the civilians and the tense en- listed men; but Captain Mboya was calm, so Scratchard kept his own voice calm as he said, "Sir?"

"Sergeant," Mboya said quietly, "you're in charge of the search. If you need me, I'll be in here."

"Sir," Scratchard agreed with a nod. "Well, get the lead out, daisies!" he snarled to the troopers, gesturing them to the street. "We got forty copping houses to run yet!"

As ben Khedda passed him, the captain saw the villager's control slip to uncover his glee. The sergeant was the last man out of the room; Mboya latched the street door after him. Only then did he meet the householder's eyes again. "Hello, Juma," he said in the Kabyle he had sleep-learned rather than the Kikuyu they had both probably forgotten by now. "Brothers shouldn't have to meet this way, should we?"

Juma smiled in mad irony rather than humor. Then his mouth slumped out of that bitter rictus and he said sadly, "No, we shouldn't, that's right." Looking at his altar and not the soldier, he added, "I knew there'd be a—a unit sent around, of course. But I didn't expect you'd be leading the one that came here, where I was."

"Look, I didn't volunteer for Operation Feirefitz," Esa blazed. "And Via, how was I supposed to know where you where anyway? We didn't exactly part kissing each other's cheeks ten years ago, did we? And here you've gone and changed your name even—how was I supposed to keep from stumbling over you?"

Juma's face softened. He stepped to his brother, taking the other's wrists in his hands. "I'm sorry," he said. "Of course that was unfair. The—what's going to happen disturbs me." He managed a genuine smile. "I didn't really change my name, you know. 'Al-Habashi' just means 'the Black', and it's what everybody on this planet was going to call me whatever I wanted. We aren't very common on Dar al-B'heed, you know. Any more than we were in the Slammers."

"Well, there's one fewer black in the Slammers than before *you* opted out," Esa said bitterly; but he took the civilian's wrists in turn and squeezed them. As the men stood linked, the clerical collar that Juma wore beneath an ordinary jellaba caught the soldier's eye. Without the harshness of a moment before, Esa asked, "Do they all call you 'Father'?"

The civilian laughed and stepped away. "No, only the hypocrites like Youssef," he said. "Oh, Ain Chelia is just as Islamic as the capital, as al-Madinah, never doubt. I have a small congregation here . . . and I have the respect of the rest of the community, I think. I'm head of equipment maintenance at the mine, which doesn't mean assigning work to other people, not here." He spread his hands, palms down. The fingernails were short and the grit beneath their ends a true black and no mere skin tone. "But I think I'd want to do that anyway, even if I didn't need to eat to live. I've guided more folk to the Way by showing them how to balance a turbine than I do when I mumble about peace."

Captain Mboya walked to the table on top of which stood an altar triptych, now closed. Two drawers were set between the table legs. He opened the top one. In it were the altar vessels, chased brasswork of local manufacture. They were beautiful both in sum and in detail, but they had not tripped a detector set to locate tool steel and iridium.

The lower drawer held a powergun.

Juma watched without expression as his brother raised the weapon, checked the full magazine, and ran a fingertip over the manufacturer's stampings. "Heuvelmans of Friesland," Esa said conversationally. "Past couple contracts have been let on Terra, good products . . . but I always preferred the one I was issued when they assigned me to a tribarrel and I rated a sidearm." He drew his own pistol from its flap holster and compared it to the weapon from the drawer. "Right, consecutive serial numbers," the soldier said. He laid Juma's pistol back where it came from. "Not the sort of souvenir we're supposed to take with us when we resign from the Slammers, of course."

Very carefully, and with his eyes on the wall as if searching for flaws in its thick, plastered concrete, Juma said, "I hadn't really . . . thought of it being here. I suppose that's grounds for carrying me back to a Re-education Camp in al-Madinah, isn't it?"

His brother's fist slammed the table. The triptych jumped and the vessels in the upper drawer rang like Poe's brazen bells. "Re-education? It's grounds for being burned at the *stake* if I say so! Listen, the reporters are back in the capital, not here. My orders from the District Governor are to *pacify* this region, not coddle it!" Esa's face melted from anger to grief as suddenly as he had swung his fist a moment before. "Via, elder brother, why'd you have to leave? There wasn't a man in the Regiment could handle a tribarrel the way you could."

"That was a long time ago," said Juma, facing the soldier again.

"I remember at Sphakteria," continued Esa as if Juma had not spoken, "when they popped the ambush and killed your gunner the first shot. You cut 'em apart like they weren't shooting at you too. And then you led the whole platoon clear, driving the jeep with the wick all the way up and working the gun yourself with your right hand. Nobody else could've done it."

"Do you remember," said Juma, his voice dropping into a dreamy caress as had his brother's by the time he finished speaking, "the night we left Nairobi? You led the Service of Farewell yourself, there in the starport, with everyone in the terminal joining in. The faith we'd been raised in was just words to me before then, but you made the Way as real as the tiles I was standing on. And I thought 'Why is he going off to be a soldier? If ever a man was born to lead other men to peace, it was Esa.' And in time, you did lead me to peace, little brother."

Esa shook himself, standing like a centipede in his body armor. "I got that out of my system," he said.

Juma walked over to the altar. "As I got the Slammers out of my system," he said, and he closed the drawer over the powergun within.

Neither man spoke for moments that seemed longer. At last Juma said, "Will you have a beer?"

"What?" said the soldier in surprise. "That's permitted on Dar al-B'heed?"

Juma chuckled as he walked into his kitchen. "Oh yes," he said as he opened a trapdoor in the floor, "though of course not everyone drinks it." He raised two corked bottles from their cool recess and walked back to the central room. "There are some Arab notions that never sat very well with Kabyles, you know. Many of the notions about women, veils and the like. Youssef ben Khedda's wife wore a veil until the revolt . . . then she took it off and walked around the streets like the other women of Ain Chelia. I suspect that since your troops swept in, she has her veil on again."

"*That* one," said the captain with a snort that threatened to spray beer. "I can't imagine why nobody had the sense to throttle him—at least before they went off to their damned fortress."

Juma gestured his brother to one of the room's simple chairs and took another for himself. "Not everyone has seen as many traitors as we have, little brother," he said. "Besides, his own father was one of the martyrs whose death ignited the revolt. He was caught in al-Madinah with hypnocubes of Kabyle language instruction. The government called that treason and executed him."

Esa snorted again. "And didn't anybody here wonder who shopped the old man to the security police? Via! But I shouldn't complain—he makes my job easier." He swallowed the last of his beer, paused a moment, and then pointed the mouth of the bottle at Juma as if it would shoot. "What about you?" the soldier demanded harshly. "Where do you stand?"

"For peace," said Juma simply, "for the Way. As I always have since I left the Regiment. But . . . my closest friends in the village are dug into the sides of the mine pit now, waiting for you. Or they're dead already outside al-Madinah."

The soldier's hand tightened on the bottle, his fingers darker than the clear brown glass. With a conscious effort of will he set the container down on the terrazzo floor beside his chair. "They're dead either way," he said as he stood up. He put his hand on the door latch before he added, pausing but not turning around, "Listen, elder brother. I told you I didn't ask to be assigned to this mop-up operation; and if I'd known I'd find you here, I'd have taken leave or a transfer. But I'm here now, and I'll do my duty, do you hear?"

"As the Lord wills," said Juma from behind him.

The walls of Juma's house, like those of all the houses in Ain Chelia, were cast fifty centimeters thick to resist the heat of the sun. The front door was a scale with the walls, close-fitting and too massive to slam. To captain Mboya, it was the last frustration of the interview that he could elicit no more than a satisfied thump from the door as he stamped into the street.

The ballistic crack of the bullet was all the louder for the stillness of the plateau an instant before. Captain Mboya ducked beneath the lip of the headquarters dug-out. The report of the sniper's weapon was lost in the fire of the powerguns and mortars that answered it. "Via, Captain!" snarled Sergeant Scratchard from the parked commo jeep. "Trying to get yourself killed?"

"Via!" Esa wheezed. He had bruised his chin and was thankful for it, the way a child is thankful for any punishment less than the one imagined. He accepted Scratchard's silent offer of a fiber-optics periscope. Carefully, the Captain raised it to scan what had been the Chelia Mine and was now the Bordj—the Fortress—holding approximately one hundred and forty Kabyle rebels with enough supplies to last a year.

Satellite photographs showed the mine as a series of

neatly-stepped terraces in the center of a plateau. From
the plateau's surface, nothing of significance could be
seen until a flash discovered the position of a sniper the
moment before he dodged to fire again.

"It'd be easy," Sergeant Scratchard said, "if they'd just
tried to use the pit as a big foxhole. . . . Have Central
pop a couple anti-personnel rounds overhead and then
we go in and count bodies. But they've got tunnels and
spider holes—and command-detonated mines—laced out
from the pit like a giant worm-farm. This one's going to
cost, Esa."

"Blood and martyrs," the captain said under his breath.
When he had received the Ain Chelia assignment, Mboya
had first studied reconnaissance coverage of the village
and the mine three kilometers away. It was now a month
and a half since the rebel disaster at al-Madinah. The
Slammers had raised the siege of the capital in a pitched
battle that no one in the human universe was better
equipped to fight. Surviving rebels had scattered to their
homes to make what preparations they could against
the white teror they knew would sweep in the wake of
the government's victory. At Ain Chelia, the preparations had been damned effective. The recce showed clearly
that several thousand cubic yards of rubble had been
dumped into the central pit of the mine, the waste of
burrowings from all around its five kilometer circumference.

"We can drop penetrators all year," Mboya said, aloud
but more to himself than the non-com beside him. "Blow
the budget for the whole operation, and even then I
wouldn't bet they couldn't tunnel ahead of the shelling
faster than we broke rock on top of them."

"If we storm the place," said Sergeant Scratchard, "and
then go down the tunnels after the hold-outs, we'll have
thirty per cent casualties if we lose a man."

A rifle flashed from the pit-edge. Almost simultaneously,
one of the company's three-barreled automatic weapons
slashed the edge of the rebel gunpit. The trooper must
have sighted in his weapon earlier when a sniper had
popped from the pit, knowing the site would be re-used
eventually. Now the air shook as the powergun detonated a bandolier of grenades charged with industrial
explosives. The sniper's rifle glittered as it spun into the

air; her head was by contrast a ragged blur, its long hair uncoiling and snapping outward with the thrust of the explosion.

"Get that gunner's name," Mboya snapped to his first sergeant. "He's earned a week's leave as soon as we stand down. But to get all the rest of them . . ." and the officer's voice was the more stark for the fact it was so controlled, "we're going to need something better. I think we're going to have to talk them out."

"Via, Captain," said Scratchard in real surprise, "why would they want to come out? They saw at al-Madinah what happens when they faced us in the field. And nobody surrenders when they know all prisoners're going to be shot."

"Don't say nobody," said Esa Mboya in a voice as crisp as the gunfire bursting anew from the Bordj. "Because that's just what you're going to see this lot do."

The dead end of Juma's street had been blocked and turned into the company maintenance park between the time Esa left to observe the Bordj and his return to his brother's house. Skimmers, trucks, and a gun-jeep with an intermittant short in its front fan had been pulled into the cul-de-sac. They were walled on three sides by the courtyards of the houses beyond Juma's.

Sergeant Scratchard halted the jeep with the bulky commo equipment in the open street, but Mboya swung his own skimmer around the supply truck that formed a makeshift fourth wall for the park. A guard saluted. "Muller!" Esa shouted, even before the skirts of his one-man vehicle touched the pavement. "What in the name of heaven d'ye think you're about! I told you to set up in the main square!"

Bog Muller stood up beside a skimmer raised on edge. He was a bulky Technician with twenty years service in the Slammers. A good administrator, but his khakis were clean. Operation Feirefitz had required the company to move fast and long, and there was no way Muller's three half-trained subordinates could have coped with the consequent rash of equipment failures. "Ah, well, Captain," Muller temporized, his eyes apparently focused on the

row of wall spikes over Esa's head, "we ran into Juma
and he said—"

"He *what*!" Mboya shouted.

"I said," said Juma, rising from behind the skimmer
himself, "that security in the middle of the village would
be more of a problem than anybody needed. We've got
some hot-heads; I don't want any of them to get the
notion of stealing a gun-jeep, for instance. The two households there—" he pointed to the entrances now blocked
by vehicles, using the grease gun in his right hand for
the gesture—"have both been evacuated to the Bordj."
The half-smile he gave his brother could have been meant
for either what he had just said or for the words he
added, raising both the grease gun and the wire brush
he held in his left hand: "Besides, what with the mine
closed, I'd get rusty myself with no equipment to work
on."

"After all," said Muller in what was more explanation
that defense, "I knew Juma back when."

Esa took in his brother's smile, took in as well the
admiring glances of the three Tech I's who had been
watching the civilian work. "All right," he said to Muller,
"but the next time clear it with me. And you," he said,
pointing to Juma, "come on inside for now. We need to
talk."

"Yes, little brother," the civilian said with a bow as
submissive as his tone.

In the surprising cool of his house, Juma stripped off
the gritty jellaba he had worn while working. He began
washing with a waterless cleaner, rubbing it on with
smooth strokes of his palms. On a chain around his neck
glittered a tiny silver crucifix, normally hidden by his
clothing.

"You didn't do much of a job persuading your friends
to your Way of Peace," Esa said with an anger he had
not intended to display.

"No, I'm afraid I didn't," the civilian answered mildly.
"They were polite enough, even the Kaid, Ali ben Cheriff.
But they pointed out that the Arabizers in al-Madinah
intended to stamp out all traces of Kabyle culture as
soon as possible . . . which of course was true. And we
did have our own martyr here in Ain Chelia, as you
know. I couldn't—" Juma looked up at his brother, his

dark skin glistening beneath the lather—"argue with their *military* estimate, after all, either. The Way doesn't require that its followers lie about reality in order to change it—but I don't have to tell you that."

"Go on," said the captain. His hand touched the catches of his body armor. He did not release them, however, even though the hard-suit was not at the moment protection against any physical threat.

"Well, the National Army was outnumbered ten to one by the troops we could field from the backlands," Juma continued as he stepped into the shower. "That's without defections, too. And weapons aren't much of a problem. Out there, any jack-leg mechanic can turn out a truck piston in his back room. The tolerances aren't any closer on a machine gun. But what we didn't expect—" he raised his deep voice only enough to override the hiss of the shower—"was that all six of the other planets of the al-Ittihad al-Arabi—" for Arab Union Juma used the Arabic words, and they rasped in his throat like a file on bars—"would club together and help the sanctimonious butchers in al-Madinah hire the Slammers."

He stepped shining from the stall, no longer pretending detachment or that he and his brother were merely chatting. "I visited the siege lines then," Juma rumbled, wholly a preacher and wholly a man, "and I begged the men from Ain Chelia to come home while there was time. To make peace, or if they would not choose peace then at least to choose life—to lie low in the hills till the money ran out and the Slammers were off on somebody else's contract, killing somebody else's enemies. But my friends would stand with their brothers . . . and so they did, and they died with their brothers, too many of them, when the tanks came through their encirclement like knives through a goat-skin." His smile crooked and his voice dropped. "And the rest came home and told me they should have listened before."

"They'll listen to you now," said Esa, "if you tell them to come out of the Bordj without their weapons and surrender."

Juma began drying himself on a towel of coarse local cotton. "Will they?" he replied without looking up.

Squeezing his fingers against the bands of porcelain

armor over his stomach, Esa said, "The Re-education Camps outside al-Madinah aren't a rest cure, but there's too many journalists in the city to let them be too bad. Even if the hold-outs are willing to die, they surely don't want their whole families wiped out. And if we have to clear the Bordj ourselves—well, there won't be any prisoners, you know that.... There wouldn't be even if we wanted them, not after we blast and gas the tunnels, one by one."

"Yes, I gather the Re-education Camps aren't too bad," the civilian agreed, walking past his brother to don a light jellaba of softer weave than his work garment. "I gather they're not very full, either. A—a cynic, say, might guess that most of the trouble-makers don't make it to al-Madinah where journalists can see them. That they die in the desert after they've surrendered. Or they don't surrender, of course. I don't think Ali ben Cheriff and the others in the Bordj are going to surrender, for instance."

"Damn you!" the soldier shouted. "The choice is *certain* death, isn't it? *Any* chance is better than that!"

"Well you see," said Juma, watching the knuckles of his right hand twist against the palm of his left, "they know as well as I do that the only transport you arrived with was the minimum to haul your own supplies. There's no way you could carry over a hundred prisoners back to the capital. No way in ... Hell."

Esa slammed the wall with his fist. Neither the concrete nor his raging expression showed any reaction to the loud impact. "I could be planning to put them in commandeered ore haulers, couldn't I?" he said. "Some of them must be operable!"

Juma stepped to the younger man and took him by the wrists as gently as a shepherd touching a newborn lamb. "Little brother," he said, "swear to me that you'll turn anyone who surrenders over to the authorities in al-Madinah, and I'll do whatever I can to get them to surrender."

The soldier snatched his hands away. He said, "Do you think I wouldn't lie to you because we're brothers? Then you're a fool!"

"What I think, what anyone thinks, is between him and the Lord," Juma said. He started to move toward his brother again but caught the motion and turned it into a swaying only. "If you will swear to me to deliver them unharmed, I'll carry your message into the Bordj."

Esa swung open the massive door. On the threshold he paused and turned to his brother. "Every one of my boys who doesn't make it," he said in a venomous whisper. "His blood's on your head."

Captain Mboya did not try to slam the door this time. He left it standing open as he strode through the courtyard. "Scratchard!" he roared to the sergeant with an anger not meant for the man on whom it fell. "Round up ben Khedda!" Mboya threw himself down on his skimmer and flicked the fans to life. Over their whine he added, "Get him up to me at the command dugout. Now!"

With the skill of long experience, the captain spun his one-man vehicle past the truck and the jeep parked behind it. Sergeant Scratchard gloomily watched his commander shriek up the street. The captain shouldn't have been going anywhere without the jeep, his commo link to Central, in tow. No point in worrying about that, though. The non-com sighed and lifted the jeep off the pavement. Ben Khedda would be at his house or in the cafe across the street from it. Scratchard hoped he had a vehicle of his own and wouldn't have to ride the jump seat of the jeep. He didn't like to sit that close to a slimy traitor.

But Jack Scratchard knew he'd done worse things than sit with a traitor during his years with the Slammers; and, needs must, he would again.

The mortar shell burst with a white flash. Seconds later came a distant *chunk!* as if a rock had been dropped into a trash can. Even after the report had died away, fragments continued ricocheting from rock with tiny gnat-songs. Ben Khedda flinched beneath the clear night sky.

"It's just our harrassing fire," said Captain Mboya. "Your rag-heads don't have high-angle weapons, thank the Lord. Of course, all our shells do is keep them down in their tunnels."

The civilian swallowed. "Your sergeant," he said, "told me you needed me at once." Scratchard stirred in the darkness at the other end of the dugout, but he made no comment of his own.

"Yeah," said Mboya, "but when I cooled off I decided to take a turn around the perimeter. Took a while. It's a bloody long perimeter for one cursed infantry company to hold."

"Well, I," ben Khedda said, "I came at once, sir. I recognize the duty all good citizens owe to our liberators." Firing broke out, a burst from a projectile weapon answered promiscuously by powerguns. Ben Khedda winced again. Cyan bolts from across the pit snapped overhead, miniature lightning following miniature thunder.

Without looking up, Captain Mboya keyed his commo helmet and said, "Thrasher Four to Thrasher Four-Three. Anybody shoots beyond his sector again and it's ten days in the glass house when we're out of this cop." The main unit in Scratchard's jeep purred as it relayed the amplified signal. All the firing ceased.

"Will ben Cheriff and the others in the Bordj listen to you, do you think?" the captain continued.

For a moment, ben Khedda did not realize the officer was speaking to him. He swallowed again. "Well, I . . . I can't say," he blurted. He began to curl in his upper lip as if to chew a moustache, though he was clean shaven. "They aren't friends of mine, of course, but if God wills and it would help you if I addressed them over a loudspeaker as to their true duties as citizens of Dar al-B'heed—"

"We hear you were second in command of the Chelia contingent at Madinah," Mboya said inflexibly. "Besides, there won't be a loudspeaker, you'll be going in in person."

Horror at past and future implications warred in ben Khedda's mind and froze his tongue. At last he stammered, "Oh no, C-captain, before G-god, they've lied to you! That accurst al-Habashi wishes to lie away my life! I did no more than any man would do to stay alive!"

Mboya waved the other to silence. The pale skin of his palm winked as another shell detonated above the Bordj. When the echoes died away, the captain went on in a voice as soft as a leopard's paw, "You will tell them that if they all surrender, their lives will be spared and they will not be turned over to the government until they are actually in al-Madinah. You will say that I swore that on my honor and on the soul of my house.''

Ben Khedda raised a hand to interrupt, but the soldier's voice rolled on implacably, ''They must deposit all their arms in the Bordj and come out to be shackled. The tunnels will be searched. If there are any hold-outs, three of those who surrendered will be shot for each hold-out. If there are any boobytraps, ten of those who surrendered will be shot for every man of mine who is injured.''

Mboya drew a breath, long and deep as that of a power lifter. The civilian, tight as a house-jack, strangled his own words as he waited for the captain to conclude. ''You will say that after they have done as I have said, all of them will be loaded on ore carriers with sun-screens. You will explain that there will be food and water brought from the village to support them. And you will tell them that if some of them are wounded or are infirm, they may ride within an ambulance which will be air-conditioned.

''Do you understand?''

For a moment, ben Khedda struggled with an inability to phrase his thoughts in neutral terms. He was unwilling to meet the captain's eyes, even with the darkness as a cushion. Finally he said, ''Captain—I, I trust your word as I would trust that of no man since the Prophet, on whom be peace. When you say the lives of the traitors will be spared, there can be no doubt, may it please God.''

''Trust has nothing to do with it,'' said Captain Mboya without expression. ''I have told you what you will say, and you will say it.''

''Captain, Captain,'' whimpered the civilian, ''I understand. The trip is a long one and surely some of the most troublesome will die of heat stroke. They will know that themselves. But there will be no . . . general tragedy? I must live here in Ain Chelia with the friends of the, the traitors. You see my position?''

''Your position,'' Mboya repeated with scorn that drew a chuckle from Scratchard across the dug-out. ''Your position is that unless you talk your friends there out of the Bordj—'' he gestured. Automatic weapons began to rave and chatter as if on cue. ''Unless you go down there and come back with them, I'll have you shot on your doorstep for a traitor and your body left to the dogs. That's your position."

"Cheer up, citizen," Sergeant Scratchard said. "You're getting a great chance to pick one side and stick with it. The change'll do you good."

Ben Khedda gave a despairing cry and stood, his dun jellaba flapping as a lesser shadow. He stared over the rim of the dug-out into a night now brightened only by stars and a random powergun bolt, harrassment like that of the mortars. He turned and shouted at the motionless captain, "It's easy for you—you go where your colonel sends you, you kill who he tells you to kill. And then you come all high and moral over the rest of us, who have to make our own decisions! You despise me? At least I'm a man and not somebody's dog!"

Mboya laughed harshly. "You think Colonel Hammer told us how to clear the back country? Don't be a fool. My official orders are to co-operate with the District Governor, and to send all prisoners back to al-Madinah for internment. The colonel can honestly deny ordering anything else—and letting him do that is as much a part of my job as co-operating with a governor who knows that anybody really sent to a Re-education Camp will be back in his hair in a year."

There was a silence in the dug-out. At last the sergeant said, "He can't go out now, sir." The moan of a ricochet underscored the words.

"No, no, we'll have to wait till dawn," the captain agreed tiredly. As if ben Khedda were an unpleasant machine, he added, "Get him the hell out of my sight, though. Stick him in the bunker with the Headquarters Squad and tell them to hold him till called for. Via! but I wish this operation were over."

The guns spat at one another all through the night. It was not the fire that kept Esa Mboya awake, however, but rather the dreams that plagued him with gentle words whenever he did manage to nod off.

"Well," said Juma, scowling judiciously at the gun-jeep on the rack before him, "I'd say we pull the wiring harness first. Half the time that's the whole problem—grit gets into the conduits and when the fans vibrate, it saws through the insulation. Even if we're wrong, we haven't done anything that another few months of running on Dar al-B'heed wouldn't have required anyway."

"You should have seen him handle one a' these when I first knew him," said Bog Muller proudly to his subordinates. "Beat it to hell, he would, Via—bring her in with rock scrapes on both sides that he'd put on at the same time!"

The Kikuyu civilian touched a valve and lowered the rack. His hand caressed the sand-burnished skirt of the jeep as it sank past him. The joy-stick controls were in front of the left-hand seat. Finesse was a matter of touch and judgment, not sophisticated instrumentation. He waggled the stick gently, remembering. In front of the other seat was the powergun, its three iridium barrels poised to rotate and hose out destruction in a nearly-continuous stream.

"You won't believe it," continued the Technician, "but I saw with my own eyes—" that was a lie—"this boy here steering with one hand and working the gun with the other. Bloody miracle that was—even if he did give Maintenance more trouble than any three other troopers."

"You learn a lot about a machine when you push it, when you stress it," said Juma. His fingers reached for but did not quite touch the spade grips of the tribarrel. "About men, too," he added and lowered his hand. He looked Muller in the face and said, "What I learned about myself was that I didn't want to live in a universe that had no better use for me than to gun other people down. I won't claim to be saving souls . . . because that's in the Lord's hands and he uses what instruments he desires. But at least I'm not taking lives."

One of the younger Techs coughed. Muller nodded heavily and said, "I know what you mean, Juma. I've never regretted getting into Maintenance right off the way I did. Especially times like today. . . . But Via, if we stand here fanning our lips, we won't get a curst bit of work done, will we?"

The civilian chuckled without asking for an explanation of 'especially times like today'. "Sure, Bog," he said, latching open the left-side access ports one after another. "Somebody dig out a 239B harness and we'll see if I remember as much as I think I do about chang-

ing one of these beggars." He glanced up at the trun-
cated mass of the plateau, wiping his face with a
bandanna. "Things have quieted down since the sun
came up," he remarked. "Even if I weren't—dedicated
to the Way—I know too many people on both sides to
like to hear the shooting at the mine."

None of the other men responded. At the time it did
not occur to Juma that there might be something about
his words that embarrassed them.

"There's a flag," said Scratchard, his eyes pressed
tight to the lenses of the periscope. "Blood and martyrs,
Cap—there's a flag!"

"No shooting!" Mboya ordered over his commo as he
moved. "Four to all Thrasher units, stand to but no
shooting!"

All around the mine crater, men watched a white rag
flapping on the end of a long wooden pole. Some looked
through periscopes like those in the command dugout,
others over the sights of their guns in hope that something would give them an excuse to fire. "Well, what are
they waiting for?" the captain muttered.

"It's ben Khedda," guessed Scratchard without looking
away from the flag. "He was scared green to go out there.
Now he's just as scared to come back."

The flag staggered suddenly. Troopers tensed, but a
moment later an unarmed man climbed full height from
the Bordj. The high sun threw his shadow at his feet
like a pit. Standing as erect as his age permitted him,
Ali ben Cheriff took a step toward the Slammers' lines.
Wind plucked at his jellaba and white beard; the rebel
leader was a patriarch in appearance as well as in simple fact. On his head was the green turban that marked
him as a pilgrim to al-Meccah on Terra. He was as
devotedly Moslem as he was Kabyle, and he—like most
of the villagers—saw no inconsistencies in the facts. To
ben Cheriff it was no more necessary to become an Arab
in order to accept Islam than it had seemed necessary to
Saint Paul that converts to Christ first become Jews.

"We've won," the captain said as he watched the
figure through the foreshortening lenses. "That's the
Kaid, ben Cheriff. If he comes, they all do."

Up from the hidden tunnel clambered an old woman

wearing the stark black of a matron. The Kaid paused and stretched back his hand, but the woman straightened without help. Together the old couple began to walk toward the waiting guns.

The flagstaff flapped erect again. Gripping it like a talisman, Youssef ben Khedda stepped from the tunnel mouth where the Kaid had shouldered aside his hesitation. He picked his way across the ground at increasing speed. When ben Khedda passed the Kaid and his wife, he skirted them widely as if he were afraid of being struck. More rebels were leaving the Bordj in single file. None of them carried visible weapons. Most, men and women alike, had their eyes cast down; but a red-haired girl leading a child barely old enough to walk glared around with the haughty rage of a lioness.

"Well, no rest for the wicked," grunted Sergeant Scratchard. Settling his sub-machinegun on its sling, he climbed out of the dugout. "Headquarters Squad to me," he ordered. Bent over against the possible shock of a fanatic's bullets, experienced enough to know the reality of his fear and brave enough to face it none the less, Scratchard began to walk to the open area between pit and siege lines where the prisoners would be immobilized. The seven men of HQ Squad followed; their corporal drove the jeep loaded with leg irons.

One of the troopers raised his powergun to bar ben Khedda. Scratchard waved and called an order; the trooper shrugged and let the Kabyle pass. The sergeant gazed after him for a moment, then spat in the dust and went on about the business of searching and securing the prisoners.

Youssef ben Khedda was panting with tension and effort as he approached the dugout, but there was a hard glint of triumph in his eyes as well. He knew he was despised, by those he led no less than by those who had driven him; but he had dug the rebels from their fortress when all the men and guns of the Slammers might have been unable to do so without him. Now he saw a way to ride the bloody crest to permanent power in Ain Chelia. He tried to set his flag in the ground. It scratched into the rocky soil, then fell with a clatter. "I have brought them to you," ben Khedda said in a haughty voice.

"Some of them, at least," said Mboya, his face neutral.
Rebels continued to straggle from the Bordj, their faces
sallow from more than the day they had spent in their
tunnels. The Kaid had submitted to the shackles with a
stony indifference. His wife was weeping beside him,
not for herself but for her husband. Two of the nervous
troopers were fanning the prisoners with detector wands
set for steel and iridium. Anything the size of a razor
blade would register. A lead bludgeon or a brass-barreled
pistol would be ignored, but there were some chances
you took in the service of practicality.

"As God wills, they are all coming, you know that,"
ben Khedda said, assertive with dreamed-of lordship.
"If they were each in his separate den, many of them
would fight till you blew them out or buried them. All
are willing to die, but most would not willingly kill
their fellows, their families." His face worked. "A fine
joke, is it not?" If what had crossed ben Khedda's lips
had been a smile, then it transmuted to a sneer. "They
would have been glad to kill me first, I think, but they
were afraid that you would have been angry."

"More fools them," said the captain.

"Yes . . .," said the civilian, drawing back his face like
a rat confronting a terrier, "more fools them. And now
you will pay me."

"Captain," said the helmet speaker in the first sergeant's voice, "this one says he's the last."

Mboya climbed the four steps to surface level. Scratchard waved and pointed to the Kabyle who was just
joining the scores of his fellows. The number of those
being shackled in a continuous chain at least approxi-
mated the one hundred and forty who were believed to
have holed up in the Bordj. Through the clear air rang
hammer strokes as a pair of troopers stapled the chain
to the ground at intervals, locking the prisoners even
more securely into the killing ground. The captain
nodded. "We'll give it a minute to let anybody still
inside have second thoughts," he said over the radio.
"Then the search teams go in." He looked at ben Khedda.
"All right," he said, "you've got your life and whatever
you think you can do with it. Now, get out of here before
I change my mind."

Mboya gazed again at the long line of prisoners. He

was unable not to imagine them as they would look in an hour's time, after the Bordj had been searched and their existence was no longer a tool against potential hold-outs. He could not have broken with the Way of his childhood, however, had he not replaced it with a sense of duty as uncompromising. Esa Mboya, Captain, G Company, Hammer's Regiment, would do whatever was required to accomplish the task set him. They had been hired to pacify the district, not just to quiet it down for six months or a year.

Youssef ben Khedda had not left. He was still facing Mboya, as unexpected and unpleasant as a rat on the pantry shelf. He was saying, "No, there is one more thing you must do, as God wills, before you leave Ain Chelia. I do not compel it—" the soldier's face went blank with fury at the suggestion—"your duty that you talk of compels you. There is one more traitor in the village, a man who did not enter the Bordj because he thought his false god would preserve him."

"Little man," said the captain in shock and a genuine attempt to stop the words he knew were about to be said, "don't—"

"Add the traitor Juma al-Habashi to these," the civilian cried, pointing to the fluttering jellabas of the prisoners. "Put him there or his whines of justice and other worlds and his false god will poison the village again like a dead rat stinking in a pool. Take him!"

The two men stood with their feet on a level. The soldier's helmet and armor increased his advantage in bulk, however, and his wrath lighted his face like a cleansing flame. "Shall I slay my brother for thee, lower-than-a-dog?" he snarled.

Ben Khedda's face jerked at the verbal slap, but with a wave of his arm he retorted, "Will you now claim to follow the Way yourself? There stand one hundred and thirty-four of your brothers. Make it one more, as your duty commands!"

The absurdity was so complete that the captain trembled between laughter and the feeling that he had gone insane. Carefully, his tone touched more with wonder than with rage until the world should return to focus, the Kikuyu said, "Shall I, Esa Mboya, order the death of Juma Mboya? My brother, flesh of my father and of my mother . . . who held my hand when I toddled my first steps upright?''

Now at last ben Khedda's confidence squirted out like blood from a slashed carotid. "The name—" he said. "I didn't *know*!"

Mboya's world snapped into place again, its realities clear and neatly dove-tailed. "Get out, filth," he said harshly, "and wonder what I plan for you when I come down from this hill."

The civilian stumbled back toward his car as if his body and not his spirit had received the mortal wound. The soldier considered him dispassionately. If ben Khedda stayed in Ain Chelia, he wouldn't last long. The Slammers would be out among the stars, and the central government a thousand kilometers away in al-Madinah would be no better able to protect a traitor. Youssef ben Khedda would be a reminder of friends and relatives torn by blasts of cyan fire with every step he took on the streets of the village. Those steps would be few enough, one way or the other.

And if in the last fury of his well-earned fear ben Khedda tried to kill Juma—well, Juma had made his bed, his Way . . . he could tread it himself. Esa laughed. Not that the traitor would attempt murder personally. Even in the final corner, rats of ben Khedda's stripe tried to persuade other rats to bite for them.

"Captain," murmured Scratchard's voice over the command channel, "think we've waited about long enough?"

Instead of answering over the radio, Mboya nodded and began walking the hundred meters to where his sergeant stood near the prisoners. The rebels' eyes followed him, some with anger, most in only a dull appreciation of the fact that he was the nearest moving object on a static landscape. Troopers had climbed out of their gun pits all around the Bordj. Their dusty khaki blended with the soil, but the sun woke bright reflections from the barrels of their weapons.

"The search teams are ready to go in, sir," Scratchard said, speaking in Dutch but stepping a pace further from the shackled Kaid besides.

"Right," the captain agreed. "I'll lead the team from Third Platoon."

"Captain—"

"Where are the trucks, unbeliever?" demanded Ali
ben Cheriff. His voice started on a quaver but lashed at
the end.

"—there's plenty cursed things for you to do besides
crawling down a hole with five pongoes. Leave it to the
folks whose job it is."

"There's nothing left of this operation that Mendoza
can't wrap up," Mboya said. "Believe me, he won't like
doing it any less, either."

"Where are the trucks to carry away our children, dog
and son of dogs?" cried the Kaid. Beneath the green
turban, the rebel's face was as savage and unyielding as
that of a trapped wolf.

"It's not for fun," Mboya went on. "There'll be times
I'll have to send boys out to be killed while I stay back,
safe as a staff officer, and run things. But if I lead from
the front when I can, when it won't compromise the
mission if I do stop a load—then they'll do what they're
told a little sharper when it's me that says it the next
time."

The Kaid spat. Lofted by his anger and the breeze, the
gobbet slapped the side of Mboya's helmet and dribbled
down onto his porcelain-sheathed shoulder.

Scratchard turned. Ignoring the automatic weapon
slung ready to fire under his arm, he drew a long knife
from his boot sheath instead. Three strides separated
the non-com from the line of prisoners. He had taken
two of them before Mboya caught his shoulder and
stopped him. "Easy, Jack," the captain said.

Ben Cheriff's gaze was focused on the knife-point. Fear
of death could not make the old man yield, but neither
was he unmoved by the approach of its steel-winking
eye. Scratchard's own face had no more expression
than did the knife itself. The Kaid's wife lunged at the
soldier to the limit of her chain, but the look Scratchard
gave her husband dried her throat around the curses
within it.

Mboya pulled his man back. "Easy," he repeated. "I
think he's earned that, don't you?" He turned Scratchard
gently. He did not point out, nor did he need to do so,
the three gun-jeeps which had swung down to fifty meters in front of the line of captives. Their crews were

tense and still with the weight of their orders. They met
Mboya's eyes, comprehending but without enthusiasm.

"Right," said Scratchard mildly. "Well, the quicker
we get down that hole, the quicker we get the rest of the
job done. Let's go."

The five tunnel rats from Third Platoon were already
squatting at the entrance from which the rebels had
surrendered. Captain Mboya began walking toward them.
"You stay on top, Sergeant," he said. "You don't need to
prove anything."

Scratchard cursed without heat. "I'll wait at the tunnel mouth unless something pops. You'll be out of radio
contact and I'll be curst if I trust anybody else to carry
you a message."

The tunnel rats were rising to their feet, silent men
whose faces were in constant, tiny motion. They carried
detector wands and sidearms; two had even taken off
their body armor and stood in the open air looking paler
than shelled shrimp. Mboya cast a glance back over his
shoulder at the prisoners and the gun-jeeps beyond. "Do
you believe in sin, Sergeant?" he asked.

Scratchard glanced sidelong at his superior. "Don't
know, sir. Not really my field."

"My brother believes in it," said the captain, "but I
guess he left the Slammers before you transferred out of
combat cars. And he isn't here now, Jack, I am, so I
guess we'll have to dispense with sin today."

"Team Three ready, sir," said the black-haired man
who probably would have had sergeant's pips had he
not been stripped to the waist.

"Right," said Mboya. Keying his helmet he went on,
"Thrasher to Club One, Club Two. Let's see what they
left us, boys." And as he stepped toward the tunnel
mouth, without really thinking about the words until he
spoke them, he added, "And the Lord be with us all."

The bed of the turbine driving Youssef ben Khedda's
car was enough out of true that the vehicle announced
its own approach unmistakably. Juma wondered in the
back of his mind what brought the little man, but his
main concentration was on the plug connector he was
trying to reeve through a channel made for something a
size smaller. At last the connector shifted the last two

millimeters necessary for Juma to slip a button-hook deftly about it. The three subordinate Techs gave a collective sigh, and Bog Muller beamed in reflected glory.

"Father!" ben Khedda wheezed, oblivious to the guard frowning over his powergun a pace behind, "Father! You've got to . . . I've got to talk to you. You must!"

"All right, Youssef," the Kikuyu said. "In a moment." He tugged the connector gently through its channel and rotated it to mate with the gun leads.

Ben Khedda reached for Juma's arm in a fury of impatience. One of the watching Techs caught the Kabyle's wrist. "Touch him, rag-head," the trooper said, "and you better be able to grow a new hand." He thrust ben Khedda back with more force than the resistance demanded.

Juma straightened from the gun-jeep and put an arm about the shoulders of the angry trooper. "Worse job than replacing all the fans," he said in Dutch, "but it gives you a good feeling to finish it. Run the static test, if you would, and I'll be back in a few minutes." He squeezed the trooper, released him, and added in Kabyle to his fellow villager, "Come into my house, then, Youssef. What is it you need of me?"

Ben Khedda's haste and nervousness were obvious from the way his car lay parked with its skirt folded under the front from an over-hasty stop. Juma paused with a frown for more than the mechanical problem. He bent to lift the car and let the skirt spring away from the fans it was probably touching at the moment.

"Don't *worry* about that," ben Khedda cried, plucking at the bigger man's sleeve. "We've *got* to talk in private."

Juma had left his courtyard gate unlatched since he was working only a few meters away. Before ben Khedda had reached the door of the house, he was spilling the words that tormented him. "Before God, you have to talk to your brother or he'll kill me, Father, he'll kill *me!*"

"Youssef," said the Kikuyu as he swung his door open and gestured the other man toward the cool interior, "I pray—I have been praying—that at worst, none of our villagers save those in the Bordj are in danger." He smiled too sadly to be bitter. "You would know better than I, I think, who may have been marked out to Esa as an enemy of the government. But he's not a cruel man, my brother, only a very—determined one. He won't add you to whatever list he has out of mere dislike."

The Kabyle's lips worked silently. His face was tortured by the explanation that he needed to give but could not. "Father," he pleaded, "you *must* believe me, he'll have me killed. Before God, you must beg him for my life, you *must!*"

Ben Khedda was gripping the Kikuyu by both sleeves. Juma detached himself carefully and said, "Youssef, why would my brother want you killed—of all the men in Ain Chelia? Did something happen?"

The smaller man jerked himself back with a dawning horror in his eyes. "You planned this with him, didn't you?" he cried. His arm thrust at the altar as if to sweep away the closed triptych. "This is all a lie, your prayers, your *Way*—you and your butcher brother trapped me to bleed like a sheep on Id al-Fitr! Traitor! Liar! Murderer!" He threw his hands over his face and flung himself down and across a stool. The Kabyle's sobs held the torment of a man without hope.

Juma stared at the weeping man. There was something unclean about ben Khedda. His back rose and fell beneath the jellaba like the distended neck of a python bolting a young child. "Youssef," the Kikuyu said as gently as he could, "you may stay here or leave, as you please. I promise you that I will speak to Esa this evening, on your behalf as well as that of . . . others, all the others. Is there anything you need to tell me?"

Only the tears responded.

The dazzling sun could not sear away Juma's disquiet as he walked past the guard and the barricading truck. Something was wrong with the day, with the very silence. Though all things were with the Lord.

The jeep's inspection ports had been latched shut. The Techs had set a pair of skimmers up on their sides as the next project. The civilian smiled. "Think she'll float now?" he asked the trooper who had grabbed ben Khedda. "Let's see if I remember how to put one of these through her paces. You can't trust a fix, you see, till you've run her under full load."

There was a silence broken by the whine of ben Khedda's turbine firing. Juma managed a brief prayer that the Kabyle would find a Way open to him—knowing as he prayed that the impulse to do so was from his mind and not at all from his heart.

"Juma, ah," Bog Muller was trying to say. "Ah, look, this isn't—isn't our idea, it's the job, you know. But the captain—" none of the four Techs were looking anywhere near the civilian—"he ordered that you not go anywhere today until, until . . . it was clear."

The silence from the Bordj was a cloak that smothered Juma and squeezed all the blood from his face. "Not that you're a prisoner, but, ah, your brother thought it'd be better for both of you if you didn't see him or call him till—after."

"I see," said the civilian, listening to his own voice as if a third party were speaking. "Until after he's killed my friends, I suppose . . . yes." He began walking back to his house, his sandaled feet moving without being consciously directed. "Juma—" called Muller, but the Tech thought better of the words or found he had none to say.

Ben Khedda had left the door ajar. It was only by habit that Juma himself closed it behind him. The dim coolness within was no balm to the fire that skipped across the surface of his mind. Kneeling, the Kikuyu unlatched and opened wide the panels of his altar piece. It was his one conscious affectation, a copy of a triptych painted over a millenium before by the Master of Hell, Hieronymous Bosch. Atop a haywain rode a couple. Their innocence was beset by every form of temptation in the world, the World. Where would their Way take them? No doubt where it took all Mankind, saving the Lord's grace, to Hell and the grave—good intentions be damned, hope be damned, innocence be damned. . . . Obscurely glad of the harshness of the tiles on which he knelt, Juma prayed for his brother and for the souls of those who would shortly die in flames as like to those of Hell as man could create. He prayed for himself as well, for he was damned to endure what he had not changed. They were all travellers together on the Way.

After a time, Juma sighed and raised his head. A demon faced him on the triptych; it capered and piped through its own blue snout. Not for the first time, Juma thought of how pleasant it would be to personify his

own weaknesses and urgings. Then he could pretend
that they were somehow apart from the true Juma
Mboya, who remained whole and incorruptible.

The lower of the two drawers beneath the altar was
not fully closed.

Even as he drew it open, Juma knew from the lack of
resistance that the drawer was empty. The heavy-barreled
powergun had rested within when ben Khedda had accompanied the search team. It was there no longer.

Striding swiftly and with the dignity of a leopard,
Mboya al-Habashi crossed the room and his courtyard.
He appeared around the end of the truck barricade so
suddenly that Bog Muller jumped. The Kikuyu pointed
his index finger with the deliberation of a pistol barrel.
"Bog," he said very clearly, "I need to call my brother
at once or something terrible will happen."

"Via, man," said the Technician, looking away, "you
know how I feel about it, but it's not my option. You
don't leave here, and you don't call, Juma—or it's my
ass."

"Lord blast you for a fool!" the Kikuyu shouted, taking a step forward. All four Technicians backed away
with their hands lifting. "Will you—" But though there
was confusion ͻͻ the faces watching him, there was
nothing of assent, and there was no time to argue. As if
he had planned it from the start, Juma slipped into the
left saddle of the jeep he had just rewired and gunned
the fans.

With an oath, Bog Muller grappled with the civilian.
The muscles beneath Juma's loose jellaba had shifted
driving fans beneath ore carriers in lieu of a hydraulic
jack. He shrugged the Technician away with a motion
as slight and as masterful as that of an earth tremor.
Juma waggled the stick, using the vehicle's skirts to
butt aside two of the younger men who belatedly tried
to support their chief. Then he had the jeep clear of the
repair rack and spinning on its own axis.

Muller scrambled to his feet again and waited for
Juma to realize that there was not enough room between truck and wall for the jeep to pass. If the driver
himself had any doubt, it was not evident in the way he
dialed on throttle and leaned to bring the right-hand
skirt up an instant before it scraped the courtyard wall.

Using the wall as a running surface and the force of his turn to hold him there, Juma sent the gun-jeep howling sideways around the barricade and up the street.

"Hey!" shouted the startled guard, rising from the shady side of the truck. "Hey!" and he shouldered his weapon.

A Technician grabbed him, wrestling the muzzle of the gun skyward. It was the same lanky man who had caught ben Khedda when he would have plucked at Juma's sleeve. "Via!" cried the guard, watching the vehicle corner and disappear up the main road to the mine. "We weren't supposed to let him by!"

"We're better off explaining that," said the Tech, "than we are telling the captain how we just killed his brother. Right?"

The street was empty again. All five troopers stared at it for some moments before any of them moved to the radio.

Despite his haste, Youssef ben Khedda stopped his car short of the waiting gun-jeeps and began walking toward the prisoners. His back crept with awareness of the guns and the hard-eyed men behind them; but, as God willed, he had chosen and there could be no returning now.

The captain—his treacherous soul was as black as his skin—was not visible. No doubt he had entered the Bordj as he had announced he would. Against expectation, and as further proof that God favored his cause, ben Khedda saw no sign of that damnable first sergeant either. If God willed it, might they both be blasted to atoms somewhere down in a tunnel!

The soldiers watching the prisoners from a few meters away were the ones whom ben Khedda had led on their search of the village. The corporal frowned, but he knew ben Khedda for a confidant of his superiors. "Go with God, brother," said the civilian in Arabic, praying the other would have been taught that tongue or Kabyle. "Your captain wished me to talk once more with that dog—" he pointed to ben Cheriff. "There are documents of which he knows," he concluded vaguely.

The non-com's lip quirked nervously. "Look, can it wait—" he began, but even as he spoke he was glancing at the leveled tribarrels forty meters distant. "Blood," he muttered, a curse and a prophecy. "Well, go talk then. But watch it—the bastard's mean as a snake and his woman's worse."

The Kaid watched ben Khedda approach with the fascination of a mongoose awaiting a cobra. The traitor threw himself to the ground and tried to kiss the Kaid's feet. "Brother in God," the unshackled man whispered, "we have been betrayed by the unbelievers. Their dog of a captain will have you all murdered on his return, despite his oaths to me."

"Are we to believe, brother Youssef," the Kaid said with a sneer, "that you intend to die here with the patriots to cleanse your soul of the lies you carried?"

Others along the line of prisoners were peering at the scene to the extent their irons permitted, but the two men spoke in voices too low for any but the Kaid's wife to follow the words. "Brother," ben Khedda continued, "preservation is better than expiation. The captain has confessed his wicked plan to no one but me. If he dies, it dies with him—and our people live. Now, raise me by the hands."

"Shall I touch your bloody hands, then?" ben Cheriff said, but he spoke as much in question as in scorn.

"Raise me by the hands," ben Khedda repeated, "and take from my right sleeve what you find there to hide in yours. Then wait the time."

"As God wills," the Kaid said and raised up ben Khedda. Their bodies were momentarily so close that their jellabas flowed together.

"And what in the blaze of Hell is *this*, Corporal!" roared Sergeant Scratchard. "Blood and martyrs, who told you to let anybody in with the prisoners?"

"Via, Sarge," the corporal sputtered, "he said—I mean, it was the captain, he tells me."

Ben Khedda had begun to sidle away from the line of prisoners. "Where the hell do you think *you're* going?" Scratchard snapped in Arabic. "Corporal, get another set of leg irons and clamp him onto his buddy there. If he's so copping hot to be here, he can stay till the captain says otherwise."

The sergeant paused, looking around the circle of eyes focused nervously on him. More calmly he continued,

"The Bordj is clear. The captain's up from the tunnel, but it'll be a while before he gets here—they came up somewhere in West Bumfuck and he's borrowing a skimmer from First Platoon to get back. We'll wait to see what he says." The first sergeant stared at Aliben Cheriff, impassive as the wailing traitor was shackled to his right leg. "We'll wait till then," the soldier repeated.

Mboya lifted the nose of his skimmer and grounded it behind the first of the waiting gun-jeeps. Sergeant Scratchard trotted toward him from the direction of the prisoners. The non-com was panting with the heat and his armor; he raised his hand when he reached the captain in order to gain a moment's breathing space.

"Well?" Mboya prompted.

"Sir, Maintenance called," said Scratchard jerkily. "Your brother, sir. They think he's coming to, to see you."

The captain swore. "All right," he said, "if Juma thinks he has to watch this, he can watch it. He's a cursed fool if he expects to do anything *but* watch."

Scratchard nodded deeply, finding he inhaled more easily with his torso cocked forward. "Right, sir, I just—didn't want to rebroadcast on the Command channel in case Central was monitoring. Right. And then there's that rag-head, ben Khedda—I caught him talking to green-hat over there and thought he maybe ought to stay. For good."

Captain Mboya glanced at the prisoners. The men of Headquarters Squad still sat a few meters away because nobody had told them to withdraw. "Get them clear" the captain said with a scowl. He began walking toward the line, the first sergeant's voice turning his direction into a tersely-radioed order. Somewhere down the plateau, an aircar was being revved with no concern for what pebbles would do to the fans. Juma, very likely. He was the man you wanted driving your car when it had all dropped in the pot and Devil took the hindmost.

"Jack," the captain said, "I understand how you feel about ben Khedda; but we're here to do a job, not to kill sons of bitches. If we were doing that, we'd have to start in al-Madinah, wouldn't we?"

Mboya and his sergeant were twenty meters from the

prisoners. The Kaid watched their approach with his hands folded within the sleeves of his jellaba and his eyes as still as iron. Youssef ben Khedda was crouched beside him, a study in terror. He retained only enough composure that he did not try to run—and that because the pressure of the leg iron binding him to ben Cheriff was just sharp enough to penetrate the fear.

A gun-jeep howled up onto the top of the plateau so fast that it bounced and dragged its skirts, still under full throttle. Scratchard turned with muttered surprise. Captain Mboya did not look around. He reached into the thigh pocket of his coveralls where he kept a magnetic key that would release ben Khedda's shackles. "We can't just kill—" he repeated.

"Now, God, *now!*" ben Khedda shrieked. "He's going to *kill me!*"

The Kaid's hands appeared, the right one extending a pistol. Its muzzle was a gray circle no more placable than the eye that aimed it.

Mboya dropped the key. His hand clawed for his own weapon, but he was no gunman, no quick-draw expert. He was a company commander carrying ten extra kilos, with his pistol in a flap holster that would keep his hand out at least as well as it did the wind-blown sand. Esa's very armor slowed him, though it would not save his face or his femoral arteries when the shots came.

Behind the captain, on a jeep still skidding on the edge of control, his brother triggered a one-handed burst as accurate as if parallax were a myth. The tribarrel was locked on its column; Juma let the vehicle's own side-slip saw the five rounds toward the man with the gun. A single two-centimeter bolt missed everything. Beyond, at the lip of the Bordj, a white flower bloomed from a cyan center as ionic calcium recombined with the oxygen from which it had been freed a moment before. Closer, everything was hidden by an instant glare. The pistol detonated in the Kaid's hand under the impact of a round from the tribarrel. That was chance—or something else, for only the Lord could be so precise with certainty. The last shot of the burst hurled the Kaid back with a hole in his chest and his jellaba aflame. Ali ben Cheriff's eyes were free of fear when they closed them before burying him, and his mouth still wore a tight smile. Ben Khedda's face would have been less of a study in virtue and manhood, no doubt, but the two bolts that flicked across it took the traitor's head into oblivion with his memory. Juma had walked his burst on target, like any good man with an automatic weapon; and if there was something standing where the bolts walked—so much the worse for it.

There were shouts, but they were sucked lifeless by the wind. No one else had fired, for a wonder. Troops all around the Bordj were rolling back into dug-outs they had thought it safe to leave.

Juma brought the jeep to a halt a few meters from his brother. He doubled over the joy-stick as if he had been shot himself. Dust and sand puffed from beneath the skirts while the fans wound down; then the plume settled back on the breeze. Esa touched his brother's shoulder, feeling the dry sobs that wracked the jellaba. Very quietly the soldier said in the Kikuyu he had not, after all, forgotten, "I bring you a souvenir, elder brother. To replace the one you have lost." From his holster, now unsnapped, he drew his pistol and laid it carefully down on the empty gunner's seat of the jeep.

Juma looked up at his brother with a terrible dignity. "To remind me of the day I slew two men in the Lord's despite?" he asked formally. "Oh, no; my brother; I need no trinket to remind me of that forever."

"If you do not wish to remember the ones you killed," said Esa, "then perhaps it will remind you of the hundred and thirty-three whose lives you saved this day. And my life, of course."

Juma stared at his brother with a fixity by which alone he admitted his hope. He tugged the silver crucifix out of his jellaba and lifted it over his head. "Here," he said, "little brother. I offer you this in return for your gift. To remind you that wherever you go, the Way runs there as well."

Esa took the chain. With clumsy fingers he slipped it over his helmet. "All right, Thrasher, everybody stand easy," the captain roared into his commo link. "Two-six, I want food for a hundred and thirty-three people for three days. You've got my authority to take what you need from the village. Three-six, you're responsible for the transport. I want six ore carriers up here and I

want them fast. If the first truck isn't here loading in
twenty, that's two-zero mikes, I'll burn somebody a new
asshole. Four-six, there's drinking water in drums down
in those tunnels. Get it up here. Now, *move!*"

Juma stepped out of the gun-jeep, his left hand gripping Esa's right. Skimmers were already lifting from
positions all around the Bordj. G Company was surprised,
but no one had forgotten that Captain Mboya meant his
orders to be obeyed.

"Oh, one other thing," Esa said, then tripped his commo
and added, "Thrasher Four to all Thrasher units—you
get any argument from villagers while you're shopping,
boys . . . just refer them to my brother."

It was past midday now. The sun had enough wester-
ing to wink from the crucifix against the soldier's armor—
and from the pistol in the civilian's right hand.

EDITOR'S INTRODUCTION TO:

ALLAMAGOOSA
by
Eric Frank Russell

When I first read this story I was not long out of military service. I have remembered it ever since, and knew that it had to be in this collection.

All good officers detest paperwork. The best know that it's necessary. That doesn't make them happier about it.

There is another class of officer which thrives on paper work. These seem to believe that if all the forms are properly filled out, it doesn't matter who wins the battles.

These two kinds of officers are natural enemies.

Each service has traditions, and among them are the means for dealing with official bat puckey. Headquarters knows of these traditions, and bureaucrats are perpetually closing loopholes. This is supposed to keep the serving officers on their toes.

The tension is generally healthy, but sometimes things get out of hand.

ALLAMAGOOSA
by
Eric Frank Russell

It was a long time since the *Bustler* had been so silent.
She lay in the Sirian spaceport, her tubes cold, her shell
particle-scarred, her air that of a long-distance runner
exhausted at the end of a marathon. There was good
reason for this: she had returned from a lengthy trip by
no means devoid of troubles.

Now, in port, well-deserved rest had been gained if
only temporarily. Peace, sweet peace. No more bothers,
no more crises, no more major upsets, no more dire
predicaments such as crop up in free flight at least
twice a day. Just peace.

Hah!

Captain McNaught reposed in his cabin, feet up on
desk, and enjoyed the relaxation to the utmost. The
engines were dead, their hellish pounding absent for the
first time in months. Out there in the big city four
hundred of his crew were making whoopee under a
brilliant sun. This evening, when First Officer Gregory
returned to take charge, he was going to go into the
fragrant twilight and make the rounds of neon-lit
civilization.

That was the beauty of making landfall at long last.
Men could give way to themselves, blow off surplus
steam, each according to his fashion. No duties, no
worries, no dangers, no responsibilities in spaceport. A
haven of safety and comfort for tired rovers.

Again, hah!

Burman, the chief radio officer, entered the cabin. He
was one of the half-dozen remaining on duty and bore

340

the expression of a man who can think of twenty better things to do.

"Relayed signal just come in, sir." Handing the paper across, he waited for the other to look at it and perhaps dictate a reply.

Taking the sheet, McNaught removed the feet from his desk, sat erect and read the message aloud.

Terran Headquarters to BUSTLER. Remain Siriport pending further orders. Rear Admiral Vane W. Cassidy due there seventeenth. Feldman. Navy Op. Command. Sirisec.

He looked up, all happiness gone from his leathery features. "Oh, Lord!" he groaned.

"Something wrong?" asked Burman, vaguely alarmed.

McNaught pointed at three thin books on his desk. "The middle one. Page twenty."

Leafing through it, Burman found an item that said:

Vane W. Cassidy, R-Ad. Head Inspector Ships and Stores.

Burman swallowed hard. "Does that mean—?"

"Yes, it does," said McNaught without pleasure. "Back to training-college and all its rigmarole. Paint and soap, spit and polish." He put on an officious expression, adopted a voice to match it. "Captain, you have only seven ninety-nine emergency rations. Your allocation is eight hundred. Nothing in your logbook accounts for the missing one. Where is it? What happened to it? How is it that one of the men's kits lacks an officially issued pair of suspenders? Did you report his loss?"

"Why does he pick on us?" asked Burman, appalled. "He's never chivvied us before."

"That's why," informed McNaught, scowling at the wall. "It's our turn to be stretched across the barrel." His gaze found the calendar. "We have three days—and we'll need 'em! Tell Second Officer Pike to come here at once."

Burman departed gloomily. In short time Pike entered. His face reaffirmed the old adage that bad news travels fast.

"Make out an indent," ordered McNaught, "for one hundred gallons of plastic paint, Navy-gray, approved quality. Make out another for thirty gallons of interior white enamel. Take them to spaceport stores right away. Tell them to deliver by six this evening along with our correct issue of brushes and sprayers. Grab up any cleaning material that's going for free."

"The men won't like this," remarked Pike, feebly.

"They're going to love it," McNaught asserted. "A bright and shiny ship, all spic and span, is good for morale. It says so in that book. Get moving and put those indents in. When you come back, find the stores and equipment sheets and bring them here. We've got to check stocks before Cassidy arrives. Once he's here we'll have no chance to make up shortages or smuggle out any extra items we happened to find in our hands."

"Very well, sir." Pike went out wearing the same expression as Burman.

Lying back in his chair McNaught muttered to himself. There was a feeling in his bones that something was sure to cause a last-minute ruckus. A shortage of any item would be serious enough unless covered by a previous report. A surplus would be bad, very bad. The former implied carelessness or misfortune. The latter suggested barefaced theft of government property in circumstances condoned by the commander.

For instance, there was that recent case of Williams of the heavy cruiser *Swift*. He'd heard of it over the spacevine when out around Bootes. Williams had been found in unwitting command of eleven reels of electric-fence wire when his official issue was ten. It had taken a court-martial to decide that the extra reel—which had formidable barter-value on a certain planet—had not been stolen from space stores or, in sailor jargon, "teleportated aboard." But Williams had been reprimanded. And that did not help promotion.

He was still rumbling discontentedly when Pike returned bearing a folder of foolscap sheets.

"Going to start right away, sir?"

"We'll have to." He heaved himself erect, mentally bidding goodbye to time off and a taste of the bright lights. "It'll take long enough to work right through from bow to tail. I'll leave the men's kit inspection to the last."

Marching out of the cabin, he set forth toward the bow, Pike following with broody reluctance.

As they passed the open main lock Peaslake observed them, bounded eagerly up the gangway and joined behind. A pukka member of the crew, he was a large dog whose ancestors had been more enthusiastic than selective. He wore with pride a big collar inscribed: *Peaslake— Property of S.S. Bustler.* His chief duties, ably performed, were to keep alien rodents off the ship, and, on rare occasions, smell out dangers not visible to human eyes.

The three paraded forward, McNaught and Pike in the manner of men grimly sacrificing pleasure for the sake of duty, Peaslake with the panting willingness of one ready for any new game no matter what.

Reaching the bow-cabin, McNaught dumped himself in the pilot's seat, took the folder from the other. "You know this stuff better than me—the chart-room is where I shine. So I'll read them out while you look them over." He opened the folder, started on the first page. "K1. Beam compass, type D, one of."

"Check," said Pike.

"K2. Distance and direction indicator, electronic, type JJ, one of."

"Check."

Peaslake planted his head in McNaught's lap, blinked soulfully and whined. He was beginning to get the others' viewpoint. This tedious itemizing and checking was a hell of a game. McNaught consolingly lowered a hand and played with Peaslake's ears while he plowed his way down the list.

"K187. Foam rubber cushions, pilot and co-pilot, one pair."

"Check."

By the time First Officer Gregory appeared they had reached the tiny intercom cubby and poked around it in semi-darkness. Peaslake had long departed in disgust.

"M24. Spare minispeakers, three-inch, type T2, one set of six."

"Check."

Looking in, Gregory popped his eyes and said, "What the devil is going on?"

"Major inspection due soon." McNaught glanced at his watch. "Go see if stores has delivered a load and if

not why not. Then you'd better give me a hand and let
Pike take a few hours off."

"Does this mean land-leave is cancelled?"

"You bet it does—until after Hizonner had been and
gone." He glanced at Pike. "When you get into the city
search around and send back any of the crew you can
find. No arguments or excuses. It's an order."

Pike registered unhappiness. Gregory glowered at him,
went away, came back and said, "Stores will have the
stuff here in twenty minutes' time." With bad grace he
watched Pike depart.

"M47. Intercom cable, woven-wire protected, three
drums."

"Check," said Gregory, mentally kicking himself for
returning at the wrong time.

The task continued until late in the evening, was resumed early next morning. By that time three-quarters
of the men were hard at work inside and outside the
vessel, doing their jobs as though sentenced to them for
crimes, contemplated but not yet committed.

Moving around the ship's corridors and catwalks had
to be done crab-fashion, with a nervous sideways edging.
Once again it was being demonstrated that the Terran
lifeform suffers from ye fear of wette paynt. The first
smearer would have ten years willed off his unfortunate
life.

It was in these conditions, in mid-afternoon of the
second day, that McNaught's bones proved their feelings
had been prophetic. He recited the ninth page while
Jean Blanchard confirmed the presence and actual existence of all items enumerated. Two-thirds of the way
down they hit the rocks, metaphorically speaking, and
commenced to sink fast.

McNaught said boredly, "V1097. Drinking-bowl,
enamel, one of."

"Is zis," said Blanchard, tapping it.

"V1098. Offog, one."

"*Quoi?*" asked Blanchard, staring.

"V1098. Offog, one," repeated McNaught. "Well, why
are you looking thunderstruck? This is the ship's galley.
You're the head cook. You know what's supposed to be
in the galley, don't you? Where's this offog?"

"Never hear of heem," stated Blanchard, flatly.

"You must have done. It's on this equipment-sheet in plain, clear type. Offog, one, it says. It was here when we were fitted out four years ago. We checked it ourselves and signed for it."

"I signed for nossings called offog," Blanchard denied. "In zee cuisine zere is no such sing."

"Look!" McNaught scowled and showed him the sheet. Blanchard looked and sniffed disdainfully. "I have here zee electronic oven, one of. I have jacketed boilers, graduated capacities, one set. I have bain marie pans, seex of. But no offog. Never heard of heem. I do not know of heem." He spread his hands and shrugged.

"There's got to be," McNaught insisted. "What's more, when Cassidy arrives there'll be hell to pay if there isn't."

"You find heem," Blanchard suggested.

"You got a certificate from the International Hotels School of Cookery. You got a certificate from the Cordon Bleu College of Cuisine. You got a certificate with three credits from the Space-Navy Feeding Center," McNaught pointed out. "All that—and you don't know what an offog is."

"Nom d'un chien!" ejaculated Blanchard, waving his arms around. "I tell you ten t'ousand time zere is no offog. Zere never was an offog. Escoffier heemself could not find zee offog to vich zere is none. Am I a magician perhaps?"

"It's part of the culinary equipment," McNaught maintained. "It must be because it's on page nine. And page nine means its proper home is in the galley, care of the head cook."

"Like hail it does," Blanchard retorted. He pointed at a metal box on the wall. "Intercom booster. Is zat mine?"

McNaught thought it over, conceded, "No, it's Burman's. His stuff rambles all over the ship."

"Zen ask heem for zis bloody offog," said Blanchard, triumphantly.

"I will. If it's not yours it must be his. Let's finish this checking first. If I'm not systematic and thorough Cassidy will jerk down my pants along with my insignia." His eyes sought the list. "V1099. Inscribed collar, leather, brass studed, dog, for the use of. No need to look for that.

I saw it myself five minutes ago." He ticked the item,
continued, "V1100. Sleeping basket, woven reed, one
of."

"Is zis," said Blanchard, kicking it into a corner.

"V1101. Cushion, foam rubber, to fit sleeping basket,
one of."

"Half of," Blanchard contradicted. "In four years he
have chewed away other half."

"Maybe Cassidy will let us indent for a new one. It
doesn't matter. We're okay so long as we can produce
the half we've got." McNaught stood up, closed the
folder. "That's the lot for here, I'll go see Burman
about this missing item."

Burman switched off a UHF receiver, removed his
earplugs and raised a questioning eyebrow.

"In the galley we're short an offog," explained Mc-
Naught. "Where is it?"

"Why ask me? The galley is Blanchard's bailiwick."

"Not entirely. A lot of your cables run through it.
You've two terminal boxes in there, also an automatic
switch and an intercom booster. Where's the offog?"

"Never heard of it," said Burman, baffled.

McNaught shouted, "Don't tell me that! I'm already
fed up hearing Blanchard saying it. Four years back we
had an offog. It says so here. This is our copy of what we
checked and signed for. It says we signed for an offog.
Therefore we must have one. It's got to be found before
Cassidy gets here."

"Sorry, sir," sympathized Burman. "I can't help you."

"You can think again," advised McNaught. "Up in the
bow there's a direction and distance indicator. What do
you call it?"

"A didin," said Burman, mystified.

"And," McNaught went on, pointed at the pulse
transmitter, "what do you call *that?*"

"The opper-popper."

"Baby names, see? Didin and opper-popper. Now rack
your brains and remember what you called an offog
four years ago."

"Nothing," asserted Burman, "has ever been called an
offog to my knowledge."

"Then," demanded McNaught, "why the blue blazes did we sign for one?"

"I didn't sign for anything. You did all the signing."

"While you and others did the checking. Four years ago, presumably in the galley, I said, 'Offog, one,' and either you or Blanchard pointed to it and said, 'Check.' I took somebody's word for it. I have to take other specialists' words for it. I am an expert navigator, familiar with all the latest navigational gadgets but not with other stuff. So I'm compelled to rely on people who know what an offog is—or ought to."

Burman had a bright thought. "All kinds of oddments were dumped in the main lock, the corridors and the galley when we were fitted out. We had to sort through a deal of stuff and stash it where it properly belonged, remember? This offog-thing might be anyplace today. It isn't necessarily my responsibility or Blanchard's."

"I'll see what the other officers say," agreed McNaught, conceding the point. "Gregory, Worth, Sanderson, or one of the others may be coddling the item. Wherever it is, it's got to be found."

He went out. Burman pulled a face, inserted his earplugs, resumed fiddling with his apparatus. An hour later McNaught came back wearing a scowl.

"Positively," he announced with ire, "there is no such thing on the ship. Nobody knows of it. Nobody can so much as guess at it."

"Cross it off and report it lost," Burman suggested.

"What, when we're hard aground? You know as well as I do that loss and damage must be signaled at time of occurrence. If I tell Cassidy the offog went west in space, he'll want to know when, where, how and why it wasn't signaled. There'll be a real ruckus if the contraption happens to be valued at half a million credits. I can't dismiss it with an airy wave of the hand."

"What's the answer then?" inquired Burman, innocently ambling straight into the trap.

"There's one and only one," McNaught announced. "*You* will manufacture an offog."

"Who? *Me?*" said Burman, twitching his scalp.

"You and no other. I'm fairly sure the thing is your pigeon, anyway."

"Why?"

"Because it's typical of the baby-names used for your kind of stuff. I'll bet a month's pay that an offog is some sort of scientific allamagoosa. Something to do with fog, perhaps. Maybe a blind-approach gadget."

"The blind-approach transceiver is called 'the fumbly,' " Burman informed.

"There you are!" said McNaught as if that clinched it. "So you will make an offog. It will be completed by six tomorrow evening and ready for my inspection then. It had better be convincing, in fact pleasing."

Burman stood up, let his hands dangle, and said in hoarse tones, "How the devil can I make an offog when I don't even know what it is?"

"Neither does Cassidy know," McNaught pointed out, leering at him. "He's more of a quantity surveyor than anything else. As such he counts things, looks at things, certifies that they exist, accepts advice on whether they are functionally satisfactory or worn out. All we need do is concoct an imposing allamagoosa and tell him it's the offog."

"Holy Moses!" said Burman, fervently.

"Let us not rely on the dubious assistance of Biblical characters," McNaught reproved. "Let us use the brains that God has given us. Get a grip on your soldering-iron and make a topnotch offog by six tomorrow evening. That's an order!"

He departed, satisfied with this solution. Behind him, Burman gloomed at the wall and licked his lips once, twice.

Rear Admiral Vane W. Cassidy arrived dead on time. He was a short, paunchy character with a florid complexion and eyes like those of a long-dead fish. His gait was an important strut.

"Ah, Captain, I trust that you have everything shipshape."

"Everything usually is," assured McNaught, glibly. "I see to that."

"Good!" approved Cassidy. "I like a commander who takes his responsibilities seriously. Much as I regret saying so, there are a few who do not." He marched through the main lock, his cod-eyes taking note of the fresh white enamel. "Where do you prefer to start, bow or tail?"

"My equipment-sheets run from bow backward. We may as well deal with them the way they're set."

"Very well." He trotted officiously toward the nose, paused on the way to pat Peaslake and examine his collar. "Well cared for, I see. Has the animal proved useful?"

"He saved five lives on Mardia by barking a warning."

"The details have been entered in your log, I suppose?"

"Yes, sir. The log is in the chart-room awaiting your inspection."

"We'll get to it in due time." Reaching the bow-cabin, Cassidy took a seat, accepted the folder from NcNaught, started off at businesslike pace. "K1. Beam compass, type D, one of."

"This is it, sir," said McNaught, showing him.

"Still working properly?"

"Yes, sir."

They carried on, reached the intercom-cubby, the computer-room, a succession of other places back to the galley. Here, Blanchard posed in freshly laundered white clothes and eyed the newcomer warily.

"V.147. Electronic oven, one of."

"Is zis," said Blanchard, pointing with disdain.

"Satisfactory?" inquired Cassidy, giving him the fishy eye.

"Not beeg enough," declared Blanchard. He encompassed the entire galley with an expressive gesture. "Nossings beeg enough. Place too small. Everysings too small. I am chef de cuisine an' she is a cuisine like an attic."

"This is a warship, not a luxury liner," Cassidy snapped. He frowned at the equipment-sheet. "V.148. Timing device, electronic oven, attachment thereto, one of."

"Is zis," spat Blanchard, ready to sling it through the nearest port if Cassidy would first donate the two pins.

Working his way down the sheet, Cassidy got nearer and nearer while nervous tension built up. Then he reached the critical point and said, "V1098. Offog, one."

"*Morbleau!*" said Blanchard, shooting sparks from his eyes. "I have say before an' I say again, zere never was—"

"The offog is in the radio-room, sir," McNaught chipped in hurriedly.

"Indeed?" Cassidy took another look at the sheet. "Then why is it recorded along with galley equipment?"

"It was placed in the galley at time of fitting out, sir. It's one of those portable instruments left to us to fix up where most suitable."

"H'm! Then it should have been transferred to the radio-room list. Why didn't you transfer it?"

"I thought it better to wait for your authority to do so, sir."

The fish-eyes registered gratification. "Yes, that is quite proper of you, Captain. I will transfer it now." He crossed the item from sheet nine, initialed it, entered it on sheet sixteen, initialed that. "V1099. Inscribed collar, leather . . . oh, yes, I've seen that. The dog was wearing it."

He ticked it. An hour later he strutted into the radio-room. Burman stood up, squared his shoulders but could not keep his feet or hands from fidgeting. His eyes protruded slightly and kept straying toward McNaught in silent appeal. He was like a man wearing a porcupine in his breeches.

"V1098. Offog, one," said Cassidy in his usual tone of brooking no nonsense.

Moving with the jerkiness of a slightly uncoordinated robot, Burman pawed a small box fronted with dials, switches and colored lights. It looked like a radio ham's idea of a fruit machine. He knocked down a couple of switches. The lights came on, played around in intriguing combinations.

"This is it, sir," he informed with difficulty.

"Ah!" Cassidy left his chair and moved across for a closer look. "I don't recall having seen this item before. But there are so many different models of the same things. Is it still operating efficiently?"

"Yes, sir."

"It's one of the most useful things in the ship," contributed McNaught, for good measure.

"What does it *do*?" inquired Cassidy, inviting Burman to cast a pearl of wisdom before him.

Burman paled.

Hastily, McNaught said, "A full explanation would be rather involved and technical but, to put it as simply as possible, it enables us to strike a balance between opposing gravitational fields. Variations in lights indicate the extent and degree of imbalance at any given time."

"It's a clever idea," added Burman, made suddenly reckless by this news, "based upon Finagle's Constant."

"I see," said Cassidy, not seeing at all. He resumed his seat, ticked the offog and carried on. "Z44. Switchboard, automatic, forty-line intercom, one of."

"Here it is, sir."

Cassidy glanced at it, returned his gaze to the sheet. The others used his momentary distraction to mop perspiration from their foreheads.

Victory had been gained.

All was well.

For the third time, hah!

Rear Admiral Vane W. Cassidy departed pleased and complimentary. Within one hour the crew bolted to town. McNaught took turns with Gregory at enjoying the gay lights. For the next five days all was peace and pleasure.

On the sixth day Burman brought in a signal, dumped it upon McNaught's desk and waited for the reaction. He had an air of gratification, the pleasure of one whose virtue is about to be rewarded.

Terran Headquarters to BUSTLER. Return here immediately for overhaul and refitting. Improved power-plant to be installed. Feldman. Navy Op. Command. Sirisec.

"Back to Terra," commented McNaught, happily. "And an overhaul will mean at least one month's leave." He eyed Burman. "Tell all officers on duty to go to town at once and order the crew aboard. The men will come running when they know why."

"Yes, sir," said Burman, grinning.

Everyone was still grinning two weeks later, when the Siriport had receded far behind and Sol had grown to a vague speck in the sparkling mist of the bow starfield. Eleven weeks still to go, but it was worth it. Back to Terra. Hurrah!

In the captain's cabin the grins abruptly vanished one evening when Burman suddenly developed the willies.

He marched in, chewed his bottom lip while waiting for McNaught to finish writing in the log.

Finally, McNaught pushed the book away, glanced up, frowned. "What's the matter with you? Got a bellyache or something?"

"No, sir. I've been thinking."

"Does it hurt that much?"

"I've been thinking," persisted Burman in funereal tones. "We're going back for overhaul. You know what that means. We'll walk off the ship and a horde of experts will walk onto it." He stared tragically at the other. "Experts, I said."

"Naturally they'll be experts," McNaught agreed. "Equipment cannot be tested and brought up to scratch by a bunch of dopes."

"It will required more than a mere expert to bring the offog up to scratch," Burman pointed out. "It'll need a genius."

McNaught rocked back, swapped expressions like changing masks. "Jumping Judas! I'd forgotten all about that thing. When we get to Terra we won't blind *those* boys with science."

"No, sir, we won't," endorsed Burman. He did not add any more but his face shouted aloud, "You got me into this. You get me out of it." He waited quite a time while McNaught did some intense thinking, then prompted, "What do you suggest, sir?"

Slowly the satisfied smile returned to McNaught's features as he answered, "Break up the contraption and feed it into the disintegrator."

"That doesn't solve the problem," said Burman. "We'll still be short an offog."

"No we won't. Because I'm going to signal its loss owing to the hazards of space service." He closed one eye in an emphatic wink. "We're in free flight right now." He reached for a message pad and scribbled on it while Burman stood by, vastly relieved.

BUSTLER to Terran Headquarters. Item V1098, Offog, one, came apart under gravitational stress while passing through twin-sun field Hector Major-Minor. Material used as fuel. McNaught, Commander. BUSTLER.

Burman took it to the radio-room and beamed it Earthward. All was peace and progress for another two days. The next time he went to the captain's cabin he went running.

"General call, sir," he announced breathlessly and thrust the message into the other's hands.

> *Terran Headquarters for relay all sectors. Urgent and Important. All ships grounded forthwith. Vessels in fight under official orders will make for nearest spaceport pending further instructions. Welling. Alarm and Rescue Command. Terra.*

"Something's gone bust," commented McNaught, undisturbed. He traipsed to the chartroom, Burman following. Consulting the charts, he dialed the intercom phone, got Pike in the bow and ordered, "There's a panic. All ships grounded. We've got to make for Zaxtedport, about three days' run away. Change course at once. Starboard seventeen degrees, declination ten." Then he cut off, griped, "Bang goes that sweet month on Terra. I never did like Zaxted, either. It stinks. The crew will feel murderous about this and I don't blame them."

"What d'you think has happened, sir?" asked Burman.

"Heaven alone knows. The last general call was seven years ago, when the *Starider* exploded halfway along the Mars run. They grounded every ship in existence while they investigated the cause." He rubbed his chin, pondered, went on, "And the call before that one was when the entire crew of the *Blowgun* went nuts. Whatever it is this time, you can bet it's serious."

"It wouldn't be the start of a space war?"

"Against whom?" McNaught made a gesture of contempt. "Nobody has the ships with which to oppose us. No, it's something technical. We'll learn of it eventually. They'll tell us before we reach Zaxted or soon afterward."

They did tell him. Within six hours. Burman rushed in with face full of horror.

"What's eating you now?" demanded McNaught, staring at him.

"The offog," stuttered Burman. He made motions as though brushing off invisible spiders.

"What of it?"

"It's a typographical error. In your copy it should read 'off. dog.'"

"Off. dog?" echoed McNaught, making it sound like foul language.

"See for yourself." Dumping the signal on the desk, Burman bolted out, left the door swinging. McNaught scowled after him, picked up the message.

Terran Headquarters to BUSTLER. Your report V1098, ship's official dog Peaslake. Detail fully circumstances and manner in which animal came apart under gravitational stress. Cross-examine crew and signal all coincidental symptoms experienced by them. Urgent and Important. Welling. Alarm and Rescue Command. Terra.

In the privacy of his cabin McNaught commenced to eat his nails. Every now and again he went a little cross-eyed as he examined them for nearness to the flesh.

EDITOR'S INTRODUCTION TO:

PEACEKEEPER
by
J. E. Pournelle, Ph.D.

In the introduction to this book, I promised to give you the results of Project 75, and to explain the basic principles of the strategic dilemma.

There's nothing pleasant about the subject of nuclear war, and many prefer to leave it to the experts. They may be making a severe mistake when they do that. The experts—at least a group of "defense intellectuals" calling themselves experts—have brought us to the present situation.

In plain language, here is the strategic dilemma.

PEACEKEEPER
by
J. E. Pournelle, Ph.D., F.R.A.S.

The United States currently faces the most serious threat to our national existence since the Civil War. The threat has long been foreseen, although the political authorities are just getting around to doing something about it.

The issues, while complex, aren't that hard to understand. The only reason it looks difficult is because of the strange terminology. The trouble is, there's not enough information, so experts can legitimately disagree. When the experts can't agree, but the problem has to be solved anyway, politicians get in the act. Some of them don't bother to learn even the facts that the experts *do* agree on; being used to "soft sciences" like sociology in which there is no "right" answer, they think strategic problems work that way too.

If our current leaders can't cope with difficult problems, then it's time we hired some who can. There must be a few citizens who are willing to put national survival ahead of politics. Maybe it's time we elected them to Congress, before the current batch kills off the lot of us.

First principles: when defensive systems are stronger than offensive ones, the situation is stable. When the offense dominates, it isn't. Example: if it takes ten attacking missiles to reliably knock out one enemy bird, no one is going to be anxious to start the war. Why should they? If the attacking side launches everything, it disarms itself, leaving the other side with fire in its eye and 90% of its force intact.

On the other hand, if one attacking bird has a high probability of knocking off ten of the other side's missiles, the situation is highly unstable. Each side has an incentive to launch, because the one who strikes first has a good chance at a clean win. Thus any tense situation can "escalate" rapidly, as President and Chairman think to themselves, "He may not want to attack, but he knows that if I attack first I'll win, and he's not going to allow that." It's then only a question of time before someone reaches for the Gold Phone.

Unfortunately, a long time ago a Secretary of Defense named McNamara adopted a national policy known as "Assured Destruction". This doctrine says that you'll never have to fight a war; you just make sure that if the other guy kills you, you can kill him back. This later got refined and was called "Mutual Assured Destruction", more properly known as MAD. The MAD doctrine says that *defensive* systems are *destabilizing*.

That logic goes as follows: as long as war is too destructive to fight, nobody will start a war. Therefore, anything that will decrease the destruction is a step toward war.

Under this doctrine, Civil Defense and fallout shelters were considered an act of aggression by the United States against the Soviet Union: by trying to protect our citizens, we'd be making it more possible to go to war with the Soviets. This argument was once very popular among sophisticated people on university campuses.

One result was that we lost a splendid opportunity to construct a nationwide chain of fallout shelters at low cost. Civil Defense structures were originally planned as part of the Interstate Highway System. There were to be fallout and partial blast shelters under most of the approach ramps. This would have been easy to do as part of the construction, and a few model shelters were actually built as a demonstration.

Then the full logic of MAD was accepted, and the project was abandoned. After pouring all the concrete for the Interstate System, we currently have fewer shelter spaces than we did in the '60's.

To this day a great many "defense intellectuals" either reject active defense, or never think of it.

In 1968, Stefan Possony and I argued for the concept

of "Assured Survival" to replace "Assured Destruction" as the strategic doctrine of the US. We argued that it made sense, and that being based on defensive systems, posed a lower threat to both mankind and western civilization. The doctrine was opposed by most "defense intellectuals." Congress explicity rejected ballistic missile defenses, and MAD remained the doctrine of the US.

Whatever one thinks of the MAD doctrine, though, one thing is clear: if our strategic offensive forces can't survive, we've nothing at all, since we already gave up strategic defenses including civil defense.

Next: what determines system vulnerability, and how can you tell what will happen if a nuclear war starts? After all, nobody ever fought one before.

First, you can't know. Not for certain, and indeed one of the best ways to keep the missiles in their silos is to increase the uncertainty; generals and marshals just *hate* it when they have to gamble without a reasonable estimate of what's likely to happen. However, you can make some calculations, and if you have enough overkill capability you can have fairly high confidence in your predictions.

The United States bases its intercontinental strategic offensive forces, the SOF, on three independent branches, which we called the "Triad". Each leg of the Triad is supposed to be independent of the other two, meaning that whatever can kill one leg ought to be able to knock out either of the other two. The Triad is composed of manned bombers, submarine launched ballistic missiles (SLBM), and land-based intercontinental ballistic missiles (ICBM). Prior to the ICBM leg we had Snark, an air-breathing pilotless aircraft capable of flying intercontinental distances—an early "cruise missile."

Each leg, then, depends on a different mechanism for survival. The manned bomber is very soft; it can be killed on the ground by nukes landing a long way off. It depends for early survival on warning: unlike the other two legs of the Triad, the manned bombers can be launched at an early stage of alert and still be recalled.

Without warning the manned bomber is a dead duck, but even if it gets warning it still has to penetrate the enemy's air defenses. Those may be pretty formidable.

We try to get around them with stand-off missiles, and electronic counter measures (ECM), and such like; but whatever we do isn't going to change the fact that the B-52 was designed in the 40's and early fifties, with the first aircraft rolled out in 1956. (I helped work on updates to the B-52 as my first aerospace job.) While it's not strictly true that the planes are older than the pilots who fly them—at least not older than the senior pilots—they're pretty old. One USAF colonel recently described a B-52 as "a mass of parts flying in loose formation."

The Soviets have had more than 20 years to design defenses against the B-52, and while Soviet civilian science and engineering may lack something, they're willing to devote a lot of resources to their military. I wouldn't care to bet my family's life on the ability of that grand old girl to get deep into Soviet territory.

Even if the bombers can penetrate, they're not useful for *fighting* a nuclear war. You can't send the bombers to attack Soviet missile bases; there'd be nothing to hit but empty holes by the time a sub-sonic bomber got to the target.

And that's what's wrong with cruise missiles: they can't be recalled, so they have to be survivable, something not so easy for a soft thing like a pilotless aircraft; they still have to penetrate; and they take quite a while to reach their targets after they're launched.

Cruise missiles can be an excellent supplement to the strategic force, but they are certainly not a potential leg of the Triad. They are vulnerable to everything that kills airplanes (on the ground or in the air) without the recall advantages of manned aircraft.

The second leg of the Triad is the submarine. Its survival depends entirely on concealment. If you can locate a submarine to within a few miles, it can be killed by an ICBM carrying an H-bomb. Bombardment of the ocean won't be good for the fish, but the Soviets aren't much on environmentalism.

Note, by the way, that all the subs in harbor—up to a third of them, sometimes more—are dead the day the war starts. You can be sure that nuclear submarine bases are very high on the enemy's target priority list. The rest, though, can make it if they can hide.

Unfortunately, the submarine's concealment isn't what

it used to be. Subs can be located in at least two ways. First, by tracking them from their bases; every submariner can tell you stories about playing tag with the Russkis when they leave Holy Loch.

Worse, though, the oceans aren't nearly so opaque as we thought. Not long ago we took a look at some radar pictures made from a satellite. "Look at that," one of the engineers said. "You can see stuff down in the ocean! Deep in the ocean." And sure enough, using "synthetic aperture" radars, the oceans have become somewhat transparent down to about fifty meters. While the subs can go deeper than that, they can't *launch* from deeper than' that. Moreover: anything that accidentally—and it was accidental, nobody expected this at all—makes the oceans transparent to fifty meters is unlikely to be limited to that. Now that the principle is known, you can expect satellite surveillance of the oceans to get much better.

Incidentally, as I write this, a Soviet naval surveillance satellite is about to fall. It carried a 100 kilo-watt nuclear power plant. The United States has yet to put a *ten* kilo-watt satellite into orbit.

So. The subs are getting more vulnerable. They've also got another problem: they're useful for deterrence, but they're not so good for *fighting* a nuclear war. Submarines have to launch their missiles from unpredictable places (by definition; imagine what the KGB would pay to find out where our subs would launch from), and this drastically limits their accuracy. I'll get back to that when I explain what accuracy means.

That leaves the third leg of the Triad, land-based missiles. These depend for their survival on their basing mode, and that's the question up for debate. Before we get to that, though, there's a prior question: do we need land-based missiles at all? Maybe it would be better to put all our birds on subs, or ships, or somewhere like that, where we don't invite the Soviets to wreck US real estate.

There are two answers to that. First, if you don't have land-based missiles, you have pretty well given up your war-fighting capability. You've bet it all on deterrence; that the other guy is rational, and that he sees things the way you hope he sees them.

But does he? Suppose one morning the Soviets knock out our Minutemen installations (not too difficult, as we'll see in a bit) and many of our subs. They still have quite a few birds left. The Red Army is marching into Germany. The hot line chatters, and the message is pretty simple: "You haven't really been hurt. Most of your cities are in good shape. Cool it, or we launch the rest of our force."

At that point it would be useful to have something capable of knocking out the rest of their strategic force.

To have that capability, you need land-based missiles. To be exact, you need MX. MX, and only MX, has both the accuracy and the Multiple Independently Targetable Re-entry Vehicles (MIRVS, and they're different from multiple warheads; MIRVS can attack targets much farther apart) that might give some counterforce capability. True, it won't be a *lot* of counterforce capability; but it'll be all we'd have.

But can MX survive?

That depends on the basing concept. Before we get into that, we have to explain vulnerability.

If you attack a target with an ICBM, your "single shot probability of kill" (PKSS) depends on three major factors: attacker's yield, attacker's accuracy, and hardness of target.

Yield is the size, in kilotons or megatons, of the attacking warhead. Yield to weight ratios are pretty thoroughly classified, but nobody really doubts that you can pack ten one-megaton warheads onto one big ICBM. Hardness is generally measured in "pounds per square inch overpressure" (PSI), which means how much pressure the target can withstand before it's made useless.

Accuracy depends on a lot of things. Some of the most important are: weather at launch site; winds over target; gravitational anomalies under the flight path; how good your gyros are; how good your computers are; how good your mathematicians are; and location errors (where are you when you launch, and where is the other guy in relation to you?). We measure accuracy in Circular Probable Error (CEP), which is the size of the circle that *half* your shots will fall inside.

Given those three factors, we can calculate the PKSS, and given that we can claculate the overall vulnerability of the force. While there are classified refinements, all the numbers you really need have long since been published in the US Government Printing Office's "The Effects of Nuclear Weapons". They've even been put on a circular slide rule that the RAND Corporation used to sell for about a dollar in the 60's.

And now, at long last, we can get down to cases. The Minutemen Missile lies in a soil that's officially hardened to 300 PSI. When we put in Minutemen—the last one was installed in the 60's—it was no bad guess that the Soviets could throw a megaton with a CEP of about a nautical mile. This gave them a PKSS of about .09, and it would take more than 20 warheads to give better than .9 kill probability. That was obviously a stable situation.

They can up the yield, but it doesn't help as much as you might think. Going to ten megatons puts the PKSS to about 35%, and it still takes more than five attackers to get a 90% chance of killing one Minuteman; still not a lot to worry about.

Changes in accuracy, on the other hand, are *very* significant. Cutting the CEP in half (well, to 2700 feet) gives one megaton the same kill probability as ten had for a mile. Cutting CEP to 1000 feet is more drastic yet: now the *single shot* kill probability of one megaton is above 90%.

If you can get your accuracy to 600 feet CEP, then a 500 *kilo*-ton weapon has above 99% kill probability. Now all you need is multiple warheads, and you're able to knock out more birds than you launched. Clearly this is getting unstable.

In 1964 we figured the Soviets had 6000 foot CEP, and predicted that by 1975 they'd have 600 feet. By 1975 I'd given up my clearances, and I don't know what they achieved. It doesn't take clearances to see what must be happening to the error budget.

Item: weather satellites; winds over target are predictable, so you can correct for them. Item: lots of polar-orbiting satellites; by studying them, you can map gravitational anomalies. Item: observation satellites; location errors just aren't significant any more. Item: the Soviets have been buying gyros, precision lathes, etc, as well as computers. They already had the mathematicians.

They're not ten feet tall, but if by 1984 they don't have several warheads per bird, each with 600 foot CEP, they're pygmies.

Now what can we do about it?

One: it does no good to put MX in Minuteman silos. Well, it does a little good: MX is a better bird. The problem is, you decrease stability, by deploying a force that both makes them nervous and which they can knock out. It can't be our best bet.

Two: in the 60's we studied lots and lots of mobile basing schemes: road mobile, rail mobile, off-road mobile, canal and barge mobile, ship mobile, etc. We even looked at artificial ponds, and things that crawled around on the bottom of Lake Michigan. There were a lot of people in favor of mobile systems—then. Now, though, there are satellites, and you know, it's just damned hard to hide something seventy feet long and weighing 190,000 pounds. (Actually, by the time you add the launcher, it's more like 200 feet and 500,000 pounds.)

Make it smaller, then. A *small* mobile missile. Unfortunately, we don't have one, and it will take both time and money to develop.

Worse, you can't harden a mobile system very much. Even a "small" ICBM rocket is a pretty big object. Twenty PSI would probably be more than we could achieve. The kill radius of a 50 megaton weapon against a 20 PSI target is very large: area bombardment becomes attractive. You've invited the enemy to use hand grenades while you barricade yourself in a room with your family. Not too bright.

Waterborne is not Triad independent, and doesn't have the war-fighting capability we'd like. The scheme for basing MX on 5-man subs in shallow water will lose its support when the full realization of synthetic aperture radar sinks in. Putting them on merchant ships, or surface ships of any kind, doesn't help much, either. And nearly every mobile basing scheme puts nukes out where they have to be protected from terrorists and saboteurs including well-meaning US citizens aroused in protest (and you just know there'll be plenty of them).

Air-mobile and air-launched were long-term favorites, and I was much for them in the 60's. The Pentagon's

most recent analysis says we just can't afford them; it
would cost in the order of $150 billion, possibly more.

The "race-track" or "shell game" has been rejected on
political and economic grounds. There's also the security problem. Synthetic aperture radars have seen old
watercourses under the Sahara beneath many feet of
sand; they can look through a lot of stuff we thought
was opaque. There's also the KGB: want to bet our lives
they can't find out which bunker has the bird?

In fact, every alternative you've ever heard of, and a
few you haven't, were analyzed in great detail back in
1964. I know, because I was editor of the final report. I
even invented one scheme myself, Citadel, which would
put some birds as well as a national command post
under a granite mountain. The problem with that one is
that the birds will survive, but if they attack the doors,
how does it get *out* after the attack?

Every one of these schemes has holes in it. Every one
of them.

However, though there isn't any absolute safe basing
system, you *can* make the other guy complicate his war
plan. The simpler the war plan, the more likely the war;
thus you don't lightly give up any leg of the Triad,
especially not now when we're just seeing new vulnera-
bilities in the wet leg.

First try the obvious: harden your birds. In 1964 we
called it "Superhard," 5000 PSI basing. Now 5000 PSI
isn't easy to come by. There are severe engineering
problems, and it isn't cheap. Worse, "Superhard" didn't
buy all that much: at 500 foot CEP's a megaton has a
95% chance of killing "superhard" targets. (A megaton
weapon makes a crater 250 feet deep and over a thousand feet in diameter even in hard rock.) Thus putting
MX in 5000 PSI silos separated by miles didn't seem
worth the cost.

Suppose, though, there were a way to foul up the
other guy's attack?

The "Dense Pack" scheme came after my time. It
makes a lot of sense. We used to worry about "fratricide"
among our MIRV's, meaning that one goes off and kills
a bunch of its brothers before they can get to their
targets—after all, a re-entering warhead in flight is a lot

softer than a missile in a silo, and thus will be killed at much greater distances.

If fratricide is a problem for us, it'll be a problem for them. If it's a problem for them, why not increase that problem by spacing the MX emplacements just far enough apart that a hit on one—or half-way between two of them—destroys only one (or none) of our missiles?

There's no magic in this, but it *does* complicate hell out of the enemy's war plan. He not only has to coordinate strikes against air bases, submarines, and missiles (including good old Minuteman); but his attack on the MX Peacekeeper base has to be timed *exactly*, down to fractions of a millisecond, or else he has to attack our Peacekeeper force one missile at a time.

Any artilleryman knows the problems involved in getting off a precise TOT (all the shells go off over the target at once) for a single battery. Imagine trying it at intercontinental distances. True, the time of detonation can be coordinated. We know how to build clocks a lot more accurate than the ones needed here. (I'm not so sure that given the exact time sequence, there aren't enough timing uncertainties in the *chemical* explosive parts of a nuclear weapon to cause some concern, but we can ignore that one.)

The real problem comes with having a hundred or more birds arrive in position all at the same instant. ICBM's travel thousands of feet per second, and we're talking about CEP's in the hundreds of feet. Since they all have to *detonate* at once, it doesn't take much error in the launch time to put a lot of them miles away from their targets when it's time to explode.

If he chooses some other means to defeat dense pack—earth penetrators, for example—he has to build and develop the missiles, which will take a while, and he probably has to test them, and we'll get some inkling of the tests. There are other clever ways to attack dense pack; but every one of them is complex enough to be a planner's nightmare.

Meanwhile, what have we lost? If the enemy's accuracy is nowhere near as good as we thought, and the fratricide argument turns out to be fallacious, then we'll lose more missiles than we would if we spaced them out. On the other hand, because of his inaccuracy and our superhardening, we'll have well over half those accurate 10-warhead Peacekeepers left after his best attack.

If we decide on active defenses—General Graham's Project High Frontier, as an example—it's a lot easier to defend the corridors to one patch of ground than a lot of installations.

The plain fact is that dispersal is usually a good idea, but it isn't *always*; sometimes you're better off hardening hell out of your fortress and concentrating inside it. (I'm aware of the Maginot Line mentality; I'm also aware of just how valuable, in a different era, fortresses and magazines were.) Just about every honest analyst who takes the trouble to work through the numbers comes away muttering "That's a goofy sounding scheme, but damned if it doesn't look like it might work . . ."

Then there's another possibility: put MX in the old Minuteman silos, but defend them. This is what's recommended by Lt. General Daniel O. Graham's PROJECT HIGH FRONTIER.

Details of High Frontier are available from Project High Frontier, 1010 Vermont Ave. NW #1000, Washington DC 20005, as well as in the Tor Book by General Graham.

Graham rejects the idea of trying to match the Soviets in tanks, guns, ships, men, planes, and missiles. Instead, he says, let's take a strategic sidestep into space. Use the space environment and our lead in high technology to construct missile defenses. They won't be perfect, but they won't need to be: the enemy can't know how good our defenses are. Thus he can't be sure of the outcome of his strike.

The Soviet war plan gets complicated as hell.

A lot of highly competent people are convinced Graham's plan is best. It has been examined by an engineering team headed by Harry Goldie, Vice President of Engineering for The Boeing Company, as well as a number of highly regarded physicists and space scientists. Predictably, Graham's enemies try to ridicule the concept; one, Professor Tsipis of MIT, says that Graham doesn't understand the laws of physics. Tsipis, who is part of the MIT Arms Control Project, says that almost everyone who argues in favor of arming the US doesn't understand the laws of physics.

Unfortunately, the laws of physics not only permit, but practically demand, that space will be an important theatre of war. The US already depends on space for command, control, communications, and intelligence—the famous "C-3 I" factors. Like it or not, war in space has already begun; the only real question is whether or not we will prepare for the decisive battles there.

We live in perilous times. Certainly we would prefer to reduce military expenditures. It's always more pleasant to consume than to save, and it always hurts when you can't even save what you don't consume, but have to "waste" it on something non-productive like defense.

Fortunately, investment in space resources is not inflationary; we can prove that it has always been the best investment the government has ever made. Whether space research pays for itself fifteen times over, as space enthusiasts say, or only twice over, as its critics say, nearly everyone is agreed that it does pay for itself—which is more than you can say for most other parts of the budget.

If we fail to provide for the common defense, it does no good to promote the general welfare.

The strategic problem is damned severe. Defense is costly, and you can't be *sure* of what you get for all that money. The only certainty is that you *can't* remove the uncertainties. Whatever we do will have flaws; but anyone honestly looking at the problem will conclude we have to do *something*, and it's getting damned late.

The stream of technology moves on; we can move with it, or try to swim against it. The one thing we can't do is stand still.

I can't say Dense Pack is the best thing to do. I don't even believe it is; I prefer General Graham's "bold stroke" approach. However, I can appreciate the risks involved, and that the President might not want to take them.

Of the "conventional" things we could do, Dense Pack makes the most sense, and is most compatible with a shift to strategic defense. We *have* to go to defense some day. Nothing else leads to a strategy of "Assured Survival" rather than MAD.

I believe our best course is to build MX and fund Graham's High Frontier defense system. By the time we have MX in production we'll know whether we need Dense Pack (with all its high expenses; 5000 PSI silos are not cheap), or can rely on space defenses. Meanwhile we've bought our children some reasonable insurance.

We'd better do something. The hour is late, and the clouds are gathering.